D1327964

10-01

DEATH FROM THE SNOWS

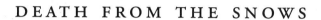

Death

FROM THE SNOWS

BRIGITTE AUBERT

Translated from the French by David L. Koral

 Welcome Rain Publishers / *New York*

Death from the Snows by Brigitte Aubert
Originally published in France as *La mort des neiges.*

Copyright © 2000 Editions du Seuil
Translation copyright © 2001 Welcome Rain Publishers LLC.

Direct any inquiries to Welcome Rain Publishers,
532 Laguardia Place, Box 473, New York, NY 10012.

Library of Congress Cataloging-in-Publication Data
Aubert, Brigitte.
[Mort des neiges. English]
Death from the snows / Brigitte Aubert;
translated from the French by David L. Koral
p. cm.
ISBN 1-56649-177-0
I. Koral, David l. II. Title.
PQ2661.U168 M67513 2001
813'.914—dc21
2001017969

Text design by Labreacht Design
Printed in the United States of America by HAMILTON PRINTING COMPANY

First Edition: September 2001
1 3 5 7 9 10 8 6 4 2

Prologue

IT'S RAINING. A thick, heavy rain pounding the windowpanes . . .

No! That's what was in the novel—the novel they squeezed out of the drama we had to live through two years ago in Boissy-les-Colombes. Atrocious child murders. At the time it made a whole lot of noise! Journalists descended upon it like flies on a trash heap. And because in some small way it was thanks to me that some light could be shed on this mystery, they came by to interview me. I even got to go on TV.

Then I sold my story to some mystery writer, and it got published under the title *Death from the Woods*.

All this commotion!

The town is peaceful again today. We're bandaging our wounds. Trying to forget. But as soon as a child is more than fifteen minutes late, his mother's heart skips a beat.

What made me think of the novel is the rain. A thick rain . . . Stop.

I'm rolling my wheelchair toward the window, pressing my forehead against the cool pane. It's January. If it won't stop raining tonight, it may turn to snow. I'm in the mood for the smell of snow. I'm happy over the idea that in a couple of days we'll be leaving for the mountains.

I'd like to see the garden. I love winter gardens in the pouring rain.

But I can't see a thing. As anyone who read the book will know, I was indirectly the victim of a bombing attack in Ireland almost three years ago, and ever since, I've remained paralyzed, blind, and mute. Up until last year, I could express myself only with the aid of my left index finger, which didn't make things much easier.

After my last operation, I recovered complete movement in the left arm. But not my sight. Or speech.

"What are you doing by the window? You're going to catch something!" Yvette calls out, running up from behind.

I raise my hand to quiet her.

"Whatever you want! Mr. Tony called," she adds. "It was hard to hear him because the sea was rough, but he sends kisses."

Yvette doesn't like Tony. She refers to him as "mister" with ostentation. As far as Tony's concerned, he doesn't give a damn whether he's liked or not.

I imagine him standing on a ship's deck swept by sea spray. Of course I'm imagining a man whom I know only through my fingers.

I don't know what his face looks like, because I met him after the accident.

It still has a strange effect on me to think that tons of people saw me on TV, answering questions by raising or lowering my hand, as you would when you play Simon Says.

Elise Andrioli, the steel-legged star, facing up to the journalists' firing line: "How were you able to solve this mystery nailed down in your wheelchair?" "Is there an 'Iron Woman' series under way?" "Will you marry Tony Mercier?"

No, I haven't married Tony. I didn't feel like throwing myself into a new romance before I was sure our feelings were mutual, true to the advice in the women's columns. Anyway, Tony hasn't asked me. In fact, he's gone back to his first profession, the one he was in before he started drinking: a sailor in the merchant marine. He travels all the time. Virginie, his daughter, is at a boarding school in Paris—an establishment that specializes in children who are victims of serious trauma requiring psychological follow-up. Yvette, my companion, has not married Jean Guillaume, either, even if they are spinning out love's perfect dream. "At our age, what use is there in going before the mayor again? Besides, I like my independence," she confided to me in private. Jean, not one to argue, and who also has his solitary little habits, readily accepted their arrangement: Yvette goes on living with me, they spend all their free time together, and once or twice a week, Jean comes over to sleep at the house.

Right now he's away. He's eked out a big, fat contract in Brittany: There's a whole mansion that needs fixing up, complete with old-fashioned slate tiles and period plumbing.

Ah! The telephone!

"It's for you!" Yvette yells.

I drive my electric wheelchair over to the phone. Yvette holds the receiver up to my ear.

"Hello, Elise. It's B* A*."

Well, well. What a coincidence. My author!

"I'm calling because I've received a letter concerning you. I'll fax it to you," she says.

I tap on the mouthpiece once, which means "Okay." Twice means no.

"I hope you're well. See you soon. I've got to run. Love you."

I'm sure you do love me, with all the money I made for you. But who's the one who almost had her throat slit and got burned alive? Me, that's who! All you did was pick up your pen and pfft! Show me the money!

The fax machine is rattling. Yvette tears out the sheet and skims it.

"I have no idea what this is about," she murmurs.

I'm champing at the bit. Will she decide to read it to me? When will there be faxes in Braille? I've been learning and I'm starting to get the hang of it.

"I'll read it to you."

Not a minute too soon.

"'Dear Miss Andrioli. You may be able to fool the public, but you can't fool me. Ever since I saw you on television, I've known the truth. You are an angel.'"

Aw, shucks! How ever did he guess?

"'One of those angels sent by God to combat the legions of Evil. I can always recognize them by their idiotically satisfied looks.'"

No, you don't say.

"Does this mean anything to you?" Yvette murmurs, then continues, "'I cannot resist: As soon as I see an angel, I can feel all my demons inside awakening. They mount me, sit astride me. The most imperious of them all is named Desire. I'm hoping that Desire will be able to lead me to you. Respectfully yours, D. Vore.' It's all a big prank, I guess," Yvette concludes, crumpling the sheet of paper.

I pick up the notepad, which always lies in my lap, and quickly scribble, *Please call B* A* and ask her where this letter comes from.*

"Whatever you want. But if you've got to take an interest in every hack who writes to you . . ."

I'm prudent. I think it's better to be sure. I'm in no mood to be prey to the delirious projections of some schizoid on the loose.

"Yes, hello, this is Yvette Holzinski. I'd like to speak with B* A*, please. Oh, well, that's too bad. Thank you. Bye-bye."

Yvette hangs up. "We missed her by five seconds. She called while she was waiting for her taxi. She's leaving for Japan. She's going on a lecture tour. Oh, well. How about a nice cup of tea?"

I nod distractedly. "D. Vore." Good citizen D. Vore sounds strangely off his rocker.

We drink our tea in silence. Yvette is peeved because Jean placed bets to win, place, and show and lost everything. Jean's very fond of going down to the state betting office. And those scratch-off things. He's always buying me Black Jacks. Not once have I won. Oh, yes, in fact: ten francs, which I gave to Virginie.

I'm very excited over this idea of leaving for the mountains. Not to take part in the Olympic wheelchair slalom, but my uncle Fernand, who lives in Nice, kindly suggested that I take advantage of his chalet in Castaing, a small family resort in the country. Clean air, sun, outings in the wheelchair through fresh snow . . . We're leaving in two days. Virginie and the guys will be joining us for vacation in February. I'm impatient. Yvette has packed three times over to make sure she hasn't forgotten a thing. Mittens, socks, Thermolactyl undergarments—we're ready for Annapurna.

Least funny of all is this ridiculous letter. Yvette's right. Surely it's only a joke. People who read these whodunits always think they're so clever, and there must be one out there who must have said to himself: "Look, I'm gonna scare the shit out of that poor handicapped woman. Let's see if she's as tough as all that . . . " I can easily imagine him as one of these nervous types, with a white silk scarf tied fastidiously around his neck, wearing big, heavy boots on his feet, and carrying a leather saddlebag stuffed with illegible manuscripts. Sitting at the rear of a café in Paris, smoking Gitanes and feverishly fingering his buttons, sniggering ferociously as he reads about my adventures, with an air of superiority. While I'm heading over to the TV, he's counting out his change to pay for his gross coffee—some robusta that's already been under the steam nozzle twice. Life's so unfair.

1

So HERE I AM, at the foot of the ski trails, sitting like a queen on her throne, bundled up all snug and warm: Always trust Yvette. I'm feeling cramped in my old duck blue ski suit, with bright red moon boots my uncle lent me, as well as a black chapka pulled down over my head. The lambskin earflaps are eating me up, and I'm sweating rivers. The sun's hot as hell, but still it's out of the question to uncover me by so much as a thread. Yvette's standing watch over me and adjusts my plaid blanket as soon as it slips a milli-meter, all the while commenting on the turn of events:

"Now, there's someone who's just taken a lovely little fall; he just narrowly missed that tree . . . And that other guy with his snowboard—a real public nuisance. How about some more tea?"

I refuse with a wave of the hand. We're set up on the terrace of the Chalet Canadien, one of the resort's strategic points. At some point or other, every vacationing biped must pass this way. Surreptitiously I reach my left hand toward the chapka when Yvette's piercing voice rings out: "That's out of the question! Cold enters through the ears. I'm sure you'll be quite happy when you've got the flu."

I don't have the flu, and the thermometer is showing a temperature of forty-one degrees. I heard it on the radio, but, fine, trying to get Yvette to understand that we're not camping out on the Siberian tundra is a bit beyond my reach. I don't feel like going into a polemic over this.

The air is ringing with the metallic clang of Teleskis, and I can hear people laughing and calling out to one another, children shouting. A baby's crying. His mother's trying to convince him that, no, he's not crying. I'm all right. I seem to be filling up with fresh air. I'm going to get a tan and look great. I feel around for my teacup and delicately lift it to my lips.

"Elise Andrioli! You're Elise Andrioli, aren't you?" a woman behind me screams.I jump and knock over my tea.

"I'm Francine Atchouel, from MRCHA," she continues.

Mrcha? Mr-what?

"Your uncle told me you'd be coming. I recognized you right away."

That shouldn't be too difficult. I don't think there are scads of ravishing young blind women in electric wheelchairs in these parts.

"Excuse us, but Miss Elise cannot answer you," Yvette puts forward in her best "Marie-Antoinette explaining to the peasants to come back during business hours" tone.

"I know, I know, Mr. Andrioli explained it to me. Your uncle's so nice! He's one of our most generous donors."

What's she talking about?

"He assured me that you'd certainly be thrilled to visit the center and get to know our residents. You're such a role model to them. And you must be Mrs. Holzinski," she continues, turning to Yvette, "the faithful companion!"

"Yes, that's right, but I didn't think . . . " Yvette boasts, flattered.

"Oh, but everyone's heard of you. Look, I've lent out the book to all my friends. What a horrible story! Even more horrible to think it's about some real-life item in the news! Brrr! You must have lived through some dreadful moments! Oh, excuse me, there goes our driver, I've got to run. I'll give you my card. Call me and we'll get together. Bye-bye!"

"She's gone," Yvette informs me. "She's getting into a green minibus with something written in yellow letters that I can't quite read from here. She left me her card. Let's see . . . ah, yes: 'Francine Atchouel, Director.' At the bottom it says, 'Mountain Recreational Center for Handicapped Adults,' with a phone number."

I'm starting to get the picture. This brave lady wants to parade me in front of her flock as proof of all one might do despite a handicap. And that son-of-a-bitch uncle of mine made sure to let me know. In any case, this is idiotic: I can't speak, and I'm not going to give them a lecture in deaf-mute language.

"She seems nice," Yvette has me know, "but a little . . . uh . . . exuberant. And that winter coat with pink flowers on it . . . frankly, it's not too flattering on her; it makes her look fat, and considering she's not too skinny . . . So what do you think, would you like some blueberry pie?"

I refuse with a gesture. We've already gulped down two crêpes each, and I don't get enough exercise to stuff my face without restraint.

"Well, fine, I'm going to take some myself. All this mountain air gives me an appetite," Yvette decides as she gets up.

I finally manage to drink a sip of cold tea. There are voices of young people laughing. Thumping and shouting. When I was a kid, I also scrambled down these slopes at high speeds, red from the cold, and with pleasure. I can still feel the tension in my ankles, the shaking from the bumps, the dizzying sensation of sliding. With Benoît, I got into cross-country skiing. Taking runs over sparkling powdery snow. Tour skating over training tracks. There must still be some brand-new equipment in the basement; we bought it before . . . the accident. It's all over. It's like being sentenced to life in prison, and the cell is my own body. All right, no more negative thoughts or else I'm going to start sobbing in public.

"Elise . . . "

To my left there's a voice; it's soft, in whispers. Is this yet another acquaintance popping up out of the blue?

"Elise . . . "

I give a vague wave of the hand to show I've heard.

"I have a present for you," this voice, with its tender inflections, goes on.

Is it an admirer? I feel a hand with warm, dry skin touching mine, closing my fingers around the strap on a plastic bag.

"See you later."

I'm left planted here, with a bag in my hand.

"There, you were all wrong: It looks delicious!"

Yvette sits down heavily.

I hold it out to her and scrawl on the pad, *Did you see someone talking to me?*

"But . . . if someone were talking to you, you must know anyway!" she replies, her mouth full. "No, I didn't see anyone, but with all these people . . . What is that? A gift package? Has someone given you a gift?"

I quickly write, *Yes, but I don't know who. Open it.*

Sounds of paper unfolding.

"My goodness! This is completely idiotic. A steak in plastic? How strange, to wrap up a steak to offer it as a present! And how strange, to offer steak!"

A steak?

Confused, I inquire, *What kind of steak?*

"Steak. Red, bloody, thick. I hope it's French meat. Mind you, we may be better off throwing it away. We'll give it to the dogs; I don't like to eat meat if you don't even know who gave it to you. A steak! I swear."

I can feel my neurons quiver in all directions. Somebody went to the trouble of coming and giving me this steak without so much as telling me his name, while taking advantage of Yvette's absence. Someone who insists on remaining anonymous. But what's the point of playing a joke, if this is, in fact, a joke?

Perhaps someone wants to deliver a message to me. It's a rebus, and the steak is the first element. Yes, these ski resorts are full of happy pranksters who give out 3-D rebuses to poor invalids who are bored. They're paid by the tourist bureau to create some ambience. Well, then, he's succeeded: I'm not bored anymore. In fact, I'm scared to death!

"Ah, here's a sticky note!" Yvette exclaims. "'Your butcher wishes you a nice stay.'" Obviously, some people are prepared to go to great lengths for the sake of publicity nowadays.

So the mystery's been resolved. Over the past two years I've had my share of adventures, and anything out of the ordinary tends to unsettle me, just like my psychologist says.

My psychologist is quite practical: I can take him with me wherever I go. One day when I was really in the mood to do myself in, I thought him up. He's a big guy in a white shirt with a matching beard, sort of a cross between God and Santa Claus, and he sits in an overstuffed leather armchair, listening to me with attention and kindness. With him, I can talk. The words come out of my mouth like they did in the past. I can see it. I can see him, the window behind him, the blue sky, clouds. I'm moving, crossing my legs, pulling on my skirt, rolling my big toes around in my shoes. Shrink gives me answers and encourages me, telling me not to despair. Thank you, Shrink.

Yvette yanks me out of my reverie, announcing that it's time to go home, the sun's going down. To hear her tell it, it's worse here after dark than it is in Transylvania: all reckless pedestrians run the risk of being frozen alive or devoured by packs of werewolves. Fortunately for us, we'll be warm inside the chalet, in front of a fire.

The fire is crackling pleasantly. I feel a bit drowsy. The end of the afternoon passed in a blink. In the time it took for me to do my muscle exercises, Yvette already had us set up in front of *Numbers and Letters*. I'm playing on my notepad. Yvette always wins. I wonder what my handwriting must look like—my new handwriting, I should say, because I've had to learn to write again, left-handed, unable to see my own progress. Hours and hours of exercises. At first Yvette seemed confused. Then, one afternoon, she exclaimed,

"That's it! I can read you! You mean to say you're hungry? Well, it's not time."

I'm smiling. I feel all right.

Finally, after a taste test turned out positive, we ate the famous steak with steamed potatoes and a perfectly suitable Côte de Nuits, and now Yvette's doing the dishes. The telephone rings. As I'm right by the side table, I feel around and pick up.

"My angel . . . "

Tony! I'm overrun with joy, yet just as soon it runs back: this isn't Tony's voice. It's a sickly-sweet voice, one I've heard only this afternoon.

"My angel, did you taste it? Was it good? Tender and juicy? Like your heart?"

"Who is this?" Yvette asks.

"Talk to you soon."

He hangs up. I grimace for Yvette, to indicate that I don't know who my interlocutor was.

"I'm sure it was a wrong number," she assures me. "All right, I'm going to get your bed ready."

We had to equip my room so that I might stay here without any problems: the bed, the anti-bedsore cushions, the bedpan, and the support bar that allows me to hoist myself into a sitting position. Now it's a real palace for the handicapped.

Who the hell could this guy be? Certainly not the butcher, a strong, hefty man with a stentorian voice. Could it be a coincidence that only a few days ago I received an impassioned message signed by a "D. Vore" in which I was called an angel as if it were some sort of insult, and that today someone gives me a steak before phoning up and calling me "my angel"? How much likelihood is there for such a coincidence? If it's not a coincidence, then it means that this Mr. Vore has been on my trail. That he knows me. That he knew I would be coming here on vacation. That he's observing me.

And that when he calls me "my angel," his voice is passionate. Ever since my accident, people won't stop telling me they love me. To the point where I've started to believe that when I could move and express myself normally, I made them run.

I don't like this call. No, not one bit.

2

AFTER BREAKFAST, Yvette wheels me down the main street, to proceed toward the ceremony we know as shopping. I feel like an empress reviewing her guard. We head over to the butcher shop on the double quick, and Yvette parks me outside, in front of the window. I imagine myself framed between a calf and a boar's head. Some kids are shouting, throwing snowballs at one another. It may be cute, but it's dangerous, and I'm really dreading that— *pow!* There you have it, I've just taken one right in the face. The little band takes off in headlong flight. The snow runs down my cheeks and chin, and I wipe it off with my one good hand.

"Well, it wasn't him!" Yvette yells as she grips my wheelchair. "He knows nothing about that steak. Oh, my, I'm telling you, we shouldn't have eaten it. With all that hepatitis and mad cow disease going around . . . "

I have a brief vision of Yvette gamboling about on crooked steps in a cacophony of discordant moos.

"What are you laughing about? Oh, there's that lady from yesterday, you know? The one from the handicapped—"

"Hello, Mrs. Holzinski; hello, Miss Andrioli," the voice with a shrill northern accent calls out. "I'm hoping you'll do us the honor of having tea with us this afternoon. Is five o'clock okay? I'll be expecting you. We'd be so pleased to have you."

Yvette's awaiting orders. I hide a sigh and scrawl, *Gladly.*

"Oh, you can write. That's fabulous! At five o'clock sharp, then. The driver will be by to pick you up in front of the tourist office. See you!"

Yvette grumbles something about some people's lack of consideration and wheels me on toward the superette. There, it will take her a good quarter hour, which should give me the chance to take in some sun.

There's panting on my left and a rough tongue over my hands.

"Stop it, Tintin! He's young, you know. He's not allowed into the store. Would it bother you if I left him with you?" asks a very soft woman's voice.

There's a silence. I'm looking for my pen, which has slipped onto my lap. The woman is starting to understand.

"Oh, excuse me, I didn't see that . . . really, what I mean is . . . No, it's okay, I'll just tie him to the fence. He's a Labrador," she adds, "he's black."

Why is her voice so sad?

I raise my hand and come across thick fur, a moist nose.

The woman walks away, her footsteps crunching on the fresh snow. The dog rests his snout upon my lap and lets out a long sigh. Yes, old boy, I know what it's like! We wait outside, and we're wise. I scratch his head, he licks my hand. Suddenly I feel like having a dog. And a cat. And a parrot who'll make conversation with me. I'll have to "speak" to Yvette about this.

Ah! No more sun. The dog has gone stiff and has started to growl softly. Oh, well, fine, something like this would happen to me! The only Labrador in the ski resort who happens to eat invalids. I slowly move my hand away, and he calms down. The sun has returned. The animal may be allergic to clouds. I hesitate to touch him again, but he's intent upon cramming his snout into my hand.

Nearby, an old man's voice: "I'm telling you, this world is crazy."

"It seems she belonged to some cult," replies another male voice, quavering.

"You think that's the reason they crucified her? It was some satanic offering?"

"They must have been dope addicts! With all their drugs, there's no reality for them anymore."

The old gents walk on, babbling away. I bury my hands deeper into the Labrador's fur, my mind made up not to let these somber tidbits spoil my good mood.

"I thought I was going to be there for hours! What are you doing with this dog?"

Just then, the sad voice interrupts: "Thanks. I hope I didn't take too long. Come on, Tintin, let's go. Good-bye, ladies."

The dog lets out a joyous woof, then is gone. Yvette leans over and murmurs, "She's one of those girls who works at the nightclub. She's got blond hair—it goes all the way down her back, and she wears a miniskirt. In the middle of winter! There was a murder last night in Entrevaux," she continues, all excited. "I bought the paper. Let's go sit at a corner."

Entrevaux's a small city nearby, a peaceful sort of town where a murder would make page one of the local paper for days and days. Now I'm thinking back to that conversation the two old men next to me were having, and expecting the worst.

We find a spot at the foot of the ski lifts, I in my wheelchair, Yvette on a low cement wall. The newspaper ruffles as it unfolds.

"It's on page one: 'The crucified naked body of a young woman was found yesterday in an abandoned house. The victim, who was not identified'—she's got to be homeless—'was crucified'—crucified, have you ever?— 'on a one-inch-thick panel of plywood with two-and-three-quarter-inch screws.' He must have used one of those screwdriver-drills. They've been advertising those lately. 'According to the earliest findings, the death, which took place two to three days ago, may be due to the forced ingestion of bleach.' How horrible! How could anyone do such a thing? And not too far from here!"

I'm feeling vaguely nauseated as I play out the scene of the poor woman who was crucified alive, then poisoned. I keenly regret that Yvette read me this piece. It's not that I want my eyes shut to my surroundings, but I've had my fill of crime. With nightmares and cold sweats every night for six months.

Yvette steadfastly continues: "'The horror intensified as the murderer removed large chunks of flesh from the victim after she died'—fortunately— 'apparently with the aid of a power saw. In Entrevaux, emotions understandably are running high. The police are on the alert. The house, a small cottage abandoned for years, was a regular hangout for squatters. The investigation will treat this as a crime committed under the influence of narcotics.' I can't quite see a drug addict going to buy plywood, screws, and all that. They're not the kind to premeditate murder," Yvette comments as she puts down the paper. "If you ask me, it was a maniac. It figures with all this unemployment."

Now she's launching into a long diatribe against the government and planetary drift. I'm trying to concentrate on the heat from the sun and children's laughter, but my head's filled with the vision of the young woman, desperately screaming while a 2.75-inch screw bores down into her wrist.

No, I refuse to think about it.

Think about the dog. The dog's nose, his warm hair. The loosening of the bladder . . . the absolute terror . . . the hum of the saw slicing through the flesh . . . No! I grab the pen and have a hard time holding it, but manage to write: *I'm going to buy a dog.*

"A dog? But those animals make a big mess all over! Look, you're not the one who does the cleaning. If you want my opinion . . . I'm sure a dog will keep you company. A small, gentle little thing you can hold in your lap. I could knit him a winter coat, considering it's always raining where we live."

Whoa! I've managed to get her to change the subject! While Yvette's rattling off all the dogs in the neighborhood, I hear a great shout: "Watch out!" Yvette shouts as well, I get pushed, and then something strikes violently. The wheelchair skids, slides, and butts against a bump, and I wind up on the ground, head over heels, in a position even less comfortable than sitting. A man's voice, contrite, says, "I'm sorry, I was trying to avoid a kid who'd fallen and . . . "

"You shouldn't be speeding up if you don't know how to skateboard," Yvette yells back as she tries to pull me up.

"I'm really sorry. Here, I'll help."

In the time it takes to say "whoa," I'm in the arms of some unknown man who smells of aftershave. His hair is tickling my face; it must be long. He seems kind of beefy; when he lifted me, he didn't even let out so much as a sigh. Yvette has turned the wheelchair right-side up, and the guy gently sits me down.

"I suppose this belongs to you—the notepad and pen."

He places them in my lap.

"I'm really, terribly sorry. May I invite you to lunch to make it up?"

Zap! There goes another! Already my incomparable charm has driven him nuts. Before Yvette can refuse, I write, "Yes, thank you." Even if it is a bit shaky for me to eat in public, I tell myself, at least we won't be talking about this grisly murder.

Wrong, Elise! The only time when he and Yvette aren't talking about it is when their mouths are full. The guy who bowled me over is called Yann, an instructor and reader of the paper. That's where he got all those passionate commentaries, which I'm listening to now with a knot in my stomach. Why is it that the only thing people find interesting is misfortune? Why not speak of the color of the tablecloth, the song of the goldfinch during mating season, or the virtues of olive oil? *You* try tasting a raclette while listening to this:

"I'm sure he cut her up while she was still alive! He's a sadist."

"Perhaps you're right. Some more cheese, Elise? If only you could see some of the things I saw during my internship at the psychiatric hospital. Things that would send shivers up your spine. Because he's crucified her, you can tell already he's got to be a bit peculiar. A mystical delirium, no doubt. Or one of those satanic cults."

"And what about the bleach? That's got to burn like hell! Let me give you some more white wine, Elise," says Yvette.

"Was it a purification ritual? . . . I don't know," Yann ventures. "The fact of the matter is that there's a dangerous criminal on the loose, in our midst."

There's the kind of thing that puts you right at ease for the rest of the day! I down my wineglass in a single gulp.

"He might even be here, at the resort," Yann says with zest. "What better place to conceal oneself than in the bustling crowd of a ski resort? A parka, a hat, sunglasses? Everyone here looks the same."

Anyway, no one even knows what the murderer looks like. He doesn't need to hide. He can go on with his activities at his own ease. Feeling melancholy, I nibble at my salad without any appetite.

"Are you here on vacation?" Yvette asks.

"No, I work here. At the center for the handicapped."

No. Am I dreaming?

"The MRCHA?" Yvette blurts out, quicker than on *Questions for Champions*.

"How do you know about it?"

Explanations, laughter, "oh, my, what a coincidence!" They good-naturedly order coffee, except for Elise, the killjoy, at your service, who is invaded by somber premonitions. I'll give ten-to-one odds that if some sicko is lurking about in these parts, his path will cross mine.

Coffee cups clatter, and the room is abuzz with the lively conversations of skiers. Yvette pours her heart out on my behalf, recounting the hardship and suffering, telling all about the book and last year's events, while I do my vase impression. It's exasperating to hear people speak about you continually as if you weren't there. I almost feel like pulling out the tablecloth and knocking everything over. Yann must understand, for suddenly I feel his hand on my wrist.

"And what about you, Elise? Is all this sudden celebrity hard to handle?"

On my notepad I write, *I completely don't give a damn. Can we go now?*

"Uh-oh. Either I'm mistaken or you're in a bad mood. You're right. Why sit around inside when it's so lovely outside? I'm going to try to go down this trail without knocking anyone off. Check, please. No, no, it's out of the question. I invited you."

Outside, the wind has picked up. Yann leaves with strong handshakes. Yvette informs me that he's wearing gray ski pants and a sweater streaked with gray, black, and orange. He's got long blond hair held in place by a headband. "He looks more like a ski instructor than a special-ed teacher," she adds with good humor. Apparently Yann has succeeded in conquering the dragon that is my companion.

We quietly head for our usual terrace, and Yvette plunges into the latest Harlequin while I throw myself into a series of mental calculus operations.

It's something I've discovered recently, and it keeps me busy. Long addition, multiplication, rules of three, and so on. When I get too bored, I can always turn on my Walkman and listen to music or the radio. The problem is, I'm not that musical and I'm not that wild about the radio. People talk, and it makes me annoyed. What I'd really like to do is read a good book, but I've "read" my whole collection in Braille, and I'm waiting for a new shipment.

$1,356 + 2,417 =$ I still can't think about anything besides that poor young woman who was murdered. 752×235, two hundred times $700 = 140,000 + 30$ times $50 =$ and then there's this Yann who jumps out of nowhere and it just so happens he works at MRCHA. Maybe it's because I'm walled up inside myself, but I tend to see plots everywhere. I must say in my defense, though, that ever since I almost died in the attack that turned me into a vegetable, I've been through several murder attempts. It tends to put one on the lookout.

I ought to take advantage of the sun. I ought to relax. Try to take a quick nap. Three hundred sixty-five sheep jump 28 times 36 fences in 13 minutes. How many fences does each sheep jump in 42 minutes?

Someone's shaking me. I yawn abundantly. I was looking for a figure, and all I came up with was forty winks. I'm in a complete daze.

"It's ten to five," Yvette announces. "The driver's here."

"Hello! My name's Hugo!" a man I take to be in his fifties calls out in a ragged voice. "Come on in, young lady, I'll get you into your seat."

The vehicle is specially fitted to transport people with handicaps. Now I'm on some sort of platform. Yvette sits in the front seat, next to Hugo, who informs us that he's one of two nurses in the center, the other one being a woman.

The driver chooses a winding route.

"We're climbing over the village," Yvette tells me, "toward a great stone structure."

The great stone structure, as she says, dates back to the nineteenth century and juts out over the village. They still call it the "sanatorium" here, even though that was closed more than forty years ago. When I was a child it was already abandoned, and my uncle strictly forbade me to go inside. I promptly made my way in through a broken window and wound up in a vast room with a wooden floor and vaulted ceiling that was dark and stank of urine. Beer cans littered the floor. A door half torn off its hinges revealed a large room with white tiles that was equipped with an enormous black furnace, the kind that brought to mind children who were a bit too curious and wound up cooked in a wine sauce by some smiling ogress. In a corner lay a naked, dismembered doll. I really felt like peeing. Somewhere a door slammed, and I took off running, terrified.

I never set foot in there again, which was just as well, since my visits to Castaing began to seem more and more old hat as I turned into a teenager, when I preferred London and, like everybody else, was dreaming of Kathmandu.

We stop. Hugo sets me down on a ramp for people with handicaps. I can tell from the rough whiskers against my hand that he's bearded, and I know he's strong from his enormous protruding biceps. Heels click against the cement. Francine Atchouel rushes our way.

"I'm so happy you could make it! Thank you, Hugo, I'll look after them. That's Italian architecture dating back to the beginning of the nineteenth century," she explains to Yvette. "Originally the building served as a barracks for Piemontese troops, and then, during the twenties, it was converted into a sanatorium before it was abandoned during the fifties."

"Did the foundation buy it back?" Yvette asks politely.

"MRCHA, yes. Four years ago. The air is very clean up here, as you know, and now that everything's been renovated, it's fabulous!"

My wheels are sliding over a parquet floor that has a nice wax smell while she leads us into a large living room, "our household," where residents wait for us in perfect silence.

"Hello, everybody!" Mrs. Atchouel trumpets. "This is Elise and her companion, Yvette."

I hear chuckles, stamping feet, and growling bellies. Yvette coughs nervously.

"Let me introduce you. They're a bit shy," Francine continues. "This is Magali.

Infantile psychosis," she whispers.

I extend my hand into the void; there's a giggle, then a hand, which clumsily grips mine. It awkwardly goes limp, then someone touches me on the shoulder without saying a word.

"Léonard de Quincey," Mrs. Atchouel announces in a formal tone. "Léonard's our astronomer. Neuromuscular handicaps," she whispers.

Léonard leaves us.

"Christian," she continues.

"Hewwo, mith!" a thick voice shouts. "Mith, mith, mith, mithtake."

"Oh, don't say such silly things! Christian's mildly retarded, with a tendency toward echolalia," Francine whispers. "Laetitia, would you come here, darling."

She's making a strange sliding sound. Oh, yes, that's a walker sliding across the wooden floor.

It goes on this way for a good quarter of an hour. Eight participants, whose handicaps affect either their minds or their motor functions: the center takes in all kinds of cases. Jean-Claude, twenty-eight years old, is a victim of Charcot-Marie-Tooth disorder, which brings about a progressive and irremediable paralysis; he's a video freak and lives with a camcorder on his shoulder. Bernard, twenty-five, has never been socialized and has been "diagnosed with Ganser's syndrome" ("what's it to you?") as well as OCDs (obsessive-compulsive disorders—these I know about: they're the people who wash their hands a hundred times a day and check six hundred times to make sure the gas really is turned off). There's Emilie, thirty-two, who has Down's syndrome. And Clara, forty-three, who's stricken with oligophrenia. Emilie claims that Clara's an idiot, but they're thick as thieves.

All these strange voices are making me dizzy; I'm mixing up their names, starting to feel tired, when finally we get to have our tea. This is a bit complicated because it's served by the residents under the supervision of Hugo and Martine, the two nurses.

"You must be wondering what we look like," Hugo says, gently. "Well, Martine looks like the head nurse in *One Flew Over the Cuckoo's Nest*," he continues, with a laugh.

"And you look like Captain Haddock, but redheaded!" she rejoins.

Francine Atchouel hands out cake "iced by our residents" and insists we help ourselves to heaping plates of seconds.

In a low voice, Yvette asks Hugo what *oligophrenia* means.

"It's the name given for backwardness," Hugo answers.

"They used to be called innocents," Martine adds. "We distinguish those who can speak and learn the rudiments of reading and writing from those who can only speak, and those who can't even master language," she goes on, all the while yelling at Clara, who's trying to grab Emilie's teacup out of her hands.

"And as far as Ganser's syndrome goes," Hugo continues, "these are patients who, like Bernard, systematically give answers that miss the point, even when they've understood perfectly (or so we think) what they've been told."

"How much does Bernard weigh?" Yvette asks, in an even lower voice.

"Two hundred forty pounds, at five foot seven," Hugo replies.

He's obese. They continue to make small talk. I'm vaguely following the conversation, but feel tense; I don't like being around strangers who can observe me while I can't see them. And I know this isn't a very honorable sentiment, but being in the company of the "backward" has always made me slightly uneasy. It's the feeling of not knowing how to respond to their expectations, their needs. And wanting to draw back from the physical contact they're always demanding. I'm not a big fan of physical contact outside of sexual relations. Benoît often criticized me for being so cold. How different I am today, Benoît! I'm so dependent now!

Cries of pleasure suddenly ring out when someone jovially calls out, "Hey, gang!" It's Yann. Apparently, he's very well liked among the residents. Emilie repeats his name ecstatically, while Magali in her enthusiasm shakes my arm, and Christian sniffles with vigor.

Francine wants to introduce us, but Yann explains that we've already met. It takes less than fifteen minutes for them to get to the savage murder in Entrevaux. Yann's got fresh news from one of his skiing buddies who is assistant to the sergeant of the local police brigade assigned to this investigation. As soon as Yann brings up the subject, Francine begins to cough vigorously, and he cuts himself short.

"Hugo, isn't it time for the soap?" she asks. "Whoever wants to watch the soap in the rec room may go with Hugo."

"You're letting them watch *Police City Blues*?" Yvette, who knows the TV schedule by heart, asks, stunned.

This calls to mind blaring gunfire, curse words, car chases replete with screeching tires, and athletic (or amorous) gasping.

"They're adults!" Francine Atchouel replies.

"You know, it's not all sweetness and light," Lactitia calls. "Well, I've got to go. I love this show!"

Feet shuffle, and someone plants a loud, smacking kiss on my cheek.

"That's Magali," Francine explains. "She never misses an episode. She goes wild for the flashing sirens."

Someone's pounding on my hand.

"That's Christian."

"Ping, pong, ping, pong, hiiii!"

The others leave without saying good-bye. "I have to wash my two hands. Tomorrow's Saturday," I hear Bernard mumbling through his teeth.

"Yann, I would appreciate it if you didn't bring up such painful subjects in front of our residents!" Francine exclaims once they've left. "You know how sensitive they are."

"You're the one who planted them in front of the TV!" Yann replies, offended.

"So? What did your policeman friend have to say?" Yvette breaks in, devoured by curiosity.

"Well, it's not too pretty. The information is correct: the girl was crucified alive, and then forced to swallow pure bleach, no doubt with the help of a funnel."

They protest in horror. I grit my teeth, ordering myself not to imagine the scene.

"Then what?" asks Yvette, her voice altered.

"At least two pounds of flesh were carved off her hips, to make damn steaks, of all things!"

"Yann! Have some respect!" Francine cries, scandalized.

I'm getting the feeling she doesn't appreciate her sports teacher all that much.

"According to the earliest findings, the woman was in her thirties, had long brown hair, blue eyes, with no features that particularly stood out," Yann continues without stepping down. "He's contacted the FRDD, but without much success so far."

"The what?" Francine asks. "Can you try to make some sense when you talk to us?"

"The Forensics Research and Documentation Division," Yann recites. "Philippe's very hooked in with scientific research methods. He's had internships with NCAPS and the ICR," he adds with delight. "The National Center for Advanced Police Studies and the Institute for Criminal Research."

"Goodness gracious!" Yvette whistles between her teeth. "Have they found anything?"

"Nothing. They're going to broadcast a photo of the victim on TV."

"Certainly a homeless person who came across some sadist in the squat," Yvette decrees.

"A sadist who'd gone out and bought all his materials beforehand . . . What I think is he lured her there, and had decided to kill her well in advance."

"Or to kill any woman, no matter whom!" Francine Atchouel murmurs. "My God, it gives me chills. I hope they catch him quickly."

"That would surprise me. Mmm, this cake's delicious. They've got absolutely no trail," Yann replies, with a certain satisfaction. "Certainly he was wearing gloves. Oh, I forgot, they found a plastic sheet covered with the poor girl's blood. He must have used it to protect his clothes."

"Stop it, you're making me ill!" Francine protests.

"Whatever you want. Oh, by the way, did the sleigh guy call?" Yann asks.

"Yes, everything will be ready for tomorrow at ten o'clock. Yann's arranged sleigh rides for our residents with teams of huskies," Francine explains.

"Oh, that must be fabulous!" Yvette exclaims, ecstatically.

"Why don't you come with us?" Yann offers, enthusiastically.

I find the idea rather tempting. A ride out in the open, wrapped warmly, with dogs panting. This might give the illusion of the Great White North. I squeeze Yvette's hand as a sign that I accept.

We arrange to meet the following day, and Yvette takes her leave.

In the minibus conversation naturally drifts toward the residents. Hugo informs us that Jean-Claude has only a few years to live.

"He's got a nice-looking face, but he's so skinny!" Yvette comments sympathetically. "The astronomer's a rather handsome young man," she adds after a brief silence, before concluding sadly, "What a pity!"

"He suffers quite a lot from his condition," Hugo says. "He's ashamed of it. He's a tormented soul. I always see he gets his medication."

"Are you afraid he'll commit suicide?" Yvette cries.

"You never know. Everyone takes him for retarded, even though he's certified to teach math. Life's a bit hard, you know."

Yes, I know it is. I remember after the accident how everyone thought I was nothing but a vegetable. I remember that horrible feeling of powerlessness to make myself heard, to show that I've understood. It reminds me that in the beginning of February, I should return to Paris for new exams. Perhaps after that, I might have another operation. Who knows? If I recover a bit more autonomy at each intervention, then ten years from now I might be able to play *"Au Clair de la Lune."* "What's more," Hugo goes on, still on the subject of Léonard, "there was a fire in his classroom when he was prepping at Polytechnique. Fifteen of his classmates perished. He suffered a terrible depression and was undergoing psychiatric treatment for years. Mrs. Atchouel preferred to keep us up to date on this; we're always more effective when we know people's backgrounds."

It's a rather sinister background, actually. Hugo's gently shifting gears. Rap thunders out of a passing vehicle with honking horns and squealing brakes.

"Some people have a knack for throwing themselves under the wheels of a train!" Hugo comments. With a laugh, he adds, "When we walk in a small group, it's not too shabby, either. Yesterday Magali gave us the slip, and I found her in front of the superette. Bernard almost got himself run over by a bus. He wanted to cross to look at cakes in the bakery window."

"You let him eat whatever he wants?" Yvette asks.

"He's supposed to follow a diet, but . . . Bernard has a hard time fitting in, he lived a long time with his mother. He's both stupid and clever, a little too gentle. They're the ones who jump into action and make really big blunders."

"What about Christian? He's a little scary," Yvette admits. "He's a giant," she adds for my benefit.

"Christian's another story. He was abused during his childhood and was taken away from his family. He's very impulsive and loves to play around with the sound qualities in words. He's no dummy, but he's incapable of acting like an adult. He's a six-foot-one-inch baby, built like a rugby player."

"They're all a bit like babies disguised as grown-ups," Yvette murmurs. "Unleashed, abandoned to their own suffering."

"Hey! What about us, the teachers? Don't we count? We're here to replace their incompetent parents."

"I'm sorry, I didn't mean to put your devotion into question. You've got to turn there, to the right!"

The tires grind, the bus skids a bit over the slippery road, and this conversation has made me melancholy.

Once we're in, Yvette dashes straight for the TV, grumbling: her show has already begun. I roll my wheelchair over to the half-open window. Night has fallen, and I can hear snow crunch beneath the boots of passersby, chains going *floc-floc-floc* as a car drives past. The smell of snow at night. The wind has picked up, sweeping aloft moist snowflakes that land on the window, my nose, my cheeks, my lips, cool and sweet. Yvette violently shouts something at the announcer about a statement that did not meet her approval. I smile to myself, then think once more of the young woman who was tortured and no longer feel like smiling. Last night was just as peaceful as tonight, and yet someone went to her death with horrible suffering.

"Elise . . . "

I jump. Was I dreaming or did someone just whisper my name under the window?

"Elise . . . "

No, I'm not dreaming. Someone's calling me. Yann? I open the window a bit more with my good hand and brush against something. Is it a face? Yes, I think it's a face. I hold out my arm, but come across nothing. Then my fingers close around a moist package.

"For you, my love," a voice whispers.

Again!

Fast, fast, my notepad: *Who are you?* I wave the sheet out the window.

A small, sickening laugh. A warm hand brushes against mine, which retracts. Then footsteps go off into the distance. My mysterious visitor has left! I roll up to Yvette, who wasn't aware of anything. Thoughtfully fingering the small, wet package, I give it a sniff. It smells of meat, just as I'd figured. The steak giver has struck again!

Steak. Oh, my God! *Steak!* It feels as though I've been punched in the gut. "Cut up in damn *steaks* . . . " I drop the package, and it falls to the floor.

"What is it? Oh! What's that? Another steak? But where'd you take it from?"

As if I'd done it on purpose! My hand is trembling as I force myself to write: *Someone just gave it to me through the window.*

"But that's crazy!"

The paper crinkles as it unfolds.

"Why, yes, it's a steak! It's beautiful red meat, just like the other package. I really don't understand this . . . "

Call Yann.

"I don't see what Yann's got to do with this steak. He's certainly not the one playing this joke on us."

Call Yann.

"Fine, fine, whatever you want," Yvette grumbles as she picks up the phone.

She explains to him more or less our little problem while I slip her a message.

"Wait, let me read this . . . Elise would like to know if your friend the police officer could do an analysis of the meat . . . I know it's a whim, I don't know what's gotten into her . . . It's no problem? You're really so sweet. I'll bring it to you tomorrow morning . . . Yes, I'll put it in the fridge. Good night, and thanks again." As she hangs up, Yvette protests, "We look ridiculous. All we needed to do was throw the steak into the trash, and that would have been that!"

The ringing of the telephone interrupts her: it's her boyfriend, Jean. A long conversation follows, and I force myself not to listen. I'm in a rush to find out what the analysis might produce. Provided that it's not what I think! I'm crossing my fingers, knowing it won't do a thing.

3

SINCE THIS MORNING I've been feverish, impatient, agitated. Yvette handed the steak over to Yann, who had it sent to his policeman friend by way of the mailman. And so we're off to the Arctic Circle. The center's shuttle bus has dropped us off at Nordic Camp.

The residents are making a hellish racket, all excited at the prospect of our trip, and the dogs are not to be outdone. Laetitia, who's afraid of them, won't let go of me, while Magali's shouting out garbled words. Hugo and Martine are stopping Christian from rolling about in the snow, holding back Emilie and Clara, who want to stick their fingers in the big dogs' mouths, all the while handing out bonbons. Bernard is asking everyone the time, assuring us that time is money. I'm still thinking about that damn steak and its mysterious donor, but I'm too busy trying to grasp what's going on around to really care.

Jean-Claude has brought along his camcorder and is filming us nonstop. He's practically an invalid, but he likes to record movements. Besides, he's always calling out, "It's in the box," as if action could be canned.

I'd like to see myself on film. To find out what I look like. To see myself lift my arm like an automated Barbie doll.

The dogs are barking in long wolflike howls, growling and snorting, impatient to leave. Yann makes sure everyone in his little crowd is settled in while chatting with the drivers, three young men endowed with strong southern accents. The temperature has dropped, and the wind has picked up. Yvette helps me button the collar of my ski suit and slips on my helmet. Hugo lifts me up. I can feel my knotted muscles, his trimmed beard, his medicinal smell. He sets me down on the fur-covered wooden bench next to Laetitia. Magali and Christian are sitting across from us. Yvette climbs in last and falls back against me, murmuring, "I'm too old for this." Hugo sits down next to Emilie, Clara, and Bernard. Martine gets in with Jean-Claude and Léonard. Yann hands out thick blankets, lavishes us with advice and encouragement, then snaps the reins. The other drivers shout out enthusiastic "yoohoos." The sleighs rumble, then gather speed. As we slip into the forest, I take in the powerful scent of firs.

"How beautiful this is!" Yvette cries. "You'd think we were in Canada."

The wind whips my face, and the wooden blades swishing through the snow remind me of cross-country skiing, briefly dragging me down in the dumps, so I calm down and listen to Laetitia, who's ecstatic over everything. This is the first time in twenty-four years that Laetitia, half paralyzed since her adolescence because of an auto accident, has come to mountains. She's laughing a joyous laugh from the simple pleasure of flying through the snow.

I wonder if she thinks back incessantly to those days when she enjoyed the normal use of her legs. She was fifteen when the accident occurred, Yvette told me, and she knows practically everything about the residents because she's become fast friends with Martine; they've even exchanged recipes for gratin dauphinois. Gratin dauphinois is a main area of common ground for housewives. The ravages it may cause are terrible. Try to make one the night your best friend is coming over for dinner. Even if she's holding her nose so tight it bleeds, she'll never be able to admit yours is better than hers. And let's not even talk about what might happen if her husband, with a mouthful of potatoes, calls out, "You shee, dear, now *that'sh* gratin dauphinois!" It gives me comfort, when I think about such tragic cases of feminine strife, that Benoît, my ex, hated it. As far as Tony goes, I have no idea. Tony makes fun of everything he eats. And because it's hard to make conversation by writing, I avoid minor subjects.

"The dog!" Magali just cried out, all excited. Yvette acquiesces distractedly.

"The dog, the dog, the dog, the dog!"

"Yes, there are plenty of dogs," Yvette admits, "we've seen them. Sit down, you might fall."

"The dog! The big dog!"

"Magali, stop fidgeting!" Yann scolds, turning around.

"Calm down, Mag. Look at the snow," Laetitia gently suggests.

"Ah, I see!" Yvette shouts. "She's talking about the big black dog over there—the Labrador!"

The Labrador? Perhaps that's the one that came to say hello yesterday morning in front of the superette . . . although his owner most likely isn't the type to take him for walks out in the forest!

But Yvette's shaking my arm: "That's the dog belonging to the girl from the nightclub! You know, the big black one. I don't see the girl . . . "

Furious barking.

"What's the matter with that dog? He's coming right toward us! Oh, my, with these huskies, it's going be quite a to-do—"

Yvette doesn't have time to finish her sentence, because the huskies begin to howl and pull on the reins, while the Labrador runs beside us, barking vigorously.

"Get out of here! Get out of here!" Yann screams.

Whips crack; I hope they're not really directed at the Labrador. Oh, how this bothers me, not being able to see what's going on, or even to ask!

"A dog! Come here!" Magali shouts.

"Stop it! Shut up!" Laetitia begs her.

"Wah! Wah! Wah!" Christian sings.

"I feel like throwing up," Jean-Claude, behind us, groans.

"We're going to turn over," Yvette prophesies, gripping my arm.

In fact, I do feel the sleigh inclining somewhat.

Then an enormous mass falls into my lap, taking my breath away. Everyone's screaming, but the sleigh hasn't turned over; I feel a rough tongue licking my face while the huskies break loose.

"Dog!" Magali says with satisfaction.

"What an asshole that dog is," Yann declares as he stops the whole team.

"Careful, Magali, don't take grab him by the neck. He might be dangerous!" Yvette sermonizes.

"Nice," Magali replies. "He likes me."

"Looks like you're right," Yann sighs as the Labrador turns around to lick Magali, joyfully whipping his tail against my face.

The dog starts making the rounds from one person to the next, so here we are with some hundred-pound Labrador who's jumping, landing on our stomachs, ardently barking and causing confusion.

Then a nervous voice calls, "Tintin! Tintin! Where are you? Come here! Here, boy!"

With a vigorous "woof" and one last jolt, Tintin's off, followed by the huskies' voracious cries.

"You ought to keep him on a leash; we almost had an accident," Yann yells, furiously.

"I'm sorry. He doesn't usually get loose. He must have recognized the lady," the voice adds, closer now, still sounding sad and gentle.

"Is this dog one of your friends?" Yann asks me, sarcastically.

I give no answer, obviously.

"We met yesterday at the superette," Yvette explains.

"I'm really sorry," the voice says, sounding sad and gentle, and so feminine.

"It's all right . . . "

Look! Look! Yann's intonation has suddenly changed. His anger has flown away. I gather from this that the owner of this voice can't be too shabby to look at.

"I didn't recognize you," Yann continues. "You're okay?"

"In your opinion?" the girl replies, which to me seems quite strange. "All right, come on, Tintin," she says. "Gotta go! See you."

That's all for our episode of "wild escapade." Now the comments begin. Before we get started again, the word *dog* is pronounced 358 times.

Why did she say "in your opinion"? Is this to imply that Yann knows she's not doing well? That she should be ill? Does she have cancer? That would explain the sadness in her voice.

"Do you know her, Yann?" Yvette asks.

"A little. She works at Moonwalk."

"Oh, yes, I know," Yvette replies before launching into a series of harsh commentaries on bar hostesses and their notorious lack of good sense.

Just like her aunt's cousin, who used to work in a house in Barbès . . .

I'm trying to concentrate on the sleigh swishing through the snow and the sound it makes as it falls from heavy branches. It's even less difficult to concentrate on snow when I receive an extremely cool lump of the very same thing square in the head. Yvette dusts me off as Magali breaks out laughing. Christian mumbles, "thnowman, thnowman," in a creepy-sounding voice. What a delicious ride this is!

But like all good things, this must come to an end, and here we are back at the camp. The brave trappers disembark, and Yann lifts me up and places me in my wheelchair without so much as an "oof." He smells of cologne, and his rough chin brushes my cheek. Not the least bit unpleasant. Shrink wags his finger, scolding me and whispering, "Tony," and I reply to Shrink that he's there to act not as my conscience but rather as my devoted analyst.

We're back in the shuttle bus and return to the center for a well-deserved lunch. It's there that I prove that even with only one hand, one can perfectly swallow ten or so crêpes as quickly as the others. I suddenly realize that I'm enjoying myself, relaxing; I feel like laughing and allow myself a feeling of well-being in the warmth of a wood fire and hot chocolate. Even the taciturn Hugo is joking with us.

"That ride positively seems to have cheered you!" Francine Atchouel repeats for the third time, though she didn't consider it right to come along and jiggle her plump figure in a wooden sleigh. "I hope no one caught cold! A bit of blackberry jam, Yvette? And what about you, darling Elise?"

No, thank you, darling Francine.

"Life is so beautiful when one knows how to love it," Martine observes.

"Martine's a real church lady," Yann whispers.

The telephone rings.

"Yann, it's for you: Sergeant Lorieux!" Hugo yells.

Suddenly I don't hear a thing. No murmuring, no clamoring, no plates clattering, no wood crackling in the hearth. I hear only Yann's firm steps as he goes to pick up the receiver.

"Hello, Philippe? . . . Yeah, hi. So? . . . What? . . . Are you sure? . . . Shit!"

"Yann, please!" scolds darling Francine.

"But that's crazy! What? . . . Yeah, well, sure, but that's going to be tough, she's mute . . . Okay, we'll be waiting for you."

I'm gripping Yvette's wrist. I'm the mute, so that means the police want to see me. Yann comes back toward me: I hear his footsteps, then feel his hair against my cheek.

"That was my friend, the police officer. He had that steak analyzed. Uh . . . well . . . uh . . . "

"It's mad cow disease!" Yvette says. "I was sure of it!"

"It isn't cow," Yann murmurs.

I feel a great big lump of crêpes immobilizing in the pit of my stomach.

"Elise, this is pretty hard to believe, but, well, it's . . . "

"Pork? Impossible! Anyway, I know how to recognize pork!" Yvette protests.

Yann presses his lips to my ear: "It's . . . uh . . . human flesh. They're coming to ask you some questions. They'll be here in an hour."

Human flesh.

Yvette, with a hint of anxiety in her voice, asks, "What did you say, Yann? I didn't hear you."

"The police will explain it you," Yann answers, giving my shoulder a squeeze.

"What are you talking about, then?" Francine inquires.

"Nothing, just a minor problem regarding provisions," Yann replies.

Of human flesh.

And I ate some. So did Yvette.

Human flesh most certainly taken from a young woman's cadaver.

The lump of crêpes takes the elevator straight for the exit, and so here I go, throwing up into my lap.

It's met with a concert of varied exclamations and chuckles from the residents; someone wipes off my mouth and cleans off my lap, assuring me that "it's nothing terrible, nothing to worry about at all, it happens to everyone!" What they really mean is, especially to everyone a bit special.

Yvette goes even further, saying, "Usually she never does anything like that. It must have been the ride that upset her stomach."

"Don't stand there babbling. Get me a moist towel. Move it!" Yann orders.

"Nothing to get excited over," Yvette grumbles, doing as he says.

I'm all cleaned up. Hugo and Martine have taken the darling residents to watch TV, and darling Francine makes us a bit more darling tea.

Shrink whispers to me that I'm foolish for feeling ashamed. That my reaction is completely normal given the situation. Yet I don't see myself as a normal person. I see myself as a monster who must constantly prove herself worthy of being taken out into the company of graceful humans.

Someone's ringing the bell.

Hugo goes to open up and unceremoniously announces, "The cops."

"The police, here? Sweet Jesus, what's going on?" Martine asks, astounded.

"I don't know. It's got something to do with all this business about steak, I'd guess," Yvette mutters, disconcerted.

"Sergeant Philippe Lorieux!" a feminine-sounding voice calls out. "Miss Andrioli?"

"Affirmative," answers Yvette, who happens to love military men. "Miss Andrioli is deprived of her speech, Sergeant!"

"Very well."

I imagine him as a smooth-cheeked, fair-haired boy, fresh out of the academy, awkwardly scratching his nose.

"I'd like to have a private interview with Miss Andrioli and her interpreter," he announces, finally, in his shrill little voice.

Yvette wheels me into the small adjoining room. "My boudoir," Francine Atchouel specifies, sounding as though she's going to faint. Is the sergeant the type of pretty man who has that sort of effect on mature ladies?

The door shuts behind us. The sergeant coughs nervously. Yvette clears her throat. I don't do a thing. The sergeant gets started: "One of the teachers at MRCHA had a piece of red meat sent to us to be analyzed, which he had obtained through your intervention. Which leads to my first question: How did you enter into possession of this exhibit?"

"Exhibit? Was the meat poisoned?" Yvette asks, surprised.

"Answer my question, please."

"Well, Miss Elise was by the window, and when I returned from the kitchen, she had this package on her lap."

I feel around for my notebook and start to write. Then I hold out the paper for the sergeant.

"So the individual who conveyed this package to you did not identify himself?"

I write more. I feel Yvette's breath as she leans over my shoulder.

"'And he had already shown up the night before,'" the sergeant reads, "'with a similar piece of meat, which we ate.' Holy shit!"

Whatever you say.

At this point the door opens, and Yann asks if everything's okay.

"Insofar as these ladies have no doubt ingested part of the victim, I really can't say that everything's going for the best," Sergeant Lorieux soberly comments.

"The victim? What victim?" Yvette asks, shocked.

Lorieux coughs nervously.

"The young woman from Entrevaux. The murderer carried out some cleaving upon the body . . . and the 'steak' that Yann had sent to me . . . well . . . it corresponds to . . . "

Here it is. I knew it—

A great *boom* yanks me from my silent lamentations. Yvette simultaneously understands and faints. Men fuss around her, and Martine is summoned, with requests for rum and crème de menthe.

Philippe Lorieux starts to cough again until calm is established, or in other words until the moment Yvette stops chanting, "Omigod, I can't believe it," breathing into her handkerchief, while darling Francine groans, "This is horrible, tell us all about it!" tapping her foot.

"I'm taking everyone to the rec room," Hugo says.

"Take them, take them," Francine answers, "and close the door, thank you. Well, then, Captain . . . "

"Sergeant Lorieux."

"As you wish. Well, then, the one who murdered this poor woman, if I've understood correctly, has given pieces of her body to our poor friends. What a tragedy! Do they risk poisoning?"

"I don't know. We'll have to wait for the complete autopsy report to know if the victim was sick."

"Because on top of it all, now we risk catching something?" Yvette groans, appalled.

"No, because you cooked it."

"Aarrrgh!" Yvette chokes.

The sergeant must feel a bit overwhelmed by these events, because he raises his voice, or rather tries to: "If you please, calm down, and let's proceed with some order. I need your complete identity. After that, we'll be taking your depositions. Schnabel, get me the forms."

"Yes, Chief," answers a voice that calls to mind the roll of a drum.

As soon as Schnabel is seated and ready to take down our answers, Sergeant Lorieux starts his questioning. Not much comes of it: an unidentified man spoke to me and on two occasions gave me bits of flesh removed from a murder victim.

"Does this even have anything to do with the murderer?" Yann wonders aloud. "Why couldn't it be some harmless kook who discovered the body and decided to indulge in some macabre games?"

I don't know why I don't believe this for a second. The guy called me "my love" with all the tenderness a cannibal might reserve for an appetizing woman.

" . . . look a bit like her," Lorieux says.

Lost in my dark thoughts, I wasn't paying attention to what he said and don't understand why Yvette's screaming again: "But she could be in danger!"

Who? Darling Francine? I pick up my notebook to ask the question.

Only silence. Then the sergeant clears his throat and in his girlish voice announces, "I was saying simply that you offer a certain resemblance to the victim. The color of your hair, your eyes, your silhouette . . . "

All right, there's no need to draw me a picture, I've got it. Some crazy killer is on the loose in the village, with his bloodred hands stuffed in his mittens, waiting for just the right moment to send me off *ad patres*. It reminds me of a million lousy films.

But killers also go to the movies.

For a few moments a feverish calm prevails over the room. Yann goes and joins Martine and Hugo. Beyond the windowpanes, we can hear the wind roar. The telephone rings. Francine Atchouel picks up.

"Excuse me? Speak up, I can't hear a thing! Who are you looking for? What? Ah, hold on! It's for darling Elise," she explains.

"Who knows you're here?" Lorieux asks immediately.

"Uh . . . nobody," Yvette answers.

"I'm taking the earpiece," he decides.

"There isn't any. It's a new wireless extension—" Francine begins.

"Good grief! Would you just give her the phone?!" Yann says as he returns to the room, interrupting her and pressing the receiver against my ear.

A horrible little voice whispers, "Hello, my love."

Goose flesh. I raise my arm, point to the phone, and form a circle with thumb and forefinger.

"It's him!" Lorieux says, understanding me. "What can we do?"

"Hit the button with the plus sign," Francine murmurs, pouting.

A finger brushes over mine searching for the button that will raise the volume while the horrible little voice goes on, "Are you still hungry? Would you like some other small gifts?"

Now the voice is resounding through the room, in the absolute silence.

"I'm prepared for anything to make you happy, my love. What about you? Are you ready to make sacrifices for me?"

Click. With this menacing question, the call is cut short. The phone's taken away from me. I realize my palm is moist and wipe it against the blanket.

"Schnabel, notify HQ! He may be in the vicinity. If only we knew where he called from!"

"Look at the screen. The number of the incoming call should be lit up for thirty seconds," Francine calls out.

"You couldn't say so?" Lorieux screams.

"No one ever lets me say anything!" Francine protests. "Anyway, there's also a call-back button!"

No one listens to her. They all trample around the telephone, grunting like rugbymen in a skirmish.

"Oh four, nine three, seven eight, seven seven, seven nine," Lorieux shouts hoarsely. "Schnabel, quick, call HQ! Call them from the shuttle bus in case he calls back here!"

Schnabel dashes off at a run; the vibrations on the floor lead me to guess that he's not all that skinny.

"It's snowing," Francine notes.

No one answers, except for Yvette, who can't help observing that "moon veiled at night, tomorrow's hope takes flight." It's a cute little proverb that matches our circumstances. Yann paces back and forth, relentlessly whistling one of last summer's top Latino hits. I'm trying to put a few things back in order inside my head: Why would a sadistic killer want to involve me in his crimes? Where does he know me from? How does he know I'm on holiday here? I feel like calling Tony to the rescue, but he's not going to come back from the North Atlantic. After all, I'm not in danger, because this guy's giving me presents.

Don't kid yourself, Elise, Shrink whispers. You're in danger. Don't you feel it in the shivers in your skin? Don't you sense it in that sugary-sweet, stomach-turning voice of his? Trust your intuition, little Elise. Get out of Castaing.

But where will I go? If some mental case is on my trail, then I have no intention of bringing him back to where we live. Now that the police have taken matters into their hands, I'm protected.

Lorieux bursts into the boudoir shouting, "He called from the phone booth across the street from the superette! That's not even a hundred yards from here! Reinforcements are on the way."

I already know they're coming for nothing. An anonymous skier makes a call and then drifts off into the crowd, a small, fuzzy silhouette under the snow. A half hour rolls by as I occupy myself with mental calculations. Darling Francine suggests we stay for dinner. Yvette accepts. Lorieux quite naturally declines and takes his leave, advising us to be prudent.

In writing, I ask what time it is. Five o'clock, Yann answers on his way out of the room. It's time for gymnastics with the residents.

Two more hours until the meal, listening to Francine and Yvette rant.

If only I too could pace up and down the room furiously, tossing off indignant commentaries, or hold my head in my hands, or contemplate nightfall, but I can't do a thing except remain seated in the darkness that envelops me perpetually.

Before dinner, which everyone eats together in the large dining room—"our darling dining room," as Francine says—the residents are permitted to watch the local news on television.

Where they speak once again of the murder in Entrevaux and the investigation, which is "progressing in leaps and bounds."

Laetitia comes to me to make conversation: "I don't like hearing about such sad things," she declares, sitting next to me. "I'd like life to be full of bright colors."

So would I, my child. Even with one, I'd be happy.

"And what I'd like more than anything else in the world is to ski. I know it's impossible. But often I dream of skiing. I'm sliding over the snow. I've seen the Special Olympics on TV. I've told my father I'd like to go into training, to do some sort of sport. But he doesn't want me to. He thinks it's dangerous."

She lowers her voice and whispers, "Yann understands me. He's trying to heist a special instrument for me. But you mustn't talk about it. It's a secret!"

Yann seems to have a penchant for women in distress. And to think I don't even know what he looks like!

"Why did the police come by here?" Laetitia continues, lowering her voice even further.

Completely thrown, I pencil a vague response: *Administrative reasons.*

"I don't believe you. They seemed too upset. And their chief, the pretty blond man who looks like a girl, was sweating from his upper lip. That's a sign of nervousness."

So Lorieux has a delicate physique. He's got no chance as a sergeant!

"You know, Elise . . . May I call you Elise?"

She may, for in any case she doesn't wait for me to answer.

"Everyone talks to me like I was retarded. But apart from the fact that I have difficulty moving, my brain is intact, just like yours or Mrs. Atchouel's."

I'm not crazy about my brain being compared to that of Mrs. Atchouel.

"What I think is the police came here because of the murder in town. They think someone here knows something."

She must be able to read the surprise upon my features, for she laughs and goes on: "I'm no medium! In fact I heard the one named Schnabel, the big heavy guy, call up his headquarters."

She leans toward me, and I can feel her breath against my cheek: "Is it true you ate a piece of the victim?"

All right, fine. Here we go. I write: *Alas, yes.* Why lie about it?

I hear an incredulous, excited whistle.

"What did it taste like? What I mean is, was it any different?"

I'm sincerely asking myself that question. Can I answer a curious young soul that it was in fact delicious? How our stomachs felt no revulsion at the contact of human flesh? I feel nausea returning at the thought of the tender, savory meat between my lips. Laetitia squeezes my hand.

"Oh, excuse me, you're all white! But it's so, so . . . you understand . . . It's not that often that one meets . . . "

Cannibals. Shit, shit, and shit! I feel a flash of rage. If that son-of-a-bitch Vore—because I'm sure it's him—were right here in front of me, I'd . . .

I'd what? He could eat me alive without my being able to defend myself. There'd be no need even to tie me up. I already am, in this wheelchair, by chains far stronger than barbed wire.

Vore. That letter I got. I'm trying to remember the exact terms. He called me an angel. Spoke as though we were to go into battle. With him representing the forces of Evil. But if that were the case, why would he give me such foul presents? Why would he call me "my love"? Or maybe that has nothing to do with anything. Vore's just some poor nut job who's got a strange little habit of writing to famous people, and the killer's another poor nut job who's got a strange little habit of falling in love with famous people. I've always appealed to maniacs. I've never been able to ride the subway without getting my ass felt up.

"Dinner is served!" Francine Atchouel suddenly announces, interrupting my rambling thoughts.

The mealtime atmosphere is more or less agitated. Growling stomachs, flying lumps of bread, sniggers, interminable coughing fits, burps—the residents are worked up. Magali, sitting next to me, won't stop chuckling, tapping me on my forearm. Yvette and Francine are playing a game of "six degrees of separation," discovering a mutual third cousin in Sydney, Australia. Clara and Emilie are arguing over a hairband. Jean-Claude's listening on his Walkman to conversations between Truffaut and Hitchcock. Laetitia's comparing the advantages of two brands of beauty products. I'm nervously picking at my plate. Yann's encouraging me to eat. Thank God there's no meat, just a raclette, a dish I'm terribly fond of ordinarily. Bernard assures us, "Whoever has drunk will drink, whoever has eaten will eat; is there any sausage left?" "You eat too much, big guy," Yann calls back good-naturedly. In hushed tones, Hugo and Martine are discussing a conference on accompanying the dying. It's a barrel of laughs. Christian, sitting across from me, is nervously kicking me under the table at regular intervals, crying, "Pa-*tat!* Pa-*tat!*" Fortunately,

dessert calms everyone, and spoons are eagerly plunging into the house chocolate mousse.

Then we're introduced to the cook, Mrs. Raymond, a solid seventy-five-
year-old woman from the village with a sunny accent who's doubling as the
maintenance woman. I'm imagining her as a sort of feminine Raimu, without the mustache: whenever I have to represent a stranger's face for myself, I
draw from the stock of images my brain recorded before the accident. No
doubt it's limited, but I've got no choice. I make robot-portraits from my
entourage and modify them according to tones of voice, smells, footsteps,
and contact.

We have full-flavored coffee. There's not enough sugar, but I can't be
bothered with grabbing my notepad to write "sugar." I feel tired, sad and
tired, and I'm in a hurry to get to bed.

4

WHAT THE HELL time is it? I've woken up and everything's quiet. You'd think I was in a tomb. For my birthday, I'm going to ask for a talking alarm clock. There's no noise outside. Not even the slightest swoosh of tires, the faintest snatch of conversation. A lot of good it will do to cock my ear, because I don't hear anything. Just the curtains rustling against the half-open window.

I've got to get back to sleep. I've got no intention of mulling over the sordid events of these past two days. No intention of remaining paralyzed in the darkness, imagining that Mr. Vore is prowling around me with a big scalpel. That he's looking at me, snickering. That he's leaning over my face, his bloody lips next to mine . . . No, it's out of the question! I'm counting sheep, tons of sheep, fat, dirty, stinking sheep, with big stupid eyes: *bahhh, bahhh.* Come on, sheep, jump! One, two, one, two, get your sweat running, there's no wolf, no, no one's chewing on your ankles, there's nothing, I tell you!

The cat jumps onto the parquet floor, trotting discreetly . . . the cat? What cat? I must be half asleep. I've dreamed of my cat, who died four years ago. There was a tumor in his liver. Okay, fine, I'm not about to start weeping over my cat. My nerves are really beaten to a pulp. I should ask Yvette to buy vitamins. But what about the sound? I've just heard a sound. A light thud on the parquet floor.

Didn't Yvette close the window before going to bed?

I hold my breath to hear better. There's a rustle on my left. So minute. My heart's beating so hard that it's all I can hear. I feel a draft of air on my face; is it a draft of air or breathing? As I brutally raise my arm, casting about to strike anything, my hand runs into something, and then there's a noise of glass breaking on the floor, deafening in the night.

"What's the matter?" Yvette yells from the room next door.

She gets up heavily.

"Elise? Is everything all right?"

There's a hiss of exasperation. I'm not dreaming, I've just heard it. A small, reptilian hiss. The floor creaks, followed by a gust of cool air. He's gone. The bastard's gone, I sent him running!

"Oh! You've knocked over your water! There's broken glass all over the place!"

Who was it? Who entered my room in the middle of the night? And to do what?

"You must have been having a nightmare. Me too, I'm not sleeping so well. I can't stop waking up. I can't wait for morning! I must have forgotten to close the window. With all this wind, it doesn't stop banging. Aw, the poor little thing!"

The poor little what?

"He must have died from the cold. He's fallen on the floor, beneath the radiator . . . "

Who? What? For God's sake, Yvette . . .

"It's a little sparrow, all shriveled up."

My grandmother used to claim that dead birds in the doorway of a house are evil omens. Was it just some silly peasant belief?

"Well, I'm putting him in the trash. Let's try to get some sleep."

Yvette walks out again.

A sparrow who died from the cold. Who dropped dead in my room in the middle of the night, through my open window. Certainly that could happen. He may even have fallen on his head. Or perhaps while making a loop, he landed under my drapes. But if this sparrow had been left there by my mysterious visitor, what's that supposed to mean? Am I supposed to understand something in this? Hit my forehead and say, "Oh, right, a sparrow, so now it's definite that—"

I'm shivering. I'm cold. I'm afraid. I have pain in my heart. Yvette and I are all alone in this chalet, an old lady and an invalid. And a sadistic killer's prowling out in the night, nearby. It surprises me that I'm hoping he really is in love with me; that he means me no harm. The ambiguity of this desire makes my stomach turn.

"It's still snowing!"

Yvette passes me the bedpan and comments on the unfavorable weather report. After a quick wash, she tosses me into the wheelchair and points me toward the kitchen. We have scrambled eggs, coffee, and grapefruit juice. After a year of herbal tea and "easy-to-chew" cornflakes, I decided this winter to go over to solid foods, and for once Yvette has obeyed. In fact, she's gone along with it herself, and at the age of sixty-five is giving up her buttered bread with jam without remorse. On Sunday we even get to have sausages and crêpes with maple syrup.

I'm chewing conscientiously. There's a foul odor. I sniffle.

"That's the sparrow. I put him in a plastic bag, but the smell's still lingering. I'll throw him into the garbage can on my way out. I don't know if I'll be taking you along to go shopping. With all this snow, it wouldn't be practical for the wheelchair."

Rapidly I scribble, *I feel like getting some air.*

"'Getting some air, getting some air,'" she grumbles. "When your wheelchair topples over and you're buried under six feet of snow, then you'll be happy."

If Bruce Willis comes to save me, why not?

Just to get some air on the stoop.

"You only want to follow your own whims. No wonder I get so tired."

The doorbell rings. It's Yann, smelling like fresh snow and gusts of cold wind. I can hear him tapping his shoes against the doormat.

"It's not too warm today. They're forecasting a nice little storm."

"Well, Elise is obstinate about wanting to go out," Yvette announces in a huff.

"She's got a point. If the weather gets any worse, then it's better to take advantage of it now. I'll go with you if you'd like. I'm not working this morning."

Yvette bundles me up, looks around feverishly for her wallet, keys, and glasses, and when she's got everything she needs and everything's in place, then we can go.

By some unspoken consensus, no one alludes to the events of the night before. My wheelchair bumps along the road, firmly guided by Yann, who's commenting on what's going on. The snowplow has just passed. The salt truck is idling just ahead of us. A little girl has just slipped on the ice. They've stopped the ski lift because some kid is stuck in the tram. There's an endless line at the service station: gas is being rationed and the truck drivers are still blocking the depot that supplies the southeast. Yvette's just gone into the bakery. He's got to buy stamps . . . and then silence.

Yoohoo, Yann? Have you morphed into a snowman? I've barely got the time to ask myself that question when something wet and warm lands on my cheek. A tongue. I wouldn't dare believe that Yann . . . It tickles my nose and, sad to say, it's a bit coated; I can feel hair and smell its breath—a dog's tongue. That explains it. My good friend Tintin. I suppose Yann's getting all buddy-buddy with his mistress. There you have it, I'm catching a whiff of Air du Temps.

"Elise, this is Sonia," Yann says, as if he were saying, "This is the empress of China." It's Sonia Auvare of Moonwalk.

"I get the impression that Tintin appreciates you very much," Sonia says in her soft, depressed voice.

"Everyone appreciates Elise!" Yann assures her good-naturedly.

"If you like her, then you'd better get her way out of here," Sonia says.

Their familiar tones lead me to understand that they know each other a lot better than what was indicated yesterday.

"Take her away, Yann," she continues in an urgent tone. "You know terrible things are going to happen."

"What are you talking about?"

"I'm talking about madness, destruction, evil. That's what I'm talking about."

I shudder. She's expressing this in such a poised way. Yann seems nervous.

"Do you know something?"

"Tintin, let's go!"

"Sonia! Wait! You can't just dangle things like that at me and then take off! Sonia!"

Their boots make crunching sounds in the distance. I'm left here all by myself.

"Where did Yann go?" Yvette calls. "I'm going to run over to the newsstand," she adds. "You're okay? You're not cold?"

I signal no. Where *is* Yann?

There's a slight yelp on my left. I finger the control on my wheelchair and advance a yard or so in the direction of the sound. Sonia's voice is low and restrained. Yann's sounds urgent. I advance some more, praying to heaven not to bump against some obstacle.

"Leave me alone. I want nothing from you!"

"Listen . . . "

"You know that nothing can stop forces of evil once they've been loosed. They're on their way, Yann. They've already struck, haven't they?"

"But . . . "

"No, be quiet. Haven't you learned that words mean nothing?"

"That's stupid. Trust me, Sonia!"

"Trust is a luxury beyond my means. Let me go!"

Yann's voice becomes very urgent: "I want to see you again."

"Maybe."

"No. Tonight."

"I'm working tonight."

"Closing time. We've got to talk."

"Let me go. You're hurting me!"

"Okay?"

"Yes. Tintin, let's go!"

I release my breath. Yann mutters something unintelligible, then says, "Oh, there you are! Where's Yvette?"

Without waiting for an answer, he grips the wheelchair and we return to the main thoroughfare.

I don't mean to take myself for Sherlock Holmes, but I'm deducing from the conversation I've just heard that Sonia knows a few things about the murder in Entrevaux. Yann shouldn't have let her go. Even if they are just stupid suspicions, she should let the police in on them. I'm getting the impression that we're all behaving as if this weren't real, as if a young woman weren't really dead, as if Yvette and I didn't eat a piece of her, and as if the killer weren't on the loose in Castaing. Is it a state of shock that's leading us to deny reality? Or has my perception of reality been altered from living as a recluse inside myself?

At this point, Yvette announces, "I've bought some nux vomica to help us with our digestion. Is something the matter, Yann? You look a little funny. Would you like some nux?"

"No, thanks. We've just run into Sonia, and she seemed a bit . . . disturbed."

"The young barmaid?"

Yann must be wincing, because Yvette explains, "The dairy woman told me she was a nice girl but a bit . . . flaky, shall we say. In fact, she gets by on her charm occasionally. She's the niece of old Mauro, an illiterate shepherd who never left the mountains. He's the one who raised her. You'd never believe such a pretty, stylish young girl was weaned on goat's milk!"

"In one week you know as much about the villagers as I do," Yann exclaims. "And I've always lived here."

"Are you insinuating that I'm an incorrigible gossip?"

"Of course not! At best, you'd make a fine psychologist."

Confused, Yvette signals to leave. I feel flakes coming to rest on my cheeks and forehead; I must be covered in a fine white layer. Statue of a sitting woman, late twentieth century.

So Sonia works as a prostitute. Could she have had contact with the murderer? He might be one of her clients. A client who terrorized her to the point where she wouldn't want to say a thing. Or her uncle? The wild shepherd descending into the village to crucify young, immodest women? Good grief! Why did Yann let her get away?

I rifle around under the blanket, take out my notepad and the pen I keep attached to it, and scribble, *Sonia must speak to the cops!*

"How am I supposed to make her?" he retorts, irritably.

This is no film!

"Oh, I know! Lorieux showed me some photos of the cadaver, if you can imagine. I almost puked on his cap."

So Lorieux's smaller than Yann. Then how tall is Yann? Oh, come on, Elise, what does it matter?

We return to the chalet in silence. Yann takes his leave without lingering. We eat our lunch with no appetite. Yvette's sighs are so heavy they can split logs. Coffee, pousse-café, soap opera—I'm boiling with boredom. Suddenly a car horn's honking, and the doorbell rings.

"I'm coming, I'm coming! Damn, right in the middle of *Fun on the Cruise.*"

"Yoohoo! I just felt like stopping by to say hi!"

It's darling Francine! Yvette mutters a sluggish "hi" and goes to shut off the TV while Francine bursts into the living room.

"I've taken the liberty of bringing our darling Laetitia, who quite appreciates the company of darling Elise, and Justine, who's just arrived. Justine Lombard. This isn't disturbing you, I hope? I haven't slept all night with this horrible business! Justine, this is Yvette and Elise."

"Hello," Justine calls out in a sexy voice, à la Marlene Dietrich.

"Laetitia, could you lead Justine to the sofa, please?"

Lead Justine? Might she be blind? Laetitia's walker slides over the floor.

"I thought about you all night," she assures me. "There, Justine, here we are, you can sit down. Justine is unsighted," she confirms for me.

It cracks me up to imagine us face-to-face, incapable of seeing each other. A light silence between us is punctuated with peeps from Francine, who's decided to help Yvette make tea. Laetitia coughs nervously. Justine clears her throat. I'm clutching my woolen skirt in my fingers. We must look like three carnival freaks in a dollhouse. Suddenly, Justine breaks the silence: "I know that you can't speak. Laetitia explained it to me. I'm sorry."

Me too.

"It seems that my hair is Venetian blond, I have freckled skin, I'm five foot seven, and I weigh one hundred twenty-seven pounds. I'm fifty-two years old. I'm telling this to allow you to imagine me."

"Justine looks a bit like Grace Kelly," Laetitia explains.

Grace Kelly, with Marlene's voice. Damn! Tony did the right thing by not coming!

"Laetitia's drawn your portrait for me. I've translated it in my own way. I'm blind from birth," Justine says.

I grab my notepad: *How does Justine represent people?*

I hold the pad in Laetitia's direction, and she reads it aloud for Justine.

"I don't know, it's hard to explain. I can feel masses, volumes . . . "

"Tea is served! Oh, isn't it cute the way all three of them are having a chat!" Francine blurts, ecstatically.

Yvette serves the tea, grumbling that she's freezing cold. Francine decrees right away that she's dying from the heat. I'm trying to pick up my teacup without knocking anything over, but it's a failed effort because Justine calls out, "Laetitia has told me all about this terrible affair."

Francine coughs nervously. Justine goes on: "As soon as I passed through the door at the center, I could feel an abnormal amount of tension. The air was distorted by a bad vibration. I hope they'll get their hands on the culprit soon. A creature who's capable of all this violence won't stop in midstream."

Unfortunately, that's just what I think!

"I've run into Sergeant Schnabel," Francine lets us know, "and they haven't found anything new, unfortunately!"

"Oh, that one's a handsome man . . . ," Yvette murmurs.

I translate this as five foot ten, two hundred pounds, a mustache, and a ruddy complexion.

"I have the notion that he likes plump women," she goes on dreamily.

"You think so?" Francine asks.

Some moments pass. They avoid getting onto the subject of the crime. Laetitia babbles about everything and nothing: movie stars, supermodels, mundane bits of gossip—she's as joyous as a girl. Justine barely steps in; she tells me that she's living off the works she's exhibited. Rather impolitely, I make her repeat it. Darling Francine says, "Oh, yes, our darling Justine is an artiste."

I'm imagining lace doilies and wicker place mats purchased by ladies from charitable organizations.

" . . . exhibited in several galleries: Barcelona, Tokyo, Paris . . . "

What, international macramé galleries?

" . . . the raw material of paint on the raw material of the support, the clash of spaces."

Well, well! If I weren't mute, I'd be speechless. Justine's a painter? I wonder what the hell these canvases must look like, painted by some woman who's blind from birth and has no idea what a color might be. The worst thing is that I've got no chance of finding out, since I myself can't see. This situation has a bittersweet taste that goes well with the tea.

I abruptly feel Justine's hand brushing my hair; she says, "Laetitia's told me that you were involved in that affair having to do with a murder. You ought to be careful. I sense a lot of red around you."

Red? Dearie, how can you possibly know what red is, or gray, or blue? Angrily I reach for the notepad: *What is red?*

"For me, red is the name given to suffering. When I bring my hands close to your face, I can sense your aura. It's red. Suffering limns you like a halo."

A blind mystic painter! Dear Shrink, may I remind you that at the beginning of this story, I'd just taken off for a few days in the snow, all right? I'd like to keep it that way! What? You mean you're not God? Well, that's rather regrettable. And what about this new one, who's giving me the creeps with her aura of suffering limning my beautiful Mediterranean face . . . I huddle in my wheelchair, feeling glum. Yvette and Francine are playing rummy, at a penny a point. Laetitia's taking it upon herself to describe the various residents of the home for Justine. I'm listening, because every new detail lets me add another touch to the mental portraits I've made.

"You shouldn't be afraid of Christian," she explains to Justine. "He seems like a brute, but he's very sweet. He reminds me of a mastiff who barks all the time."

"How old is he?"

"Around forty, I think."

And I imagined him as a teenager!

"Then there's Bernard," she moves on. "He's very fat and very scary. He only speaks in little sayings; it's funny. There's also Emilie and Clara, they're the best friends in the world. Emilie's a brunette, with a typically Mongoloid face."

"I've never seen one," Justine gently reminds her.

"Oh, yes . . . Uh, Clara has chestnut hair, she's not very pretty, she squints a bit, and always has her mouth open. Magali, on the other hand, is ravishing, with a magnificent red mane of hair. To see her, you'd never guess she's got the intelligence of a five-year-old. Only when you talk to her or your eyes meet hers do you realize this. You know, it's . . . I don't know . . . a little different with her. She's always lived in a home. Her parents never wanted to take care of her."

"Really? How sad! I was also placed in a home at a very young age, after the death of my parents. What about you, Elise?" Justine asks.

What should I answer? That I lived very happily with my parents, had a good time in school, ran my movie theater with pleasure, and loved Benoît with passion? That I consider myself in transit in a tunnel? I scribble, *Normal*. Laetitia reads it for her.

"It's a pleasure to meet normal people," Justine says, with a smile in her voice.

That's an original comment from someone talking to a person who's paralyzed, blind, and mute. Laetitia continues, "Jean-Claude is nice but he always thinks he knows everything. I think that because he can't move, he tries to prove that he still has some worth."

Do I also do that? Do I give the impression that others are stupid and I'm always right? No, Elise, not you, dear girl! You're so modest . . .

"Léonard's motor functions are impaired, but he's qualified to teach high school math. He doesn't talk much: it's too hard for him to express himself. And then again he's not too interested in our chatter. His passion is astronomy. That's why he's come here, because of the sky. You can't see the stars that well in the city."

"I came here for the sounds. In the mountains they're more pure, more distinct. You can hear the bark crackling on the trees. I get the impression of moving through a crystal palace," Justine explains.

And *I* get the impression that I'm stuck in a layer of mud. Tsk, tsk, be positive! Let's imagine me in a space capsule, cruising through these fucking stars I can't see anymore . . .

"More tea, girls? Your tea's delicious, Yvette!"

Now, there's someone who's positive! Always the optimist, Mother Atchouel.

"Are you the one who made these shortbread cookies?" she goes on. "You must make some more for our darling residents; they're so crispy."

The residents are so crispy? That's a bad play on words, Elise. Sinister, vulgar.

"And then there's Martine . . . she acts a bit like a nun, but you can count on her," Laetitia continues, inexhaustibly. "Watch out for Hugo, he doesn't like slackers. I wonder if they're together," she concludes, lowering her voice.

The rest of the afternoon passes this way, in muffled chitchat set against the backdrop of the whistling teapot. When I had use of my body, I hated staying inside. The very idea of hanging around for hours at a tea party would give me the hives. I needed movement. Fresh air. I would have taken my skis and raced down the slopes . . . attacked Tony with snowballs. I have a hard time imagining myself with Tony in these dream sequences, because when I met him I was already nailed into this wheelchair and never saw his body, his face. I've made an impression of him by touching him; I know he's thin and wiry like a boxer; I know that he has a straight nose, a square jaw, and that there's no hair on his temples. But I've never *seen* him. So in these films I play for myself in my head, I'm often alone.

Suddenly I realize that Francine has signaled to leave. She shakes my hand, Justine gives my shoulder a squeeze, and Laetitia kisses me. Yvette sees them to the door and returns with the mail. Several letters are for me. Ever since my adventures appeared in a novel, I receive many letters from readers. They're always wondering to what degree the author romanticized the facts. Unfortunately, she only related them in all their sad truth. If she knew that at this very moment, I'm once again caught up in a drama . . . The publisher should be happy. No cynicism, Elise, not when human lives are at stake. Elise Andrioli, spokesperson for wheelchair detectives, must be politically correct.

The evening goes by slowly. Yvette watches a TV movie about school gangs, then the debate over violence in schools. I'm half listening. Isn't this the same debate they were having last year and the year before? With the same people invited? I feel sleepy. All these words, like the wind through the branches . . .

5

$\mathscr{I}$ AWAKE WITH A start, in my bed. Yvette must have laid me down. What time is it? I can hear her moving next door. Is she sleeping or awake? My door opens without a sound. I raise my hand to show I'm awake.

"Oh, I was wondering . . . You just conked out last night! It's still very early, barely five o'clock, but I can't sleep anymore. I'm going to take a shower, and then I'll be with you."

Five o'clock. What an idea, to wake up so early. It must still be the dead of night. To tell the truth, it doesn't change much for me . . . Yvette slips into the bathroom. I yawn profusely, stretch out my good arm, and rub my eyes. Then I execute a series of windmills. My morning workout. The ringing of the phone makes me jump on the inside. The answering machine picks up and my uncle's voice begins: "Hello, you've reached Château Montrouge. Please leave your message at the beep. Thank you."

"Oh, my God, help me, help me, I'm begging you. He's going to . . . Oh, no, *no!*"

My blood freezes. It's the girl with the sad voice! But what's . . .

"No! He's coming! He's coming! I don't want to! I'm begging you, please help . . . "

I'm petrified; I can hear the shower running in the bathroom, I can hear this terrified voice, and *I don't know what to do.*

"Help me, I'm begging you. I don't want to . . . "

There's a noise in the background. Some sort of humming. *The humming of an electric drill.*

A painful spasm contracts my stomach. I'm dreaming, tell me I'm dreaming, tell me this can't be.

Sonia's screaming now, screaming like a woman possessed, while the buzzing grows closer; I can hear a door slam shut, and against that door the pounding redoubles. The blows are powerful, determined. I roll over to the phone and grab it with my good hand, but I can't speak, I can't ask where she is; then there's Yvette, who won't come, can't hear a thing, and whom I can't call! I drop the receiver and roll toward the bathroom like a madwoman, bumping against the furniture, then throw my wheelchair against the plywood, once, twice, while at the other end of the line the door abruptly gives way; I hear the wood crackling and once again the roaring of the drill . . .

"Is something wrong? What's gotten into you?"

Screams and frantic pleas are coming from the living room. Yvette takes off in their direction, smelling of hot water and soap.

"What's going on?"

I hold out my arm toward the telephone, from which a mix of indistinct groans and cries for help are escaping.

Yvette starts running, her bare feet flop-flopping over the floor.

"Hello? Who's there? Hello?"

"Too late," Sonia murmurs, with infinite sadness. "Too . . . late . . . "

"Who's there? Where are you? Where are you?"

"The dog . . . managed to save the dog . . . please . . . "

"Where are you? What's going on?"

Silence. A silence interrupted by the breathing of two people. One of them whistles laboriously; the other is slow and deep.

Click. Someone's hung up. The buzzing of the dial tone takes over.

"I think it might be the girl with the dog! I'm calling the police. Maybe it was a joke, but—"

I don't think that it was a joke. I think that Sonia has just died, live, at the other end of the line. That if she'd called someone else, she might have been saved.

Yvette's phoning the police. Lorieux's not on duty, so they pass her to his assistant, Morel. She splutters a description of what just happened, then hangs up.

"They'll be going to her home. To the nightclub as well. No one's reported her disappearance to them, though."

It's hard to report a disappearance before it happens.

The buzzing of the drill. I can hear it ringing in every single nerve. My jaw is clenched so tight, my teeth are grinding. Yvette's pacing back and forth, wailing, "I can't believe this! Those screams, that young woman . . . It's all a farce, this can't be, and the dog, she said that the dog was safe . . . I can't believe that . . .

Yann had a rendezvous with Sonia. He was supposed to meet her when the club closed. What could have happened? Yann . . . No, it's impossible.

A half hour passes in this way, I with my forehead pressed against the cold windowpane, and Yvette in the kitchen, furiously wearing grooves in the floor.

The telephone rings.

Yvette picks up after the second ring.

"Yes . . . Oh, no! Are you sure? . . . Yes, excuse me. No, no, we're not going anywhere."

Click. Yvette's hand is on my shoulder.

"They've found her. In the basement of the nightclub. She's . . . she's dead."

My fist is clenched so tight I can feel my nails.

"They'll be here right away," she continues.

We keep quiet a long while. Yvette turns on the radio and quietly listens to the news. There's been an airline crash in Malaysia—225 missing. A deputy's under investigation. There are going to be new arrangements in the matter of the school curriculum; they'll be going back to the old one. And it's the fourth day that the gas station in Puget-sur-Argens has been blocked off. A gas shortage is in sight.

Gas. People leaving for work, taking their cars, listening to the same news at the same time we do, lighting their cigarettes or swearing they'll stop smoking. And there's a body in a basement that's not moving.

"Why did she call here?" Yvette suddenly asks.

That's exactly the question I'm asking myself. If she were being followed by some insane murderer, why would she go through the trouble of looking for a phone number that leads only to a mute? No, no, Elise, your reasoning's all wrong. Maybe she wasn't trying to get through to Yvette or me. Maybe she dialed a number she knew by heart. My uncle's number. Was my uncle a regular at the Moonwalk? Let's be frank: Was my uncle one of Sonia's clients? After all, he's been a widower for twenty years, and he's still quite lively. He's only sixty-three years old, and except for his paunch, the last time I saw him, he was looking pretty good, with thick gray hair, a lofty stature, and a patrician face.

Lorieux's breathless arrival keeps me from pursuing these musings of mine. Before he even says hello, he asks, "Is Yann here?"

"Yann?" Yvette repeats. "Here? At six in the morning?"

"Yann had a rendezvous with Sonia Auvare last night, didn't he?"

"Oh, but I don't know a thing about that!" Yvette protests.

"Elise! Answer me!"

I raise my arm, wondering why Lorieux seems so agitated.

"If he's the one who did it, I'll kill him!"

"I beg your pardon?" Yvette hiccups.

"Nothing. He had no right to try to see her again!"

"Are you okay, Sergeant? Don't you want a little coffee?"

"She's dead!" he snaps back. "If only you'd seen her body, if only you'd seen what that bastard did to her! There was blood everywhere . . . on the walls . . . on the ceiling . . . and her belly . . . Oh, my God . . . "

"Uh . . . calm down. Look, it's pretty hot."

I guess she's talking about the coffee. Lorieux blows on it noisily. He calms down, then takes a deep breath.

"I'm sorry."

I can't help it. I scribble, *Were you intimate with Sonia?* and blindly hold out the sheet.

"Yes," he answers in a voice that suddenly sounds tired. "Oh, yes, we went out for a year. We were supposed to get married. It was a dream, a beautiful dream, that's all. She couldn't ever give up the dope. And to pay for the dope . . . well, you get the point. We broke up more than six months ago. Yann knew that . . . that I was very attached to her. I never would have believed he'd . . . well, that he'd . . . "

That he'd decide to pick her up?

"Yes. Still, I should have figured as much. Yann's incapable of resisting a pretty girl. He's a hunter."

So is the killer we're looking for. I'm thrumming my fingers on the arm of the wheelchair, irritated, my stomach in an uproar. Yvette's drinking her coffee; the sergeant's drinking his as well—I can hear them slurping.

So the officer in charge of the investigation has slept with the victim and, it seems, is still in love with her. His best friend had a rendezvous with the victim on the night of her death, and then disappeared.

"I've got to listen to her call," he suddenly shouts through clenched teeth.

"It sounds so horrible," says Yvette.

He doesn't answer. He plays around with the phone and then Sonia's crazed voice rings out through the room. I know I'm listening to a dead woman speak, and yet I can hear her dying over and over.

He doesn't make a single comment. When the final beep sounds, he cracks his fingers before articulating with great effort, "It's a digital answering machine. There's no cassette. Don't erase this message. I'll come by and have it recorded."

"Would you like some more coffee?" Yvette asks miserably.

He doesn't reply. He continues, "She was found in the toilet in the basement. She must have tried to lock herself in, as the door was broken down."

Yvette's cough interrupts the silence that follows.

"There she was, on the floor, the telephone about a foot away from her face. It was a wireless," he says mechanically.

Just at this moment the phone rings, sending me jumping on the inside. Yvette goes running over.

"It's for you, Sergeant," she says.

"Sergeant Lorieux speaking . . . Where? . . . Dead drunk?! Yes, I'm coming . . . I'll be there in ten minutes."

He hangs up.

"They've found Yann, in the snow, at the foot of the trails. He's in an alcoholic coma—half frozen. They're taking him to the hospital. There was an empty bottle of vodka next to him. Miss Andrioli, I need a quick deposition. Can you write down for me on this sheet everything you know of the events of last night?"

I comply, describing Yann's meeting with Sonia, the rendezvous, all of it.

He reads it back aloud and smacks the sheet against his hip.

"She knew something! Why didn't she tell me anything? Why?"

Ten thousand reasons come to mind, but I won't venture to express them. Yvette keeps quiet, apparently hooked up to a coffee drip. Lorieux has me sign, then walks out with heavy strides.

"I've got a bit of a headache. That poor girl . . . and knowing that we heard her . . . Oh, I think I . . . "

She goes running for the toilet. I also feel a bit out of sorts. These painful events have been a bit too jarring, and I'd really like to step down from the ride. Yvette returns, making her apologies. She offers me a glass of almond milk. I take a sip; it's cool. It calms the burning sensation in my esophagus.

"We've got to go back to Boissy," Yvette suddenly suggests.

I don't think it's possible. We're witnesses.

"Well, I don't give a hoot!" she cries. "They'll just have to come and interrogate us there. I'm going to call Jean. We can't stay here, what with that madman on the loose, those women murdered, this lovesick police officer, Yann in the hospital . . . Maybe you think it's fun to play detective, but not me. Not when real people are dying."

She runs off to the living room. I can hear the radio again: there's a gas shortage. Who'll take us to the airport, assuming the planes aren't on strike? That's the case every time I want to get around, and I avoid long trips by train or bus because of the peeing problem. And then again, we won't really be safe in Boissy. Ultimately, I'd prefer not to be too far from our friends, the police.

Yvette comes back into the kitchen and starts wiping the dishes the way she does when she's mad.

"There's no more gas in the region. Air International has sent out a strike warning for the day after tomorrow. And it takes twelve hours by train, with three changes. Frankly, getting around in France in the year 2000 is worse than during the Middle Ages!" she says, suddenly blowing up.

On my notepad I write, *Anyway, all alone up there . . .*

"I thought Jean might be able to return, given the circumstances, but no, His Highness has to finish up his job, he completely doesn't give a damn if we're killed! And when I told him we could join him in Brittany, he seemed annoyed. Annoyed! If that doesn't take the cake! Even if the living arrangements are a problem there or it's bitter cold, then we could go to a hotel."

And how would we get to Quimper? Rent a limousine with a chauffeur?

"Oh, fine, now your wrist doesn't seem to be bothering you. Usually it's 'I'm hungry! Thirsty! Let's go out!' But now you're taking your time, writing down everything!"

Excuse me, but I think we're getting a little excited.

She grumbles her agreement as she places the dishes back in the cupboard.

"Well, if I understand things correctly, we're stuck here. Jean promised he'd call every night. Men, men. You can never count on them!"

Oh, but you can. To kill. To destroy. Is the simple-minded sexism in my remark hiding a secret hurt? Shrink's looking at me through wide, haughty eyes. (I'll assume full responsibility for "haughty.") Go see for yourself, Shrink! You're also just a dirty old man.

The telephone rings. The ringing's starting to get on my nerves. The answering machine picks up: "This is Sergeant Lorieux!"

Yvette picks up right away.

Her long silences are punctuated by "can't be" and "really?" and finally, "I'll pass her the earpiece."

By chance, my uncle's phone is an old model. Yvette presses the earpiece to my ear.

Lorieux's voice sounds tired and hollow.

"I was saying to Mrs. Holzinski that you must be wondering why Sonia"—he catches his breath—"called your uncle's chalet."

"It's true," Yvette says approvingly.

"Sonia confided to me that she had a godfather who would give her money sometimes. An old country boy, who was a choirboy with her uncle Mauro. Someone named Fernand. I hadn't thought about it until this morning. What's your uncle's name?"

"Fernand Andrioli," Yvette confirms for him.

"That's what Schnabel told me. That would explain her phone call. Your number was the first on her cell phone's speed-dial."

His voice has become practically inaudible as he adds, "She must have hit it while she was trying to get away."

Louder now, he continues, "Do you have a number where we can reach Mr. Andrioli? He's her only relative, since Mauro Auvare passed away six months ago."

Yvette passes on my uncle's cell phone number, explaining to him that he's in the construction business and that he should be in Poland right now, for a trade show. She puts down the receiver and exclaims, "Oh, dear! Your uncle was Sonia's godfather! Were you aware of that?"

What if I am aware that my uncle was Sonia's godfather? Funny that he never said anything about it to me. It's funny as well how suddenly everyone has some connection to this second victim, even though no one knows a thing about the first, right down to her name. In fact, I'm even getting the impression that no one gives a damn about the anonymous victim. What if there were two killers? What if Sonia's murder were a "classic" murder, one motivated by jealousy, hatred, or money, and the murderer took advantage of the circumstances to commit it, thinking they'd pin it on the crazy killer?

But how would Vore fit in to the affair? Think, Elise, get your little gray cells moving, as Poirot would say. Vore's a psychopath who's in love with you. He crucifies some poor woman and then offers me pieces of the victim. Similarly, someone murders Sonia Auvare with an electric drill. The violence of these murders would suggest the same author, so the second killer might think he's beyond suspicion. Yeah, that stands to reason. Still, that doesn't tell me who Vore is, or the other one, the copycat.

Telephone!

Yvette, out of patience, answers, "Hello! Oh, hello, Francine . . . Yes, I know . . . We were even the first ones notified, unfortunately . . . I'll explain it to you . . . What? . . . Oh, it's horrible . . . Oh, okay, see you soon."

She hangs up.

"Sergeant Schnabel's just been to the center to check up on Yann's schedule. He was very upset. He said it was unimaginable how this monster could go to such lengths on that poor girl with his electric drill. Schnabel confessed to Francine that he nearly threw up, and yet he was in Algeria."

Yvette shuts up, fortunately. I'd very much appreciate it if no one felt obliged to describe for me in detail what Sonia must have gone through! I'd prefer to think of anything else. Schnabel, for example. Let's say he was eighteen in 1961, it's now the year 2000; that would make him fifty-seven years old. Must be odd to be commanded by such a young officer.

"Francine invited us to go . . . where's my purse?"

Have tea?

"How did you know? It'll do us some good to see people. I'm going to run out to the bakery. Don't open up for anyone!"

No, and I'm not going to run the hundred-yard dash, either, don't worry. The bolts click shut. Finally a bit of calm and silence. I propel myself toward the window. Is it still snowing? Are there people passing by outside who can see me sitting here? Vore, for example? I move back my wheelchair. Yvette's forgotten to get the fire going. Too bad; I like the logs crackling. Sitting in the middle of the living room, I listen to the silence while ruminating on sinister thoughts.

My second-murderer theory doesn't quite jibe with the conversation Sonia had with Yann yesterday. Only yesterday! This conversation gave me the impression that she knew she was in danger. If she thought she was in danger, then it was precisely because she feared some action from the man who murdered the first victim. So there's only one! Good grief! Why didn't she run away if she was afraid? Her voice was quavering: "Terrible things are going to happen." And then that abominable death . . . Vore. D. Vore, the devourer.

The doorbell's ringing imperiously. Yvette must have forgotten her keys again! I roll my wheelchair up to the door, feeling my way down the wall in the corridor with my fingertips. I raise my arm to pull back the bolt. But from the other side of the shutter, only silence. Not knowing why, I suspend my motion.

He's there, he's there, on the other side of the door, I'm sure of it! Some seconds pass. I hear the lid to the mailbox rise and an object fall inside. Footsteps fade in the distance. Even if I were to open up, I wouldn't know who it is. I would yell, "Arrest that man!" into the emptiness. Either it's the mailman, and I'd look like a nut. Or it's *him,* and he might turn around and stab me. I'm not opening. I'm afraid.

I feel about in the mailbox and my hand closes around a small square package. If it's another piece . . . I hesitate awhile before unwrapping it. Come on, Elise, where's your nerve? Somehow I rip off the paper and discover a wooden box the size of a pack of cigarettes. I lift the lid and move my hand forward. The box contains two round, soft objects, like rubber balls. Are these anti-stress caps? I squeeze them a little, not too much, for fear they might break. Chocolates? I sniff them, but they don't smell like anything . . . oh, yes, they've got a pharmaceutical odor. Ether, perhaps. What the hell can they be?

The door suddenly opens on Yvette, who's raging against all this snow that will never end, the baker and the way he takes so long, and all those little old ladies who spend hours yakking while there's such a mad world out there.

"With all that, I'm going to wind up missing the news! You did the right thing by not coming, with this weather . . . Ahhhh!"

Yvette's piercing scream freezes me. What's going on?

"Oh, my God! The eyes!"

What about my eyes? I'm getting an image of an enormous hairy spider stepping up to my eyes. Speak up!

"The eyes . . . in your hand!" Yvette pants.

I beg your pardon? *Eyes* in my *hand?* Oh, nooo! Those gelatinous balls! My heart drops to my heels. I open my fingers and hear two small plops on the floor. This can't be. I can't quite understand. I roll toward Yvette. Even more screaming.

"Stop! You're going to crush them. Oh, quick, the police, quick! Where did you get those eyes?"

As if I'd gone looking for them on purpose to play some prank! I write, *the mailbox,* with trembling hand. I feel like I'm in a surrealist film.

"In the mailbox," Yvette repeats, in a sinister tone. "This madman knows where we live. He's going to come and cut us into pieces. We can't stay here. Hello, get me Sergeant Lorieux, it's urgent! . . . What do you mean, busy? . . .

I'm telling you, it's urgent . . . Why? Because I've got a pair of blue eyes on my living room floor, that's why! . . . No, I'm not joking, young man, and I'm not drunk! Tell him to come to Château Montrouge immediately! And don't delay!"

She slams down the phone.

"You're lucky that you didn't have to see that . . . Oh, my, how am I going to get into the kitchen? I can't trip over those . . . those things! You especially, don't move, Elise. Could you imagine if you rolled over them?"

Yes, I can imagine. The chair's rubber wheel flattening a blue eye, making it crack open like a soft-boiled egg . . . Stop thinking about that right now; think about little birds in the trees, their little eyes as black as grapes, ready to pop; no, pretty butterflies, yes, that's it, butterflies, fluttering about through bunches of flowers. An eye. A human eye. Ox-eyed daisy in science class. Enormous. Dead. Dead. Dead.

Yvette rifles nervously through her wicker basket; the papers rustle. I realize I'm gripping the arm of the wheelchair as if it were a life buoy.

"You've given me such a shock!"

I have? What about me? Didn't I just have a shock? To know that I've held eyes in my hand, that I've felt them, squeezed them, almost put them in my mouth! The eyes of a cadaver!

"You think these are poor Sonia's?" Yvette asks in a low voice.

There's a chance they are, unfortunately! And when Lorieux sees that . . . The doorbell rings. My hand grips the arm of the wheelchair. Yvette looks through the peephole, then opens.

"Oh, Sergeant, it's horrible . . . Look."

Two steps are taken in my direction. A breath is drawn. And then there's a dull thud.

"Sergeant! He's passed out!"

Yvette gives him a few quick slaps. The door opens with a gust of fresh air and Schnabel's big voice: "The sergeant told me to come join . . . What's happened to him?" he inquires, surprised.

"He saw the eyes," Yvette soberly explains.

"The eyes? What eyes?"

"The eyes, over there . . . "

"Oh! Holy shit! Whose are they?"

"I don't know!" Yvette rages. "They've got to be Sonia's! Give me a hand, we'll put him on the couch."

Schnabel complies, muttering, "Thirty years on the force, and I've never seen anything like this!"

A mild groan rises from the sofa, then Lorieux's tattered voice croaks, "Sonia's eyes . . ."

"I'm going to notify the boys from the lab, Chief. We're in luck. They stayed in Alpe d'Azur for lunch."

"We're in luck? Did you see that, Roger? Did you see what that bastard did?" Lorieux screams, jumping to his feet.

"Calm down, Chief, calm down! Yvette, don't you have a little hooch?"

In a voice vibrating with hatred, Lorieux bellows, "If I catch up with that son of a bitch, I'm going to feed him his—"

"Here, drink up, it'll do you some good, Sergeant. It's genepi, the real thing."

Glug, glug, glug. I hear glasses filled. Personally, I wouldn't spit on a splash of good, strong alcohol, but no one's offering me any. Schnabel's calling the restaurant where the crime-scene technicians are having lunch. Lorieux's pacing back and forth in the living room. Yvette's knocking back some genepi. And I'm all alone in the corridor with the goddamn eyes, not daring to move for fear of rolling over them.

"Schnabel, take Mrs. Holzinski's deposition," Lorieux says suddenly, regaining control of himself. "I'm going to handle Miss Andrioli. Do you have your notepad? Write down for me what happened," he commands.

His voice seems harder, strained by anger and despair. He reads through my brief notes.

"This bastard came here to bring it to you. But what does he want, anyway? You'd almost think he was playing with us!"

I think about how cats bring their prey back to their master. Maybe he's playing around. Maybe he wants to show me how strong, clever, and unpitying he is. But why me? Could it be that I know him? On the notepad I write, *Maybe he knows me . . . from before my accident.*

"Exactly. I hadn't thought of that. That would explain why he's bringing you his . . . his hunting trophies, the sick freak!"

I've never met a police officer who expresses himself quite like this. I almost feel like I'm in the middle of one of those American crime shows with cops in leather jackets saying "fuck, fuck, fuck" from start to finish.

The doorbell rings. The boys from the lab are getting out, moaning because they didn't get to finish their meal, and start dusting things throughout the place. A flashbulb crackles amid their voices: "Pass me that plastic bag." "Watch out, he stuck that one on the wood. Take it easy." "I didn't think there'd be such wide filaments like that behind there . . . " "And how do you think this stays up?" "Wait a second, I'm going to take one more; there, that's it."

I swallow slowly. Lorieux's grinding his teeth. Literally. There's a new gust of fresh air.

"So, Lorieux, what's going on now? I haven't even had time to drink my coffee."

"See for yourself, Doctor."

"Good God, your man's not exactly a doily maker!"

He must be leaning over, because I can hear his breath getting stronger.

"I'd say it's an eighty percent possibility that these belong to this morning's client, since she was enucleated," he lets out. "It's really gross to see things like this. Well, boys, do what you must. I'll be getting back to you."

"We'd better get a move on if we want to catch up with the lab in time. It's still snowing, and the road's going to be cut off from here tonight. We'll give you a call tomorrow, Chief!" someone calls out to Lorieux.

They leave in a whirlwind, just as they arrived. It's an hour's drive from here to civilization. The doctor's tapping on an object that must be a pipe. That's it! The sweet smell of Amsterdammer pervades the hallway.

"Dirty little business, this case of yours . . . Have you got a trail?"

"No, not really."

"Is it one man murdering women in Alpes-Maritimes?"

"What's your opinion?"

"The wounds don't lead me to this conclusion, but my general impression is, yes, we're talking about the same man. Pretty twisted individual we've got here, by the way. It reminds me of . . . ," he begins, apparently determined to tick off every fascinating case he's ever worked on.

"This one I'm going to get, believe you me!" Lorieux interrupts, full of resentment.

The doctor gives a contrary sniff and taps on his pipe.

"I hope so. That's what they're paying you to do! Well, I'll do a preliminary report for you. I suppose the judge is going to ask for a complete autopsy, in Marseilles."

Lorieux acquiesces. The doctor takes his leave. Schnabel and Yvette join us again, the smell of genepi hanging heavily in the air. Lorieux lets out long sighs. Schnabel coughs nervously. Yvette blows her nose. I'm scratching myself. You'd think we were nothing more than sad, confused animals.

"I haven't managed to get a hold of Mr. Andrioli," Lorieux says suddenly. "We can't get through to his cell phone just now. You can't stay here by yourselves," he adds in a definitive tone of voice. "Can't your friend Mrs. Atchouel put you up?"

"Uh, I don't know. I hadn't thought about it. I wouldn't want to disturb her," Yvette mutters, taken by surprise.

"Find out from her and keep me posted."

He leaves, followed by Schnabel, and we're left alone with the unappetizing prospect of staying at MRCHA.

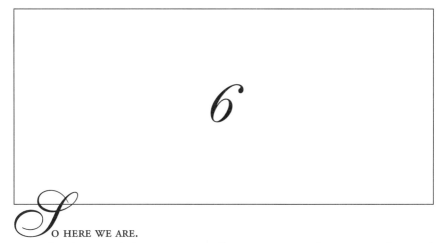

S O HERE WE ARE.

We've been settled into two small attic rooms with pine paneling and views of the mountain peaks, *dixit* Yvette.

Darling Francine has once again given us a brief history lecture, reminding us that at the turn of the century there was an attempt to convert Castaing to a thermal station, thanks to a sulfur spring that today is depleted. It was during this period that the center was transformed into a residence for puny, sickly, unhealthy children: malnutrition, anemia, tuberculosis, you name it. They were sent to the mountains, to what was called the sanatorium. The accommodations of the former dormitory have since been rethought with the new residents' handicaps in mind—treatment rooms, converted showers, an so on. A huge elevator, recently modernized, serves all three floors in the building.

Darling Francine has given me a map in Braille and Hugo has had me visit everything so that I might get around all by myself, more or less. Justine, Laetitia, and Léonard are staying on the same floor as us. This wasn't with the intention of annoying me. The most disturbed residents are put together on the second floor, near the instructors. Jean-Claude has the use of a special room on the ground floor, across from Yann's.

I roll my wheelchair into my new space: there's a bed, a dresser, and an armoire that gives off a pleasant lavender fragrance. The window's positioned above my head; raising my hand, I can reach the lock. Someone's knocking. I don't shout "Come in," but someone enters.

"Elise? Are you there?"

It's Justine. I slowly roll toward her by the sound of her voice and bump against her extended arm.

"Hello! I hope I'm not disturbing you. I just wanted to find out what's new with you."

I remain silent, obviously, and it's useless to write anything since she can't read it. I give three quick, lively taps against the rail of my wheel.

"You know Morse code?" Justine asks matter-of-factly.

No answer.

"I'll teach you, it's easy. This way we can have discussions."

That should be a change from using my index finger and the notepad.

"I'll leave you be. Until tonight."

She bumps into the doorframe with a little laugh, then she's off into the hallway. A door shuts. She still isn't very familiar with the premises, so she must be having a hard time finding her way about. For me, in fact, it's easier, since most of the time I'm led around. Not necessarily where I want to go, but . . .

I'll take advantage of this moment of calm to try to relax. I take in a deep breath, and then exhale, ten times or so. I'm trying to create emptiness in my mind. I'm concentrating on the image of a pointed summit hooded in white, the sepulchral peace of the mountaintops. Seagulls are passing again and again in a sparkling blue sky, sending out their long calls. Okay, I know there aren't any seagulls up in the mountains, but there they are in my meditation. Snow and salt have the same brilliance, the horizon the same intensity. White, blue. The blue of an iris in the white of a cornea. Well, now it's all been screwed up. Someone's knocking, and I jump.

The door opens. The footsteps are uncertain. Someone's coughing. A man's cough. I'm nervously tightening my grip around the rail of the wheel.

"Wewww . . . come" is articulated with difficulty by a serious-sounding voice.

The man allows a pause, his breath whistling.

"Neigh . . . ba . . . Léonard."

Ah, the famous Léonard! The mysterious young savant with a speech impairment. I feel about and hold my hand out toward him. His warm fingers envelop mine. After a slight grasp, he lets go. I hear his awkward footsteps, silence, then a door closing.

Well, these little evenings among friends are going to be pretty sad. One who sees but doesn't speak. One who speaks but doesn't see. And then there's me, who can't speak or see. I'm trying to recapture my train of thought. To give my images free rein. A stream of violent, multicolored visions is charging through my head. A seagull plucking at the empty eye sockets of some cadaver abandoned on a mountainside. A sergeant with long blond curls screaming himself to death under the moon. Yann, with his eyes hidden behind dark glasses, his incisors stained with blood. Calm down, Elise. Think hard.

Two women have been killed. Why? By whom? I've been offered two pieces of the first woman, and the eyes of the second. Is there a plan? Some progression? Sergeant Lorieux, who's in charge of the investigation, was in love with Sonia Auvare, the second victim. The aforementioned Sonia, more or less a prostitute, was the goddaughter of my uncle. Her own uncle, a wild shepherd, lived in the mountains. Sonia claimed to know something about the first murder, of the unknown woman. So the only link between all these elements is Sonia. If I could draw a diagram or use one of those magic computers like the kind you see in the movies . . . Someone would feed in all the data I possess and, wham, the face of the murderer would slowly appear on a dot-matrix screen while the audience held their breath.

And as I can't see a thing, I'd be the only ass who wouldn't know what was going on.

Yann's out of the hospital. When he came back, we were in the middle of tasting one of Francine's "it's delicious, darling" teas. Francine gave him a rather cool reception, and he went to great lengths to explain himself: Sonia didn't show up at the rendezvous, he waited in vain, pounded on the service door with no result, and then decided to get bombed on a bottle of vodka he had in his trunk.

On this, Francine asked him if he was in the habit of stocking his car with bottles of vodka, and he retorted that he'd gone shopping that afternoon, keeping in mind the possibility of an eventual invitation to have a drink back at Sonia's place. Francine harrumphed, Yvette harrumphed, and Yann went into a huff. If she wanted his resignation, then all she had to do was say so, and anything he did outside his hours on the job was his business and no one else's, et cetera, et cetera.

"You're aware that you're putting me in a delicate situation," Francine replied.

At this point, everyone calmed down. Yann excused himself, saying it was the residents' time for gym. He walked out stiffly.

"He could have shaved!" Francine called out, acerbically.

"He's still got bloodshot eyes. He must have some hangover!" Yvette said.

"I'm really worried. It's far from me to suspect Yann of being able to . . . But after all . . . he's got no alibi, has he?"

"Still, you don't believe that Yann would be capable of—"

"My darling Yvette, if only you knew what people are capable of . . . "

"Oh, but we know only too well, don't we, Elise?"

You said it. Last year I was able to experience from up close the duplicity of the human soul. In a way Yvette and I are the survivors of an expeditionary force thrown across the burning limbo of madness. And when I say "burning," I mean it literally, because we were almost burned alive. First fire, and now ice. Will someone try to freeze us under a fir tree?

I know, Shrink, I know. To deny emotions by taking refuge behind self-deprecation leads to self-destruction. But I've always been that way. I've always been the kind to laugh nervously at burials. To be unable to resist making a wisecrack. To protect myself behind an impassable wall of humor. It's my system; it's got its drawbacks, but I don't know any other. And anyway, what difference does it make today, now that I can't really communicate with anyone? I don't risk offending anybody.

Francine must have turned on the radio. It's playing commercial jingles. Because I have no intention of leaving for Singapore on Transtour, trading in my scooter for a Range Rover, or buying the Doc Persil box set, I listen distractedly. The news items rumble past.

" . . . Tornado in Polynesia . . . Brussels: still no agreement on the grading of bananas . . . Murder victim in Entrevaux has been identified! Marion Hennequin, a homeless woman who lived in Digne for about three years . . . "

"I told you it was a homeless person!" Yvette says, triumphantly.

" . . . the young woman regularly came for meals at a drop-in center, whose director was surprised by her absence . . . "

Marion Hennequin. Rest in peace, Marion. What's the chance that Marion, a homeless woman in Digne, and Sonia, barmaid in Castaing, knew each other? What was Marion doing before she lived in the street? I hope Lorieux will fill us in on this.

"I'm dying!" Laetitia calls out, bursting with laughter. "Yann's killing us!"

The joke falls a bit flat, and Francine hastens into the kitchen to supervise the tasting. MRCHA should stand for Mountain Recreation Center for Hungry Adults. It seems to me I'm spending my days eating. I'm going to wind up looking like a barrel on a shelf.

Little Magali, who's taken a liking to me, has thrown herself at my knees, roaring, "Sports, great!" I say "little" because her voice and her comportment as a five-year-old child always make me forget that in fact she's twenty-two. I pat her head. She's taking it upon herself to braid my hair. She loves coiffing me. This is a good fit, since I love it when people play with my hair. I always wanted Benoît to brush my hair, and he always answered that I could brush it myself . . . It always made us double over with laughter. When I imagine how he must have been thinking about his mistress while joking around with me! When I think that he's dead. The explosion, the sharp pieces of glass flying all over, the shouts, the panic, the shard embedded in his neck, his incredulous stare. Full of shock and terror. The last look I ever saw, before I woke up and was blind. Only a few months ago the memory of this scene where my life was turned upside down invariably provoked an outburst of tears. Now it's like a film whose colors are fading. I ought to make an effort to "see" these details again with precision. To tell you the truth, I'm avoiding it.

" . . . Marion Hennequin, a homeless person . . . ," Yvette's saying.

"It's funny, it means something to me," Yann mutters pensively.

" 'Funny' really isn't the word!" Francine corrects him, sweeping back in like a whirlwind. "All right, it's time to have our refreshments. Léonard, darling, would you like to help me carry the tray?"

Grunts. I can imagine what a trial this must represent for a man who can't quite coordinate his movements. The teacups clink and clatter as they collide. I'm crossing my fingers that he won't knock anything over.

"Good, Lenad, good!" Christian says encouragingly, clapping his hands.

Someone with a mental handicap is congratulating a man certified to teach math because he managed to place a tray on a table. How does Léonard feel? What good is all the intelligence in the world if the body refuses to obey? I remember a boy from Boissy who used to come to the movie theater often. When he walked, he threw his arms about in all directions like an epileptic, and his head used to roll around on his shoulders. To earn a living he used to sell flowers in restaurants and on the subway. He spoke with enormous difficulty. People often chased him like a dog. He was bothering them, scaring them, causing an embarrassment. At that time I still could see, and one day in the local paper, I read an interview with him, within the framework of an investigation on the homeless. He explained that his thoughts and feelings were exactly the same as those of anyone else, and that he refused to live in a home, receiving aid, preferring instead to confront the gazes of others and earn his living like a "normal" man.

I've often thought of this boy since my accident. I've been lucky to have something to live on, to have Yvette, a roof over my head, an uncle. I'm free and independent. How would I live with my handicap if I were locked away in a center with a ton of darling Francines? There, there, Elise dear, you've been having some morose thoughts today, haven't you! Well, yes, dear Shrink, but these current events don't exactly lead to joviality, even though, it's true, I still have all the things I do.

It's stopped snowing. A radiant sun is shining over the resort, and with this good weather, calm seems to have returned. No more phone calls, no more morbid "gifts," no more mutilated cadavers. Two days' respite. I'm savoring them, filling my lungs with cool, dry air. A light breeze is making the fir branches swish. I've begun hoping ever so selfishly that the killer has left for other horizons.

I'm settled on the terrace overhanging the main road, with the roofs of the village at my feet. Sounds are dulled by the time they reach me. A raven passes with a squawk. Martine's wrapped me in a Scottish wool blanket, and only my nose sticks over the top.

"If only you could see what a beautiful day we've got!" she calls before going away. "Truly a God-given day!"

Behind me, Yvette's and Francine's shrill exclamations are coming through the half-open bay window in the living room, as they indulge their mutual passion for rummy. They play late into the evening. Listening to them in the morning, I can guess which of them has won by either the triumphant or tight-lipped tone of voice. For the moment, Yvette's in the lead, and she's chuckling with glee.

Yann's taken the able-bodied residents on a long walk in the hills—snow-balls and downhill slides.

Laetitia and Justine are in the sauna. They asked me to join them, but I declined their offer. I'm in no mood to suffocate inside a wooden shack. What I'm in the mood for is fresh air and sunshine. I'm in the mood for sharp, shimmering peaks, crows flying, and hares scampering through snow-banks. If I concentrate really hard, I can almost see them.

Footsteps. Someone's coming up the stairway leading to the terrace. Is it Martine already? A shadow passes across my face. I'm looking for my pad to tell Martine that I'd like to stay outside a bit longer.

"Why don't you love me as much as I love you?"

Oh, no! It's like being punched in the stomach. I tense up, my heart pounding. Yvette and Francine are right here, just behind the curtains. They can see him. He's not going to try anything, he won't try anything at all. My notebook!

What do you want? Who are you?

He laughs a small laugh, small and unpleasant, like a vicious child.

"What do I want? You. Who am I? Me. You and me, my angel, a footbridge between good and evil."

It sounds like he's reciting a text he's learned by heart. It's unbearable to feel him so close and not know what his hands are ready to do next. Once again he's whispering.

"Did you like my presents?"

No.

While I'm writing, I can hear him breathing rapidly, can sense him against my cheek, giving off an odd, spicy odor—pepper!

Why did you kill those girls?

"Why does the sun shine? Why does night fall? You ask silly questions." His voice turns hard. "I believe you're an idiot. I believe I was mistaken about you. I believe I will have to love someone besides you," he concludes, jubilation in his voice.

His whispering quickens, his lips lightly brush mine, and I can feel the fullness of his breath; I can no longer hold in a belch. His hand tightens around my hair like a raptor's claw.

"You little bitch! You think you can do anything! But you're nothing, nothing but a pile of meat sitting in a wheelchair! And I eat meat!"

I feel drenched in cold sweat. Won't Yvette lift her head from her rummy? Won't Martine show up humming a tune? My heart's beating so hard, it feels as if it's been replaced with a drum.

There's something cold against my face. Right away, I know what it is: a knife. Someone already used one on me last year. I know what it can do when it cuts through flesh. I know pain. I know fear. I know hatred. Hatred and anger are rising inside me, almost nullifying the fear. But there's nothing I can do. The blade is held flat against my throat. His stinking breath is suffocating me. Is he going to kill me? Slit my throat on this beautiful winter afternoon?

My wheelchair's moving forward. The blade is still pressed flat against my carotid artery. Where's he taking me? The fear's returning in great gusts. If he picks me up, I'll be at his mercy, at the mercy of a man who crucifies women or rapes them with an electric drill.

We're moving straight ahead. Though not toward the staircase. No. Over to the long drop. He's going to throw me off the terrace, and I'm going to be crushed on the road. The wheelchair comes to a stop. The wind has picked up strength. The blade moves aside.

"The angel's leap. Do you know it, my sweet? You're going to make a magnificent exit!"

I'm going to die. I'm going to die in a few seconds. Foolishly enough, here, ten yards away from Yvette. My skull's going to be splattered on the frozen asphalt. All because of this trash! I swing my good arm behind me, trying to grab him, but he's laughing contentedly.

"I'm going to count to three, my angel! One . . . "

No, no, this can't be!

"Two . . . "

I don't want to. This is too silly!

"Thr . . . "

A deep, dull growl, terrifying me. Is that him? From behind there's a shock, then a strangled cry. Did Martine arrive on the sly? I hit the reverse button on the wheelchair, and bump against something on the ground; the growling intensifies—it's a dog, a dog! It's whimpering now. The man's crazed footsteps run off in the distance. The dog's barking and whimpering.

"What's going on?"

Yvette, at last!

"That's Sonia's dog! Look, Francine!"

"Well, of all things! What's he doing here?"

He's just saved my life! I'd like to scream at them. Brave Tintin.

"Oh, he's bleeding! He's hurt himself on the side!"

"We'd better call the veterinarian; it looks deep. Don't move, boy, we're going to take care of you. I'm going to give him something to drink," says Yvette, "he looks dehydrated."

I stay here with Tintin, alone. He's resting his burning nose on my hand, and I pet his head. That son of a bitch stabbed him in the side. I hope the dog had the time to give him plenty of bites.

Yvette returns and gives him something to drink.

"Was he there a long time? You should have tapped on the window."

Oh, of course. Why didn't I think of that? I should have asked my attacker politely to be patient a few minutes before sending me over. With a tired hand, I grab my notepad, and in shaky letters transcribe what's just happened.

The police are called, and when Francine is informed, she joins her voice to the Yvettian exclamations in a concert of lamentation. Martine's next, repeating to me a hundred times how sorry she is, and if only she'd known. I work at breathing calmly, telling myself how marvelous it is to be alive. Justine and Laetitia show up, and Francine gives them the scoop.

"Oh, poor Elise!" Justine exclaims, squeezing my hands in hers. "I warned you! Your aura is so disturbed."

She suddenly lets go of my hands as if they were burning.

"Oh! He's here, he's just next to you!"

Who? This is ridiculous!

"Evil is enveloping you like a shroud," she whispers to me in an urgent voice. "Take warning, your soul is in danger."

My soul? Don't worry about my soul; it's my body that almost wound up like a pancake at the edge of the road.

"Well, what's happened? Step to the side, please."

It's Lorieux. Everyone starts talking at once until he cries, "One at a time, please!"

"Here," says Yvette. "Elise wrote everything down."

Dead air. He must be reading. Then he calls for Hugo and goes off to a corner to be alone with him, before returning to Yvette and Francine. They cough nervously.

"So if I've understood correctly, Miss Martine Pasquali, a nurse associated with the center, placed Miss Andrioli on the terrace to 'take advantage of the sunshine.' She then went to the main office to 'fill out paperwork.' During this time, an unidentified individual attacked Miss Andrioli and attempted to push her over the side. He was prevented from doing so by a dog, a black Labrador identified as the dog of the late Sonia Auvare"—he breathes in— "and the aforementioned dog was wounded in the right side. Mrs. Holzinski and Mrs. Atchouel arrived at this point, discovering the wounded dog and Miss Andrioli in a state of shock."

That state of shock he's talking about is a bit of an exaggeration. I think I can take a beating remarkably well.

In all this commotion, the veterinarian's arrival has gone unnoticed, and he has to raise his voice to be heard. As he gives first aid to Tintin, I make my way toward Lorieux by the sound of his voice and hold out a sheet from my pad: *Did you know Tintin?*

"Of course. I'm the one who gave him to Sonia. She used to come home late at night, and I thought a dog might be a good . . . "

His voice breaks. The veterinarian interrupts us: the dog's wound isn't so deep and no vital organs were touched. He's taking him to the dispensary to stitch him up, and we can come pick him up tomorrow. Pick him up?

"The problem is, the owner of the dog is deceased," says Lorieux, who's pulled himself together.

"Keep him here!" Magali exclaims, childishly.

"Well, dear, I don't know . . . "

"But he saved Elise's life!" Jean-Claude shouts.

"It's true he's a brave animal," Yvette admits, with a tone in her voice that makes me think she's wondering what Jean Guillaume would say upon seeing her return home with a hundred-pound Labrador packed in her bags.

Darling Francine finally gives in. Emilie lets out a big "whoopee!" which makes Clara cry, no one knows why. Magali shouts, "No cry! No cry! Go without dessert!" Bernard declares that he should take a bath and that he's a good hunting breed. "Check him out!" shouts Christian, before starting to bark.

I can feel Justine's presence by my side. Like me, she can perceive this scene only by sounds. Yet does she have the same representation as me? Perhaps it's not Emilie crying, but Clara. Perhaps Christian's not the one crying, but rather Léonard. Perhaps Yvette is not pushing my wheelchair inside, promising me an herbal tea to get back my strength, and perhaps Tintin didn't intervene, and perhaps I'm dead and my spirit, still functioning a few more seconds, is continuing to fabricate these familiar images.

No. The stomach-turning odor of herbal tea can belong only to the real world.

Tintin has returned. He follows me around everywhere. His presence is very reassuring, and I like holding out my hand and feeling his rough fur. He's being spoiled rotten by everyone from the cook to the residents, who force-feed him cake from the kitchen. Darling Francine passes her time wringing her white hands to bring back some calm. It's got a way of exciting the dog. Amid all this brouhaha, I'm trying once again to plot my position, and for a blind woman, it's pretty tough. That's a lamentable joke, Elise.

Schnabel has confirmed for his friend Yvette that Yann was in fact out on a walk with the residents while someone was trying to turn me into a glider. In any case, I know Yann well enough by now to be able to identify him by his touch, odor, and voice. The man who attacked me was smaller, with bad breath and an odd smell of pepper . . . Lorieux asked me how I knew this man was smaller than Yann. I explained to him that by reflex I continue to lift my head toward my interlocutors when they speak to me. I've managed to situate approximately the height of the sound, and therefore their mouth. Vore's voice came from about eight inches above my head. Lorieux began rapid calculations: "Let's see . . . notwithstanding that you're sitting in a wheelchair and that the summit of your head reaches . . . Schnabel, get the measuring tape! . . . Four feet four inches, and that an individual's mouth is situated about . . . Schnabel! . . . two-thirds down the face, then subsequently, the suspect should stand at five feet seven inches."

"Like you," Francine remarks. "Who wants more tea?"

I'm starting to imagine darling Francine as a giant samovar gifted with speech. Lorieux rejects her offer rather . . . impatiently, I might say, and departs to write his report, leaving us in Schnabel's care, who himself is under Yvette's watchful eye.

Five feet seven. According to Laetitia, Yann's taller than five eleven. Oh, why am I so intent on suspecting poor Yann? He didn't know me before I came here, and he couldn't have sent me that fax the evening prior to my departure!

The evening prior to my departure. Why, yes, Vore did contact me. He can't be in Castaing at the same time I'm here purely by coincidence. So either he followed me here or he knew of my arrival. But from whom? Answer: only my uncle was aware of this. New theory: Vore lives in the region. He's some psychopath who's obsessed with me. He finds out from my uncle incidentally that I'm going to be staying here. And comes to challenge me. Killing first a homeless woman and then my uncle's goddaughter.

Which leads me to this hypothesis: is it someone who holds a grudge against my uncle? Someone kills his goddaughter, then tries to kill his niece . . . Is it someone from Castaing who secretly hates him? But if that's the case, why did he kill Marion Hennequin? To throw off the investigation? Perhaps I've put my finger on something important.

"I did a portrait of you this morning."

I was lost in thought; Justine's voice gives me a sudden jolt. My portrait?

"It's incredible, it's really quite a success!" Laetitia exclaims, continuing, "Oh, I'm sorry, I didn't mean to say—"

"Not important," Justine says, cutting her off.

How do you do it?

"I let myself be guided by colors," she answers as soon as Laetitia has read her my question. "Their textures on my skin. I paint with my fingers. That's often why I touch people. To feel their material configuration."

Saying so, she lightly touches my chin, temples, and eyebrows. It feels like being brushed by a raven's wing.

"Don't be afraid of me," says Justine, her beautiful voice serious. "I'm not a witch."

I try to laugh to show her I'm in no way afraid of witches, and Laetitia whispers in my ear, "Do you want to go into the little corner?"

I raise my index finger to say no. If someone misreads my face so that the challenge of skepticism is confused with the desire to urinate, I'm not out of the woods when it comes to communicating.

"Ah, there you are, Justine! I was looking for you. It's time for your lesson!" says Yann, bursting in among our little group, smelling of snow, freshly washed hair, and tobacco.

"Justine's going to take her first skiing class," Laetitia explains. "Do you want to come see?"

Yvette grouses a bit: she's in the middle of mopping the floor with Francine, but Laetitia can't push my wheelchair because of her walker.

So here we are in the snow. Tintin's trotting beside me, amicably nuzzling my thigh with his head every now and then. Yvette pulls my bonnet over me with one big unamicable sweep.

"A ski lesson," she mutters. "Now I've seen everything. That poor woman's going to break her face."

"No, look!" Laetitia leans over to me and says, "Yann's holding her by her frame, and he'll be going down the slope with her. It's to give her the sensation of sliding. You can't know how marvelous it is to slide!"

I can see myself again, sliding toward the edge of the terrace.

"Sensation, sensation; it's not all that proper anyway," Yvette gripes; the altitude, the rural setting, and her passion for gaming are transforming her into a duenna.

It's cold. Some snowflakes flit about and melt on my cheeks. Branches are rustling.

"By the time they go back up the hill on foot, we'll be frozen," Yvette grumbles.

"Oh, a squirrel!" Laetitia cries.

I can imagine a plumed tail skipping under the trees. Tintin lets out an indecisive "woof." Should I or shouldn't I race the little furry creature? I pat his head, and he sits back down.

"Let's go!" says Yann, far above our heads.

A pair of *skis* go swish. I conscientiously try to watch the spectacle I can't see. Justine's laugh. A throaty laugh, rippling, very feminine. Justine in Yann's vigorous arms. Schnabel and Yvette going at it in a cowshed. Darling Francine, in black leather, whip in hand, directing Martine and Hugo's lovemaking. Oh, my, a libido attack looks imminent, and there's no Tony at hand!

"And here's our work!"

"Super!" says Laetitia. "You didn't even fall down!"

"Yann's a remarkable teacher," Justine agrees. "I almost believed I was a skier."

"We'd better go back, it's really starting to get cold," Yvette mutters.

"What about you, Yvette, don't you want to give it a try? You'll take a little ride in the ski tow and then, whoosh! We'll let you go down on the bunny slope!"

"Poor Yann. That bunny slope of yours is just a slide for babies!"

"Ah, because you know how to ski?" Yann asks, mockingly.

"You bet! My father was a mailman."

Stunned silence.

"In the Jura. I spent my childhood following him around, delivering mail to farms. And not in a four-by-four."

"My, how secretive you are!"

And what a liar she is! Her father was a postmaster. I can hardly see him dashing through the woods with a saddlebag slung over his shoulder and Yvette in tow.

" . . . do a demonstration?" Yann is saying, guiding Justine, an arm around her waist.

Laetitia's humming, Tintin's sniffling, and I'm listening without listening, pleasantly cradled by wheels sliding through fresh snow.

We spend the evening beside the fire. I'm slowly savoring the cognac Yann offered me after our meal. Laetitia's playing Chopin on the digital piano. Justine's stretched out on the rug, doing her relaxation exercises. Francine and Yvette are dueling it out in crapette. Magali, Christian, and the others are sitting in the rec room in front of a TV movie that's talking about differences (take your pick: size, class, gender, beliefs).

A sound of footsteps works its way across the wooden floor, which is certainly well waxed.

"Would you like a cognac, Léonard?"

"No. Coca-Cowa."

"Go ahead. Help yourself."

I hear him pant, can sense his wavering mass; the bottle goes *pssht* as it's opened, and the glass shatters, crashing to the floor.

"Don't worry about it, we'll pick it up," says Yann.

Léonard's silent.

"How come you're so soaked? Did you go out?" Yann goes on.

"Stars . . . tonight."

He pauses, breathing heavily.

"Mizar and Alcor. Sup . . . sup . . . "

"Super!" Justine finishes for him. "The atmosphere out here is so pure!"

Like she's ever seen a star in her life. Learning the constellations only to put on an act!

Laetitia strikes a chord a little too loudly. Yann serves some more cognac, and I hear him empty his own class in a single gulp.

"Good Lord!" he blurts from out of the blue. "If only I could understand!"

What about me?

"Yann! Yann! Come watch the race on TV! Come on!"

Magali's suddenly rushed out, excited and filled with joy.

"They're rebroadcasting the men's snowboarding finals from La Colmiane," Hugo explains.

"Hmmm," Yann acquiesces distractedly.

He gets up and trudges off.

"Lise, come watch TV. The race! Come on!"

"Magali! You know very well that Elise can't see the TV!" Laetitia calls out between two thirty-second notes.

"Too bad! You're friend's in the TV."

Friend? What friend?

"Your friend who give presents to you. Presents, presents, pretty presents, thank you."

Does she mean that . . . Vore? On TV? Quick, my notepad. *Please, ask Magali to show you my friend on TV!*

I randomly hold the sheet in front of me. Turn around, Laetitia, Justine can't read!

"Lae-ti-tia . . . ," Léonard articulates. "Lae-ti-tia . . . "

"'Please, ask Magali . . . ' Oh, dear, this is illegible!"

Fast! Good God, fast!

"'To chew you'? No, that doesn't mean anything. To . . . ah . . . 'show . . . you my friend on TV.' Uh, I'm not getting this."

Ask her!

"Magali, would you show me Elise's friend on TV?"

"Friend gives presents, why not to Magali?"

"Would you show him to me?"

I cock my ear over the walker's swishing and Magali's chuckles.

"Gone! Gone!"

Obviously. Magali was watching the ski races. What race, and where? I ask these questions once again in writing and blindly hold out my note.

"What are you up to?" Yvette asks, lifting her eyes from her sacrosanct cards for half a second.

I furiously scribble, *Magali saw Vore on TV!* resisting the urge to throw a ball of paper at her head.

"How? Magali doesn't even know who Vore is! Where would she have seen him?"

Good question. Obviously in my company, since she's describing him as the friend who gives me presents. But when? Oh, maybe I haven't understood anything!

"Magali, who did you see on TV?" Yvette asks.

"The man, the man, Lise's friend. The man on the terrace."

"On the terrace?" Yvette repeats, with less assurance.

"The man, play with Lise on the terrace. Why not play with Magali? Magali want play wheelchair! Right now!"

"Stop that!" Francine says, cutting her off. "Elise's wheelchair is not a toy, and you know it. What's this man like?"

"Don't know. Don't remember."

"Magali! Come back here!"

Their small shouts grow distant.

"She's going to throw a fit," Martine predicts. "She's very sensitive."

"She saw the murderer!" Francine cries. "I don't give a damn about those lousy fits of hers! Go get her."

"But . . . Mrs. Atchouel," Martine protests, bewildered by this sudden outburst.

"Francine's right," says Yvette, "this is no game. Someone almost killed Miss Andrioli, after all! Let's notify Lorieux."

They make the call. Yann returns to find out what's going on. Laetitia explains.

"But wasn't Magali on a walk with you during that unfortunate incident on the terrace?" Justine asks.

Yann thinks about it for a few seconds.

"Lorieux's on his way," says Francine, hanging up.

"Chris-tian . . . left," Léonard says, suddenly.

Yann smacks his palm.

"Exactly! I must have gone after Christian, who was speeding downhill on his ass. Magali could have slipped away from us for a few minutes. Now I remember she didn't want to come, she said she had a headache."

"Could she have been present at the attack against Elise and then quietly met up with you again?" Justine asks with surprise.

"Come on, straight ahead!" Martine orders someone (no doubt Magali). "No one's going to eat you up!"

Pretty sad words, given the context.

"Excuse me, I heard what you were saying," Martine continues, "and I think I'm holding the key to the mystery. As I was leaving the office, I saw Magali in front of the garage, and I went with her as far as the group. Yann was down below, behind the snowbank, tugging on Christian. I hurried to get back, as it was time to go take care of Jean-Claude."

So we know Magali's not lying. Lorieux arrives, followed by Schnabel. The situation's been explained to them: Magali claims to have seen my attacker on television, during the rebroadcast of the men's snowboarding finals in the Europe Cup in La Colmiane, a ski resort thirty miles away. Lorieux's asking just what makes us think that "Elise's friend" is in fact Vore and not just some country bumpkin. This business of "presents" is explained to him. From this he concludes that Magali did see the man approach me before the scene on the terrace. Everyone turns toward Magali, who starts crying, saying she's got a headache.

"When young ladies weep, the sun loses its wings," Schnabel tells her.

"The sun doesn't have wings!" Magali protests in a muddled voice.

"No? How do you think it flies through the sky?"

Magali seems to be considering the question with interest while Francine mutters, "As if she needs to be told such foolishness."

"Would you like a piece of candy?" Schnabel continues.

"What kind of candy?"

"A candy with a magic potion. It takes away your headache."

I can hear the sound of the cellophane crumpling.

"Better?"

"Yes," Magali says hesitantly.

Schnabel forges on: "So, just like that, you saw me on TV?"

"No, that's not true! Lise's friend!"

"I'm also a friend of Lise," Schnabel says, maneuvering with finesse.

"You're too fat! Your head's too high!" Magali shouts. "You weren't on TV, you liar!"

"But I've got blond hair," Schnabel, the consummate strategist, replies.

"Black!" Magali chirps. "Elise's friend is like the dog! Tintin! Tintin!"

A quick yapping.

The man's got dark hair, and he's smaller and less corpulent than Sergeant Schnabel.

"Okay, okay. What was Elise's friend doing? Was he skiing?"

"Pff! Silly! He was watching, like us!"

Vore, an anonymous spectator watching the race, was pinned by the cameras. What an incredible stroke of luck! Lorieux's getting busy with his special-frequency radio-telephone. Everyone's commenting on this recent turn of events. Magali's demanding another piece of candy for her stomachache. After spending half an hour palavering with his counterparts at La Colmiane and with the organizers of the race, Lorieux finally gets someone from the TV crew who was getting ready to go back down to Monaco. The tape of the broadcast may be viewed only on their equipment. Lorieux arranges a meeting with them for nine o'clock the next day.

"I'll come by at seven-thirty to pick up Magali. Someone should come with us."

"I'll come," says Yann, beating out everyone else.

I can hardly believe that tomorrow we'll know what Vore's face looks like! And I'm the one who's always criticizing the media for being omnipresent. We're all very excited, though the residents must be wondering what's happened to us. Schnabel offers Magali another piece of candy, and then the police take their leave.

"Champagne!" Yann cries.

"You shouldn't count your chickens before they're hatched," Yvette begins.

"Yvette dear, until Magali's miraculous intervention, I was the prime suspect in this whole affair. Don't argue, Lorieux can't stand me!"

"He's your best friend. You're just speaking off the top of your head!"

"I thought he was a friend. I realized that he couldn't ever get over his breakup with Sonia. Ever since I started to show an interest in her, he's hated me."

I for one think Yann's analysis is on the money.

"You should try not to wash your dirty laundry in public, Yann, if you don't mind," Francine declares, tightly. "As far as champagne goes, there isn't any. I'm sorry, but this is a care facility, not a nightclub."

"How about taking me out to see the stars, Léonard?" Justine says with affection.

"There are plenty of clouds!" Laetitia calls out.

"No, the sky's perfectly clear," Martine says ingenuously.

"A whole lot of good that'll do for Justine!" Laetitia blurts.

"The stars emit vibrations other than light waves," Justine replies, "but only certain trained individuals can pick them up."

Laetitia keeps her mouth shut.

I can sense Léonard passing nearby, recognizable from his disorderly movements, followed by Justine's perfume.

"I'm happy for you, Elise," she says to me on her way out. "I hope we'll finally put an end to this creature's state of harmfulness."

Judging from her intonation, one might think she's talking about a supernatural being, some sort of werewolf from the mountaintops.

The door slams shut.

"Vibrations from the stars! Better not be hearing those! The things some people go on about!" Laetitia mutters.

On my notepad I write, *Is Léonard handsome?*

"Ha . . . If you go for someone who's dark and skinny with an intense emerald gaze . . ."

"Like Dracula suffering from Saint Vitus' dance," Yann confirms.

"Yann! Really!" Francine shouts.

"Yes, really."

"You know what I mean!" Francine goes on in hushed tones. "Hugo, isn't it time we put all these people to bed? Would you like to play one last game, Yvette, or perhaps your finances may not permit it? Darling Yvette has done nothing but lose today," she adds for our benefit.

"How about going down to the village for a drink?" Laetitia says.

"I think I'm going to bed myself," says Yann, whose mood has changed. "Well, good night."

"What super ambience this place has!" Laetitia comments. "Oh, well, I'm sure you don't care!" she calls in my direction before she too leaves the room.

So here I sit, slumped by the hearth, waiting for Yvette to remember I exist. I'm not bored, though; I've got a lot to think about. I'm so impatient for tomorrow to come so I can find out!

7

I CAN'T STOP yawning. It was impossible to fall asleep until I don't know what time, and I've been up since seven this morning to be around for Magali's departure. She needed every bit of persuasion from her friend Schnabel to get into the shuttle bus—she thought they were taking her to jail. Those magic candies were back in service. By now, the bus should be approaching the coast. I can already "see" handcuffs closing around Vore's wrists—bony, hairy wrists, covered with scratch marks from his victims.

Hugo has wheeled me into the living room, where we had our breakfast. Darling Francine and Mrs. Raymond have drawn up a list of all the necessary supplies. Martine and Hugo are seeing to it that the residents are washed. Jean-Claude is delivering a dissertation on the concept of narrative structure in the films of Abel Ferrara. Léonard hasn't come down; he's working in his room. Justine, right on form, is explaining to Laetitia the latest theories on quarks and quasars, while Laetitia asks Yvette to pass her the butter. "And here I lie by the shores of silence, where the soft lapping of these waves of boredom gently soothes my melancholy." (Elise Andrioli, winner of the Nobel Prize for Poetry, 2000).

The rest of the morning drags out this way until the phone rings. Yvette dashes over, knocking Hugo aside.

"Hello? Yes, hello, Sergeant . . . Yes, you're coming through loud and clear . . . What? . . . Uh . . . Obviously . . . Of course . . . All right, I'll talk to you later."

She sounds disappointed.

"What did he say?" Laetitia asks avidly.

"Magali pointed out a man for them."

"A man?" Martine and Hugo repeat in unison.

"A man in a red ski suit."

"A ski suit?" darling Francine calls out as she comes out of the kitchen.

"An instructor's suit from the skiing school in Castaing. He was wearing a black ski cap, glasses, and gloves."

"If that's the case, then how did Magali recognize him?" Laetitia asks.

"She recognized a ski instructor," Justine says.

On my pad I write, *Anyway, it means my attacker was dressed as an instructor.*

"So maybe it was an instructor," Yvette adds.

A ski instructor from Castaing, calmly moving about through town, whose face is so familiar that no one pays attention to him anymore. Or is it Vore disguised as an instructor? With sunglasses and a cap, anyone in the world can be whoever, and vice versa. Way to go, Elise. After poetry, you've walked away with the Grand Prize in Contemporary Philosophy, awarded by Professor La Palice.

So Lorieux's going to direct his investigation toward the ski school. I for one doubt that Sonia or Marion Hennequin ever took lessons.

Francine's trying to remember all the instructors from the ski resort, and realizes that she's almost always seen them sporting reflecting sunglasses, painting their faces with those new multicolored kinds of makeup, and hiding their hair under bandannas or ski caps.

"Well, in the long run, you'd recognize them by the sound of their voice," she concludes.

"Red again," Justine sighs. "You see, Elise, I was right. Red is evil, and it's blazing a trail through the white snow like a starved animal."

I'd really be curious to see some of her paintings. And I'm eaten up with frustration at the idea that I'll never see anything again. How is this possible? Why me, one who so loved to see things, look at them, observe them?

I must be clenching a fist, because Francine whispers, "You ought to spread out your fingers to get rid of the stress."

At this moment I'd be thrilled to spread them out to smack you across the face and make you shut up. I've had enough of these aggravations without anyone coming to give me lessons! Doesn't anybody realize that I've been spending my time taking a beating without being able to say anything about it, like a groggy boxer under an avalanche of blows?

"What I don't understand," says Laetitia, "is why Vore went to the race in La Colmiane in his ski instructor suit."

"Maybe it's not Vore. Magali *thought* she recognized Elise's friend," Justine snaps, in the tone of voice of a teacher who's patient yet exasperated.

"We see instructors in town every day, and she's never said anything," Laetitia observes.

That's because Magali, like us, sees the global picture of an individual—his weight, his size, his attitude, and doesn't need to make out features to realize who it is. When I could see, I could recognize someone by his shoulder, his hand, his way of walking. Does that mean it's really Vore on the videotape? And if he's going around dressed as a ski instructor, does it mean he really is one? I'm getting the impression that I'm going in circles asking myself these questions. Fortunately I wasn't the one who wrote the book on that matter in Boissy. The readers would be committing suicide from sheer boredom.

This makes me think that my author will be thrilled to know I'm mixed up in new murders. Bingo, looks like another big printing! The new adventures of the sack of potatoes on wheels. One might imagine a whole new series: *Elise in the Congo, Elise Goes to Serbia, Elise Meets the Head of the Fundamentalists, They've Marched on Elise.*

And if I die, it'll sell even better: *The True and Tragic Tale of Elise Andrioli, Devoured by the Cannibal from the Snows.* With an eye-catching cover.

Fortunately no one knows the horrors I can think up all by myself in my little corner. I feel as bitter as sage herbal tea. Or, given my surroundings, a glass of gentiane.

"Ma'am," says Mrs. Raymond suddenly, "Father Clary's here, for butter and cheese."

"I'm coming."

Father Clary? A priest who sells dairy products?

"You should come, too, Yvette," Francine goes on. "All his products are a hundred percent natural. He brings them from the sheepfolds. All dairy products, but also honey from the mountain pastures and donkey sausage . . . "

A shepherd. Was he a colleague of poor Sonia's uncle? I press down on the wheelchair's electric release and roll in the direction of the voices. I pass through the doorway to the kitchen without hitting too many obstacles (getting just a black-and-blue mark on the knee). There's a draft of fresh air, which tells me the French windows must be open. They're in discussion. I can hear a gruff man's voice, with a thick accent. Yvette's ecstatic over everything, ready to eat lavender honey off the brush for the rest of her days. At least we won't be going home without presents. If we do go home, that is.

I hear Father Clary say, "What about something for the poor lady? Take a bit of goat cheese for her, with green pepper. That ought to pick her up."

I sense he's talking about me, and as I wait to be force-fed goat cheese, I grab my notepad: *Did you know Mauro?*

"Ah! You can't speak anymore, either? Look, for all the nonsense we say most of the time—"

I shake my sheet of paper again.

"Oh, yes, Mauro, poor fellow!" he answers laconically.

"He died six months ago, I believe?" Yvette says.

"Soon it will be seven. He took off for Les Aiguilles. The sheep came back with the dogs eight days later. But no Mauro."

"Did you call the police?"

"What police? I wasn't going back down. I looked for him fifteen days. I know the mountains better than the police."

"And . . . ?"

"He'd fallen into a crevasse. Dead stiff, poor guy. Half eaten by wolves."

"Wolves!" Yvette exclaims.

"Oh, yes, the new wolves who've come from Italy. They've eaten up ten or more lambs of mine, the bastards. When I came back down, I notified the cops and his niece, the whore."

"Mr. Clary!"

"Don't 'Mr. Clary' me! A whore's a whore. A brave whore, maybe, may she rest in peace."

I guess he's crossing himself while I quickly write, *Fernand Andrioli, my uncle, was her godfather.*

"You're Fernand's niece? How about that! What a rascal, that one! When we were small fries, we used to get into such scrapes together. Now he's become a real gentleman, that Fernand. It's true, you do have a family resemblance."

Did Sonia inherit anything?

"Hell, yeah! I brought her the old man's hat and his sculpted olive cane."

That doesn't seem like a great motive for murder. After a few niceties, Clary takes his leave; other customers are waiting. And with him goes a whole other life: mountain pastures burned by the sun, the odor of fresh grass, gray stones rolling down hillsides. Oh, those memories of mountain runs—the frozen torrents, the tremor in air set abuzz with cicadas.

Yvette goes and puts our purchases away. I drive into the living room and position myself in front of the big window. This is my favorite corner; I get the feeling that I'm seeing everything that's going on, that I'm close to the light. It's so tiring to be in darkness for perpetuity. It's like being in a room whose shutters are always closed. It smacks of sickness, of being locked away. I take a deep breath, several times.

"Yoohoo! They gave me a cassette! Lucky Luke! Faster than his own shadow!"

Magali shoves an object under my nose, half crushing me.

"Easy there, young lady!" says Schnabel, pushing her to the side. "She's a bit overexcited, that's all," he explains.

"McDonald's!" Magali cries. "Lots! Lots!"

"Uh, we stopped at McDonald's; the poor little thing was dying of hunger."

"Fries! Three fries for the general!"

"You've been hiding your promotion from us, Schnabel!" Lorieux jests.

Schnabel stammers something unintelligible.

"She's not going to eat anything at the table," Francine complains. "Where's Yann?"

"He needed a little calm, so he went for a ski run after dark," Lorieux answers mirthlessly. "We haven't gotten much farther," he continues for my benefit. "Has Yvette explained it to you?"

I raise my hand.

"I've sent two of my men to the ski school to get all the employees' names and photos," he goes on, "but I don't think much will come of it."

On my pad I write, *Where can someone get an instructor's suit?*

"Hmm . . . I guess he could make it himself. All he needs to do is get a red ski suit, stitch 'Castaing Skiing School' in blue on the back, and glue a patch onto the sleeve."

I can't quite see Vore doing the work himself. Did he go to an embroiderer? We'd better find out for sure. I write it down.

"You're right. We'd better check up on that. All that aside, I forgot to speak to you about the report concerning the Hennequin woman. She was originally from Entrevaux. Twenty-nine years of age. Her maiden name was Gastaldi. A very good family, bankers. She was married to one Mr. Hennequin from 1990 to 1992, the same Hennequin having died of an overdose toward the end of '92. He and Marion were constantly drinking and shooting dope. She was fired from her job as a cashier in 1993. Amid all this turmoil, she stopped paying her rent and got herself kicked out six months later. After that, she left town, and from then on we lose track of her."

And six years later she's found dead in Entrevaux.

What do her parents have to say?

"They're dead. Gastaldi senior died of Alzheimer's disease last year. Mrs. Gastaldi died in '97, without ever seeing her daughter again. The neighbors say there were always arguments going on in the family the whole time Hennequin was around."

What was Hennequin's occupation?

"A computer programmer. He was unemployed when Marion married him. He'd already been through detox twice. They met in a methadone program."

That's romance for today. Replaces the sanatoriums of our great-grandparents.

Lorieux takes his leave, followed by Schnabel, who thanks Yvette for the cup of coffee, and a yapping Magali, who has to be held inside. Exeunt the forces of order. Enter the thoughts of disorder. "My head's just a mess, where I drive in distress." After playing for a moment with the idea that this composition might actually reach the top of the charts if it were performed on a voice synthesizer, I return to the gloomy depression that's been gripping me since early this morning.

Two young women are dead. A man tried to kill me. Who? Why? For whom? Is Vore being manipulated by someone? Perhaps Lorieux should check up on some of the mentally unbalanced patients who are being released from psychiatric hospitals.

Marion Gastaldi. Sonia Auvare. Who were Sonia's parents? Surely they weren't rich bankers. I note that question on my clipboard. I should ask Lorieux, too, who's going to inherit the Gastaldis' money now that Marion's dead.

"Lunch is served!" Francine cries, just next to my right ear, practically making me jump straight to the ceiling.

Without waiting for an answer, she wheels me toward the long guest table, which I'm assuming is loaded down with food. The residents enter as a group, with the usual clamor. So here I am, sitting next to Martine again.

I feel around a bit for my plate, piled with ham and steamed potatoes, while she's murmuring grace. Suddenly I feel horribly unbelieving. And horrified when suddenly she suggests, "How about going to Mass on Sunday? The new priest is really quite invigorating."

Okay, I'm playing the deaf-mute stuffing her face. She's not pushing it. Jaws are clicking amid satisfied groans.

"So where's darling Justine?" Francine asks.

"Why, you're right, she hasn't come down," Martine says.

"Nor Léonard!" Hugo observes. "I'll go get them."

"I would like it if order and discipline at the center were not too greatly disturbed by these dramatic developments we've been experiencing," Francine says dully.

Christian starts to let out lascivious sighs.

"Christian!" Martine shouts.

"Ha, ha, ha, Lenna, Juthine. Ha, ha, ha! Dirty!"

"What's dirty?" Emilie asks. "Dirty cocky?"

"Cocky! Cocky!" the others start to shout, banging the table with their silverware.

"Come on, come on, let's calm down!" Francine orders. "Or else you'll go without dessert!"

There's an instant silence in the ranks.

"Christian started it!" says Magali.

"Not another word! Martine, would you be good enough to see if Christian is taking enough of his medicine; I'm finding him a bit . . . agitated."

"Christian has testosterone attacks," Martine whispers in my ear. "Often I find him in the middle of you-know-what. I've prayed for him and doubled up his doses, but nature's stronger. I'm a little worried; imagine what might happen if he turns it on children? Such innocent souls!"

Yes, I can imagine. Just as I can very well imagine Léonard and Justine. Hugo returns, preventing me from imagining any more.

"Well?" asks Francine.

He clears his throat. "They're not hungry."

"Neither one?" she asks, stunned.

"Léonard's got a migraine, and Justine has a stomachache. They'd rather lie down."

"They might have let us know," says Laetitia. "After all, we're a team."

"Exactly!" Francine says with approval. "A bit more ham, dear?"

Laetitia refuses and asks permission to leave the table. She's left her nose drops in her room.

"I'll go get them for you," says Hugo.

"Don't worry, I can get around on my own."

"Exactly. Go ahead and eat, Hugo, it's going to get cold. Laetitia's not helpless."

"I'll go with you," says Martine.

"I *do* know where my room is!" Laetitia protests.

"I left my *Voici* in my room, and I feel like reading some of it out on the terrace," Martine explains, and no one asks her a thing.

"You buy that?" Francine says.

"For the word search," Martine explains.

"Is this the latest?" Yvette asks. "The one where you see Richard Gere in his briefs?"

Laetitia's already outside. I'm sure she's racing as fast as she can toward Justine's or Léonard's room. Martine finally manages to get rid of Yvette and dashes out herself. After the drama comes vaudeville.

The next ten minutes pass in relative calm. Then a door on this floor slams and an angry woman's voice screams, "How could you? She could be your mother!"

"Laetitia!" Martine calls out.

Another door slams shut. Then silence. Apparently, Léonard's motor handicap doesn't extend to all his members. That's a good one, Elise! Very chic, very dignified!

Martine returns. I can hear her whispering, and Francine says, "I might have figured. We'll look into it later. No reason to panic, let's have dessert."

I've had two cups of coffee, nice and strong, with plenty of sugar, just the way I like it. Yvette's going through the "people" pages in her magazine, commenting aloud on the articles she's reading. Francine's holding great consultations with Mrs. Raymond. Hugo's leading the creativity workshop, with puzzles and early-learning games. Martine's straightening things in the medicine cabinet. Everything on the floor seems calm. I'm elaborating on a dark tale: Someone's killed Mauro before killing his niece. The killer is pursuing an ancestral vendetta that extends to the Gastaldis as well. Perhaps it's the son of a farmer who'd been ripped off, a lover who'd been spurned, or a robber who'd been blackmailed? However, if a vendetta really did put opposing clans at odds, then one might suppose that even the local constabulary would have caught wind of it. For the time being, I'll pack away this theory of mine, but I've got a feeling these murders have dark roots plunging deep into this region's harsh earth.

"I think I'm going to have a siesta," Yvette says, laying down her weekly. "Would you like to go upstairs and rest a bit, Elise?"

I acquiesce. Take the elevator. I manage to maneuver the wheelchair all by myself to get out and advance down the hallway. A door opens.

"Is that you, Elise?" Justine asks. "I heard the sound of your wheelchair."

"Yes, it's us," Yvette answers. "We're going to rest awhile."

"Why don't you come in for five minutes," Justine suggests.

"No, thanks, it's nice of you, but I'm really tired," Yvette says.

I pivot my wheelchair toward Justine's voice and slowly advance.

"All right, I'm going to leave you here," says Yvette. "You'll know where to find your room, I suppose. It's the second door on your right as you leave Justine's."

I move forward a bit more and bump against an obstacle.

"That's my leg," says Justine. "I'm backing up; follow me."

We slowly pass through the door to her room. She shuts the door. It smells like incense. Justine grips my wheelchair and pushes it across the room, counting aloud, "One, two, three, four. There! You're right in front of your portrait. It's on the wall, at eye level."

I raise my arm, hold out my hand, and brush against a canvas. The paint is thick. I let my fingers slide over it. A white canvas. Paint. A long stroke. A sinewy curve. I can feel subtle differences in thickness and variations in all its directions. Horizontal, vertical . . . a fat oval blotch brushed over with vertical strokes. Is that my face?

"Do you like it?" Justine asks.

This woman's incredible! Does she think I can see through my fingertips?

"I've put you in a violet dress. Like a stormy sky."

The picture my fingers are deciphering by following the tracks in the paint is shaped like the letter *L*.

"You're sitting, of course. Sitting in the interstellar void," she goes on, ecstatically.

How charming. With the blood red aureole of evil knotted around my neck, I suppose. And then again, what does she know about using violet for my dress? Maybe she's mistaken and she's used yellow. Sun yellow. Yellow looks good on brunettes.

"I've started to paint Léonard," she continues. "He came by just a little while ago to pose."

That's right, to pose, and in the nude, I suppose.

"I've passed my hands over his face, his body . . . "

Well, well!

" . . . to capture its essence, so that I may then project it onto the canvas."

I don't know who projected what, but . . .

"Laetitia interrupted us, which was unfortunate, for it was such a fragile, delicate moment."

I'm holding back, or else I'll start giggling.

"So much anger in such a young, innocent heart . . . Sometimes I get the feeling that even though she can see and move about, she suffers from her difference more than you or I. You ought to speak to her."

Sure. With my computer that reproduces the voice of Maria Callas.

"Tell her how her youth should keep her from any jealousy. Léonard loves her very much."

Okay, but it's with you that he's . . .

"He has respect for her."

I've heard that one about three thousand times before. When a guy respects a girl, it means he doesn't hold a grudge against her, that's all.

"Did you know that Léonard knew the husband of the young woman who died?"

The husband of the young woman who died? Hennequin?

"They were in high school together, in Nice. A real asshole, according to Léonard."

Does that mean, maybe, that Léonard also knew Marion? I grab my pad and write, *Tell Lorieux,* then hold out the sheet in front of me, casting about, before I remember that Justine can't read. Her hand runs into the sheet.

"Ah, you want to tell me something. Wait, I'll pass you my sandbox."

The dumb idea of kitty litter crosses my mind, but she sets a rectangular box filled with fine sand on my lap.

"Trace your letters in the sand so that I can reread them."

To keep it short, I print *Police.* Justine traces the letters for herself.

"The police? Do you really think that would interest them? Some vague friendship between students, before Hennequin was even married?"

I erase my message and trace, *Sure it's the same H?*

"I suppose so. Léonard doesn't speak in long sentences, you know. Hennequin can't be such a common name, and it was a Hennequin who was heading into computers. In any case, what connection can he have with these horrible murders?"

And why did Léonard feel the need to go and tell you all that? Especially when he has such a hard time expressing himself.

She takes back her sandbox. That's the end of our visit. I start driving toward what I believe to be the door. *Bing.* I mechanically move my hand forward. A curtain falls. Now the bed. I go into reverse. *Bang.*

"Good God!" Justine blurts out, sounding exasperated. Then, continuing, she says, "You're not using your internal sonar, Elise. What I call our infrared vision, which enables us to make out forms in the dark. Thermal masses. Solid volumes. Your sonar must sweep your environment, constantly, and you'll see . . . you will see!"

She guides me toward the door, counting again. Once again I'm in the hallway, brushing my hand against the wall to find my way. The second door to the right is my door. I open up. I must have left my radio on; it's a contralto interpreting Haydn.

"Who dere?" says the radio.

Léonard? In my room?

It's a gesturing mass whose thermal radiance I certainly can sense.

"Wha want?" he asks.

Just the question I've been meaning to ask him. This conversation's getting off to a difficult start. On my pad I write, *Did you know Hennequin?*

"Yeah. School."

Marion, his wife?

"No. Elise . . . take shower."

Is this his elegant way of telling me I stink? Has this poor boy lost his head or what?

"Get oout, please."

What's he talking about? I raise my hand to protest, and it falls upon a belly. A naked, hairy belly. I pull my hand back as if I'd just plunged it into a nest of red ants. His belly jumps backward. He's naked, in my room! I'm having images of being raped in the shower, hanging by my hair from the plastic curtain rod, while Léonard sings Haydn.

"Get oout," Léonard repeats.

No one asks someone to leave if he wants to savagely abuse her. A certain suspicion comes to me. On my pad I ask, *Where are we?*

"My voom."

In fact, I've always confused my left from my right. I lose myself in silent excuses and go back out, more or less. I head straight across the hallway. Finally, at my door! I open up, enter, and *bing. Bing*—into two sneakered feet.

Two sneakered feet? I lift my hand apprehensively and grope the obstacle, feeling my temperature drop several degrees. Yes. There, level with my face, are feet, ankles, and legs, slowly swinging. Oh, no! No! I back up and bump against the door. Assuming that Laetitia didn't . . . Oh, my God! The hallway. I've got to warn Yvette, fast! I bang on her door.

"I don't want to see anyone!" an agitated voice shouts back.

Laetitia! I bang again. And again. Two doors open.

"Are you the one making all this racket?" Yvette asks sleepily.

"Elise, I want to be alone!" Laetitia exclaims.

My room, quick!

Yvette, bracing for the worst, runs to my room, followed by Laetitia, who's leaning on her walker. Yvette's scream confirms my fears. Two more doors open.

"What's going on?" Justine asks, sounding worried.

Laetitia lets out a scream as well.

"Laetitia?" says Justine. "What's going on?"

"Magali! Magali!" Laetitia stammers in a mechanical voice, while Yvette shouts, "Help me, hold on to her feet, we've got to cut the rope!"

"I can't!" says Laetitia. "I'm not strong enough."

Yvette grips my wheelchair and sets me beneath the sneakers. I shiver with revulsion but I've got no choice. I hear her pull out a chair and climb onto it while shouting, "Justine, go notify somebody, right away! Léonard, pass me those scissors!"

Léonard brushes against me; he's in terry cloth. Laetitia's making indistinct sounds somewhere between a sob and a scream. The sneakers are touching my face lightly, smelling of earth and leather. After one good shake, a mass abruptly falls on top of me, taking my breath away. With my one good arm I try to hold on to the body, and when Léonard comes to my aid, I can breathe in the scent of his eau de cologne. I can feel hair, a face, and though my hand withdraws, I force it to pass over this face. Eyes wide open. The eyebrows feel strange, tickling my palm, as if in a bad dream. I follow the bone in the nose; the cold, soft lips; the moist, protruding tongue; suddenly I feel nauseated, but keep descending, looking for the carotid artery. Nothing. Yvette, out of breath, asks, "Anything?"

She slaps her and shakes her inanimate body, saying, "Breathe, damn it, breathe!" I don't move; instead I'm frozen in place, and all the sounds and smells seem exceptionally sharp. Magali's lying across my lap, like a big, unmoving doll. I know she's dead. She's not giving off any heat; under her skin, the river of life has stopped running. She's nothing more than a mass of solid particles, like the seat of my wheelchair.

A cavalcade comes running in.

"This can't be!"

Hugo dashes over, tears the body out of my arms, and starts giving cardiac massage. His fists are pounding against her rib cage. Laetitia's crying now, noiselessly. Léonard's next to me, trembling. Is it from the cold? From emotion? I'm trembling, too.

"How could she? . . . " Yvette groans. "Where did she come up with the idea to take clothesline and wind it around the beam? She might have seen it in one of those satanic films! My second cousin died like that, he was just playing around and wound up hanging himself from a radiator."

I reach for my notepad: *Where was the chair?*

"Knocked over on the floor," Yvette answers. "Well, Hugo?"

"I think she's gone," he answers, panting. "Damn it! Where the hell's the ambulance?"

Feet are stamping down the hallway.

"That way," says Francine.

A thick voice says, "We were on our way out for a broken leg. Clear the way, clear the way! Oh, shit! Come on, let's get her in! One, two, three, go! Push!"

"Do you think . . . ?" Yvette asks.

"I don't think anything, lady. The doctor will tell you all about it. But frankly . . . "

The feet are stamping again. The ambulance siren is fading in the distance. Hugo's gone with them.

"She's dead, isn't she?" Laetitia asks, sniffling.

"I think so," says Yvette.

"But what was Magali doing in your room?" Francine asks.

That's what I'm asking myself. Francine leaves to go question Martine, all the while shouting, "Would you mind getting dressed, Léonard?"

Yvette lays her hand on my shoulder. I lay my hand on hers. Magali was twenty-two years old. I think she was redheaded. I've still got the sensation of her face beneath my fingers. Of her unblinking eyes beneath my palm. I don't believe for a second that she committed suicide. Not even playing around. What would she be playing? In my room? It doesn't make sense. I feel oppressed, I'm having a hard time taking a deep breath.

"Let's not stay here," says Yvette, leading me toward the elevator.

We all go down. Francine suggests we have tea, and I'd love to take that teapot and send it flying at her face. Yvette takes the opportunity to uncork the flask of cognac and with authority pours us two drinks. The alcohol starts to dissolve the knot bundled in my stomach. I hear footsteps in the hallway. I can recognize Lorieux's gait, the way he strikes with his heels.

"The police," Justine announces at that very moment.

"Ladies," Lorieux says.

"Is she . . . ?" Yvette asks.

"Dead for more than half an hour. There was nothing they could do. Mrs. Atchouel, would you please be kind enough to give Sergeant Schabel all the necessary information for the registry office. We also must notify her family."

"Everything's in my office. If you'll follow me, Sergeant."

"What was Magali doing all alone in Miss Andrioli's room?" Lorieux continues.

I suppose all eyes are on Hugo, because he stammers, "I . . . I don't know. We were in the middle of creativity workshop, and Magali likes that very much, you know, cutouts, puzzles, and—"

"You didn't notice she was absent?" Lorieux cuts him off, icily.

"They were occupied. Everyone was calm, so I just went to the kitchen to listen to the match results, five minutes, tops," he suddenly admits.

"What match?" Lorieux asks.

"Tennis. Ladies' finals."

Magali sees my attacker during a snowboard race and dies during a tennis match. I don't know why, but I find that even more pitiful.

"And when you got back?" inquires Lorieux, clapping his notebook against his hip.

"I heard Justine calling all the way from the hallway, I went to see what was the matter, and then . . . ," Hugo mutters in a tired voice.

He must have been away a good ten minutes for Magali to have the time to climb up to my room, knot the clotheslines, and . . .

"I want the schedule of every person present, minute by minute, from lunch until now!" Lorieux roars. "Sergeant Mercanti will take your depositions. I also want the patients' schedules."

"Residents," Martine corrects him, mechanically.

"If it pleases you. May I have a word with you?" he continues, laying his hand on my arm. "You seem to attract death the way honey draws flies!"

On my pad, *Stupid and mean.*

"That's true. I'm sorry, but I'm starting to get a bit edgy. This kid now . . . and anyway, it was in your room!"

He's gone silent, ruminating over I don't know what thought. We stay like this for a moment, quietly, listening to the questioning led by Sergeant Mercanti, a newcomer whose poised voice reveals a cold, methodical spirit.

Supposedly at the moment in question—when our meal was over—Yvette was taking a nap. Laeititia was in her room, pouting. Martine was discussing something with Francine. Léonard was getting ready to take a shower. Justine was having me over in her room for a visit. Hugo was listening to the match on the radio. What about the other residents? Jean-Claude was lying down, watching TV, but as far as the others go, no one knows a thing. There's a fifteen-minute gap. They're saying they haven't moved from the rec room. Did anyone see Magali leave? No, nobody. "Magali din't leave!" says Christian, who must be afraid she'll be getting a scolding.

"But when did Hugo leave?" Sergeant Mercanti insists.

"Hugo din't leave!" Christian shouts. "You leave!"

The sergeant sighs. Christian howls.

The rest of the afternoon plays itself out in the same sort of mournful confusion. Yann sweeps in at around five, his snowboard under his arm, carting along the smell of fresh air, and stands shocked by our despondent faces. He's apprised of the latest events and then asked where he's been. He swears like a trooper, reels off a list of slopes, and runs down the names of all the buddies he met while he was up in the mountains. But no, he can't say exactly where he was at around two o'clock. On his way to Dog's Head, no doubt. He doesn't go snowboarding with his nose glued to his watch, which by the way was covered over by his glove. Mercanti's taking it all down, without a comment.

When he's through giving his deposition, Yann collapses onto the sofa, next to me, and offers me cognac. I refuse. I want to keep my mind clear. I'm like a soldier in some war movie, during a bombing. Charging ahead, one foot in front of the other, making his way no matter what it takes. I know that Johnny's just been shot, and that Frank's legs have been blown off, and that the lieutenant's going to die, I know it, and it's causing me pain, but I've got to move forward. Toward safety. And in this case toward the truth.

The walker's sliding past.

"Her parents will be sending their lawyer to handle all the formalities," Laetitia says. "They have a hotel in Fort-de-France, and it's high season. They really haven't got the time to worry about their daughter's cadaver."

"Magali's mother never wanted to see her again once she understood her little girl wouldn't be developing normally," Yann explains. "A reaction like that is fairly uncommon, but not as uncommon as you'd think. Martine will tell you how mothers like that are under this impression that they've given birth to a monster, and the sight of such a child continually awakens unbearable feelings of guilt. It's better to place them in an institution. On the other hand, infanticides often take place, disguised as accidents. Or there are real accidents."

Was Magali's death a real accident?

On my notepad: *Where did she get clothesline?*

"Good question," says Sergeant Mercanti's cold voice. "Household products are usually stored in the cellar, which is always locked. Every staff member has a copy of the key in his locker."

Was any rope missing?

"According to Mrs. Raymond, no," he answers. "The spare roll she keeps is still there."

Is it the same kind of rope?

A sigh. "Exactly. It's a brand that's sold in neighborhood grocery stores. If you'll excuse me . . . "

He takes off.

What kind of man is Mercanti?

"A dead fish," Yvette says. "He's all beige, with pale blue eyes. You might even say he's a robot disguised as a police officer."

I return to my feverish thoughts. If no rope is missing, then Magali had to have found it somewhere. I don't see her going to the superette to buy any! So someone must have provided her with some. From this, we can deduce that this someone passed it around her neck . . . but wouldn't she have cried out or fought back? She was pretty heavy! Unless he persuaded her that this was all a game. "Get up on the chair, you'll see . . . " Not very convincing. I notice that I'm shivering. I put my hand on top of the heat—it's burning.

"Yann," says Justine, "would you take me for a bit of fresh air?"

Yann mutters one of his least enthusiastic "yeah, sures," and the sofa squeals as he gets up.

"If only you could see her," Laetitia hisses. "Always teasing and flirting, it's ridiculous. Mrs. Atchouel was saying that she might be leaving sooner than we thought, for some expo in Berlin, I think. Well, so much the better! Why doesn't she just take that artsy-fartsy attitude of hers and leave us the hell alone!"

I thought my portrait was a success.

"Well, all right, I guess there is something to her work, a force, I don't know, but that still doesn't hide the fact that she's a . . . a . . . real bimbo!" Laetitia says in conclusion.

Translation: She's an extremely seductive woman. Who took special pains to lure me into her room at precisely the moment when Magali . . . A solid alibi. The same goes for Léonard, whom I could verify offhand as being in his room, in his birthday suit, at the fatal hour. He couldn't have anticipated that I was coming. He really was singing while he undressed.

Singing? Damn, I'd forgotten about that! Just like everyone else. That's perfectly understandable. It was a beautiful contralto, and I thought it was coming from the radio. He's a guy who can't speak without stuttering and yet can sing without a hitch? A guy who knew the first victim's husband.

Please call Lorieux.

Laetitia gets right on it. Lorieux comes over.

"It's too hot here. You wanted to see me . . . uh, speak with . . . uh, have a meeting with me?"

Léonard de Quincey knew Hennequin, the husband.

"Yes, I know. Some minor acquaintance when they were in high school. Because of his handicap, and because of his higher grades, Quincey never made many friends."

Did Hennequin know Sonia?

"I don't see . . ."

Neither do I. But we'd better bring these hidden ramifications to light. Somewhere there's a connection among all these people. Maybe it's something in their past. Only it's just an intuition, too complicated to explain in writing.

"Did Marion and Sonia know each other?" Lorieux goes on, thinking aloud. "I'd better check."

He heads off and I can hear him calling Léonard over.

"Night's falling," says Yvette.

Night is the coldest tomb.

8

HE SUN'S SHINING. I can feel it on my cheeks. We're set up at the foot of the slopes. I wrote to Yvette that I needed to get some air and escape from the suffocating atmosphere of the center. From that orgy of blueberry pie, swallowed without pleasure.

The doctor's transferred Magali's body to Nice, and from there she'll be shipped to her parents, in Martinique. The autopsy confirmed that she died by strangling. I'm growing more and more certain that this was a murder. Magali just might have recognized Vore on TV. He set up her suicide and hung her in my room to serve as a reprisal, warning, or message.

"I'm going to the toilet," Yvette announces.

The instructors at the ski school were all questioned, as were the staff. What came out is that only three had no alibi for either the night Sonia was murdered or the time I was attacked. Only three, and the same three: two instructors—Hervé Payot and Véronique Gans—and a ski buff named Kevin Destreille. And for the time when Marion was murdered, even that's a bit fuzzy: Destreille claims to have been out in a club in Nice capping off the evening in his car before midnight, when he returned to get back to his job. Payot insists he was playing poker until three in the morning with some vacationers. As for Gans, she claims to have been in bed with some gorgeous stranger whose first name was Sammy, whom she met in a nightclub and hasn't seen since. Payot and Destreille have the build required to be Vore, while Gans is out of the running. Vore spoke to me and I'm seventy percent certain he's a man.

"Naturally there wasn't any soap! Fortunately I held on to the wipes they were giving out in the restaurant the other day," Yvette shouts on her way back.

What if you've been mistaken, Elise? What if Vore is a woman? He always whispers when he speaks to me. Some skinny, muscular sports type wearing a padded ski suit could have fooled Magali. Véronique Gans is in her thirties, and it makes sense to think she's the same age as Sonia Auvare and Marion Hennequin. Were they friends of hers? But why would she go after these two young women so resolutely, and with a typically masculine sort of violence? All right, Shrink, I know such an observation is stripped of all objectivity. But I'm boring the shit out of you, because you're not helping me, because I'm having a hard time, I'm in pain, I'm afraid, and I've had enough! Enough, I say! I want to be the Elise from before. I can't take it anymore!

"Elise!"

It's Yann.

"Don't tell anyone, but I gave them the slip."

"Oh, you're silly!" says Yvette, laughing. "Would you like a coffee?"

"No, thanks, I'd like a Suze," Yann answers, apparently in fine form. "You know," he continues, "I've been doing some thinking. No one could have known Hugo was going to walk out to listen to the match. Therefore, no one could have known ahead of time that Magali was going to run up to your room. So someone was watching her. Somebody who was on the premises," he finishes in a sinister tone.

"Oh, that's impossible!" Yvette exclaims.

Yann's reasoning is correct. No one could have known that Magali would be going up to my room. So the killer was there, ready to act when given the slightest chance.

It isn't the nicest conclusion.

"In any case," says Yvette, "it hasn't been confirmed that this wasn't an accident or a suicide."

"Somebody had to have gotten the clothesline for her!" Yann responds.

"You're really going on about that clothesline!" Yvette replies. "She could have picked some up anywhere. Just the other day Christian came in with an old drainage pipe, saying it was his trumpet. Magali might have mistaken the clothesline for jump rope. You know quite well that she behaved like a little girl."

"I have to go," Yann sighs, "or else Mother Atchouel is going to attack."

"Francine takes everything that concerns the center very close to heart. She's very worried about us all," Yvette says, stiffly.

"She's especially worried about the reputation of her establishment. People who get rid of their loved ones by sticking them in institutions don't enjoy being accused of sending them off to be killed."

I can't let that one pass. On my pad I write, *You think everyone has the time and money necessary to worry all day about a handicapped person?*

"Oh, what a speech! Excuse me, but I'm also feeling a bit cranky, and you must have noticed that there's no great love between me and Mrs. Atchouel. I can't wait for my contract to be over! I really have to get out of here!" he concludes, and gets up.

Tintin shakes himself and gives a small yap. Apparently he's tired of having tea. I give him a pat on the head. On my pad I write, *Would you mind walking a little?*

Yvette gets up with a sigh. We move slowly up the main street flooded with sun. There are two solutions: Either someone secretly snuck onto the premises to kill Magali if the occasion presented itself, or else the killer is one of the residents at the center. It's either a caregiver or a resident. After all, what could be easier than to fake disability? Obviously not so for Magali or Jean-Claude. But who says Justine is really blind? Or that Léonard is really handicapped? Léonard, the contralto. Naked in his room, ready to take a shower. To eliminate any trace of Magali's red hair?

Yet how could it be that the dog would not recognize the person who murdered his mistress if he lived at the center?

The pepper! The odor of pepper! To throw off his scent!

If that's it, then it would confirm that it's someone among us.

Let's go back.

Before I left for vacation, I receive a threatening letter signed D. Vore.

Shortly after my arrival, Marion Hennequin, age twenty-nine, is murdered by a sadistic killer.

The same day, I meet Sonia Auvare, a barmaid and a prostitute in her spare time, whose godfather is my uncle.

Not too much later, I meet Yann, an instructor at the center for the handicapped.

Somebody gives me a steak, which in fact is a piece of Marion. I eat it.

Later, I'm given a second one. We have it analyzed.

Just a little later, Sonia herself is murdered.

Yann had a rendezvous with her.

The police officer handling the investigation was Sonia's lover.

No, no, this isn't working. I've got to make a diagram, otherwise I'll never make it out. On one side we'll have Marion, on the other we'll have Sonia, with all their connections. I'll try to draw it in my head.

"I'm going to buy the paper."

Okay. Where was I? Oh, there are too many questions, too many facts to be lined up, everything's getting mixed up. For example, the two victims were mutilated. But not in the same manner. Is there a meaning to that? Then someone gives me a piece of her thigh. So that I might walk? And a pair of eyes. So I can see? Stop it, Elise, this is getting to be delirium. The murderer isn't some primitive who's trying to come to your aid by colorful methods, awkward though they may be: he did try to throw you off the terrace! So that you might fly, perhaps?

"They're talking about you!"

It's impossible to do any thinking with a word machine permanently plugged in beside me. What was that?

"It's a small paragraph on Magali's death. 'Castaing: A tragic death has struck at MRCHA. Magali Delgado, a young resident, died accidentally in the room of Elise Andrioli. Elise Andrioli is the courageous young handi- capped woman who, though confined to a wheelchair, helped solve the sordid child murders two years ago in Boissy-les-Colombes.' Not a single word about me. Not even to say that I got a fractured skull trying to help you!"

There you go, in five minutes, it'll all be my fault! I'm the one who drives people to kill and mutilate their fellow man. What's that, Shrink? What if it's true? That I really bring out an evil force, this bloodstained aura that Justine, the seer with closed eyes, is talking about? Thanks, Shrink, that really reassures me. From now on, you'll keep your mouth shut unless I ask you for some- thing.

We trundle along for another moment in silence when suddenly Tintin lets out a dull growl. I tug on his collar, but he keeps growling, frozen in place, fur bristling.

"What's wrong with this dog?" Yvette asks, astonished. "He must have seen a cat."

A predator much larger than a cat, if you ask me. On my pad: *Where are we?*

"Near the ski school."

What's around us?

"Well . . . a family. Two instructors. A man who's just parked his car. A policeman directing traffic. Some kids who are coming back from skiing."

What's Tintin looking at?

"The parking lot."

A lot of people?

"Pretty much so."

Too bad. I let go of the dog. But he's not running ahead. He's pressed against me, shaking. He's scared.

Yvette, Vore's got to be here.

"Because Tintin saw a cat?!"

He's not afraid of cats. He's afraid of whoever stabbed him!

I'm writing so fast, the pen's getting caught in the paper. Yvette's reading over my shoulder.

"You think so?! My God, there is a man looking at us. An old man, with vicious eyes. Oh, no, he was waiting for his wife. What about those two instructors?" she whispers. "I'm going to take a closer look."

She takes off. It's too late; the dog's not growling anymore. Vore has fled. Frustrated, I thrum my fingers on the arm of the wheelchair, waiting for Yvette to return.

"They had their names embroidered on their patches: Hervé and Véronique."

That's troubling. They're exactly the two instructors under suspicion!

"I asked them the prices for an hour of classes while observing Tintin. He had no reaction."

Exactly. If he'd believed Yvette was in danger, he would have leaped, even if terrified.

"Are you Elise Andrioli?" a young, firm feminine voice suddenly asks.

"What do you want from her?" Yvette intervenes.

"They're talking about you in the paper," the young woman says, ignoring her question. "It's because of you that the cops are coming around and hassling us."

"It's Miss Gans," Yvette explains. "The ski instructor."

Miss Gans leans in close: "If I lose my job . . . "

I play it cool. On my pad I write, *So sorry somebody tried to kill me!*

"Maybe that's not your fault, but that mongoloid who killed herself told the cops your attacker was an instructor!"

That's my fault?

"Oh, you think that's all right? While we're waiting, everyone's keeping an eye on us. They've asked us a ton of questions about our schedule the day Sonia and that bag lady were murdered. Obviously you're sitting pretty in your wheelchair; what difference does it make to you?"

What a nice young lady! Lively, with plenty of vigor, and communicative.

Yvette balefully grumbles, "That's about enough!" I'm afraid that during one of these brief gaps in conversation Véronique Gans might get whacked over the head with a handbag.

On my notepad, *If there's nothing against you, then what's the risk?*

"That's easy for you to say! The cops are like dogs: when they bite, they never let go."

Denounce one of your friends, then you'll rest easy.

"Oh, very funny! You mummy!"

Bang. There goes the handbag. "I said that's enough!"

"That silly old bag's nuts! I'm gonna tear her apart!"

"*Grrr.*" It's dull and guttural, yet makes quite an impression.

"Get the hell out of here or I'm letting the dog loose!" Yvette shouts.

"I'm not going to let it go at that! I'm going to press charges. All I want is for that guy to catch up with you!"

Captivated onlookers are murmuring all around.

"That Gans woman is completely mad! And to think people trust her with their kids!"

Mad, no. Maddened, that's for sure. Maybe she's been involved with the police in the past; that might explain the violence in her reaction.

"Please excuse Véronique, she's really a bit edgy right now," says a masculine voice with a sunny accent. "I'm Hervé Payot," he continues, "I'm also an instructor. One of those without a satisfactory alibi," he adds bitterly. "You know, in a small resort like this, things get around. The slightest suspicion about your morality can lose you all your clients. Imagine what murders might do!"

I'm sorry.

"I imagine you are. Véronique does know that it's not your fault. But it's not easy for her; she's barely back on her feet, so . . . "

"What are you talking about?" Yvette asks.

"If you'd seen her two years ago," Payot whispers, "you wouldn't even recognize her. She was like a skeleton, with wild eyes . . . Fortunately for her, she lost consciousness in the street and she was automatically taken into custody; that's what saved her."

"Drugs?"

"I shouldn't be talking to you about it, but I might as well, because it should explain a few things . . . She really had a tough time of it, you know . . . but she picked up sports again, kept to an iron-willed regimen. That's how she found her job. Now she won't even go near a cigarette, and then to see the police getting out of their car, that's got to be hard."

"That's still no reason to be vulgar!" says Yvette.

"You've got to understand her," Payot says. "She's coming out of hell."

I'm smack in the middle; it's been going on for three years, and I think I've got twenty or thirty left. But obviously that's not going to console sweet Véronique.

"The whole story's so absurd," Payot goes on, "visibly" in the mood to talk. "As if one of us is a killer! As if one of us could have killed Sonia! She was so pretty and yet so . . . so . . . Anyway, there was no reason to kill her!"

"So you did know her?" Yvette asks, in a voice filled with innuendo.

"Once, at the start of the season," he answers, without beating around the bush, "but please don't scream it from the rooftops. Especially since the sergeant was really crazy about her. Everyone knows that. Véronique doesn't know, either," he adds, lowering his voice even more, "I've preferred to keep quiet about it, if you see what I mean, and besides, she didn't like Sonia, because Sonia had seen her while she was in rehab. She was always afraid she might talk about it. As if Sonia were that kind of person—"

Sonia was in rehab?

"No, she came to visit a friend and, pfff, she bumps into Véro! You should have seen Véro's face when she told me about it!"

Who did Sonia go to see?

"I don't know. It's not important, what's important is—"

"Hervé!"

"Shit, it's Véro! Gotta run. See you later!"

"What a word machine!" Yvette exclaims. "I thought he'd never stop. Oh, my, if only you could see the way she's hollering at him!"

Uh, no, I can't see. I'm busy playing back Mr. Payot's soundtrack. Two years ago Sonia paid a visit to a friend who was in detox. Was it Marion Hennequin? How can I find out? From Lorieux. He can go through the hospital records. I'm finally starting to get the impression that this is moving forward and that the threat is fading.

But even if I do figure out the link tying the victims together, what the hell does it have to do with me?

I'm back at MRCHA. What a morose atmosphere. The residents are quite disturbed by Magali's tragic disappearance. For some, like Emilie, the concept of death is too abstract, and the inability to grasp a final absence leaves nothing but waiting and prostration. For others, such as Jean-Claude, Magali's disappearance is a reflection of their own illness, a harbinger of a seemingly inescapable end.

And quite simply, we miss Magali's gaiety and gusto. Laetitia won't stop blaming herself for having been in the room next door and without hearing anything. "I had techno on the radio, all the way up," she told me. Still, the partitions here are thin, and if Magali had cried out or put up a struggle, Laetitia would have heard her despite the music. I'm pretty comfortable with the possibility that Magali didn't suspect a thing and was not afraid of the person who persuaded her into my room.

Unless she went in by herself and someone followed her. But what would she have wanted there? To see me?

You're going around and around, Elise, like a squirrel in a cage, dulling its teeth and claws on reasoning as rigid as the bars. Try to "see" things differently. To think otherwise. If I imagine murder as the wording of a problem, then I'll have to learn to read it. Because in the wording is the solution. Hidden beneath an abstruse formulation.

"I've finished Léonard's portrait. I'd like you to tell me what you think of it, Laetitia. You too, Elise, of course."

I slowly emerge from my cogitations. Justine's wearing a musky perfume. Laetitia, reading an article on alternative rock, is nervously ruffling the pages.

"I'm no expert on painting," she answers flatly.

"I'm not looking for the advice of a professional critic. I'd simply be happy to find out your opinion on my work. From one human being to another."

One point for Justine. Laetitia sighs, "Okay." Someone pushes me toward the elevator.

Now we're in Justine's room. Someone's inside. I detect a thermal presence.

"They've come to see your portrait, Léo. Is there any tea left?"

"He-wo."

Laetitia's fine fingers tighten painfully around my clavicle. Léonard's rifling through the dishes, banging objects together. What a beautiful demonstration this is: "Look at my pet. I've got him house-trained."

"Would you mind turning over the painting, please?"

She didn't say "dear," but it's as if she had.

"Voilà!" says Justine, behaving in every circumstance as if she could see normally.

"My God!" Laetitia murmurs. "Such . . . such violence! All this black and this green . . . it's so dark!"

"It's the abysslike depth of the interstellar spaces that are bubbling under Léonard's skull!" Justine exclaims theatrically.

"My eyes . . . gween," Léonard stammers, in my direction, I suppose.

"But they're so cold, so opaque!" Laetitia exclaims. "You'd think they were two stones at the bottom of a pond!"

"Léonard's filled with ice," says Justine, "ice that's cracking, moving; ice under which spring flowers are peering through."

"I don't know, I . . . Frankly, I find this painting unsettling."

"Everything that does not function according to the norm is unsettling, don't you think? You, me, Léonard, Elise, we're monsters. Oh, tea, thank you. Give a cup to Elise."

The interstellar show dog places a teacup on my lap, I wrap my fingers around the superheated porcelain, and in spite of myself, I drop it. The cup goes crashing to the floor.

"What was that?" Justine asks. "Did the cup fall? It's not important. There are some wipes on the shelf. Laetitia, I'd very much like to do your portrait before I leave," she continues.

"When are you leaving?"

"Next Saturday, I think. Francine has to take care of the plane tickets. Hugo's taking me to Nice, to the airport. I'm going to Berlin, for a pre-revivalist exhibit."

"Uh . . . pre-revivalist?" Laetitia repeats.

"Yes, postmodernism is what has been lived. We have to look forward. The return to tradition, reaction. We're at the turning point between aftermath of the aftermath and the prelude to tomorrow."

I can imagine Justine as a police commissar with entire brigades of inspectors on Prozac. "Tell me, did you kill her to take from her what she has lived, or did you live to steal her death from her?"

"Oh! It's *PsyGot'yK!*" Laetitia exclaims.

What's she talking about?

"Do you know this magazine?" Justine asks, astonished.

"No, but it looks funny."

"I don't know if it's funny. Interesting, yes. It's an art magazine that deals with the connections between personality problems and creativity," Justine explains. "I've done one or two exhibits for them, and written a few conceptual articles on experimental art."

Personality problems. That expression calls to mind a voracious Vore.

"By the way, what time is it?" Justine asks out of the blue.

"Six o'clock," Laetitia answers.

"Oh, I've got to make a call," she says, excusing herself. "My cell phone must be somewhere around here."

"Here it is. We'll be on our way. See you later."

We leave, and Léonard leaves as well.

"Watch out, Léonard," Laetitia tells him. "Justine's trying to steal your soul."

"I don't got one," Léonard calmly answers.

He makes his way back to his room limping. We go downstairs.

"If only you'd seen that," Laetitia hisses as she leads me to the living room. "It sent shivers down my spine. Black strokes cutting across the canvas in all directions, and big splotches so green they looked almost mineral. You'd think it was opening a gate onto something quite evil."

On my pad I write, *What about my portrait?*

"It's softer. You're sitting within a blue sky, like a big sunflower, and your hair's floating in a corolla. You'd think you were Ophelia, stretched out in a van Gogh painting."

Ophelia drowning in the blue sky of the Alps.

Are you posing for her?

"I don't know. I think I'd feel ridiculous posing in front of someone who can't see me. All that to-do about her being a medium gives me the creeps. On the other hand, I'd be curious to see what she could make of me," she concludes, dreamily. "I can really see her dressing me in goose-shit brown with my eyes in off-white."

How girls get their sense of humor . . .

"Excuse me, Elise!" she whispers suddenly, all excited, "but Léonard's just come down and he's waving to me!"

Poof! Mommy's left in her Caddie while she glides as fast as she can over to the green-eyed monster. I'm getting the impression that I'm a little shrimp in a big basket of crabs. When Lorieux arrives, it has the effect of a lungful of fresh air. I hold out the page on which I've noted down questions that concern me. He reads them out loud, then clears his throat.

"All right. Concerning point number one, I can already give you an answer. Gastaldi's the one who held the purse strings. His wife had pulled off an excellent scheme by marrying the heir to a family of bankers. Their savings —two million francs, by the lowest estimate—will go to their descendants, very traditionally. Because Marion, their only daughter, has passed away, their attorney is looking up possible surviving relatives who are eligible to become legatees.

"As for point number two, I'm going to find out if this Hennequin woman was hospitalized at the same time as Véronique Gans. Do you think there's any possible drug connection? A settling of scores?"

I don't think anything. I'm just throwing out some questions like so many hooks, wondering what will bite.

"Sonia also went through rehab two or three years ago," Lorieux continues, cracking his phalanges. "Sonia, Marion Hennequin, Véronique Gans . . . "

What about Yann? His internship at the psychiatric hospital?

"Are you suggesting that . . . Might he have met them during the time he was at the hospital?" he's asking himself in a low voice. "I'll be leaving; I've got to check up on a few things."

He's already gone again. The names are swirling around in my head. Sonia. Marion. Véronique. Is dope the connection? What about Yann? Or Yann and dope? Is Yann a dealer? Let's imagine that Sonia and Marion ripped off their suppliers and that they're taking out a hit on them. And that Vore's only a professional killer. Okay, but where do I fit into this? To muddle the trail? Is Véronique Gans in danger? My head's crammed with question marks. I never realized the importance of this damn thing before. If they were to purge it from the French language, I couldn't think anymore. Let's imagine a whodunit without any question marks: no more questions, no more answers. Without question marks, my thoughts would be like a stagnant sea. Inert. Like me.

On the first day of our stay, Yann fell upon me, literally. Was it a fortuitous encounter? (Look, another "?" With me, the guys who manufacture "?" would be billionaires. Perhaps, to be fair, I'll try to put in a few "!") What if Yann had deliberately instigated this encounter!!! (Pow! Three in one.)

What if, even worse, they purged "." as in Latin inscriptions. How would anyone think clearly without punctuation? My God, I'm coming apart. It's a synaptic short circuit. Get the firemen! Elise is burning up! Get the firemen! Elise is going up in flames. Elise . . . Add a *g*, and that's *church* in French. The temple of bullshit. I know, Shrink, I shouldn't devalue myself like that. I'm a person who's as worthy as the next. I should love myself. Well, you've got a point there, old fella, because if I don't love myself, I don't know who will.

"You poor asshole," Shrink confirms for me in his sickly-sweet voice.

What?!

"You poor little asshole, you're really gonna get it!"

Good grief! He's here!

Vore's here, just outside the window, quick, look, move! I back up the wheelchair briskly, bump against the table—ouch!—something's gone through my shoulder; it's burning, sharply, like when you step on a nail—ah, again, in the pit of my belly, better lift my arm, protect my heart—ah, it's in my wrist, but what's—ah, my cheek, oh that really hurts, there's something big and hard driven deep into my cheek, scraping my gums like a scalpel— better back up, back up—this fucking table's blocking my path, liquid's running down my lips.

"Don't you think it smells like blood?"

"Blood?" Yvette asks.

My eyes, hide my eyes, if ever . . .

"Are you okay, Elise? Oh, no! No!"

They stampede over. Something in my arm again, right on the bone, is vibrating. I want to grit my teeth. Inside my head, I hear myself screaming.

"The window! Get away from the window, Justine!"

"Where's the window?" asks Justine.

"Oh, my poor dear, my poor dear!" Yvette laments as she pushes me.

She's pulling out things planted in my flesh. The shock is painful and deep, burning me.

"Hugo! Martine!"

"Shit! What the . . . ," Hugo exclaims.

"Someone's attacked Elise with darts!" Yvette cries. "Through the window, over there!"

Now it's a cavalcade.

"Martine, get bandages and alcohol," Yvette goes on, her voice somehow different. "It's all right, it doesn't look too deep."

Maybe so, but it hurts a lot. Especially my cheek. My mouth is filled with the acrid taste of blood. I try to wipe it off as best I can, and Yvette suggests that I just hold still.

Hugo comes back, saying he didn't see anyone. If the opposite were true, then it would have been really surprising. I'm daubed with alcohol, someone's wiping up the blood, which has flowed all over the place, Justine's asking questions no one's answering, and I'm in a state of shock. I know so, because I'm trembling, yet I don't feel a thing. Emptiness. It's a terrifyingly false sense of calm. It feels as if I'm isolated from the world by a layer of cotton. It's silence within silence. They're talking and getting excited. Elise Andrioli, a dartboard in an Irish pub! Pretty ironic turn of fate, especially after that bomb in Ireland reduced my life to nothing. Or almost nothing.

"Lorieux's in Digne, he won't be able to make it before tonight. They're sending over Mercanti," Francine announces.

Mercanti arrives almost right away and asks precise, pertinent questions. He tells me that the doctor will examine me to draw up a medical certificate. "With something like this, you'll have orders not to move for at least fifteen days," he calls out before suddenly cutting himself short and adding a pitiful "uhh."

He quickly goes on, asking why the dog didn't intervene. "He was outside with Laetitia and Léonard," Yvette answers. "Mr. de Quincey, Miss Castelli, you didn't see anything?"

"No, were down below, on the hillside, in front of the barn. From there, you can't see the French door or the front walk," Laetitia explains. "We were playing around, throwing a stick to Tintin." That's something else Vore couldn't have foreseen. Unless he was surveying the house. Perhaps he's constantly spying on us, with binoculars, hidden in the woods. I clench my fist and it renews the pain in my wrist.

The doctor makes his appearance, grumbling about how swamped he is.

"Let's have a look . . . Oh, my, you poor thing! Well, all right, it's not too bad, I'll give you a tetanus shot just in case, pass me my bag, thank you, and a shot for your gums so that they don't get infected. The mouth is always a pain. To shoot darts at someone who's not well—frankly, what a world we're living in! Has to be some suburban teenagers on vacation. There, it's okay. I've got to go. Excuse me, would you come over to the office so we might take care of the bill?"

9

I'M LYING IN BED with an anti-bedsore pillow between my knees, my back's propped up with pillows, there's an ice pack around my wrist and a cold compress on my cheek. It must be late. There's no sound. No birds singing. No horns honking in the distance. Nothing. Just a little wind in the branches. They've forecast heavy snowfall for tomorrow. I can hear Yvette snoring from the other side of the partition. I dreamed that Magali was crying, standing barefoot in the snow, and that she didn't want to put on the big white nightgown Francine Atchouel was holding out to her. Her red hair was shining in the night, and Laetitia was making her eat snow, telling her it was a magic potion, and she was fighting back, choking, spitting up snow, she was filled with snow, drowning in snow, and when I woke up, her eyes were madly rolling around in their sockets.

I'm sweating. It's too hot. This blanket weighs a ton. This feels like being buried alive. How did I ever get a kick out of reading "The Fall of the House of Usher?" Oh, to sit up. To just push off the cover and sit up. To punch the pillow. To lean over and reach for a book. To read. Oh, to read! To turn the pages. The smell of pages. To read quickly, indifferently, thinking I can read as much as I want to, whenever I want to. To read.

What was Magali thinking when her feet were beating in vain in the emptiness, when no breath came? What did she feel? The silence of the night is making you morbid, Elise. Picture yourself instead in your pretty sunflower yellow dress, floating in a pure blue mountain sky.

I was never too wild about that painting *Sunflowers*. Sunflower . . . I can still hear Justine: "I've put a violet robe on you. Like a stormy sky." Ever since the accident, my aural recall has become as trusty as a tape recorder. Laetitia must be mistaken. Or maybe Justine's lied to me. Or maybe it's Laetitia. I'll have to ask Yvette to go look at the painting tomorrow. Yvette's the only trusty scanner I've got at my disposal.

Will this night ever be over? I'm not at all sleepy. My arm hurts; so does my mouth. I feel like turning on my side. Like looking at the moon up in the sky. Is it a full moon? Hugo made sure three times that the shutters were shut tight. It's impossible to get into my room without a ladder. Tintin's asleep in the hall.

Someone's walking below. The idea of Magali, naked and trembling, jumps out without warning, and I push it away. Someone's walking. I'm sure of it. Has Tintin gone out rummaging through the trash cans? No, that's impossible, everything's been double-locked. Is it a wild animal looking for something to eat? That's not an animal. I can hear the characteristic crunching of boots digging into the snow. It's a human being prowling around. Is it Hugo making his rounds? Yes, of course. He's walking slowly, evenly. That's it, I'm silly, always panicking over nothing.

I know quite well it isn't Hugo. I feel like peeing. With my good hand I search for my bedpan, and wedge it under myself for better or worse.

Someone's whistling "Marinella." It's impossible to urinate; everything's blocked up. I wasn't dreaming, I really did recognize the first few measures whistled softly. So it must be Hugo. A killer wouldn't be dumb enough to stroll around under our windows whistling "Marinella."

"Marinella, I took your legs for your arms, and when I found out . . . " My God, Elise, what's happening to you, girl? Maybe someone's drugging me without my knowledge. Perhaps it's the doctor's injection. Or the food here. The herbal tea. A brain tumor. Asbestos in the wheels of my chair. Is someone going to start whistling again outside? I can't hear any more. No more footsteps. Sometimes people are unconscious as they sleep. Perhaps I closed my eyes only a few seconds and imagined it all. We'll see tomorrow. Now everything's calm. I don't like calm. I don't like this calm.

I've got a foul taste in my mouth and need some good strong coffee. I've slept really poorly. I've asked Yvette if anyone heard anything last night. "I went out for a walk around one o'clock," Hugo said, "and I saw nothing." So it really was Hugo in a modern version of "Sleep, good souls!"

"It's snowing," says Laetitia, sighing. "They've forecast snow for the next three days."

"Every season has its reason!" Martine exclaims in that positive tone of hers that's really starting to get on my nerves.

"Let's go out and make a snowman!" Yann decides. "Mrs. Raymond, I'll need a carrot, two potatoes, and a tomato. Emilie, go with Mrs. Raymond. Christian, you'll help Emilie. Tintin, you'll help Christian."

Through their laughter I can hear the dog's claws rattle on the floor as he gives a yap and follows them out.

"What about me? What am I supposed to do?" Jean-Claude asks as he zips from a documentary on wildlife to one on geography.

"Oh, you'll help out, guy," Yann answers. "In fact, I forgot to tell you that you're the one we're gonna cover in snow."

Jean-Claude lets out a chuckle. Laetitia's gotten a chill and doesn't feel like going out, so Francine advises hot tea with honey, Yvette, an herbal infusion with thyme, and Mrs. Raymond, an eggnog. Laetitia says she has her own medicines, thank you.

"I've written to my father," she says to me as she drops onto the sofa. "I don't want to stay here anymore. I'd like to go to the United States. There's an institute in Florida where they go swimming with dolphins. I can swim pretty well, with my arms. Dad's gonna start whining because it's very expensive, but he always does whatever I want. He's dying of guilt ever since the accident. He was driving too fast. It's because of him that I'm handicapped. Ever since then, I've always gotten whatever I want!"

That's why you don't understand that Justine's picking Léonard off you. Picking. Picks. I mechanically bring my hand up to my cheek, which hurts like hell. I'm running my tongue up and down my gums. They're all swollen.

"It looks like you've got a hard-boiled egg in your cheek," Laetitia says, laughing. "A red egg, because of the iodine."

She giggles some more. Oh, the joyous imbecility of youth. Suddenly I hear the sound of dashing footsteps.

"I've got news!"

Lorieux turns my wheelchair around without giving me the time to say "Oof!" and pushes me off to the side.

"Marion Hennequin and Véronique Gans were hospitalized at the same time! The receptionist at the hospital recognized Sonia from the photos. 'She was a ravishing girl; she came to see her cousin regularly.' And the cousin in question was Marion, for sure. They knew each other!"

In all his exaltation, he shakes my wheelchair in every direction.

"She told me that she used to go there to see her shrink. In fact, it was to see that Hennequin woman! But why?!"

It sounds to me like he's biting his nails.

"And there's something else: it was during this time that Yann was doing his internship in psychiatry. I remembered this morning that Sonia told me she saw him once, and that she hid because she didn't want him to see her."

I myself remember Yann telling me that Marion Hennequin's name was not unknown to him.

"We're getting somewhere! We're finally getting somewhere! I'm going to get that freak who's done this, I swear to you!" Lorieux suddenly assures me.

The desire for vengeance is vibrating in his voice. As well as the secret desire that it will be Yann. I'm sure he's wondering whether or not Yann knew Sonia at the hospital, and whether or not they were having an affair while she was still going out with him. The demon of jealousy has the sharpest claws and pointiest fangs. I know a thing or two about him. He took a cheap shot at me not too long ago when I found out that Benoît . . .

You cherish the memory of the deceased; you'll take refuge in an idyllic past; and then suddenly you discover that the bastard was cheating on you for two years! I wouldn't wish that on Lorieux.

"The record of people coming and going at that time has been computerized, but the girl who takes care of that won't be in until tomorrow. We're going to try to find the patients and screen staff members."

I get my notepad. Because of my wounds, writing hurts like hell. I go for the basics: *What if Sonia-Marion really were cousins?*

"I asked the lawyer that question. Apparently there's no family bond between the Gastaldis and Auvares. But they could have been cousins in the style of this area, meaning third cousins or something like that."

Maybe my uncle knows?

"I tried again to get a hold of him," he says with a sigh. "This time I got the voice mail of his cell phone. I asked him to call me back."

Fine. There's nothing more to do but wait.

"The superette sells dart sets," he continues. "No one bought any this week. I insisted, and the manager went to check on the stock. A set was missing."

Vore's walking through town, gets a little bored, and a dartboard set catches his eye: "Look at that. What if I took a shot at old lady Andrioli?"

"Oh, there you are!" Yann's manly voice rings out over my head. "Hi, Philippe. I was coming to get Elise, just in case she wants to get some air."

Philippe Lorieux slaps his pad. "Have you got a minute, Yann?"

"The residents are waiting."

"Just a minute. Do you remember your internship at the psychiatric hospital?"

"Naturally."

"Did you ever get the chance to meet drug addicts?"

"Do you mean Sonia? I don't remember seeing her there."

"You didn't answer my question."

"Of course I had the chance to meet them. They had their group therapy sessions in the TV room of the psych section. Why are you asking? Oh, damn, I get it. Marion Hennequin! That's where I saw her!"

The pad slaps again.

"Can you tell me anything else?"

"Wait, let me think." Some dead air, then he says, "It's coming back to me. She was different from the other patients. She was cold, reserved; she had pale skin and dark eyes; she looked like she came out of some romantic painting. The woman with camelias dying of consumption while the hero's hooked on drugs. She could have been an idiot, for all we know she had a touch of class. She refused to participate. Just stayed in her corner. Rebuffed anyone who tried to help her."

Right up to her death, she was a girl from a good family.

On my pad I write, *Lorieux told me that I look like her physically.*

He seems to be thinking for a moment, and then says, "Well, yes, now that you say so. But you've gotten so tan ever since you're here that you don't look at all sick anymore."

Gallant, that Yann.

"In fact, I think you look more like Sonia," he continues. "Besides, it's funny, but Sonia resembled Marion a lot. Do you think it's important, Philippe?"

"Let's not get lost. Did Marion receive any visits?" Lorieux asks matter-of-factly.

"I don't know. Oh, yes. Once I saw her in conversation with a visitor. A girl. Blond, I think. I saw her from behind, passing her by in the hallway. What . . . wait a minute! Wait a minute. Was that girl Sonia?"

Yann's pretty lively today.

"I'm not authorized to answer," Lorieux says.

"Oh, cut it out. You've been talking to everybody about the investigation!"

"Elise isn't everybody. She's a victim with a lot of potential. Uh . . . excuse me, I meant to say, uh . . . "

I lift my hand as if to say, "Let it go."

"And what am I, potentially guilty? Is that it?" Yann asks, a bit aggressively.

"You're a witness, that's all."

"But I didn't see anything!"

"You saw Marion Hennequin."

"A pure coincidence!"

"Is there anyone else you can identify from the time of this internship?"

"It wasn't Club Med."

"Okay, if you ever do remember something or other . . . see you later."

"Just what is he thinking?" Yann snaps as Lorieux heads off. "That I was screwing Marion and Sonia? That I killed them because they wanted to dump me? When I think how he and I went through hell together and now he's wearing some asshole uniform!"

On my notepad I ask, *Since then friends?* I feel like I'm acting in a Tarzan movie. "We were in high school together. After that we lost sight of each other, but we did some catching up when I came here to work."

He still with Sonia?

"No, I didn't even know he was dating her. There's a total blackout on that matter. I found out from Payot, one of the instructors. He told me that Lorieux was coming out of a serious depression because of a barmaid from Moonwalk. It was a passion that had the whole village talking. The policeman and the prostitute. Now that I think about it, it's bizarre that they should both be murdered the same week. But I surely don't see what it has to do with you, aside from the physical resemblance. Well, the dog's watching over them, but I've really got to go. Can I take you?"

I gesture no. I don't feel like moving. Correction: I don't feel like being moved. It seems like I'll fall to pieces with the slightest jolt. I've got shooting pains in my arm, my cheek feels tight, and my sternum's burning. All very sidesplitting, isn't it? Elise, the crass comedian. Well, you would have liked something like that, wouldn't you? Striding up and down the Alcazar in Marseilles, shouting out moronic refrains in an ostrich-feather negligee. Now

I roll around through the big living room, drawing figure eights at random, just like a bee.

"Your uncle's on the phone!" Yvette shouts, breathlessly.

She must have pressed the button raising the volume, because I can hear crackling over my uncle's voice.

"Where are you?" Yvette asks. "We've been trying to get you for a week!"

"I was in Krakow, and now I'm in Italy, in Carrare, for an order of marble. I tried getting hold of you several times, but I kept getting the answering machine!" he adds, sounding a bit incensed.

Damn, no one thought to tell him that we weren't at the chalet anymore.

"How's Elise?" he continues.

"Uh . . . okay, everything's all right, what I mean is—"

"I got a call from the police station, little Lorieux. Apparently, it sounded pretty serious."

Yvette's all muddled up in vague explanations. On my notepad I scribble *Tell him everything!* After a long sigh, she complies. My uncle listens in silence, except when she reveals that Sonia has died.

"Yes, I'm aware of that," he lets out in a low voice. "Has the investigation been progressing?" he adds.

"No, unfortunately!" Yvette's yelling, because the connection's no good.

"I can't hear anything anymore!" he shouts at the top of his lungs, while I rapidly note down all the questions to ask him, forgetting the pain.

After a succession of "hellos?" the line becomes clear again.

"I'm calling up the police," my uncle says. "I'm coming as soon as possible."

Wait! Quickly, I hold out my sheet to Yvette.

"'Did you see Sonia often?' Elise wants me to ask you," she says.

"She used to call me sometimes when I'd come for the weekend. She felt very much alone," he adds, in a voice that's somehow changed.

"I'll continue to read you Elise's questions: 'Did you know she was taking drugs?'"

"Of course! Everyone knew about it. I'm the one who convinced her to go for detox."

"'Did you know Marion Hennequin?'" Yvette reads.

There's a brief silence at the other end of the line. Then my uncle goes on in a tone of voice that sounds a bit too casual: "No, not at all. Should I?"

"I don't know a thing about it!" Yvette protests.

"Listen, my suppliers are waiting for me, and the meter's running! I'll call back tomorrow! And don't do anything foolish, Elise!"

On this note, he hangs up.

"He was calling from Italy! Frankly, that must be costing him a fortune!" Yvette says disapprovingly.

I furiously crumple the sheet with all my unanswered questions between my fingers. My scabs start to crack open.

"Look, you managed to make yourself bleed! My God, you weren't so much trouble when you were four years old!"

Naturally. Back then I still believed in Santa Claus.

Yvette goes and gets alcohol and cotton. I'd put my good hand into the fire that my uncle knows something we don't. Yvette returns, daubing my forearm and hand relatively gently. "This time, Francine's had it!" she says under her breath before dashing over to the game table in the next room. Who could have imagined that Yvette would metamorphose into a fanatic gambler? Pretty soon, they'll be able to stab me under my eyes before she'll put down her ace of diamonds.

"Elise, are you there?"

No, I'm schussing down the slopes.

"Elise? If you're there, tap the wheel of your chair," Justine continues.

I don't know what sort of demon's gotten into me, but I'm not moving. I hold my breath. Fortunately all that racket from Mrs. Raymond's vacuum cleaner covers the sound of my breath. Now it's my turn to hold out my ear to situate Justine in the room.

"No one's there?"

If I were a needle pointed south, then she'd be at three o'clock, to my right.

"This is no time to be kidding around!" she adds in a strained voice.

Oh, I quite agree, but I've got this horrible urge to be mean. My only fear is that someone neither of us can see is observing us from the doorway. It would be the unmasking of nice, genteel Elise! I could always pretend I was asleep.

Justine moves and bumps against something. The big, low table.

"Oh, damn it!"

She waits a little more. First silence, then the vacuum cleaner starts humming in the hallway. Then *beep, beep, beep, beep.* It's the telephone! She's memorized the touch pad, like me, and now she's dialing a number.

"Hello? Yes, it's me. I can't talk too long . . . No, I'm not yet sure, it's not so simple! . . . Okay, tomorrow, at four."

She hangs up.

She passes by, and I take in the scent of her perfume, retracting in my seat to melt in with the wall.

"I know someone's there!" she suddenly calls out.

My heart jumps ten feet. She makes a move forward and I prepare to feel her claws digging into me when she cries out in pain. The pedestal to the marble tabletop. Everyone bangs into it. Cursing through her teeth, she turns back.

"Oh! Miss Lombard! Did you hurt yourself?"

Providential Mrs. Raymond.

"It's nothing. I just bumped into a piece of furniture," Justine answers, sounding detached.

"Aw, give me your arm, I'll guide you."

Their voices fade in the distance as I charge over to the telephone, feel around, and catch it in midair as it goes tumbling to the floor. I've got to find the redial button. On my phone it's at the bottom, on the right. I've got it! The number she called must surely be on the screen. But that does me no good. I turn the wheelchair around, set the turbo in motion, and drive toward the living room. The first try's a no-go: I flatten myself against the wall. I score on the second try! I land on somebody.

"Ouch! Watch out!"

It's Hugo. I hold out the telephone, the way a beggar holds out his wooden bowl.

"Do you want to call someone?"

Here we go. I shake the phone under his nose. Quick! The number might disappear. He takes it and reads it mechanically: "Oh six, oh nine, one eight, two six, three three." I take it down on my pad.

"Okay, I'll dial it for you . . . Oh, no one's there, it's the answering machine. Do you want to leave a message?"

I motion to him with my hand that I want to listen. He brings the receiver close to my ear. An electronic voice repeats that the number I've requested cannot be reached, but I may leave a message. I give it back to him.

"We'll try it again," Hugo says. "Excuse me, but I've got to go get the hydrotherapy room ready for Jean-Claude."

He heads off with the phone. I continue to roll straight ahead, guided by the voices of Yvette and Francine bitterly arguing over a few points. No doubt I'm bestowing too much importance on this phone call. But there's something troubling about Justine's insistence in wanting to know if someone else was in the room. And on the other hand, if she wanted to make a phone call in peace, then why didn't she use her cell phone up in her room? Because she didn't want anyone to trace anything back to her using the list of calls received by her correspondent? Speaking of Justine, I realize that I've forgotten to ask Yvette to go look at the painting. I write a quick note and head toward the game table.

"I'm sorry, Yvette dear, but you've taken a card from the deck twice," darling Francine is saying.

"Not so! Look, I've only got six cards!"

"I assure you that . . . Yes, Elise?"

I hold out the little note.

"It's for you, I suppose," Francine says, grabbing it.

"Oh six, oh nine, one eight, two six, three three," Yvette reads.

Damn, I've gotten the papers mixed up.

"Do you want to call your uncle?" she continues.

The sky's falling on my head! Justine called my uncle! Oh, but . . . what does that mean?!

"Don't you think he's already been upset enough? We'll call him tomorrow. Hey, it's my turn to play!"

"Oh, no, you're mistaken!" Francine protests.

I back up slowly. Justine and my uncle. Sonia and my uncle. What's going on? Is everyone here part of a comedy? Are these paid actors trying to trick me? Paranoia's starting to kick in, Shrink, I know, but . . . my uncle and Justine!

What if Lorieux were also involved? What if all this is some kind of joke? Aside from what I've been told, what is there to prove to me that there have been any crimes? No, no one shoots darts at people to play a joke. And Yvette was the first one to read the local paper to me relating the murder in Entrevaux. Yvette couldn't be taking part in a plot!

Calm down. Breathe. Don't let yourself be overwhelmed with confusion. Catch a thread and hold on to it. You've held Magali's lifeless body in your arms. Cold and without a pulse. You've been hurt physically. Yvette's seen human eyeballs in your fingers. Either Yvette's lying or everything's true. The mere thought that Yvette could lie to me gives me frozen chills. She's the only crutch I've got to lean on to face the world. What's happening to me? I really need stable guideposts, something tangible, and here everything's swirling around and running through my fingers.

There's a draft of cold air on my fingers. Following it, I go up to the window, lean my forehead against the cool pane of glass, and through a small opening breathe in air from outside. The residents' excited shouts and the dog's joyous barking ring out in the clearing.

"Emilie, would you lend me your nose for the snowman?" Yann asks.

"No! No!" Emilie screams. "That's the carrot!"

"Okay. Jean-Claude, would you pass me Emilie's nose?"

"No! No!"

I smile in spite of myself. A bird lands nearby and trills out a few lively notes. What does he care for all this human butchery? Except during hunting season. One really has to make the whole planet sweat to feel one's own existence.

"I'm ti-i-red."

It's Léonard. Nearby. Just below, under the window. I cock my ear.

"I'm tired, too. Everybody's tired!"

It's Laetitia. She's speaking in a low, urgent voice. I can practically hear her heart beating.

"I . . . I . . . "

"Yes?" says Laetitia, encouraging.

"Not poss-ible. Too sick."

"You mustn't speak like that. You've got to go forward. You shouldn't let yourself get caught up in their dirty normalness!"

So Justine was right to say she was ashamed of her condition, that she didn't accept it.

"Often . . . want to . . . end it."

"You've got no right to say that! We're all here, with you!"

They're both breathing heavily. I can hear their movements, their footfalls.

"Oh, Léonard!" she stammers again.

I can imagine her pressing against him, and Léonard trying to hold her close in his clumsy arms.

"Hello, my lovebirds, are we cooing?" Mrs. Raymond's sunny voice calls out. "Be careful you don't turn into pigeons!"

She passes them by, laughing at her own joke.

"See you later," says Laetitia, who must be blushing scarlet.

Léonard acquiesces with a groan. Footfalls again. I lean over as far as I can. Ten seconds pass in silence. A match crackles, followed by the smell of tobacco. I didn't know Léonard smoked. Or maybe it's Hugo and Martine. Okay, then, I think I can shut my window.

"Marinella"! Someone's whistling "Marinella" just below! The person who's smoking.

"Be careful you don't catch a cold!" Hugo says, crossing the room.

Hugo. In here. Inside. That means he's not below my window. So then it wasn't Hugo whistling "Marinella" the other night. Léonard? An animal who can sing and whistle, yet is incapable of stringing together three words? I've got an idea! I'll lift the blanket that's lying on my lap, roll it up into a ball, more or less, and I'll let it fall out the window.

"What the . . . ?" Lorieux grunts. "Is that you, Elise? You've dropped your cover! I'll bring it up to you."

Damn! Why did he need to be passing by just then! Just when I was about to unmask Léonard. I back up, feeling a bit annoyed, and wait.

"Here it is. I'm wondering how it could have slipped off your lap. By the way, talking about the window . . . I'd like to try a little exercise. Do you mind?"

His question's a pure formality, as I've been pushed all the way across the room, as far as the dining room.

"Let's see . . . Mrs. Holzinski, please."

"Yes?" Yvette asks grudgingly.

"Exactly where was Miss Andrioli's wheelchair placed when she was attacked with darts?"

"Here, more or less," Yvette answers, getting up and coming over to position my wheelchair.

"Take this down, Schnabel. Three feet from the window and eight and a quarter feet from the table where I believe you ladies were playing cards."

"Uh, yes, that's right."

"The chair was not situated at the halfway line of the window, but moved to the right-hand side. However, all her wounds are on the right side of her body, and the tips of the darts have been driven into her flesh perpendicularly, not at an angle, as the doctor confirmed for me."

"So?" asks Francine, confused.

"So whoever was shooting darts was facing Miss Andrioli."

"So?" asks Yvette.

"See for yourself. If I go out on the terrace—follow me, Schnabel—you'll find that in order for my shot to follow a perpendicular trajectory to its target, I would have to be situated on the left-hand side of the terrace, according to a diagonal line like this."

"So?" Yvette and Francine ask in unison.

"Zorro's he-ere!" Yann calls out, facetiously. "What are you up to?"

"Unmasking the murderer," Lorieux replies coldly. "I'll continue. If you'll admit that our man necessarily stood here for Elise to be hit this way, then"—he comes back inside—"then everyone sitting here had to have seen him! Who was occupying this seat?"

"Uh . . . I think it was me," Francine ventures, "but . . . "

"Think hard!"

"I wasn't paying attention. We were playing cards, everything was calm."

"Perhaps you saw someone familiar, so familiar that you paid him no mind, but certainly your brain registered the information?"

Francine silently racks her brain for a moment. Lorieux's right. Everyone comes and goes as he or she pleases, so it's hard to recall with any kind of precision whether so-and-so was present at such-and-such a place. Francine could quite easily have seen a familiar silhouette without realizing it.

"I can't see anything," she says. "I'm sorry, but I don't remember looking out the window."

"The sun!" Yvette exclaims. "You were complaining that too much sun was getting in your eyes! Remember? I was beating you three hundred to twenty . . . You went to pull one of the curtains."

This is getting better and better. I, who thought I was facing the mountain, was really staring at a bolt of tulle, and Vore was able to approach calmly and take aim through the small opening.

Lorieux's tapping his foot, as he does whenever he gets excited. *Tap, tap, tap,* the point of his shoe is beating out a fast little rhythm on the wooden floor. Schnabel clears his throat. The tapping suddenly stops.

"All right," Lorieux continues, "where are Laetitia Castelli and Léonard de Quincey?"

"Here we are," says Laetitia, breathlessly.

"You claimed you were down below, near the barn, and that you couldn't see the terrace. Is that correct?"

"I suppose you're talking about the attack on Elise?"

"No, the fair of Saint John."

"Very funny. Yes, I was near the barn, with Léonard and the dog."

"I thought you had trouble getting around."

"I use my walker or my crutches. It takes me longer than you, of course, but I'm used to it. I'm not going to spend my whole life indoors."

"You never fall down? What with all the snow?"

"Yes, that happens. Or getting stuck. The other day, I had to wait for Hugo to come and lift me, the snow was so deep."

" 'Beneath the thick coat of white/where the earth goes to earth/and sleep without wrath/far away from our cries.' "

"Ah . . . Madame Lombard!" Lorieux says, with a long sigh. "I believe you'll be leaving us soon?"

"Next Saturday, absent any complications. What's going on? Anything new?"

"Insofar as we never bathe twice in the same water, we can say that there's always something new, can't we?" Lorieux replies dryly.

Everyone's dazed. I think we're all very tired and edgy. Justine's asking if she can have a glass of water, Laetitia if she can sit down, and Francine if she might tell Mrs. Raymond to get ready to serve everyone.

"You're not at attention!" Lorieux says, carried away. "And as far as I'm concerned, you can all go—"

"I can't believe my ears!" Francine cries out, scandalized. "I'm reporting you to your superiors!"

"So much the better! I'm asking to be off this case. I've had it up to here with this mental asylum!"

There's a long, strained silence, especially so since the residents have returned. Then darling Francine says, "Very well. These gentlemen from the constabulary will have to excuse us, but it's time for us to sit down and eat."

"Co-stab-lary!" Christian shouts. "Co-stab-lary! Come-stab-shit!"

"Shitshitshit . . . " three voices enthusiastically repeat in unison.

"Listen, I've let myself get carried away," Lorieux says.

"Don't worry," Laetitia retorts, "you didn't even say 'museum of horrors.' "

"This case isn't like the others . . . Sonia . . . "

His voice is trembling. This is worse than a reality show.

"Shitshitshit . . . "

Tintin starts to bark along with them.

"That's enough! Hugo, do something!"

"Would anyone like port?" Yvette suggests in a soothing tone.

"I don't think alcohol would be appropriate; these gentlemen are on duty, and they're in a hurry!" Francine murmurs, irritably.

"I'd be glad to have a brandy," Lorieux says.

"Why don't you try some of this; it's from old man Clary!" says Yann, uncorking a bottle.

"Is that organic brandy?" Justine inquires.

"Completely organic. Do you want a taste?"

"Being of age, I suppose I have the right to taste some," Laetitia says.

"Of course! Everyone's going to get a taste!"

"Taste, taste, taste, shit, tasteshit, tasteshit."

"Even Elise!"

I must be delirious. Perhaps they really have gone mad. But when I think about it, it's so easy to behave strangely, so what I mean by this is strange, in relation to television sitcoms.

We drink down our brandy with lip-smacking gusto. Francine's the only one to abstain. I suppose she's got her hand on the doorknob, waiting for these unruly officers to clear out. What would happen if our investigator started to lose it? Would they give us Mercanti as his replacement? Or maybe some guy from Nice. A hairy Maigret who smells like garlic and socca. Too bad; I sort of like our little police officer. I'll always imagine him as a courageous Tom Thumb, doggedly following a trail of pebbles, determined to kill the ogre and his hydras. I can even see him with a big pointed hat, as he is in my picture book. A bonnet with a little bell? Oh, no, that's Oui-Oui. He was nice, that Oui-Oui. Terrible, this brandy, especially on an empty stomach. Doesn't forgive.

"Bye-bye. Thanks for coming."

I've got to leave? Why isn't this wheelchair moving?

"Quit banging into the wall! It's getting on my nerves!"

That's Yann. The lady-killer. Is he the one who's been killing ladies? Elise, lie down. My head's spinning. Yann's given me two refills, two nice doses. Should've been a bartender, that Yann.

The telephone's ringing, stridently.

"Helloo?" shouts Yvette, who also seems to have hit the sauce pretty good. "Yes . . . yes, he's here—hic—poor thing, oh, my, I've got the hiccups, I'll—hic—get him for you . . . Sergeant—hic—it's for you. It's Elise's—hic—uncle."

Lorieux must have taken the phone and walked off; I hear his voice but can't make out the words. Would you ask that bastard uncle of mine why

Justine called him? Where's my pad! Shit, it's lost. This can't be. Oh, no, there it is, buried under the blanket. The pen. Now I'll get back to Lorieux.

"That's enough, Elise! You're bumping into everybody! Where do you want to go?"

Why don't you go have a look for yourself to see if I'm there, Francine darling? Come on, stupid wheelchair.

Yvette, shaking from her hiccups, trumpets, "Do you want to—hic—pee?"

"Hoo-ha!" Christian shouts.

I wave my pad to say no. My pad, on which Lorieux's name is written. Perhaps someone might think to pass the sheet to him. Apparently not. Okay, I'm going to charge right in.

"Enough already! What's gotten into her?"

"She's had too much to drink," says Yvette, that big phony. "You shouldn't give her too much—hic—alcohol, Yann; it doesn't go well with her sleeping pills. Come on!"

She shoves me into a corner. I start waving my pad as if I had Parkinson's disease.

"You want to—hic—write something? Your pen's over there!" says Yvette, tugging on the cord I keep around my neck.

Hasn't she seen that I've written something? I raise my arm so suddenly that I smack her right in the face. I can feel my hand smashing into her nose.

"Ouch! Oh, that notepad of yours! I'm going to toss it out the window! You almost broke my nose with it! Oh, look, it's gotten rid of my hiccups, I guess. I wouldn't recommend that method, but . . . Well, may I find out why you're waving that pad around like a madwoman? Let's see . . . I don't understand, there's nothing written here. You really are a bit tipsy."

Yvette's abandoned me. I'm sure I wrote: *Ask my uncle if he knew Justine.* Damn! That means someone's torn the sheet off the pad.

I'm trying to clear my mind. To concentrate. To put up a mental shield against these weird attacks from the alcohol. What was I supposed to be thinking about? Oh, yes, the sheet! Who took the sheet? The most obvious answer would be Justine. Yet if that were so, then she must have read it. And she must have been able to see it, for that matter. If she saw it, then it would also mean she could see me this morning in the living room when she came in to use the telephone. So it isn't Justine. If it's not Justine, then it's her brother. An accomplice, I mean; someone who read the message intended for Lorieux and wanted to protect Justine. What good would such a maneuver do, though? I can ask myself that question another time, whenever I want. Unless I die in the next five minutes, poisoned with brandy. Laugh, Elise, laugh, you've really got some good reasons to laugh right now! Isn't there something bizarre about the way my stomach's burning? And my throat's itching. It hurts when I swallow. Yvette, are you there? It feels as if I've been sent to stand in the corner. Yoo-hoo, am I all puffed up with red spots all over my face? My tongue's swollen, I'm sure of it.

"So, Elise, feeling any better?"

Just perfect, Yann dear, I'm just suffering a bit from cyanide poisoning.

"Is this yours?" he continues. "'Please, Lorieux, ask my uncle if he knows Justine.'"

The room goes silent.

"It was crumpled up on the floor. Someone must have stepped on it."

"Give me that!" Lorieux orders.

"Your uncle?" Justine says through the silence. "Oh, my poor dear, I didn't even know you had an uncle."

"You deny knowing Mr. Fernand Andrioli?" Lorieux asks in his official-sounding voice.

"Fernand? Of course I know Fernand! He's the one who recommended MRCHA to me."

Badda bing, badda boom!

"Fernand Andrioli is Elise's uncle," Lorieux explains.

"Oh? Delighted," she answers mechanically.

"I'll have a few questions to ask you, Madame Lombard," Lorieux says. "Can you come this way, please?"

"Uh . . . yes, I'd be happy to. Would you give me your hand, Sergeant?"

Schnabel must be leading her over to Lorieux, who's standing next to me.

"If you wouldn't mind going back into the other room, ladies and gentlemen. Schnabel, would you please accompany them."

All of them head off. Nobody's moving me. I'm trying to change into a piece of Chinese pottery. Lorieux clears his throat.

"May I ask you to explain the exact nature of your relationship with Mr. Andrioli, ma'am?"

"Nature is the exact explanation, Sergeant."

"In other words, he's your lover?"

"Ooh, that dirty word! He's above all a friend, and sometimes a little more. We've known each other ten years or so, you know."

He's never told me about her!

"I met him during one of his trips to Italy. I was on vacation, visiting some friends, he was visiting a marble quarry, and my car crashed into his."

Lorieux jumps. "Your car? You drive, then?!"

"Just because I have a car, it doesn't mean I was at the wheel. My chauffeur was driving."

"Doesn't matter. Go on. Your relationship with Mr. Andrioli."

"Excellent."

Lorieux sighs.

"He started screaming," Justine continues, "and then he realized I was—"

"Nonsighted?"

"French, and he calmed down. That very evening, he asked me out to dinner, and that was it. We became friends. I meet him from time to time, he comes to my openings, that sort of thing."

"He never spoke to you of his niece?"

"He told me he had a niece once. He speaks very little of his family. He's a very discreet man who travels a lot and never asks questions."

You'd think she was painting the portrait of a spy or a killer for hire. Is it possible that my Uncle Fernand, a great practical joker, is leading a double life?

Lorieux remains silent a moment.

"If you won't be needing me any further . . . ," Justine says.

"By all means. Schnabel!"

"Doesn't it worry you that I didn't sense your presence this morning?" Justine whispers rather coldly. "Maybe it's because you're starting to dematerialize."

Talk all you like, you traitor, you uncle-stealer! What's more, you're cheating on him with Léonard!

Schnabel leads her out by the arm. The sounds of scurrying high heels and clunking boots fade in the distance.

Lorieux coughs pensively, tapping his foot. "There's something rotten in the kingdom of MRCHA," he says finally. "There are too many coincidences. Too many people who know each other. You'd think it was a family reunion! Then there are all these murders that make no sense! And you, inside all. The judge is starting to lose his patience. He's leaving on vacation tomorrow, and he'll certainly want results by the time he gets back next week. They're going to start making fun of the cops again—those bumblers in kepis. To think we'll have to entrust this investigation with a real cop, a Navarro in Nikes. That's not gonna bring back Sonia."

His voice is starting to tremble. Let's hope he doesn't start crying. It's terrible when men cry; it gives me a lump in the throat.

Something wet has fallen on my hand. There it is, he's crying! I can feel my own eyes mist over as I hear him sniffling discreetly. I'm crossing my fingers that no one comes bounding in and catches him in tears; that would look pretty bad for him. His hand rests on my shoulder, and he starts to squeeze convulsively.

"I'm nothing!" he stammers. "I don't even give a shit about understanding what women are all about, that's what you're thinking!"

This little asshole's going to make me start bawling.

"I don't even know why I chose the police. Honor, country, justice; if only you knew how I don't give a damn about all that today! The world's dirty; people are gross; life is sinister; am I supposed to put some order into it? To protect them and all their bullshit? To defend them against their own evil, their greed, their stupidity? All they do is die with their mouths open, clutching the wheel in their rolling death traps, doing a hundred twenty-five. All they do is burn stop signs, screw up everything with those scooters, beat up the elderly, eat their pesticides. They can just go on killing themselves without me!"

"Is everything okay?" Schnabel asks from a distance.

"Yeah, I'm coming!" Lorieux calls back. "Talking to you really has done me some good, Elise."

He takes off, leaving me planted here, brimful with everything he's spewed. Elise, the trash can for emotions. Is your soul wishy-washy, and rife with pain? Well, call Elise, she's just like a valise. Shut the lid tight, and go home feeling light. But I'm filled with sadness, mourning, and suffering, as though with a rising black tide that one day will submerge me. They should take me to the pavilions for the incurably ill and place me between the beds; I'd listen to confessions, death throes, better than a priest, because a priest can talk. The advantage with me is that I always keep my mouth shut.

And then Fernand. Fernand, who's been sleeping with that woman for ten years and who's never spoken to me about her; Fernand, who must have figured we'd meet here. What does that mean? Oh, maybe I'm always struggling to look for meaning in things that have none. To look for a reason in this universe of madmen. I guess Lorieux's pessimism has infected me.

"So what did your friend Justine tell you?"

Yvette's sprung up beside me. I grab my pen.

"For ten years!" she exclaims when she's done reading. "Well, what do you know? What a secretive one your uncle's turned out to be! It looks like butter wouldn't even melt in his mouth, and meanwhile he's juggling women behind our backs. Who knows if he and this Sonia . . . ," she says, forging on. "Anyway, like they say, he's of legal age, he's got all his shots, and he's still got a lot of life left in him."

Sonia was his goddaughter.

"He's the one who says so. The number of handsome old men who go carrying on with their nieces, cousins, goddaughters!"

It's true; he told us so, and neither old Mauro nor Sonia could contradict him. It's an unsettling vision of my uncle: James Bond in a fleece-lined jacket, surrounded by venal creatures.

Yvette pushes me out onto the terrace, into warm rays of sunlight; breathing in fresh air does me some good. Tintin follows behind, nibbling on our shoes. I'm trying to recall Justine's words: "No . . . it's not so simple . . . " It calls to mind a romantic rendezvous, or maybe a plan. A premeditated act. Given the present situation, a plot. I'm crossing my fingers, hoping my uncle has nothing to do with any of this. I love my uncle. He's bounced me on his knee, taken me out on his boat, taught me to appreciate good wines. Taken me out on his boat . . . something about those words has a sinister echo.

"I've just been on the phone with Jean," Yvette's saying. "What with that storm the other night, part of the gutter's been torn off. He spent the whole night on the roof, soaked to the bone, trying to keep the slate tiles on without falling. I didn't dare insist that he come. He sends his love, and tells you to watch out for yourself if you want them go on writing the rest of your adventures!"

That's just like good old Jean. I have no greater wish than to become a recurrent heroine, the kind that never dies. For the time being, I've got ten or so holes in my body, and things like that don't inspire wild optimism.

On my pad I write, *You don't have to stay. Francine can take care of me.*

"As if I would abandon you! And what about that poor little Lorieux—we ought to give him a hand, shouldn't we? After all, his fiancée was murdered!"

His ex.

"Feelings don't end on a set date," Yvette answers with dignity.

10

At four o'clock! "Okay, tomorrow, at four." That's what Justine said on the phone. And tomorrow is today. My uncle should be seeing her today. But he didn't tell us he'd be coming. Unless they meant a rendezvous by telephone. I've got to get Yvette to keep an eye on her. If she moves about without a sound, Justine won't find out.

Can Yvette move about without a sound?

"Bon appétit!" Francine calls out in a cheerful tone, as if she were in a commercial for breakfast.

All around are the sounds of people chewing food. I'm not very hungry. I dreamed of Magali again and woke up with a lump in my stomach. It's strange to dream of someone whose face I never saw. I knew it was Magali, yet her features were the same as those of Botticelli's Venus, with plenty of freckles and hair down to her feet, hair that got in the way of her ankles and made her trip at every step; I backed up every time she approached; I backed up because I was afraid she might touch me, because I knew she was dead and that her eyes were no more than two dark, empty holes. I wasn't in my wheelchair, no, I was walking. Oh, the sensation of walking, so real, so strong, I almost believed I would just get up and . . .

And nothing.

The metal clicks tell me it's Jean-Claude in the machine that allows him to stand and move around just a little. We haven't seen much of him these past few days: he's suffering enormously and is staying in his room.

"Smile! You're on camera!" he calls out.

"Don't you get tired of keeping your eye screwed to that camera?" Laetitia asks.

"I'm a witness of my times. So where's the investigation at?"

"Vest-vest-vest-vestigation!"

"Christian! Stop!" Martine shouts.

"The local law enforcement seems a bit out of their depth," Francine observes, sarcastically. "I'm afraid the sergeant," she continues, stretching out the word, "may soon be replaced by someone more competent in matters of crime."

"Columbo?" Yann says, laughing.

"Funny, but I don't remember hiring you for your sense of humor," Francine responds without missing a beat. "Where are you with that snow-scooter outing?"

"I'll get on it in just a bit."

"I reread all the papers last night," Jean-Claude continues. "If this Vore really wanted to kill Elise he would have done it a long time ago. We're not such hard targets to track down."

"Jean-Claude! We don't talk of such things at the table!" Francine protests.

"It's better to talk at the table than in the cemetery," Yann can't help but observe.

"Jean-Claude's right," Laetitia says suddenly. "Elise isn't in hiding. All Vore's got to do is take aim at her with a rifle that's got a scope or something."

I'm getting the nasty feeling that Vore's in a corner somewhere, saying to himself, "Now, that's a good idea!"

"Then what's his goal?" Yann asks, crumbling bread between his fingers; I can hear the crust breaking.

"To scare us?" Francine suggests.

"To maneuver us!" Jean-Claude says. "To draw away our attention while he plots some scheme or other. Like a magician."

"You can't be saying that he's just pretending to hurt Elise," Yann observes.

"But it wasn't serious," replies Jean-Claude, who hasn't taken ten darts in his hide.

"And then again, what's he trying to turn our attention away from?" Yann goes on. "He's carrying out these schemes anyhow."

"Still," Jean-Claude continues obstinately, "here's an individual who's threatening Elise in some outlandish fashion, who commits atrocities on two women, and then nothing. Radio silence. If he were a maniac, he'd go into action. Why would he lead us down his trail with provocations against Elise?"

"You mean to say someone's acting like a maniac?" Yann asks with interest.

"Mm-hm," Jean-Claude agrees, his mouth full. "That's why he's putting on such a spectacle, what with the letters, the steaks, et cetera. In fact, he's pursuing a very precise goal."

"To turn Elise into carpaccio?" Yann quips, drawing the scandalized protest of everyone gathered.

He gives my shoulder a vigorous squeeze to make up for his joke, which was somewhat beyond questionable taste. The fact is, it would have made me laugh if it had to do with anyone besides me. The fact is also that he smells slightly, yet undeniably, of gin.

"I think he's really insane!" says Yvette. "When I think back to those eyes in Elise's hand . . . A man who's capable of cutting up a woman certainly isn't just a joker."

"Sadistic doesn't necessarily mean crazy," Jean-Claude says, obstinately. "We'll see if he strikes again."

Just now Lorieux should be making his entrance, saying, "He's struck again!!" I expect to hear his nervous, rapid steps with Schabel plodding behind, and I wonder if I'm hallucinating when in fact I hear the front door open and two men coming up the hallway at a lively pace.

"Is Véronique Gans here?" Lorieux asks in a voice that's sharper than usual.

"Véronique who?" Francine asks.

"One of the ski instructors," Yann replies. "Why would Véronique be here?" he says, addressing Lorieux.

"I've just been to the ski school to ask her a few additional questions. Kevin Destreille told us that she came to MRCHA to see someone to whom she wished to pass some important information."

I imagine they're exchanging suspicious glances.

"So no one's seen her?" Lorieux continues.

Everyone remains as mute as I. The French door slides open.

"Hewwo."

"Ah! Mr. de Quincey! I'm looking for Véronique Gans."

"Don' know huh."

A chair makes a sound as it's pulled out, a glass is knocked over, and Léonard sits down.

"Perhaps she went up to see Madame Lombard," Lorieux says.

"Is someone asking for me?"

The elevator doors swish open and close behind Justine.

"You wouldn't have met Véronique Gans?" Lorieux inquires for the fourth time.

"I don't know this person," Justine answers in a husky voice, "and for you to say that I've come across her . . . "

She elegantly leaves her sentence hanging and passes in front of me, leaving a trail of violet perfume and menthol inhaler in her wake.

"I've got one of those colds!" she says to me as she sits down.

"Schnabel, go through the upper floors to see if she's there!" Lorieux orders.

Immediately Francine yelps, "Have you got a warrant?"

"What kind of warrant?" Lorieux replies, slyly. "We're looking for someone who said she'd be coming here. I suppose you see no inconvenience if we check to see that she hasn't gotten lost in the corridors?"

"Or rummaging through the rooms," Yvette says, dryly.

I pinch the flab on her arm to get her to shut up.

"Oh, go on and pinch me all you want! That creature's capable of anything! Some unheard-of obscenity!"

"I see that at least you know her!" says Lorieux.

Schnabel's footsteps are ringing through our heads. We can hear doors opening and closing, not gently.

"I don't appreciate it that your police officer is traipsing around through our dear residents' private rooms," Francine says.

"Just what is he looking for?" says Justine between two coughing fits.

"He's planting microphones everywhere," Yann replies.

Laetitia giggles. I can hear liquid going *glug-glug,* and make out the smell of Suze. Yann smacks his lips with satisfaction. In the room next door Hugo's instructing the dear residents in modeling clay. Laughter breaks out amid small shouts and noises, in contrast with our silence and Schnabel's footsteps, which echo through the building.

"That's good, Clara, that's good. Your lady's quite pretty. No, Bernard, you can't eat that, you know that. I don't care if the clay is all white, like a Christmas pudding. What about you, Christian? What nice thing have you made for us? A dachshund? But your dog's missing his paws."

Footsteps on the stairs.

"I didn't find her, Sergeant," says Schnabel, out of breath.

"Well. I'm sorry to have disturbed your breakfast. If Véronique Gans shows up, I'll thank you to notify me right away."

On my pad, *Why are you looking for her?*

"Her alibi doesn't hold water," Lorieux whispers in my ear.

"Perhaps someone's been bothering you," Francine says, icily.

"No more than usual," Lorieux replies before carefully closing the door behind him.

"That guy's got a face that needs a good smack!" Francine shouts.

"Philippe always took himself seriously," Yann says. "Well, I can use another glass."

"Don't you think the sergeant smelled of edelweiss?" Justine asks.

"He seems to be standing on the edge of a professional cliff," Francine jokes. "Does anyone want some more tea? Elise, do you want toast?"

With my hand I refuse. Why did Véronique Gans claim that she had to come here? Why would she say that to Destreille if it weren't true? I would have preferred it if Schnabel had found her going through my things. I'm distractedly listening to the hubbub going on around me.

"Let me see, Clara. No, my little muffin. You've got to put the snowman's head on his shoulders, not on his side! Christian, try to make something besides bananas and oranges for a change."

"I forgot my Walkman upstairs," Laetitia says.

"I think I'll install my easel out on the terrace; there's a nightingale sun," Justine coos.

"The scooter guy's gonna call back in an hour. We've got to start thinking about picnics," Yann grumbles in a thick voice.

"No, Clara, I've just told you that the head goes on the shoulders! Come on! You don't carry your head under your arm, do you?"

"I'm going upstairs!" Laetitia calls out.

There goes her walker. The elevator doors swish open. And then a scream freezes me to the bone. A scream that won't stop. Someone jostles me on the run, a chair is knocked over, and Justine asks, "What's going on? What's going on?" Francine and Yvette also start yelling, I feverishly clutch my blanket, the elevator doors open and shut, open and shut, and Laetitia hiccups, followed by Yann's deep voice on the phone: "Notify Lorieux right away! Get him to come back to MRCHA immediately!"

"What's going on? Can somebody answer me?"

People are rushing about. And those doors keep hitting against each other.

"Hugo, close the door to the rec room!" Yann calls out amid aggravated shrieks. "Don't touch a thing!"

"But—"

"And block off that fucking door!"

"Yann!"

"My God, Atchouel! Can't you see we've got a murder on our hands? That somebody killed this girl while you were serving your fucking tea?"

Killed. Girl. Véronique Gans. In the elevator. Oh, Lord!

"Who was killed? Léonard! Léonard, where are you?" Justine squeals.

"I'm here. In-struc-tor dead. Off . . . cuh off . . . "

"What are you trying to say? Calm down. Take a deep breath. Go on, all the way down. What happened?" Justine's asking, breathlessly.

"Cuh off . . . off . . . "

"Her clothes were off? Was she stripped naked? Did someone attack her?"

"Cuh off . . . "

The odd idea that he wants coffee crosses my mind.

"Head cuh off," Léonard finishes in one breath.

Have I heard correctly?

"That's horrible!" Justine cries. "I told you there was evil here, Elise. It's close to us! All this red, all this red!"

Véronique Gans was decapitated in the elevator. The last person to take the elevator was you, old girl. You and your fucking red blood.

"Oh, my poor dear, my poor dear!" Yvette stammers as she holds me tight. "Luckily you can't see it! She's stretched out on the floor of the elevator car, with her head between her ankles. He cut her head off! Her eyes are wide open, she's looking right at us. The blood is still flowing!"

Blood gushing out of an elevator. Like *The Shining,* by Stanley Kubrick. No, stay in reality, Elise, concentrate. Véronique no doubt came to MRCHA to see somebody. Somebody who murdered her in the elevator. Without a sound. The elevator Justine took to come down and have her breakfast. Didn't she sense the thermal presence of the body? The sharp odor of blood? Did she forget to turn on her sensory detector? I can imagine Justine grimacing and disheveled, handling a meat cleaver with the dexterity of a woodsman. By the way, what was the murder weapon?

Beside me, Yvette's still muttering "whys" and "hows" and getting no answer. Francine Atchouel's demanding two aspirins and suggesting them to everyone else. Somebody sits Laetitia down on the sofa, and Yvette passes a wet cloth over her forehead and has her eat some sugar. Mrs. Raymond comes out of the kitchen and nearly passes out. She clings to my wheelchair, groaning, "Omigod, omigod." For once I'm glad I can't see anything. To be too far away to smell death. Not to touch the rigid body, the clammy skin. To be alive, and not to have felt the affection for death that brings insurmountable sorrow. Only the compassion that is due to anyone who has died, to any among us who has broken the human chain to return to limbo.

Footsteps, admonitions, many men. Lorieux, Schnabel, and Mercanti, among others. Lorieux's directing the crime-scene technicians, who can't help but toss around their comments. Four violent deaths in so little time in a peaceful region like this is shocking. I move forward to hear more, taking advantage of the fact that Schnabel is deep in conversation with Yvette.

"I want a full sample," says Lorieux. "Ah, Doctor! I'm sorry, but we'll be needing you again."

"I can see that. Good God, we've got to put an end to this! Who's the girl?"

"Véronique Gans, one of the ski instructors."

"Oh, yes, I recognize her. My grandson took a few lessons with her. Talk about butchery! Between that little Auvare girl and this . . . It's the first time in thirty years I've seen anything like it! Usually I get the broken legs, a severed spinal column maybe, an accident on the highway, and it's not so pretty, but this is revolting! A little more light please? Thanks."

"How long has she been dead?"

"The body's still warm. Half an hour? One hour, tops. You see the edges of the wound?"

"Yes. Very irregular."

"Exactly. And the same marks are on the other side. It's intriguing. Have you found the weapon?"

"No, not yet."

The doctor continues working in silence. Someone jostles me, and a young-sounding voice says, "I don't feel so well—" and vomits right beside me.

"Good grief, Morel, why don't you pay attention!" Mercanti says, scolding.

"Sorry, Sergeant," Morel apologizes.

"I'm starting to think it's a double-bladed instrument, like shears," the doctor's saying.

"I beg your pardon?" Lorieux asks.

"The flesh was scissored, not sawed, so I'm leaning toward a pair of shears or bolt cutters, the bigger models used for cutting padlocks, iron bars, et cetera."

"Something like that is hard to hide under your clothing."

"No more than a saw. And then again, under a down jacket . . . "

Always the same old song. A fly's buzzing nearby.

"Don't let it land on the victim, it's sickening," Morel says.

"It's just doing its job. In any case, forty-eight hours from now the body will be infested with larvae."

"You really think somebody got on the elevator at the same time as the victim, took out a bolt cutter from underneath his parka, put both blades around her neck, and—*crack!*—squeezed hard until her head came off?" Lorieux asks incredulously.

"We'll see what the lab says."

"Wouldn't she have screamed?"

"Maybe she was knocked out beforehand. The exam will tell us."

I hear footsteps.

"Apparently no one knows a thing, no one heard anything, as usual," Mercanti says in a low voice.

"Well, she definitely snuck into the building. Either someone was waiting for her, or someone followed her here. Are you sure no one used the elevator after Madame Lombard?"

"According to the statements we've taken, no. Schnabel took the staircases to go up and down to make sure Véronique Gans wasn't hiding there."

"And to think she was here, in the elevator! At precisely what time did Madame Lombard come down?"

"Nine-sixteen, according to the nurse. He said he'd looked at his watch at that moment," Mercanti explains.

"He looks at his watch every time the elevator doors open?" Lorieux growls. "Who came down before her?"

"Clara Rinaldi, Emilie Domengue, and Christian Leroy at eight-forty, with the nurse. Mrs. Holzinski, Miss Andrioli, and Miss Castelli at around eight-fifty."

"What about Quincey?"

"He came down earlier, at around eight-fifteen."

"Didn't he come for breakfast?" Lorieux asks, in a tone that suggests "but he had blood on his hands."

"He went out for a walk. He wasn't very hungry. Stomach trouble," Mercanti answers.

"Right," Lorieux grumbles.

"Uh, excuse me, Sergeant, but . . . "

They start whispering. Then someone grips my wheelchair and pushes me over to where everyone else is gathered. Damn! Why does he need to be so zealous? Fine, now I can't hear anything else. What's more, everyone's chattering. I'm trying to concentrate. The murderer had about half an hour between the time we came down and the time Justine took her elevator ride in the company of Véronique Gans's cadaver. Did somebody sneak off during breakfast? How might I find out? What about Léonard? Something about his absence is troubling. And then there's another question: Why did Véronique Gans take the elevator? Did she have a rendezvous on one of the upper floors?

A bolt cutter. I won't even dare imagine what a human neck must look like, gripped between the two sharpened blades of a bolt cutter. What is the diameter of a neck? Let's see . . . more or less the distance between my thumb and forefinger, perhaps even less. So that's around eight inches. No, it's not all that thick. She must have been attacked first. Unless . . . can someone cry out when two steel blades are driving deep into the flesh, cutting off the breath and the carotid artery?

"Are you okay, Elise?" Laetitia asks. "It was really something atrocious to see," she goes on without waiting for me to answer. "They've just put her in a plastic bag. They're going take her away. I'll never dare take the elevator again. I'm going to ask Mrs. Atchouel to give me a room on the ground floor. It's full of blood that's dripped all over. Yvette wasn't feeling well, so Mrs. Raymond had her breathe in some vinegar. They wouldn't stop asking us who took the elevator and at what time, who did what since seven o'clock this morning. Fortunately, all three of us came down together. Can you imagine, Justine came down in the elevator without knowing there was a decapitated body right behind her? Maybe even the killer!" she adds, overexcited.

The idea of a man crouched behind Justine, eyes blazing with madness, sends a shiver down my spine. No, the elevator remained on the ground floor; someone would have seen it leave. Just a second, Elise, think hard. Nobody saw Véronique get on the elevator. She must have gone up the stairs before we were all downstairs for our breakfast. Paper, pen, and reasoning.

The elevator opens onto a hall that looks out on both the living room and the dining room, which are separated by only an archway. From either of these rooms, sighted people can see the elevator doors—and hence the person or people getting in.

Breakfast is served between eight forty-five and nine-fifteen, because before then, the residents are having a wash with the help of Hugo and Martine. Yann sleeps on the ground floor, as does Jean-Claude, in the rooms located behind the rec room and the kitchen, which have no direct view of the elevator. Let's say Véronique gets here at around eight-thirty. She's waiting for the moment when the living room is empty, and sneaks her way into the elevator to make it to her mysterious rendezvous.

What was she doing until 8:50, when all of us took the elevator and when we knew that her body wasn't there?

She goes to a room. A room where somebody knocks her out, before dragging her into the elevator, blocking off the doors, and killing her. Then the murderer takes the stairway, which lets out on a dark corner in the hallway. From this corner he could enter the living room through a side door, which would still be open; there he would wait with us until someone discovered the body. A bloody game of chance, and one that assumes no one would decide to go back up to his room to get something—and that Justine would not come down before nine-fifteen, her usual time, something that always makes Mother Atchouel start to bray. So the killer knows Justine's habits.

So where was brave Léonard during breakfast? Walking around.

Véronique's body is loaded into the ambulance, which slowly drives away.

A black horse-drawn carriage gallops through snowy Transylvania toward the somber towers of a Gothic castle, carrying the livid body of an unfortunate young woman tossed into her casket . . . Well, this is somewhat less poetic. The casket is a plastic bag, the horse-drawn carriage is a red-and-white ambulance that goes *bing-bong,* and the driver's some tired guy who's sick to his stomach. The only constant is the predator: a creature who must kill to survive. In the first case, it's to avoid the destruction of his physical body; in the second, it's to avoid the implosion of his mental structure. You see, Shrink, pretty soon I'll be taking your place: you'll be the one stretched out on the couch, telling me the story of your life. How many times a day do you pick your nose and wonder if that symbolizes a desire to possess your mother and all that?

"Now they're going through this whole dump," Laetitia informs me, pulling me out of my jumbled thoughts. "We're not allowed to leave the living room."

"The shadows are enveloping us in their long, icy fingers," Justine pronounces in a nasal, prophetic-sounding voice. "I told you so; all this red, all this hatred, piled up, concentrated, ready to jump out."

"Her face was all white," Laetitia adds, "like wax, and she was looking at me. Just thinking about it . . . excuse me."

Her walker slides across the room.

"The face of death always has an icy pallor," Justine continues, after sneezing. "When a being expires, its temperature drops and the atmosphere becomes crystal."

Right. Go tell that to people who die in the Tropics, with stench and flies.

"Ms. Lombard, we've found this in one of the victim's pockets," Mercanti says in a schoolteacher tone of voice.

"What's 'this'?" Justine asks him.

"Touch it," the sergeant replies.

There's a short silence. Mercanti gives off the smell of cheap aftershave and strawberry Malabars.

"Well, I'd say . . . a pack of cigarettes," Justine says, finally.

"Pass your hand over the case and tell me the initials engraved on it."

"An *F* and an *A*," she spells out in an uncertain voice.

"Do you have one similar to this?"

"Yes, the one Fernand gave me," Justine quickly replies, "but . . . "

Deep down in my chest, there's a small point of childish jealousy and anger.

"How is this possible?" she continues.

"Apparently, Gans stole it from you. Were you aware that this object had disappeared?"

"No, I stopped smoking six months ago."

"If you don't mind, I'll have to hold on to this for the time being. Thank you, that will be all."

No, this will not be all! If Véronique had picked up the cigarette case, it's because she went into Justine's room! Justine, who did not come down until nine-fifteen! Justine, who must have realized that someone was rummaging through her room!

"When I told you she was a thief, it's because drug addicts are always thieves," Yvette says.

"Did this girl take drugs?" Justine asks.

"Yes, just like Marion Hennequin and Sonia Auvare. Apparently it's the in thing in these parts. All druggies!"

"And all murdered," says Jean-Claude, who's come back to join us, with the clicking of his metallic shell. "Seems to me that if I could move, I'd have better things to do than bump off my peers."

"Well, if you watch the news on TV, you'll see that about half the planet doesn't share your opinion, Jean-Claude." Someone next to me is pouring himself a drink. Is it Yann again? This is his sixth, at least, and it's not even noon. Justine blows her nose, then vigorously inhales something that smells like mint and pine resin.

"It has come to my ears that Sonia and Marion knew each other," she says.

Come to her ears? "It has come to my ears"? Really! What comes to anyone's ears these days?!

"They all knew each other!" Yvette answers. "I'm telling you, this is a village full of nuts!"

"It's the times that are nuts," Lorieux comments somberly. He's returned without my hearing him.

Mercanti lets out an irritated sigh.

"Tell me, Madame Lombard," Lorieux goes on, in a gloomy tone, "you never heard anyone enter your room this morning?"

Finally!

"I received no visits," Justine answers.

"No one opened the door? You heard no suspicious noises? You, who have such a fine ear . . . ?"

"Nothing. Unless someone entered while I was in the shower . . . with the sound of water . . . I like to turn it up all the way, like a rushing cascade, chasing away the shadows of—"

"Thank you, Madame Lombard," he says, cutting her off. "You've taken this down, Mercanti?"

"He's gotten some of his strength back," Yvette whispers to me.

"Where's Schnabel?" Lorieux adds.

"Chief!" Schnabel shouts at that very moment. "Chief!"

The hammering of heels punctuates the panting.

"Come quick!"

"What's going on now?" Francine demands.

"It's in the big retard's room. Come on," Schnabel insists.

They race out. Yvette, who wants to follow, is stopped by the police.

"Sorry, ma'am," Morel's young voice says, "but nobody leaves, those are the orders."

"Who's been done in this time?" Yann asks, his voice husky.

"I cannot give you an answer, sir. Please wait here."

"'Please wait here,'" Yann, completely sloshed, says, aping him, before adding, "I'm sick of this asshole circus of yours!"

"I beg your pardon, sir? I don't think I've heard you."

"A perfect asshole circus. You'd do better to get your hands on the killer than give us shit."

"I'd advise you to calm down, sir. I'd seriously advise you to calm down."

"And I'd advise you to go fuck yourself!"

"Can I see some ID!" Morel barks.

"How about pissing in your kepi?"

"What?!"

Morel calls for his colleagues, and I hear the sounds of fighting amid protests from Yvette, Francine, and Laetitia, and groans and noises from Yann.

"Making a spectacle like that when a woman's just died," Jean-Claude says to me, "I find that very disheartening. Don't they have any respect for the dead?"

"You know quite well that modern man rejects the idea of death," Justine calmly tells him, as if people were not fighting just beside her.

"I, too, reject the idea of my own," Jean-Claude replies in the same tone. "That doesn't prevent me from feeling compassion for those of others."

While they're continuing their philosophical debate, I receive a kepi in my lap, then Yann collapses on top of me—good grief!—just where my wounds happen to be. Someone picks him up, I take an elbow to the stomach, and then there's a stampede: Tintin growls, Laetitia cries "ouch," there's a sound of someone falling over, Justine grabs my hair—"Is that you, Elise?" No, it's the goldfish—"They're scaring me," "Stop pulling so hard, damn it!" and finally the flat sound of blows. Handcuffs click shut.

"What the hell is going on here?!" Lorieux screams. "Atteeen-tion!"

"This man has insulted us and attacked us!" Morel explains.

"We'll see about that later," Lorieux shoots back. "Mrs. Atchouel, where are the residents?"

"In the rec room, with their nurse, in case you haven't noticed."

"I appreciate your cooperation. Morel, stop bleeding from your nose and follow me."

"Bunch of assholes!" Yann screams. "Take these handcuffs off me immediately!"

"Shut up, Yann!" Lorieux snaps. "I've had enough of your clowning around."

"You've got no right, you loser! I'm a free citizen!"

"Take the free citizen to dry out in the paddy wagon."

"Already drunk at eleven o'clock in the morning! What's this world coming to?" Francine sighs, apparently more shocked by the early-morning drunkenness of her instructor than by the decapitation of a young woman in her elevator.

"I know why Sonia was cheating on you with every ski instructor!" Yann's still shouting.

A deadly silence. Someone clears his throat. Yann's dragged outside. The front door shuts.

"Doesn't surprise me," Yvette whispers. "She really looked sleazy."

I wave aside Yvette's gossip like a bothersome swarm of flies. What interests me more than Yann's drunken comments is what Schnabel found.

The door to the rec room opens, and Hugo's indignant voice calls out, "This is ridiculous; he'll tell you anything just to sound more interesting!"

"Mrs. Atchouel," Lorieux announces, "I'm obliged to take this person down to the stationhouse. I'd appreciate it if you would notify his family."

"What's poor Christian done?" Yvette asks indignantly. "Can't you see he's an innocent man?"

"An innocent man in whose room we've found the murder weapon!" Schnabel replies.

"Schnabel! Not a word!" Lorieux orders.

"Christian wouldn't hurt a fly! Come on!" Francine cries. "None of our dear residents is dangerous!"

"Tell that to Véronique Gans," Lorieux retorts. "Let's go! We're taking him in!"

"Ve'onique, nique, nique," Christian starts to sing.

"Sometimes guys like this are moved by irresistible drives," Lorieux tells us again. "Didn't you ever read *Of Mice and Men*?"

" . . . nique, nique, nique your mother . . . "

"He seems rather vicious," Mercanti observes in his virtuous pastor's voice.

Addressing Christian, Lorieux says, "Come on, buddy, we've got a couple of questions to ask you. Mercanti, tell the boys up there to do whatever it takes. Tell them to go through everything with a fine-tooth comb."

"I'm coming with you," Martine says. "He's going to be terrified if he's all alone with you, and I'm the only one who understands him."

"Well . . . up till now, it doesn't seem too hard for us to grasp, right, Chief?" Morel jeers.

"That's enough, Morel! Go get the van."

"May I remind you that I took the elevator with him at eight-forty; it's in my deposition," Martine proclaims. "I don't see, then, how he could have killed someone, since, at eight-fifty, the elevator contained no cadaver. It's not right to set upon a defenseless soul."

"He may have gone back upstairs during breakfast. Apparently, surveillance isn't one of the center's strong points," Lorieux snaps back treacherously.

"You know," Martine adds, "the poor child has a habit of picking up everything he finds."

"And hiding it under his mattress?"

"That depends. He makes up functions for objects other than what we know them for."

"The problem is not so much knowing why he hid the exhibit, but rather how he got it."

"Are you suggesting that this uncontrolled force was in the presence of the young instructor's lifeless body?" Justine asks.

Lorieux understands faster than I that "uncontrolled force" means "brute without a conscience."

"There are three hypotheses, Madame Lombard," he answers in a tone drier than the Gobi Desert. "(a) He did in fact find the evidence next to the cadaver and stole it; (b) he's behind the murder and tried to hide the object that served to vent his rage; or (c) someone hid the murder weapon in his room. So you understand why it's necessary that I question him."

"Sergeant, Sergeant! Somebody's let the air out of our tires!"

"Are you kidding me, Morel?"

"All four of them, Chief. It's unbelievable."

"Where's Yann?"

"You mean the boozer? Inside. He's singing bawdy songs."

"He couldn't get out?"

"No, he's handcuffed to the separator."

"I am fed up with this shit!" Lorieux screams like a man possessed. "I'm going to call for backup and take in the lot of you for questioning! No more joking around!"

"Laugh, laugh, laugh, she laugh too much!"

"Who was laughing too much, Christian?" Martine asks.

"Girl. Wed. Wed-thwoat. She go 'way."

"Where did she go? In the elevator?"

"And ya sista? Go 'way, go to heaven. Wit' Ma-gali."

"How could he know that somebody died?" Jean-Claude asks before Lorieux can get a word in.

"C'ara, start whining, Christian. C'ara."

"He means Clara," Martine explains. "Did Clara see something? Tell us what she saw."

"Saw nuttin', took nuttin'!"

"He's very excited."

"Where is this Clara?"

"She's over there, to the side," Hugo says. "Now that I think about it, she was behaving a bit oddly this morning."

"Meaning?" Lorieux sighs.

"We were working with modeling clay, and she insisted on putting the head of her snowman on the side."

"On the side?"

"Yes, at his feet."

Suddenly Lorieux dashes out. Apparently, everyone has followed him, and I stay here, alone with Justine and Jean-Claude.

A̶FTER A BRIEF SILENCE, Jean-Claude observes, "This investigation really doesn't seem to be conducted according to the rules. The officers seem very excited, the staff of the center are agitated, Yann has lost his head, and the residents are more than a bit shaken."

"Help from the outside would do us the most good," Justine says approvingly.

Don't worry, I say to myself, laughing inside. Uncle Fernand should be arriving at four. Perhaps Uncle Fernand's been dispatched from Scotland Yard to settle everything in two shakes of a lamb's tail.

"From the beginning I felt something wasn't right," she continues after two coughing fits. "There were stains from sparse matter, no cohesion, permanent explosions. We're at the center of a spiritual disturbance on a wide scope, and going mad will do nothing but accelerate the process."

Okay, but it's hard to keep one's cool when a killer hidden in the shadows is massacring one young woman after another! From the room next door I'm hearing voices clamoring and shrill cries breaking out.

"I suppose it's Clara," Justine says, sniffling. "Where did I put my tube of Vicks?"

Of course! No wonder she couldn't smell anything in the elevator! She was busy cramming a tube of Vicks Vaporub up her nostrils. A perfect excuse.

Someone's running toward us, followed by Tintin, woofing.

"Elise!" Yvette screams, out of breath. "Clara saw Vore killing Gans."

"Unbelievable!" Jean-Claude shouts. "I'm going to recharge my camera and take a picture of you, Yvette."

Tintin pipes up even louder, excited by all this commotion.

"Shut up!" Yvette yells. "Hugo remembered that at around nine, she asked to go to the bathroom," she goes on. "But in fact she wanted to go up to her room to eat her bonbons on the sly. Emilie's the one who told us that she hid her bonbons there. So Clara started crying and confessed everything. She wanted to take the elevator, but it was stuck. She walked up to the second floor and pressed the button again, the doors opened up, and she saw! She saw!"

"Saw what?" Justine asks nervously.

"The body of that unfortunate woman stretched out on the floor and the killer, who was holding her head in his hand! Like the head of Saint John the Baptist! He turned his horrible, grimacing face toward her and placed a finger to his lips, saying, 'Shhh.' Then he snipped the giant scissors toward her! She peed on herself, she was so scared, and ran back down as fast as she could and didn't say a word to anyone. She's just had a nervous breakdown in there; Martine's going to give her a shot."

"But what did the killer look like?" Justine asks in a strangled voice.

"A vampire!" Yvette whispers. "He was livid, and wrapped in a great black cape, with big teeth covered with blood and bulging eyes!"

"That's ridiculous," says Jean-Claude doubtfully. (He subscribes to *Tales from the Crypt*.)

"Once she gets her claws into something, she won't let go!" Yvette assures us, with unintended humor.

"Vore, the devourer," Justine murmurs. "You've brought us a particularly cruel and powerful demon, Elise."

"You really think this has something to do with a supernatural creature?" Jean-Claude asks.

"What do we know of the universe?" Justine replies, before sneezing.

"Pfff! Everyone knows vampires don't exist," Yvette retorts.

"Can you swear to that on Elise's head?" Justine replies treacherously.

Yvette remains silent.

"That would explain everything," says Jean-Claude.

I don't see how it would, but fine. What interests me is that Clara saw something at 9:00, or let's say 9:05. While Lorieux was questioning us downstairs. At 9:20, Schnabel walked upstairs to search the building. The only person to have come out of the elevator is Justine, at 9:15. If the killer didn't step out of the elevator, then he walked down from the second floor. He would have to have come across Schnabel. Unless he hid out in one of the rooms. No, Schnabel didn't find anybody. So where did he go? He couldn't have evaporated!

Unless it was Justine. This idea's threading its way in. Justine, getting rid of her disguise and weapon in Christian's room, on the second floor in fact, before calmly returning downstairs to rejoin us at nine-fifteen. Come on, Elise, says Shrink, pulling on his beard, just because Justine's sleeping with your dear uncle, it doesn't mean she's a sadistic murderer!

I hear voices, Lorieux's alto dominating all the others.

"So, Morel? What's happening with our backup?"

"The problem is, Gendreau and Pollain are on highway patrol. They're in the middle of booking some suntanned perp, and when they're finished, they'll be right here."

"A vampire," Lorieux grumbles. "Where the hell did that freak stash his disguise?"

"You might watch your language in front of our dear residents. You're a representative of the nation's armed forces, besides!"

"Ha, ha, ha!" Lorieux jeers. "Can't you keep those dear residents of yours from squalling?! They're making my head throb."

"They're disturbed, as one might expect!" Francine protests, her claws bared. "Besides, whose fault is it, if not your own incompetence?"

"She's insulting you, Chief."

"Peace, Morel. Mercanti, I want everyone to go through the premises with a fine-tooth comb, a second time."

"To look for a rubber mask and a cape, like in *Scream*?" says Morel, who's apparently got cinematic references.

"Exactly. Where's the witness?"

"She's calmed down," Martine answers, "but I think it would be better to wait awhile before taking her in to give a deposition."

"And what'll we do about that Leroy guy?" Morel asks, zealous.

"We'll see. He's not running away."

Lorieux and Mercanti are holding a private consultation, speaking in low voices.

Laetitia and Léonard join us, both moving hesitantly. Comments are exchanged. Exclamations of shock and disbelief fly about. You'd think we were in an aviary.

Who let the air out of the van's tires? The question keeps jarring me, like a surface-to-surface missile. I'm convinced the answer to this question, however insignificant it may seem, would resolve all the mysteries.

I hear the front door opening and catch the smell of wet cloth. A policeman is coming to announce that the weatherman is forecasting that the storm will pick up. The access route to the village—a winding road that runs through deep gorges—is being closed as a precaution.

"What storm?" Lorieux asks.

"Well . . . it started to snow at dawn, Sergeant. The road from Isola is already impassable."

"What difference is that supposed to make to me?"

"Well . . . Gendreau and Pollain have just called, and they're stuck below, directing traffic. There are a lot of stranded tourists. We won't be getting backup, and we're going to have some problems getting back to the station-house with the witnesses."

"What about the lab car?"

"Well, there are already four in there, Chief."

"I believe the center has a minibus?" says Lorieux.

"That's right," Hugo answers. "It's in the garage."

Lorieux has the keys handed over to him by an extremely reluctant Francine and orders Morel to go get the vehicle. Morel takes off running. I wonder what he must look like. I imagine him as a lummox with floppy ears. He reminds me of a poodle who'd like to pass himself off as a German shepherd. Schnabel's the mastiff: solid and serious. I see Mercanti as a pit bull. What about Lorieux? Lorieux's little; he's black and white, with a pointy snout, big ears, a keen eye, and a moist nose. "His master's voice": I can't remember the exact name of that breed of dog anymore.

I rather like the idea of a snowstorm. There's something fascinating about nature in all its upheavals. Well . . . not human nature.

"I didn't even realize it was snowing," Laetitia's saying. "What with everything that's happened."

"I'm totally in a whirl," Yvette says. "I'm going to make some herbal tea. Anyone want some?"

"Sergeant, Sergeant, you won't believe this!"

"What now?" Lorieux growls.

"The minibus tires. They've got nails in them, all four of them!"

"For God's sake!" Lorieux swears.

Recovering, he adds, "It's not important. We can set up temporary head-quarters here. I'm requisitioning this room."

"But you need a written order!" Francine cries. "It's out of the question to put up ten policemen who smell like wet dogs in my living room!"

"You'll just have to take things as they come," Lorieux snaps back. "We'll straighten out the situation later. In cases of flagrante delicto, an officer of the criminal investigation department, which I happen to be, is duty bound to take necessary measures in stopping any manifest disturbance to the public order, and we may consider a murder and the willful puncturing of tires as manifest disturbances. Morel, I want three men to stand guard around the house; nobody enters, nobody leaves."

"What about the guys from the lab?"

"They're staying here. We may need some more."

"They're going to start griping," Morel comments. "Besides, the commander isn't wild about overtime—"

"I don't give a shit! We're talking murders here, Morel—that's murders, in the plural, not just taking Girl Scout cookies!"

"Well, we're not getting paid any more for this," Morel mutters between his teeth, as if to say, "If I'd have known, I wouldn't have come."

"Yann must be freezing out in your van," Yvette says.

"That ought to sober him up," Lorieux retorts dryly. "Mercanti, please call everyone together in the dining room. What time is it?"

"Twelve-twenty."

"Schnabel, tell the cook to serve us something to eat."

"That's right. Pillage my supplies, bunch of Huns!" Francine shouts.

"We'll pay you back."

"Oh, I know you will! Mrs. Raymond!"

There's a sudden clacking of heels toward the kitchen. A certain weariness runs through me. A familiar feeling comes over me: This is a play being performed unbeknownst to me. Maybe that's what we're really doing. We're acting in a drama written by Vore, and we're jumping up and down like puppets while he enjoys the show.

Lunch is fairly quaint, with the investigation team on one side, the residents on the other, Yvette and me in between. The two contingents avoid talking to each other. Yvette passes the time by passing salt and mustard. Lorieux had a sandwich carried out to Yann, who threw it in the policeman's face.

"You should have made him lick it off the floor," Mercanti spits out, coldly.

In these strange situations, one's real instincts are revealed. Mercanti's not only a cold and well-trained pit bull, but a pit bull in a black leather jacket.

After polishing off the meal quickly, the police start bustling around again, the way ants pursue goals that are mysterious at first glance. The residents, grouped around darling Francine, pretend to look for distractions without paying attention to the ants. Every now and again, someone moves my wheelchair and says sorry. I may be on a strategic line of the highest importance.

Emilie comes prowling around, asks if I like some guy whose name I don't know, then starts playing out whole scenes from a soap opera. I recognize *Emergency* when she screams for the tenth time, "Shtethoshcope! Shtat! Get him into the intensive care unit! Prepare a solution of solution!" Suddenly, while practicing a delicate "mouse removal," she exclaims, "That stinks," lets go of the wheelchair, and takes off running.

It's true. Following my nose, I slowly roll ahead to get closer to the smell. I hold out my hand: there's emptiness in front of me. To my left is a metal partition. It's the elevator, its doors left open. Didn't anyone think to clean it up? Is there blood everywhere, with scraps of flesh and bone stuck to the walls? Brrr! I back up, but it's too late; someone has grabbed the wheelchair and given me a shove in the other direction.

"This is off-limits! Go back with the others!" Morel calls out, his hair bristling.

I move off, discreetly giving him the finger.

"What's this?! What's this?!"

Caught! Quick, my pad: *Pee.*

"'Pee?'" he reads, incredulous.

I confirm it for him. *Need to pee. Help me.*

It's a surefire trick for getting rid of pains-in-the-ass: they take off in a flash. I rejoin the group, finding my way by sound.

Bernard jumps out next to me and puts a book into my hand. He loves having young-adult novels read to him. *Phantomette,* in particular. I give it back to him. He insists. It's no use writing to him that I can't see any of it, since he doesn't know how to read. You'd think every obstacle to human communication was meeting up right here! He finally walks away with his book, muttering, "There's no use running, you'd better leave right away; in any case, Phantomette wins every time." Well, good for her. Elise also wins every time, doesn't she, Shrink? I approach Yvette.

What time is it?

"Three-ten," she answers distractedly. "So you were saying about duck à l'orange . . . ?"

Where's Justine?

"Justine, Elise wants you."

No, you damn moron!

"Where are you, Elise?" Justine asks.

"She's over there," Laetitia answers, "by the window."

I always wind up next to this damn window, like a moth drawn to the light. Is this a characteristic of all ephemeral creatures? Justine joins me.

"I, too, have wanted to speak with you," she says in a low voice. "I'm going to need you."

She remains silent, as if I might answer, then goes on: "I need a vector to communicate with the higher powers."

I'm getting the impression she's going to unnerve me.

"Something taken from the sky, in a manner of speaking. An immobile mass of energy crossed by powerful currents."

Does she want to electrocute me?

"Through you, I might be able to connect to the entities from beyond and get some answers. Your damaged brain should allow the waves to circulate more freely."

My "damaged brain"! I pretend to hit the wrong button and with delight run over her feet.

"Oww! You know, you can be—"

She cuts herself off with a bout of coughing.

"Léonard and Laetitia have agreed to participate. We'll get set up in the kitchen while Mrs. Raymond takes her nap."

There she goes, catching my chair and wheeling me without asking my opinion. After a few minor bumps, we enter the kitchen, where it's hot, and the fragrances of roasts, rosemary, garlic, and chocolate cream hang in the air. The ogress's kitchen. Yvette told me the room has been restored to its former look, with black-and-white checkerboard tiles, a stove with six burners, and a vast fireplace from the nineteenth century in full working order. Perhaps the terror experienced in this building at that time was a warning. Perhaps I should have known terrible events would unfold here.

Someone's tapping a fingertip on the long table in the middle of the room.

"Stop that, Léo," says Justine. "Is Laetitia here?"

"Here I am, at the end," says Laetitia. "Next to Léonard."

Justine advances cautiously, pushing the wheelchair along the table. She brings me to a stop, pivots the wheelchair around so that I'm facing her, then takes my left hand— the good one—and places it on the table. The right one stays in my lap, just as Yvette left it this morning.

"There."

She backs away, pulls out a chair, and sits down.

"Won't we be closing the shutters?" Laetitia asks.

"No. Let's let the elements impregnate us with their rage! Let's let the snow's white cloak absorb the fury and the blood."

It's like stepping back thirty years to the time we tried to hold a séance in school. Even then I found it ridiculous. I sigh, but no one pays any attention.

"Let's go. Laetitia, give Léonard your hand. Léonard, give me your hand. Elise, give me yours."

I awkwardly raise my hand and feel about, and her warm, dry fingers forcefully grasp mine.

"Now we're going to concentrate!" she orders us.

We remain silent a few seconds, and Justine breathes deeply, murmuring phrases in a language I can't identify, at a slow rhythm. A gentle torpor runs through me, the calm of the kitchen, the welcoming heat, the sweet smell of familiar food, the rustling of the falling snow . . . snow . . . falling . . . what's buried under the secret of the tires?

"O forces of the underworld, O migrant souls, come to us!"

I jump; I was just drifting off to sleep. Justine repeats her sepulchral injunction, and I suppress a sigh.

"Deeaad," a child's voice murmurs.

Huh?

"Did you hear?" Laetitia calls out, a shade of panic in her voice.

"Shhh!" Justine orders. "Yes, we have heard. Come, don't be afraid, deliver your message to us!"

Suddenly, I'm aware of the fact that it's not warm anymore. It's cold. And the room no longer smells like the kitchen, but of withered flowers.

I'm afraid.

"Deeaad," the voice repeats, fragile yet steady. "Deeaad. Everyone deeaad!"

What kind of trick is this? Laetitia's tightening her grip around my paralyzed hand, to the point where she might crush it. Léonard's fidgeting in his chair.

"Dead? Who'll be 'dead'?" Justine asks in a low voice.

"Everyone!"

"Oh, my God!" Laetitia stammers.

"Silence!" Justine orders again. "Spirit, of whom are you speaking?"

The spirit doesn't answer. A certain tension fills the room. Laetitia's keeps crushing my fingers.

"Spirit, I summon you to respond!"

A laugh. A dirty, vicious laugh.

Something brushes lightly against my face, like a wing or a spider's leg, but I'm unable to cry out; I can only gulp. The room's smell has changed again. An unpleasant odor. Like rotten egg. Sulfur. The sulfur that's associated with a diabolical presence. No! Justine repeats her question, the child repeats, "Everyone," with a perverse chuckle, and I suddenly understand.

I back up my wheelchair and Laetitia lets go of me, but I'm still holding on to Justine, who starts to shout; I tighten my fingers around hers again, and amid a series of deafening explosions and an acrid smell of smoke, Laetitia screams; without letting go of Justine, I continue to move backward. I get to the window, bump against the pane, and the smoke gets even thicker; a struggle breaks out beside us, Justine stumbles, and with the strength in my wrist I pick her up. Laetitia screams again, I advance once more, pick up momentum, then lurch back as fast as I can.

The window breaks under the impact, there's a violent explosion, like a cannon shot, cold air, then hot air, and I take off! I fall backward in a whirl-wind and hear Justine cry out above me; I'm suspended in the void—my wheelchair, where's my wheelchair? I fall, I land in the snow, a body falls on top of me, and I feel violent pain in my injured arm, my cheek; the wounds reopen and I taste blood, smell fire, fire, up above, screams, a dull thud, the odor of burned flesh, Laetitia's cries nearby, then silence, heavy breathing, the crackling of flames. Finally the fire alarm goes off.

"My hair, my hair," Laetitia groans.

Justine leans on me to get up and I can't cry out. I hear her groping her way through the snow.

"Laetitia?" she calls out in a broken, inaudible voice.

"My beautiful hair . . . "

The snow's coming down in buckets. The flakes are sticking like shards of glass. There's a funny noise: *clack, clack, clack*. I realize it's my teeth chatter-ing. Inside the house, people are running in all directions; the sounds come to us a bit muffled, but distinct: "Over here with that fire extinguisher!" "Shit! Can't see a thing through all this smoke!" Yvette's calling my name over and over, and Justine's trying to answer, but all she can give is a "We're here!" that sounds like a mouse squeaking. I feel horribly cold. This feels like being shipwrecked in the Arctic Ocean. Next to the rail of a ship I cannot reach is a radio, broadcasting some drama.

"It's okay, we're getting the situation under control."

I recognize Mercanti.

"Chief, Chief, there's one of the gagas, in the hallway."

Morel.

"De Quincey! De Quincey! You hear me? What happened?"

Lorieux.

"B-bomb," Léonard manages to articulate.

"Is anyone hurt? Who threw the bomb?"

"S-ski mmask . . . "

"He's passed out!" Morel states.

Justine's still trying to call out, without result, and Laetitia's repeating, "My hair." I tighten my arm against myself as I wait for someone to find us; there's warm, fishy blood flowing through my fingers, and I've also got a mouthful, disgusting me, so I spit, I smear my mouth with cold snow; my fingers are sending shooting pains through me, and the cold is burning my cheeks.

"Chief, look!" Morel cries. "It's a box of sulfur—that's what blew up, it must have combusted by itself. You've got to be a real ass to keep something that dangerous in the kitchen."

"The explosion broke all the windows. It must have made one hell of an in-draft!" Mercanti states.

Two seconds later, "Oh, shit, they're over there!"

"Who?" Lorieux asks. Two more seconds later, "Oh, no, I must be dreaming! Go get them. We're coming!" he shouts.

No one answers.

"Honey, sweetheart, where are you?" a powerful voice suddenly calls out.

Uncle Fernand! Finally! Several men, breathing heavily, rush over.

"Let me through! Justine, are you there? Are you all right?"

My heart stops. I'm crying blood.

"What about you, Elise, are you all right, sweetie? What's happened? Oh, my, you're not such a pretty picture. And someone ought to take care of that girl over there; her scalp's peeling!"

"Move to the side, sir, you're in the way."

Somebody with solid hands is pulling me out of my heap of snow, lifting me up, placing a blanket on top of me, and leading me inside. Inside—an empty inside—where I fall down in slow motion; my uncle and Justine are entwined like two bumbling idiots; I'm the one who saved your Justine's life. Laetitia's been picked up; her hair caught on fire, and fortunately her fall into the snow put out the flames. Léonard threw her down; he tried to fight the man in the ski mask who was hidden in the vast fireplace, but he couldn't, so he crawled out of the room while the other guy fled. Fled where? Lorieux's shaking a stupefied Léonard, who is having a harder time than usual expressing himself.

"Where did he go?" Lorieux screams.

"Can't you see the boy's in a state of shock?" says my uncle.

"I'll have a few questions to ask you!" Lorieux yells, not too affably. "Mercanti, take the gentleman into the rec room. I'll be over in a minute."

"I'm not leaving these ladies," my uncle says firmly. "Not until they receive care."

"The ambulance can't get through. There's been a rockslide," Schnabel cries over the sputtering of his radio-telephone.

As quick as a wink Lorieux asks my uncle, "By the way, how did you get up here?"

"I had myself dropped off by the mountain emergency helicopter; the pilot and I go way back."

"Our chopper!" Morel roars. "Chief, he took off with our chopper!"

"He had to come up to look for some kid who hurt his head, and he urgently needed to go down to Nice. It was a skull fracture," my uncle explains without missing a beat. "How about taking care of our own wounded?"

"I don't think anything's wrong with me," says Justine.

"What about you, Elise, are you okay?"

Just swell, Uncle! All this red smeared over me from head to toe is only strawberry jam!

"You can see for yourself she's hurt," says Yvette, who's come running up like a whirlwind.

"Ah, Yvette!"

"My condolences for your goddaughter," Yvette proclaims, always mindful of niceties, even in the middle of a bombing.

"Thank you. It's a painful subject for me to get into," my uncle replies under his breath, and I recognize his repugnance for bringing up personal feelings. "I'm happy to see you," he continues. "You haven't changed a bit."

"Well, neither have you. You've lost weight!"

"I've been on a diet, just a matter of getting back in shape."

Yada, yada, yada. I'm bleeding and no one gives a shit. Fortunately, Hugo and Martine arrive. Martine says she'll go tend to Laetitia; the burns are only superficial, and with Biafine, it'll be all right. She takes Laetitia into the nurse's room, muttering soothing words to her. Laetitia's crying, "I'm bald. This is horrible." Yvette takes off running, summoned by Francine's great screams. Hugo verifies that Léonard's suffered nothing more than a few contusions due to his struggle with the masked attacker.

"We'll be able to get by with what we have here," he assures us. "I'll redo your bandages, Elise."

Not a moment too soon! He passes something over my wounds that stings me horribly, then rinses my mouth with something or other that stings even more, and after some gauze and a Band-Aid, the mummy on wheels is all patched up; he leaves me to go on to Léonard. I can feel a tongue vigorously lick my hand; it's Tintin, all worked up over the smoke and excitement. I pat him on the head, and he wants to climb up on my lap, but where am I sitting? It's soft, made of leather: the sofa. Where's my wheelchair? Tintin jumps on my stomach and snuggles close.

"Are you the one who's adopted Sonia's dog?" my uncle asks in an emotional voice.

Oh, look, he remembers I exist.

"I'll go get you water. You have to drink something after a shock," he adds. "You sit down, too, Justine."

She sits down next to me. Tintin wriggles around for a caress.

"Oh, is that the dog? I thought it was your old blanket. I'm sorry," she adds, "I didn't think that . . . "

What?! You mean you didn't read in the crystal ball that serves as your brain that Vore would jump out and toss a bomb? What was he doing in the kitchen? He couldn't have been hiding there since this morning; Mrs. Raymond would have seen him. Unless Mrs. Raymond is Vore. I've got a headache. What if Lorieux were Magali's grandfather? And what if darling Francine's a heroin-addicted transvestite? My mind's open, go right ahead.

Uncle Fernand returns with two glasses of lukewarm water. I drink voraciously. He pats my head, as if I were Tintin; it's a shame I can't wag my tail for him. I can feel his corduroy pants against my arm. In a flash his image comes back to me—Uncle Fernand with his eternal corduroy pants, a poplin shirt in summer, a wool turtleneck in winter—and with him come all the scents of my childhood, the laughter, my family.

"You can't stay here," he says. "It's too dangerous. Starting tomorrow, I'm taking you to Nice. Three murders, one of which took place only this morning! And now a bomb!"

Justine coughs so hard her soul might break. I haven't got a notebook or a pen anymore. So here I am.

"How's Léonard?" my uncle goes on. He seems to be bursting at the seams with energy.

Léonard says, "Wo-kay."

"Our hero's in fine form," Hugo replies on his behalf. "By tomorrow, he'll be looking as good as new."

"If Elise hadn't broken the window, we might all be dead," Justine observes.

There are times when I like Justine.

"Elise has always been tough as leather," my uncle says, not seeming to realize how matter-of-fact he sounds.

"Mr. Andrioli, I'm sorry to interrupt these touching family moments, but if you wouldn't mind following me," Lorieux says, cutting him off.

"See you later, girls. Behave yourselves."

Tintin jumps off and follows Fernand. As the door closes, I hear my uncle's voice: "Who are you questioning first, the dog or me?"

"He's very nervous," says Justine. "He always acts silly when he's anxious."

I know, thank you. I hear approaching footsteps.

"Lae-ti—"

"She's okay. She went to lie down," Martine says. "You should, too."

Léonard grumbles something.

"It's pandemonium in the living room," Martine continues. "Clara's hiding under the table, Emilie's locked herself in the toilet, Bernard's eating his book, and Christian's jumping up and down on the couch. I haven't got the strength to make him get down."

"I'm coming," Hugo says with a sigh.

"And Francine dropped her favorite teapot."

"Now, there's a real drama!" Hugo says as he walks out, followed by Léonard and Martine.

Justine and I are alone again. Policemen are passing on the run, growling into their walkie-talkies. Even the crime-scene technicians seem disturbed by these events; they've begun hollering at each other. The smell of smoke has gotten into everything. Mixed with that of the snow, it brings to mind a romantic wood fire. I'm tired of acting like a lump, so I'm lumping it.

"Did you know that Santa Claus is really an old Scandinavian demon? That's why he's dressed in red," Justine says suddenly.

It must be fatigue, but I'm gripped by wild, nervous laughter. I hear myself bray, unable to stop, and the more Justine asks if I'm okay, the more I hiccup. Santa Claus! Rappeling down chimneys and coming out of the fireplace, with a knife between his teeth! A Communist demon, Santa Claus, coming all the way from Siberia, oh, this is making my belly hurt!

Fireplace. The fireplace! The enormous fireplace in the kitchen! That's how he got out! Vore! I grab Justine's arm and start shaking. Paper, pen, quick!

"Fernand!" Justine squawks uncertainly.

When I keep shaking her, she screams, "Fernand!" far more loudly.

"What's going on now?" Lorieux demands, half opening the door.

"Let me in," my uncle protests, forcing his way through. "I'm right here, everything's all right!"

"No, not really, Elise seems very . . . uh . . . tired," Justine mutters.

I let go of her arm and lift mine to fervently mimic the gesture of writing. Lorieux is quick on the uptake and holds out his pen and pad—finally.

The chimney duct.

"Good God!" he exclaims. "Morel, take two men and go explore the chimney. Get someone up on the roof!"

"On the roof? But it's so damn slippery with the snow."

"I don't give a shit. I want to know if someone can make it through the kitchen fireplace and if there are footprints in the snow on the roof! That's an order!"

"Pretty clever, that Elise," my uncle says. "She's always had a gift for mysteries," he adds, backing up my legend. "She always solved all the puzzles in *Mickey's Times.*"

I get the impression that Mercanti's chuckling. We all remain planted here, like strangers in a dentist's waiting room. The weird atmosphere of MRCHA in a state of siege has apparently rubbed off on my uncle already. Someone coughs nervously. Someone's cracking his fingers. Mercanti cracks his boots. Justine starts humming, "*Tombe, tombe, la neige,*" and my uncle starts to whistle "La Madelon." Without realizing it, Mercanti follows close behind— a few notes, a measure, then two. Then Lorieux gets started. By the time Morel returns he finds two blind women curled up on the couch and the three men who are supposed to give them support and comfort whistling "Come serve us something to drink" in rounds.

"Uh . . . excuse me, Chief?"

"Ah, Morel! Not a minute too soon!"

"Dupuy's fallen off the roof, Chief."

"Shit!"

"Yes, Chief, seeing that the snow is slippery, and that there's a heavy layer."

"Is he hurt?"

"No, Chief, he landed in the water tank, which was full of freezing water."

"So everything's all right, then?"

"No, Chief, because it took a minute for us to get him out, and he's all blue, and his teeth are chattering as if he had a pair of castanets in his mouth."

"Tell the women to get him some herbal tea, put him under a blanket by the fire, and soak his feet in a bucket of warm water," Lorieux orders.

"Which women, Chief?"

"The old ladies, Morel. For goodness' sake, can't you see that everyone else here is indisposed?"

Morel takes his leave.

"Halt!"

His heels screech.

"Were there any footprints on that fucking roof?"

"Yes, Chief, near the chimney top. Someone was recently walking there. The footprints went all the way to a drainpipe; in fact, it was from leaning over to see better that Dupuy—"

"That's fine. Dismissed!"

Morel runs out.

"My niece was right!" Uncle Fernand says triumphantly. "That's how your man slipped into the premises, and that's how he must have taken off after killing poor Véronique."

"You knew Véronique Gans?"

"Are you kidding? Yes, I knew Véronique Gans. Everyone did. Not such a nice girl. She got into a big fight with Sonia over Payot."

"Payot?" Lorieux repeats.

"Yes, the instructor. He liked Sonia, and Véronique didn't like that. Anyway, that hasn't got much to do with your investigation. We were talking about the chimney."

I can practically hear Lorieux grinding his teeth as he answers, "Exactly."

"The only thing," my uncle goes on pensively, "is that he couldn't have gone through the fireplace this morning while Mrs. Raymond was making breakfast. She would have seen him. He must have come in, then, before she got down to work. What time does she start?"

"Mercanti, when does the cook start in the morning?"

"Seven-thirty, Sergeant."

"Where did he hide for an hour and a half?" my uncle asks.

"He could have hidden in the staircases. No one uses them," Mercanti answers.

Or in a room. In Léonard's room; he'd gone out for a walk. In Justine's room; she didn't hear Véronique enter and steal her cigarette case from her. Besides, isn't it kind of funny to go steal something like that? And has anyone checked to see whether she took anything else? I wave my fingers and Lorieux passes back his pad. I write down my question.

"'Did anyone make sure that Véronique Gans didn't steal anything besides Justine's cigarette case?'" my uncle reads aloud. "What cigarette case? You don't smoke."

"I don't smoke anymore," Justine corrects him.

"The case you gave her," Lorieux says at the same time.

"Ah!" says my uncle.

"To tell you the truth, with all this commotion, I didn't think to make sure if anything else had disappeared," Justine explains. "Would you like to come with me, Fernie?"

Fernie! I've never heard anything more ridiculous. "Fernie-Branca"? Why not Féfé? Everyone knows that the diminutive for Fernand is Nanou; in any case, that's what my aunt called him.

Fernie and his lady love leave the room with Tintin. I dig my finger into the leather cushion as if I'm drilling a hole in it. And I'm absolutely not imagining that this could be Justine's eye. What are that liar's eyes good for, anyway? Why do I say liar? Oh, yes, the cigarette case! My uncle seemed to have fallen from the moon. Watch out, Elise, there's an important deduction in sight: if my uncle didn't offer her a cigarette case, then Véronique couldn't have stolen it from her. Yet she had it on her. There was a cigarette case on Véronique bearing my uncle's initials.

"Would you like another glass of water?" Lorieux asks, affably.

He's made me lose my train of thought! I shake my hand.

"All right, I'm going to leave you here awhile. Try to get some rest."

Okay, ciao! Where was I? Oh, yes. (a) If Véronique didn't steal Justine's cigarette case, then why did Justine make claims to the contrary? (b) Does this case belong to my uncle? (c) Why was it in Véronique Gans's possession the very morning she came to MRCHA to meet someone to whom she had "important things" to confide? (d) Did she steal it from my uncle? If she did, that brings us back to (a). (e) Did my uncle give a large silver cigarette case to Véronique Gans? (f) Am I going to wear out the entire alphabet without finding an answer?

I'll need to have a face-to-face conversation with Uncle Fernand.

I'd like to get back my wheelchair so that at least I'll be able to get around. Right now I feel like a rag doll left on a shelf. Policemen are coming and going without speaking a word to me. Ahoy! Here I am, I'm alive! Perhaps I've become invisible? A ghost. When I think how this jerk Vore claims to be . . . But why? Why?! Why! There's got to be a reason for this whole mess. No one kills people just for fun. No one throws bombs for the pleasure of it. Did he really want to get rid of us? Or, according to Jean-Claude's theory, is it all just smoke and mirrors?

Why is Tintin always following my uncle?

I try to move on the sofa; I'm ordering these fucking legs to move to the side. It's a wasted effort. Ah, I've got an idea: I'll grab onto the back with my good arm and try to hoist myself up with the strength in my wrist. Plop! I fall back down on the cushions, completely askew. I wonder what I must look like, turned over halfway, with my legs all crooked. Apparently I'm the only one interested.

12

How long have I been left to rot on this sofa? Perhaps Vore's killed everyone. Don't kid around like that, Elise. "Vore." What is this "Vore"? A concept. An abstraction. The representation of Evil. I can't even imagine a flesh-and-blood being anymore; if someone says "Vore," it's as if he's said "Bogeyman." I don't get the point of the spectacle in the kitchen. Jean-Claude's right: if this guy wanted to kill us all, it would be pretty easy. So?

Ah, someone, finally! Someone drops down onto the sofa, next to me, beside my bad hand. Someone's going to put me right side up again. Someone's not putting me right side up. Someone's breathing slowly. Exhaling tobacco. Tony's Gitanes. I start to dream that Tony's come to give me a surprise.

"There's one thing you must understand," whispers a voice I don't know; I can't tell if it belongs to a man or a woman. "There's one thing you must understand: Life is like a shit sandwich."

Then the person who smokes Gitanes gets up. His footsteps make their way to the door. Wait! The door slams shut. I remain with my nose in the cushions. I have no idea of the identity of my interlocutor. I can't quite say his cheerfulness has picked me up. What was the exact quote? "Life is like a shit sandwich—you eat a little bit of it every day." Well, there goes someone on an even kilter. I'm fed up with being stuck here! I'll tap my fingers against the wall. The door opens again. If this is to lay another lousy quote on me, I'll—

"What are you up to? Your panties are showing!" Yvette says, scolding.

So what else is new, I'm acting like a silly little girl on the sofa. Yvette grabs my wrists and goes to great pains to lift me back up.

"That frozen cop's starting to warm up," she says. "We took off his wet clothes and gave him some of Yann's pajamas. Speaking of Yann, Lorieux agreed to let him back inside, considering how cold it is. He's handcuffed to the radiator in the dining room. Funny, that. They've picked up your wheelchair, it's intact. Would you like someone to put you back in?"

I open and shut all my fingers to say yes; it's a signal Yvette and I have agreed on. We've got plenty of shortcuts like that.

"I'll go get someone."

So my unknown visitor must have had an unrestricted view of my panties. I've got to hope he wasn't too titillated by it. Or at least that this deplorable sight isn't what inspired his reflection on life!

Yvette returns with Morel, and they sit me down in my favorite seat. I feel the armrests, the wheels, with love. Oh, dear wheelchair, how happy I am to have found you again, with your pretty little buttons and your smell of steel and hospitals! You're the spirited chestnut steed who lets me prance across the world; once again Elise, the lonesome cowgirl, can take off for adventure! I'll take full advantage by slamming into the tibia of Morel, who doesn't dare complain. I'm getting facetious as I grow older. Wait until I've got Alzheimer's, too; then we'll really be whooping it up!

Yvette pushes me all the way to the dining room. In the rec room, the TV's playing cartoons. I can hear Clara laughing.

"Mrs. Raymond and Francine have gone to assess the damage," Yvette informs me. "Feeling any better, Sergeant?"

A male voice grumbles, "I'll be all right."

"I'll make you another grog."

I'll take one, too. I'm frozen stiff. I raise my hand, but Yvette ignores me. Sergeant Dupuy sniffles and sneezes every ten seconds. The fire's crackling in the fireplace. I approach the hearth. The heat is good, the smell calming. Yvette returns with grog, then leaves again, all busy. I jealously breathe in the smell of hot rum.

"Ah, there you are! We were looking for you!"

It's my uncle.

"Apparently nothing's missing from Justine's room."

Obviously. It's hard to make up something Véronique might have stolen once the police have checked her body and found nothing.

"I saw your portrait—superb! Léonard's, too—quite impressive. And the photos are nice. Who took them?"

"What photos?" Justine asks.

"What do you mean, 'What photos'? The ones you've tacked up over your bed."

"I didn't tack up any photos."

"You didn't? Maybe it was Yvette or Mrs. Atchouel. You can see Elise sitting on the terrace in her wheelchair and in front of the dining room window, behind a curtain . . . very artistic. And a redheaded girl playing with a jump rope."

"What are you talking about?" Justine says.

"The way they're centered is skillful. I don't know the red-haired girl; she's fairly pretty, about twenty years old, with magnificent hair. Strange-looking face, though . . . "

"Magali . . . ," Justine whispers. "There was a photo of Magali over my bed?"

"Elise, too, like I was just saying. Very clean. No doubt they were taken with a zoom."

A photo of me on the terrace. A photo of me behind the window. He took a photo of me before attacking me. And then he came by to post it in Justine's room, knowing she couldn't see them. What about Léonard, then? Pen.

Did Léonard see these photos?

"I've got no idea!" my uncle protests.

"What's she written?" Justine asks.

Ask Léonard.

"To do what?" my uncle retorts, perplexed.

"What are you talking about?" Justine asks, irritated.

"Oh! Two minutes, Justie, please."

Justie! "Justie and Fernie, sitting in a tree!"

"Elise wants me to ask Léonard if he's seen these fucking photos," he explains, sighing.

"Don't be crude, Fernie, it doesn't suit you. If Léonard had seen them, he would have said something about them to me, I suppose."

"Does he also ask you permission to take a piss?" my uncle quips.

"Fernie!"

"But why are you two getting so excited over these photos?"

"We've got to find out who took them," Justine replies. "Fernie, be nice and go get the photos and call over the chief sergeant."

"You're off your rocker!"

"No, I'm not off my rocker. Elise has understood me quite well. Do what I tell you, please. The redhead is certainly Magali, the girl who supposedly killed herself with a clothesline. And you're saying she's photographed with a jump rope."

"Damn! I said jump rope, but it's a plastic cord, and she's holding it in front of her, so I thought—"

"Dear, stop thinking so hard and go get the pictures."

My uncle suddenly rushes out. I cough, Justine coughs, and the policeman coughs.

"I've overheard your conversation," he tells us. "Matter of fact, you kinda wonder who might've taken those pictures, see what I mean?"

Undeniably, even policemen have a hard time expressing themselves correctly nowadays.

After sniffling and sneezing, he goes on, "There's something dirty about this environment, something isn't clean. I come from Auvergne, and I can pick up on things like these. You don't need cops here, what you need is an exorcist. Some kids died on these premises, back in the days of the sanatorium, and something like that, that always brings bad luck."

I think back to the naked doll lying around in the center when it was abandoned, and the sensation I had of being watched by an ogress.

"It's the egregores," Justine sighs, "the egregores hovering over us are very harmful. We're giving off too much anger, too much bitterness."

"When I was up on the roof, and I saw those footprints leading toward the void"—he lowers his voice—"I leaned over and saw this white face with no eyes and that black cape flapping in the wind. My heart jumped! And then that asshole Morel starts hollering, and I jumped with a start, and boom-bada-boom!"

He's silent for a moment . . . Is it to meditate on Morel and his bullshit?

"When they took me out of the water tank, I looked up and there was nothing! Nada!"

"Did you speak about this with your sergeant?" Justine inquires.

"Yes, he says it's the murderer in disguise. But I'm not sure this is a disguise. Maybe this guy's the cold wind of night taking form. Maybe he can't be caught."

Here we go. The mystic club's getting bigger.

"You know," says the sergeant, going on, "when I fell into the dark, freezing water, I felt like I was slipping into a gelatinous tunnel with a light at the end."

"No doubt you lost consciousness," Justine says, "and glimpsed a vital force."

"Maybe so, but I'm sure there was something at the bottom of the water, and who's to say I fell in by chance?"

"The murderer hid something inside the water tank?" Justine wonders aloud.

"Here are the photos," my uncle cries as he bursts in. "Where's little Lorieux?"

"I'd advise you not to speak that way about my boss," Schnabel returns as he passes on the run. "He might look like a kid, but believe me, he could really hurt you! He's a kick-boxing champion."

Too bad kick boxing is ineffective against the wind of night armed with a bolt cutter!

"Were you looking for me?" Lorieux asks.

"I found these photos in Justine's room, and she insisted I show them to you," my uncle explains to him.

"I didn't know these photos were above my bed. I knew nothing of their existence," Justine makes clear.

"Let's see . . . Elise, Elise again, Magali with—oh, no! She's in your room, Elise, I can make out the wallpaper, and she's holding a clothesline in her hand. She didn't see that someone was taking her picture, she's looking at something through the window."

"She's watching somebody?" my uncle suggests.

"Did you arrange to meet her in your room?" Justine asks.

I sweep through the air with my hand.

"Someone might have told Magali that she had to wait for Elise in her room," Lorieux mutters.

"Why would she have to bring a clothesline?" asks my uncle.

"The guy could have told her anything."

I pick up the pen: *Magali recognized Vore on TV. She thought he was my friend.*

"Yeah, that makes sense. He convinces her to go up there, joins her, takes her picture, and then kills her," Lorieux concludes in a sinister tone. "Just as he photographed Elise before attacking her. Out there, on the terrace, in broad daylight, and over there, when the French door was half open. The idiot. By the way, I was right about the disguise. Dupuy saw it hanging on the drainpipe."

"He told us he didn't manage to catch it," says Justine.

"It wasn't there anymore!" Dupuy protests.

"It must have flown off in the wind. We'll find it later on, in a tree or somewhere."

Why didn't he take the bolt cutter with him?

"Good question, Elise. Would anyone like to answer Elise?"

"What's the question?" asks Justine.

Lorieux reads it to her.

"He wanted it to be found in Christian's room," she says.

To what advantage? And then something else is bothering me: He couldn't have vanished into the fireplace disguised as a vampire after killing Véronique for the very good reason that we were all downstairs, and Mrs. Raymond was by her ovens. So he took the disguise upstairs later on. Thus the real question is, why didn't he leave it in Christian's room, along with the bolt cutter?

An idea's taking shape. He kills Véronique, stashes the murder weapon, hides the cape and mask under his sweater, takes the elevator, and comes down to join our breakfast without attracting any attention to himself, because he's one of us. Hugo, Yann, or Léonard, for example.

With all these clues crashing together like bumper cars, it feels like someone's driving a dentist's drill through my brain. I've got to stop thinking, for ten minutes at least. Two minutes. One minute, one minute of mental silence!

I can't take it anymore, I'm choking, I've got to think!

Wait, where have they all gone? They've left me alone with the hothead from Auvergne?

"Poor lady," the visionary in a kepi's saying. "Looks like it can't be too much fun for you every day. My father knew how to undo the tightest knots. Maybe he could have helped you."

If he knew some spell against Irish bombs, why not? For the time being, my little troubles are of secondary importance. What counts now is to stop the massacre. Stop playing God, says Shrink, who's really starting to bug me. I'm not trying to play God, I snap. Besides, God never stops massacres. Shrink just snarls and pulls on his beard.

Yvette, true to her nurturing nature, brings a second helping of grog to Dupuy, who greedily laps it down. I'm silently wetting my lips.

"Ah, that does a body good!" says Dupuy. "Reminds me of Mauro's."

"You knew Mauro?"

"Sure did! Just three months ago, we were still having drinks together. You know," he continues, lowering his voice again, "Mauro confided in me a secret that's got something to do with that Auvare girl."

My ears are cocked like those of a hunting dog. I bring my wheelchair closer, until I'm touching a hairy ankle and a damp blanket.

"So tell me, Dupuy, when you're finished guzzling down all the rum in the place, do you think you'd mind coming to help out?"

Schnabel's voice is rude, like a slap. Dupuy excuses himself, and gets up with great difficulty, sneezing. With a grumble into his beard he goes and gets his uniform, which Yvette has dried and ironed. I'm left hanging in the scent of rum on his breath, which marks where he stood; my jaws are chattering like a cat who just missed his bird.

Someone approaches, with an ultraclean smell. It's Mercanti, letting out a small laugh. "You remind me of a spider in the middle of a web," he remarks. "You tirelessly spin your threads, you lay your traps, and you don't give a damn at all about what the hell might happen to anyone else."

Now, that really takes my breath away! What right has he got to say that? What would he like me to do? Scream? I can't. Cry twenty-four hours a day? That I could do, but the fact is, it's just not my temperament. The passion for tomorrow always wins out over today's sadness.

"But that's not important," he goes on, laying his frozen hand on the nape of my neck, "I like stubborn little creatures better. Getting them to bend is more enjoyable."

Beyond taking my breath away, what is it about him?

"With the cold, your blouse is very suggestive," he whispers again. "It could give some ideas to people with ill intentions."

My blouse. I can feel my nipples, hard from the cold—damn! I'm fumbling with the buttons; obviously one of them's open, and I clumsily close it, but he places his hand over mine and uses it to stroke viciously.

"There, there, let me help you. You're a very proper little girl, buttoned up and all."

If someone doesn't get this guy away from me, I'm going to vomit. Fortunately Yann's calling from the other room.

"Shit! I'm dying of thirst. Give me something to drink, damn it!"

"Duty calls. See you later, pretty little doll!"

He goes away, but not before dragging his long, frozen fingers over my mouth. This guy sends shivers down my spine. There's an inaudible conversation on the other side of the partition. I hope he's not going to beat Yann to a pulp. Tintin starts growling, low and dull, and Yann orders him to be quiet. Mercanti's footsteps rapidly fade in the distance.

I move my wheelchair forward to the door, cast about for the knob, and give it a turn: nothing. I'm locked in! Panic's starting to get the better of me. I tap against the doorframe. No one's coming. I'll tap some more.

"Why on earth would you want to go into the pantry?" Yvette asks suddenly, in a tired voice.

All my bearings have disappeared. I'm too flustered, I've got to calm down. I let her bring me over to the fireplace and pull a sweater over my head while sharing her worries with me. It's been a short while since night has fallen, and the police are going to set up a guard, and so on. You'd think we were in a war movie.

"Your uncle's outside with Justine," Yvette continues, an uninterrupted stream of words. "They needed some air. The police are searching the premises for the murderer's disguise. The boys from the lab have dusted the whole kitchen with their whatsit and now we've got to clean up everything. The residents have gathered in the rec room with Martine and Hugo—even Laetitia. Lorieux didn't want her to stay all by herself in her room. She's got this big bandage around her head, like a turban. You'd think she was a Hindu!"

I'm wondering what the hell Mauro's secret could be concerning Sonia. Was she in fact his own daughter? Or a child someone left in his care?

"Just a minute ago, I was saying to myself we might have done better to go to the northern Alps instead, but when I see all those avalanches," Yvette continues, "we might have been buried under snow or burned alive in a tunnel of fire. Deep down, I think it's just as well we've come here. At least we know we're in danger, while all those poor people were hit just like that—*pow!*— without expecting it. Must have been terrible."

Now, there's someone with a positive outlook!

"I'll be leaving you; I'm gonna help Mrs. Raymond. She's not too keen about staying all alone in her kitchen," Yvette adds in a low voice.

Yvette leaves and Francine enters. A whole new stream of words.

"I can't take it anymore," she begins, letting herself fall onto the sofa, which whines back. "What a horrible day it's been! I should have figured it would turn out so rotten after Yvette won last night. I'm ruined! And then all these hussars running around through my establishment! Lucky for you, you can't see any of this. It's enough to make you scream! There's hardly any difference between this and locking us in the basement with one ration of bread and water per person. To think they could suspect poor Christian! Even Clara! Why not me while they're at it? They'd do better to worry about Yann. That's what I've said from the start. Anyway, I hope your uncle will get them to listen to reason. How about some tea? I've put some water on to boil. Like I always say, you can't let yourself get run down!"

Exit the tea bearer. I turn my head from right to left, wondering whom I'm facing.

"Someone used a portable, battery-powered electric drill to let the air out of the tires."

Now it's Lorieux.

"We've just found it. Guess where. In the water tank. Dupuy remembered seeing something shiny at the bottom of the water. We spent an hour fishing it out with some line we improvised. You know what? I'm sure that's what he used to crucify Marion Hennequin. Why would he have hidden it here? Because the owner lives here. Everything brings us back to this fucking center. The answer's here, somewhere within these walls. Starting tomorrow, I'm sealing off everything and everyone. It's going to the police in Entrevaux. I'm going to ask to be relieved of this investigation, and I'm passing this baby on to my successor. Then I'm off to the Balearic Islands for fifteen days."

Then he gets up and leaves. What the hell time is it? I'm not hungry, but that doesn't mean anything: I'm not that hungry at just this moment. Tintin's barking in the room next door, and Yann raises his voice: "Is anybody there?"

I roll toward him, with the sound of his voice as my guide.

"Elise! I'm so happy to see you."

I approach until I'm touching him, and hold out my hand. He takes it and holds it in his, which are handcuffed.

"You're really kind. I'm going to press charges for police brutality. They haven't got the right to hit me and keep me chained up. It cracks me up that someone let the air out of their tires while I was locked up like an animal in their lousy van. And what about the bomb? Was I the one who threw it, perhaps? They haven't got any reason to treat me this way anymore!"

"There's someone else here who thinks otherwise," says Lorieux, who has returned without my hearing him.

"Payot!" Yann exclaims. "What the hell are you doing here?"

"He came by ski," Lorieux explains. "He found Véronique's diary in his laundry basket."

"You son of a bitch," Payot suddenly yells, as though he could no longer control himself, "you were really making a fool out of me!"

"I don't understand . . . ," Yann protests, without much conviction.

"I know everything, do you hear me? How many times, and when, and how! She wrote it all down!"

"Listen, Hervé, don't start dramatizing this!"

"I'm not dramatizing anything. You were doing it with Véronique behind my back! You screwed Sonia and she's dead, and now it's Véro's turn!"

"What did you say about Sonia?" Lorieux inquires, in an undertaker's voice.

"Bullshit!" Yann answers. "This is nothing but bullshit."

"Bullshit? Tell me right now Véronique was a liar!"

"A junkie and a liar!" Yann shouts, scornfully.

"What?! You hear that?! I happen to know a couple of things myself!"

While they're hollering at each other, I grab my pen: *Does Véronique talk about her hospital stay?*

"Yes, she talks about it," Payot screams after Lorieux reads him the question. "It's even in there how she met that jerk, that jerk over there! She talks about Sonia, who often used to come to see her cousin, Marion Hennequin. And that son of a bitch, you think he didn't know Marion? Did you do her as well? Huh?"

"It looks like you're all suffering from an ego problem here," Yann quips.

"I oughta break your face!" Payot screams.

"What's going on?" my uncle asks. "We can hear you screaming all the way in the rec room."

"Hervé Payot is a friend of Véronique Gans," Lorieux tells him, as if that explains everything.

"Véronique was a very impetuous young girl," my uncle says.

"I thought you barely knew her?" Lorieux says, astonished.

"I met her when I was going to see Sonia, while she was in rehab. Véronique was still coming for psychotherapy."

I thought it was the other way around.

"Did you also know Marion Hennequin?" Lorieux asks, following a sudden prolonged silence.

"Yes, I knew Marion," my uncle says, his voice cracking. "Poor, poor little things. It's all so absurd!"

"What's so absurd?" Lorieux suddenly lets out. "That you killed them?"

"Killed them? What do you think? That I would go and kill my own daughter!" my uncle screams.

Sonia! There it is! That's the secret!

"But you don't have children!" Yvette exclaims, just entering the room.

"What do you know?" he shoots back. "My wife was sterile, and I . . . I happened to be a womanizer," my uncle mutters. "I couldn't resist a pretty woman—excuse me, Justie—so sometimes . . . there were some mistakes, you know."

"Some?!" Lorieux presses.

"They weren't taking the pill like they are today!" my uncle protests. "And condoms, for me, that's . . . "

"Fernie! Why don't you discuss all this with the sergeant in private?" Justine suggests firmly.

"You're right."

"Shit. For once, this was starting to get good," Yann cries.

"Son of a bitch!" Payot repeats. "You won't be laughing so much once I speak to the sergeant!"

"Calm down!" Lorieux orders. "Morel, release the suspect, give him something to drink, and watch him. Payot, follow us. I've got some questions for you."

A door slams shut.

SHOULD'VE THOUGHT of that!" Francine says when the quiet returns. "Such a proper man . . . "

"That's all men think about," Yvette proclaims. "Well . . . not my Jean, of course."

"You have my condolences!" Yann shouts. "My hands are completely numb here! Would someone get me a glass of water?"

I'm listening to them distractedly. My uncle is Sonia's father. Okay. Then who's her mother? Justine? No, Justine would have no reason to abandon her child; she's single and cares little about what people might say. A married woman, then.

"With all this, when do we get to eat?" Francine laments. "I feel like making a special dinner for the residents."

"Better wait for the sergeant's orders," Morel replies.

"Oh, don't be ridiculous, young man. I'm not going to wait for his permission to feed my guests!"

"From what I understand, you're all under arrest! So starting now, button it!"

"'Button it'?" Francine repeats. "Button what?"

"What he means is 'Button your lip'!" Yann explains.

"Oh, please! I'm not letting myself be intimidated by some country cop!" Francine cries. "Over to the kitchen, everybody with me!"

She bounds toward the kitchen, followed by Yann, who's delighted by the insurrection, Yvette, and the residents, who are all happy to be running, all while Morel calls for help. Mercanti and Schnabel show up.

"Listen, buddy, if you bother us one more time for some bullshit like this, I swear you'll be heading back to finish up your vocational training certificate!" Schnabel snaps after listening to Morel. "And put away that gun, it's not made out of chocolate!"

"These days you can't find the right people," Mercanti comments. "Everything okay, Elise?"

In my lap, my fist is clutched tight. He's raising my chin with his hand, which reeks of scouring powder.

"You seem tired. Would you like me to help you into bed?"

I'd rather die. I shake my head to free myself, but his fingers tighten their grip.

"The sergeant's waiting!" Schnabel yells. "Get a move on."

He lets go of me, as if he regretted it, and in a voice too low for Schnabel to hear murmurs, "Okay, you fat pig, I'm coming." This guy's making me sick. I'm going to ask Yvette if I can sleep in her room.

While the insurgents are kicking up a joyful racket in the kitchen, Morel's pacing back and forth, muttering things through his teeth. Too bad I haven't got a rubber ball to toss his way. That might keep him busy.

But something's bugging me. Something I ought to remember. Snatches of sentences. Lorieux speaking to me about Marion? Or was it Yann? No, right at the start of the investigation, it was Lorieux: "I was saying simply that you offer a certain resemblance to the victim. The color of your hair, your eyes, your silhouette . . . " And then there was Yann: "In fact, I think you look more like Sonia. Besides, it's funny, but Sonia resembled Marion a lot." Why am I thinking about the resemblance between Sonia and Marion? Between Sonia, Marion, and me. Sonia is the daughter of my uncle. My uncle and . . . Yes! I snatch up my pen.

Heels are clacking, and two people arrive. Morel rushes over, shouting, "Chief! Chief!" Lorieux listens for five seconds, then tells him to go outside to see if he's there. Morel steps out, happy to have a mission.

"Elise, we've made some progress," Lorieux says. "Payot's waiting for me in Mrs. Atchouel's office, so I'll be as brief as possible. Your uncle has admitted to quite a few things . . . "

Before he can finish his sentence, I proudly brandish my notepad for him: *Sonia was Marion's sister.*

"How did you know that?" my uncle asks, stupefied.

"How does she know what?" Justine wants to know, sounding suspicious.

He doesn't answer. Quickly I scrawl, *My deduction. Sonia resembles Marion*

because they have the same mother. But Sonia resembles me, too, and I resemble
you, so . . .

"This girl will always amaze me!" my uncle calls out to no one in particular. "Yes, it's true, I had an adventure with Marcelle, uh . . . I mean Mrs.
Gastaldi, when she got married. In fact, she was pregnant with Marion. That
went all right—neither seen nor heard, as they say—but then her husband
had some serious prostate problems, and unfortunately she became pregnant
again, with Sonia this time, and it couldn't be his, and she didn't want to
abort—"

"What?" Justine shouts. "What are you telling us, Fernie?!"

"Remember, Justie, the world was a lot different then!" my uncle answers.
"Marcelle was a respectable woman in a small town in the hinterlands, mar-
ried to a rich, powerful man, okay? Marcelle went to 'take her waters,'" my
uncle goes on, "and then she just abandoned the baby, under the name of X.
I . . . it was my baby all the same, and I recognized her and entrusted her to
Mauro. So there."

"So there?" Justine repeats. "But, Fernie . . . "

"No, not 'so there,'" Lorieux says in his sharp voice. "Continue."

"It all happened nearly thirty years ago. Things weren't going so well
between your aunt and me, Elise. I had . . . uh . . . relations with more than
a few women."

No so well? I remember them as a close-knit couple, always in agreement.
"Now, Huguette's a lucky woman," Mom always used to say. "Fernand treats
her like a little queen." She wasn't so much a little queen as a woman who
was cuckolded to the marrow, Mother dear. Suddenly the idea comes to me
that Mom and Fernand might have . . . unbeknownst to Dad, and that I . . .
My heart's pounding, but no, cut out the moviemaking, Elise; this need of
yours to always be a heroine is a bit ridiculous!

Fernand continues, "It's a little complicated. To make a long story short,
about ten years ago I met Justine; I was a widower, a bit wiser in my old age,
and things went well between us, so we became good friends. Last year she
made a trip to Venice in the company of some people who were physically
challenged, and when she got back, she informed me of a rumor going
around to the effect that I'm the founder of MRCHA, and that I have a son
who lives here!"

I raise my arm, but my uncle lowers it for me.

"I'm getting to it. Yes, I'm the founder of the center, and, yes, I insisted on remaining anonymous. You'll understand why, Elise. I received a letter one day—a very simple letter telling me I had a son. The mother, who at the time was very young, tried to give birth all alone, under the conditions you might imagine. They were able to save him, but he remained handicapped. There was a problem with his brain, I never really knew, she refused to ever see me again or tell me the child's name. For me it was quite a realization, I was really distraught, and I decided to correct my wrongdoing however I could."

My head's spinning. With all these kids leaping out of thin air like rabbits out of a hat, and my uncle their tormented progenitor, and hundreds of cousins with black hair and my distinguished nose, does anybody really care about me anymore?

"And I'm told that this son is here now!"

"Hmm," says Lorieux, apparently warmed by this dark family saga, "excuse me, but I've got to go back and see Payot."

"Where was I?" my uncle wonders aloud (and I understand). "Oh, yes," he continues, "I was up to MRCHA. Mrs. Atchouel thinks I'm just a generous donor, and I'd prefer it to stay that way. I'm not too keen on coming forward, you understand?"

That's right, you've already put enough into it that way. Elise! Shrink thunders. Mea culpa. But what about this boy? I've got my own little ideas on that matter.

"Exactly how many children do you have?" Justine asks in a shrill voice.

"Uh . . . I don't know. Listen, Justie, I never wanted to bore you with my family stories . . . "

"I realize by now that there must be some really wild ones!" she explodes. "You'd think it was a bad pulp novel. All these secrets!"

"There's no reason for them to be secrets now that my poor Sonia is no more!" my uncle finishes, wearily.

I can imagine him with his head in his hands, full of dark reflections. Justine's tapping nervously against the marble pedestal, quite far from her Zen fullness. People are busily passing by. Jean-Claude's camera is humming. He shouldn't miss a speck of this. This must be a real change from those wildlife films. Still, here like anywhere else, it's always the law of the jungle. "Human beings are not animals, Elise!" Shrink asserts. Yeah, well, that's a pity, because other mammals don't kill each other, do they?

Someone bumps into me without saying sorry, as if I were a piece of furniture.

"You knocked something over, Elise," my uncle says suddenly.

I fumble around; oh, yes, my notebook's not here anymore. I hear him bending over and picking it up.

What's he doing? Ah, he must be reading my notes. He's clearing his throat. He must understand the extent to which we're living in a nightmare.

"Ah!" he exclaims. "Well, uh . . . "

He suddenly cuts himself off. Morel's just come in—I can recognize his youthful footsteps.

"What is it, Fernie?" Justine inquires.

"Nothing, nothing," my uncle grumbles.

"Don't mind me," Morel calls out. "Apparently I don't count for much around here! I'm just an auxiliary police officer," he adds, "and I really don't give a crap!"

"The problem here is all these negative energies," Justine whispers to me. "It keeps me from seeing through the shadows. You really should eat something, Fernie," she says aloud, "and bring back a sandwich for Elise."

He heads off, muttering, "What a mess—no, really, what a big mess this is!" followed by Morel, who's asking him questions about his career as a professional entrepreneur. Justine puts her hand on my arm.

"Now I understand why he wanted me to discover who his son was! When he found out that the Gastaldi daughter was murdered, he must have been shocked, but when he found out that Sonia, too . . . the coincidence was too enormous! Two sisters, in the same region! And his son—right here!"

Was he afraid someone might kill his son as well? Or that . . . The answer hits me like a tons of bricks: who would profit from this crime? The last surviving relative, whoever that may be. To him would go the Gastaldis' two million francs, through Marion and her sister Sonia, and therefore . . .

"It's horrid," says Justine, suddenly, "but now I'm telling myself that Marion was the Gastaldis' only heiress, that she had no family aside from Sonia, and that Sonia herself had no family aside from this half brother, whom Fernand's spoken of. I hope he's not—"

She leaves the sentence hanging.

In my head, I'll finish it for her: a murderer.

But if in fact it is Léonard they're talking about, and if he really isn't well, then how could he have committed these crimes? Marion was killed in Digne, and Sonia in the basement of the nightclub. I'm rapidly writing down the question—but damn, she can't read it, and I'm stuck here with my paper in hand, going over this and a thousand other questions.

Nothing's holding up.

And I'm finding that my uncle's showing very little sorrow over the murder of what turns out to be his own daughters!

The idea that he's lying has occurred to me, but I really can't see the point in coming up with such a device. Justine's having difficulty breathing. She must be having a hard time digesting the news.

I feel a bit strange, as if I were drugged. That happened to me only once, in Boissy, when I was carried off by that child killer. It's the same gritty feeling in my mouth and the impression that everything's mixed and muddled. Something's not quite right. *Everything's* not quite right.

"You'd think it was bright and sunny," Justine says, all of a sudden.

It's true. I feel something hot beaming down on my shoulders. Is the storm finally over?

But there's no sunlight at seven or eight in the evening.

"I'm wondering what Fernie's up to. Where've they all gone?"

I think I've just heard someone laugh. Justine must have heard the same thing, because I sense her pivoting briskly.

"Is someone there?"

As usual, there's no answer. I grab her arm and tap on her voice watch. I've got to remember to tell Yvette to buy me one like that.

"You want to know the time?"

She presses the small button and the watch coos, "Eight-two and four seconds," with a Japanese accent.

"My God! Already!" Justine exclaims.

Wake up, Justie, there's no sunlight at eight! The cops must have turned on the floodlights. They've got to be looking for Vore's disguise. But why are the floodlights trained inside the building?

"Wait here, I'm going to see what Fernand's doing," she continues.

You're talking like I'm going to wait here all by myself. I grip her arm, forcing her to drag me forward as she advances.

"Let go of me, will you! I can't pull you, this is ridiculous. I need both my hands to find my way."

Someone's laughing again. Well, now I'm really scared to death.

Justine's trying to get loose, while I'm tightening my grip; my hand feels like an eagle's claw around a lamb's thigh.

"Fernand!" she bleats as she starts running ahead.

My wheelchair jolts back, and I go bumping against all sorts of things; so does Justine. "Fernand, Fernand!" But there's no Fernand. Justine takes a tight turn, sending the wheelchair toppling over; I let go of her and fly off-course like an arrow into the scenery.

Bang! Something falls on top of me; something burning—it's a lamp; someone screams, "Watch out!" and pushes me back, and I can hear glass breaking. "You really do nothing but foolishness!" Mercanti says, letting his dirty fingers run over my chest. I hear myself crying, "Uncle!" in silence, and suddenly the image of Mercanti raping and killing Marion and Sonia seems horribly realistic.

He steps up his fondling, as I remain powerless, openmouthed in my silence; he's going to abuse me, right here, while everyone else is in the kitchen stuffing their faces and the cops are running around outside. I manage to get my hand free and raise it, extending my index and middle fingers. In a split second it thuds against his face. I grab his nose and press hard while he growls, "You cunt!" I've located his eyes and let go of his nose, and my stiff little fingers go bursting toward his eyeballs; they make contact with something soft, and he screams, grabs my wrist, and twists violently, but this is nuts! Footsteps, two men arrive quickly. "Stop it!" Schnabel suddenly screams. "Stop it immediately! Have you lost your mind or what?" With all my strength, I'm thinking "unfortunate accident": Schnabel inadvertently pulls the trigger on his gun and sends two bullets into that bastard Mercanti's knees. Keep dreaming!

"I oughta break your face!" Schnabel adds when it's quiet again.

"What's going on?" murmurs the cop who's with him.

"Schnabel! Fazzi!" Dupuy suddenly calls from outside. "Come have a look! Quick!"

"You've got nothing to lose if you wait!" Schnabel calls back before he runs out with Fazzi.

"Oh, you're bleeding again. It's reopened," Francine states. "I'll tell Martine."

"What's the matter?" Martine asks, as if it were exactly what she was expecting.

I don't listen to Francine's answer. I listen instead to a sound I know all too well: the humming of Jean-Claude's camera. Why do the cops let him film all this? Something's trying to leap out of my muddled brain, something I know yet don't know. I let Martine manipulate me without reacting, while in my mind I'm busily trying to squeeze the gray matter to make the truth jump out.

Crashhhh! I startle, and so does Martine.

"It's the lights!" Francine cries.

"Everything's blown up!" Yann answers from a distance.

"It's got to be because of the storm," Lorieux shouts from a nearby room. "Hey, out there, is there any light coming from the village?"

"Nothing, Chief!" Morel screams.

Outside, I hear Schnabel hollering at Dupuy: "So where's the fucking cape, Alphonse?"

"It's flown off again!"

"Schnabel, have we got any emergency lights in the van?" Lorieux shouts as he walks into the room.

"I'll go see!" Schnabel answers through the window.

"What are you doing?" Martine asks in a low voice. I don't know who she's talking to.

"We're stopping awhile," Mercanti answers, in the same tone of voice.

"This is really rotten luck," says Francine.

That remark doesn't sound like Francine. Suddenly I feel like being close to Yvette, to my uncle, and even to Justine, because I think I'm losing my head. I hear voices, I'm imagining absurd dialogues, I'm going crazy.

I'm listening as they bustle about in the darkness, when suddenly a chorus of "Ayyys" breaks out. Sighted people panic quickly in the dark. For someone like me, who's in a perpetual state of blackout, nothing changes.

"What should I do with the others?" Martine asks.

"Nothing for now," Mercanti answers. "She almost took my eye out, that cunt," he adds in a loud, intelligible voice.

Are these auditory hallucinations? I grip the armrest on my wheelchair. It seems real.

"Well, in any case, we're almost finished," says Mercanti. "We'll see the rest tomorrow."

Someone grabs hold of my wheelchair and pushes me forward. If this is Mercanti . . .

"What a madhouse!" whispers the voice that smokes Gitanes, placing my wheelchair against a wall.

"Here's a flashlight, Chief!" Schnabel calls out in his powerful voice. "I've tried GPHS," he continues, articulating carefully. "I was able to call the barracks. The road is open again for special vehicles; they're sending us backup. They'll be here during the night."

These words are followed by silence. Lorieux's shoes go *tap-tap*.

"Okay, get the men together, give them something to eat, and then we'll organize guard shifts. Mercanti, go tell Mrs. Raymond to prepare something for them."

"In the dark?" Mercanti replies insolently.

"She's got a storm lantern and some candles, so that ought to do."

"Okay," Mercanti grumbles as he walks out.

Wow, good riddance!

"I'll be back," says Lorieux, turning on his heels.

A lighter clicks, someone breathes in, and it smells like Gitanes. The man next to me is smoking.

"What are we going to do now?" he asks, without my knowing whom he's addressing.

"We'll do whatever's necessary," Martine answers, closing the double-sash window. "Would you put out that cancer stick? You're making a perfect target."

"A target for whom?" my neighbor asks, surprised.

"Have you forgotten that there's some psychopath on the loose?"

"He only attacks women," the smoker replies nonchalantly.

"God only knows what's in the future."

"That's understood!" the man growls, sullenly.

Here's somebody who doesn't seem traumatized. And Martine seems to be on familiar terms with him! Why haven't my uncle and Justine returned?

And what's Jean-Claude up to? I've heard his camera, but he hasn't uttered so much as a peep.

"Ah, the lights are back on!" Martine exclaims joyfully. "Hallelujah!"

I hear a series of detonations. Outside. Like an exhaust pipe backfiring. But exhaust pipes don't cry out. Did I really hear crying out? The storm's making such a racket that it's smothering everything. Am I the only one who's heard someone cry out?

"Everything's all right," Mercanti calls out, cracking open the door. "Schnabel's trying to get the van started."

Oh, it's so phony, the way he says that! I'm sure he's lying. Something happened outside, something serious. Did I hear gunshots? But if that were so, why would Mercanti lie? . . . Unless . . . Oh, my God! What if it's him, what if he's Vore, what if he's the one who killed them all?! My pen, quick.

"'Are you sure about Mercanti?'" the smoker reads over my shoulder.

Damn.

"Sure I'm sure!" he replies. "I've known him for four years! He's solid, that Mercanti, you can count on him."

No, you're mistaken, he's a vicious liar! But how can I prove that? If I write *Mercanti felt me up,* I can already imagine the comments: "She's dreaming, the homely thing! Hasn't she seen what she looks like?" All those niceties of our macho world.

The door flies open, letting in a gust of icy air, and a few flakes drift over to me.

"Everything's in order," says Mercanti, his voice sounding poised, quite different from the one he used with me.

"What about Léonard?"

"He's in his room."

So they suspect Léonard.

"When is our backup supposed to show up?" Mercanti asks again.

"During the night, three or four hours from now, I think; they've slowed to a crawl, with all this ice and snow."

They're having a little consultation, speaking in muffled tones. It's no use cocking my ear; I can't hear a thing. My neighbor's joints crack as he stretches, then to no one in particular he calls out: "How about we get a bite to eat? After this, we're not going to have any time."

They pass in front of me, toward the kitchen. I'm listening attentively but can't make out any presence in the room. Apparently, I'm alone. I finger the button on the wheelchair and slowly advance along the wall, coming to a halt once I encounter some obstacle. If one follows a wall, one will have to arrive at a door. Then the hallway. And then the front door.

My shoulders tense with the expectation that a hand will be placed on them while a hateful voice says, "Yoohoo!" But I'm rolling through the hallway without a hitch. About another yard left, then half a yard, and then I hold out my hand to open the door, but I shouldn't have bothered—it's ajar, blowing back and forth in the irregular puffs of wind. I push aside the storm door and take the ramp made specially for wheelchairs; the wind blasts me, whipping me with whirling masses, but the cold does me good after the confined atmosphere inside the house.

Once I've reached the bottom of the ramp, I hesitate. I can hear nothing except the roar of the wind through the woods. My wheelchair's advancing with difficulty over the layer of fresh snow, which won't stop growing. I don't quite know where to go but I'm moving straight ahead. There's no sound of voices. Where are the men who are standing guard? Suddenly I feel the urge to urinate, and my hair is standing on end. I know this sensation. It's fear. Real fear. Fear of heading into the dark, knowing a monster's waiting for you there.

Ahhh! Someone's just touched me! A big, wet hand! I let out a scream no one can hear. The hand softly slides along my neck, down my shoulder—is this Mercanti?—then moves aside; a great, panting mass drops beside me, blocking the wheelchair.

I lean forward as far as I can. My fingers brush against rough, wet cloth, decorated with buttons. It's a pea coat. Don't panic, stay calm. It's a pea coat covering a man's torso. A pea coat with holes in it; my fingers are grasping the tattered edges of cloth, and a damp flow of something that smells of copper floods down my face. Oh, my God! It's blood, a geyser of blood, spraying me—there's nothing I can do to avoid it. I shake my head crazily; the blood's dripping, it's hot, so hot, giving me spasms of terror. I seem to be peeing on myself, unable to hold it in anymore, and while hot urine's running down my thighs, and hot blood runs down my cheeks, I finally manage to back up!

But no, I've got to see if the man's alive. I advance again and, as best as I can, place myself diagonally to him. My heart hurts from beating so hard, but come on, fingers, be brave: There's the pea coat, a massive chest, a fleshy chin, and a thick moustache, like wet dog hair. Schnabel!

I touch his lips. No breath, not even the slightest. Someone's killed Schnabel! He's just died, right here, before my useless eyes! Stupidly I stick my fingers into his breathless mouth, touch his teeth and tongue, but I get an absurd sensation that the mouth might bite so I quickly remove my fingers. The mouth doesn't bite any more than it breathes.

Retreat! Go warn Lorieux! I back up, pivot my wheelchair around, and slowly advance. Now I can distinguish the smell of metal from the gas from the van. And the odor of blood. I let my hand drag against the wheel. They're under my fingers. Bodies. Tangled. At least five or six. Lorieux's brigade.

Oh, no! They can't all be dead! I'm all alone with them. Is somebody watching me, is the barrel of a pistol pointed toward my head? I've got goose flesh and bristling hair. I've got to get back to the center, quickly, shit, I've made a mistake, the wheelchair bounds forward—yikes! I've just collided with some new obstacle—something that's leaped back up, bumped against my knees, and remained there, leaning upon them.

I stick out my hand. Then pull it back, as if I'd plunged it into a nest of spiders. I've just touched hair. This is a head—leaning against my motionless knees.

Feeling repulsion, I raise it to move it aside, and it says, "A pity . . . Just wanted to find . . . job . . . "

It's Morel! Morel's alive!

I hold him by the hair, as if his head has been cut off, and his tremblings reverberate in my hand; I don't know if I should let him go; what should I do?

" . . . Should have stayed in technical school," Morel says again.

Then, sobbing, he adds, "Mama!"

He drools some liquid into my lap that soaks the blanket, and I feel tears running down my cheeks—are these tears of fear, distress, or compassion? I don't know. I know he's going to die. Someone's got to help me, and I can't call out, nor can I leave him. Leave him? To go look for help? "Mama!" Morel repeats, then he goes silent, gets all soft, and falls back down with a clang, certainly against the van.

Snow seems to be falling inside me, filling me, piling up, turning hard—dangerously hard. The smell of fresh blood and dead men is mingling with the ozone scent of snow. I no longer feel my soiled thighs or the layer of blood on my skin; all I can feel now is an immense anger taking over me.

Someone's just killed these men. Mercanti?

"You really are too curious," someone says quite affably, as in answer to my question.

But this isn't Mercanti. It's Dupuy, the brave Auvergne man.

A metallic object presses against my temple. The barrel of an automatic pistol?

"This gun isn't supernatural," he says into my ear. "Did you like that little conversation we were just having?"

To think Dupuy is Vore. The fact that he more than adequately pulled the wool over my eyes puts me beside myself even more. Of course he found the drill; he's the one who stashed it in the water tank! He must have really had a laugh with all that talk of a disguise on the roof! Suddenly a sentence returns like a slap in the face: "Just three months ago, we were still having drinks together!" Three months ago, old Mauro was dead. I'm too stupid!

"Old Mauro's secret," he whispers. "You know what it is? He was a lecher! The old pig used to screw his sheep. Come to think of it," he adds, "you're a bit like a sheep: panic stricken, and you can't defend yourself."

He's passing the barrel of his weapon over my nose and chin—go on, have your fun. Unseen I tighten my fist against the wheel of the chair in frustration—I'd like to clock him! But there's something against the wheel. Leather under my phalanges. Leather. Damp cloth. A body.

He forces me to open my lips and shoves the barrel of his weapon between my gritted teeth; what kind of effect would a bullet have, fired at point-blank range, inside the mouth? A bullet digging its way through the palate, pulverizing the brain; would anyone even realize what happened? I feel the cold steel against my lips. "Suck it," he says. "Suck or I'll shoot." You weirdo! Weirdo!

My hand's fumbling over the body sprawled at my feet . . . that's leather—a belt; I'm sucking on the cold metal; my fingers are running along the leather, inch by inch—there! A grip, solid and rigid. Come on, fingers, put yourselves around it, take it out of its holster, there you go. "Oh, that's good; my, but you're very well behaved!" Dupuy says. Come on, index finger, slide under the trigger, yes, like that.

His pants unzip. "You know what? I think you're going to show me what you can do!" Oh, yes, you're going to see just how much I know. He puts aside his weapon, no longer thinking it necessary to point it against my head. I hear him put it down. He's breathing fast and heavy; he grabs me by the back of my neck, brutally digging his fingers into my hair and pulling me toward him; his warm flesh, smelling of sweat, is pressed against my lips; my index finger's on the trigger; I raise my hand along my hip, bend my elbow up at a right angle; the cold steel brushes his hot, naked testicles; he jumps—too late, Sergeant!

There's a strange sensation about this fraction of a second when I spring into action. And this action already belongs to the past.

He screams. Like Sonia on the answering machine. Like Marion in the squat. The smell of gunpowder is suffocating. Certainly his cries will attract someone. I listen without emotion; I'm hoping he'll die. I didn't know I was so cruel. I didn't know I was capable of being deaf to screams of suffering. He collapses, groaning. Perhaps he might shoot me; I back up six feet and pivot around: I've got to get back to the house before he gets his bearings back.

"What . . . what the . . . ," people stammer as soon as I make it to the door. What does that mean?

Lorieux.

I can hear him running, racing over to where all the bodies are piled up. A few more seconds go by, and Dupuy's still wailing.

"They're all dead! All dead!" Lorieux lets out, stupefied. "All except Dupuy . . ."

"Good grief!" cries someone else who's just leaped up beside us.

It's Mercanti.

He runs over and gets in my way, shouting, "She's gone mad!"

Oh, no! No! Quick, my pen. I put the weapon in my lap so that I can write. *Dupuy is Vore!*

Lorieux clears his throat: "Give me that weapon, you might hurt someone," he says, picking it up.

He attacked me! He killed them all!

I don't know if he's read it, because he mutters, "Schnabel, little Morel, and everyone else, my God! I can't believe it!"

Anyway, he won't believe that . . . How could I? The first blind shooting champ!

I can hear Mercanti speaking comforting words to Dupuy: "Hold on, we're gonna take care of you, it's gonna be all right."

"I'm gonna die," Dupuy answers, "and this bitch killed me!"

"What's got into you?" Lorieux asks. "What's got into you?"

Can't he see the mass grave right before his eyes? I'm pressing down so hard that the pen tears through the paper.

Dupuy killed your men! HE'S VORE!

"I've got to warn Martine!" Mercanti cries. "He's bleeding to death!"

Lorieux takes off running, leaving me planted under the snow to listen to Dupuy die. There's a big commotion behind me. Someone shoves me aside. I can hear Martine's frenzied voice: "We've got to make a tourniquet!"

Laetitia's voice comes from inside: "So?"

"So Elise shot Dupuy!" Mercanti answers, sounding morose.

"Is he seriously hurt?"

"He's a goner."

Dupuy's not crying out anymore. Only a few seconds of silence. Then Martine says, "He's gone to meet his Creator . . ."

I've just killed a man. This is the first time I've killed a human being. Perhaps the absence of vision reduces sensibility. Perhaps if I'd seen him die, I might have felt like vomiting or crying. But I feel as cold and dry as a Larzac stone.

I hear the sound of the body as they drag it away. As they throw it on top of the others. It's a sad field of honor for police officers fallen in the line of duty. Dupuy does not belong.

It smells like Gitanes. The smoker comes up the front steps; I can hear his cigarette crackling. More footsteps follow, and then I hear Martine's voice: "Poor Dupuy! He was so cheerful!"

And what about those guys there, lying on the ground. Weren't they cheerful? Are you an asshole or what?!

"Why did he seem suspect?" she continues.

"Suckspet, sucks pets, suck pets, suck and pet!"

"Oh, shut up!" she shouts at Christian.

I didn't hear him come in. Why did Dupuy seem suspect? Well, let's just say there was a pile of bodies on the ground, and Dupuy was armed and threatening me, so by some unexplainable mental aberration, I found him a bit suspect!

"Keep an eye on her," Martine adds, without waiting for an answer from me. "I should be back."

Keep an eye on me? Now, that takes the cake! I sit seething with indignation, in the company of a guy who's smoking and Christian, in the relative shelter of the leaded-glass awning.

Mercanti's busying himself with I don't know what. It's curious that no one else has come to see what's going on. Lorieux no doubt forbade all the residents to leave. It would make no sense to traumatize them further. Christian must have threaded his way out. Surprisingly, he's staying calm. A match crackles, followed by a cloud of nicotine.

Someone's whistling "Marinella," the first measures.

"'Marinella, I took your legs for your arms, and when I found out—"

"Had my mouth on your ass!" Christian blurts out.

The whistler goes on, but then Christian brays, "Ma'inella, your breath stinks, an' you smell like tobacco!" The other guy starts to whistle again, but then something cold, colder than true coldness, penetrates me.

When Christian sings, nobody whistles. When somebody whistles, Christian doesn't sing.

Am I alone with him? With him, who's smoking Gitanes? With the one who's smoking Gitanes and can express himself perfectly normally?

"Did you know Dupuy's first name was Alphonse?" the smoker asks.

"Pounce on Alphonse!" Christian barks.

"Did you know that Francine's middle name was Thérèse?"

"The gir' who waffs when she's getting laid!" Christian screams.

"And did you know I nicknamed you killjoy?"

"Killjoy, killjoy, kill!" he says, pressing his lips to my earlobe.

If only I could close my eyes. If only I could no longer see inside my head, no longer hear, no longer understand . . . No longer picture a gleeful Christian inside my head, leaning over me, no longer hear him say, "I really got you, didn't I?" No longer understand that I understood nothing.

Christian! Not Léonard! Christian!

But what was Dupuy doing just now?

"Would you like me to read to you a bit?" Christian suggests.

His words take a moment to work their way into my understanding. He's already begun to read, fumbling ahead: "'Author's notes: Can one have Vore torture Yvette without altering the reader's emotional capacity? Be careful about reactions that may cause them to reject it on account of such outrages! No clowning around!'"

Huh?!

He's already continuing: "'On the other hand, I should find a way to make Elise less annoying. Should there be a lover? Should I make her sleep with Vore?' Vore and Elise; ha, ha, ha!" he says, gasping.

I feel my mouth go dry. The pages rustle as he quickly turns them. He goes on, "'Chapter two: Elise meets a sad little girl who knows a few things . . . Chapter four: Yvette and the director play cards. Elise dozes off near the terrace . . . Chapter eight: Elise enters her room and finds a young handicapped girl who's hanged herself . . . ' How do you like it, Elise my heart?

Elise, openmouthed, arms dangling, stares into the emptiness. The emptiness before my eyes, the emptiness inside my head.

Was all of this *written?*

"OKAY, LET'S GO BACK," Christian says in conclusion.

He pushes me inside.

How could all of this be *foreseen?* The absurd yet agonizing idea that I'm really just a character in a book crosses my mind. Do I not exist? No, how could I have any sensations? In fact, I haven't got any, except that of being a blob of aspic bobbing about in my wheelchair, soft and tasteless.

Inside, people are chatting. They turn silent when we come in. Someone runs up, making the floor vibrate.

"Elise!" my uncle cries. "Where'd you go?"

"She took down Sergeant Dupuy," Mercanti responds. My uncle laughs. Yes, he's *laughing.*

"Now, that's a bit rich!" he calls out, good-naturedly.

Is he drunk?

"I'm telling you, this bitch of a niece of yours—"

"I won't stand for that!" Fernand growls.

" . . . has just killed Alphonse!" Mercanti says, hammering it home.

"What? How can it be? Weren't they blanks?" says my uncle, astonished, his voice trembling.

The aspic is seeping into my ears and spreading through my brain. The sticky synapses refuse to transmit my thoughts. I feel like pulling out my hair and screaming, "I don't get it!"

"They don't use real bullets in the movies!" my uncle says, losing his temper. "You're kidding me!"

Oh, of course, movie—there's even a pile of walk-ons sprawled in the snow and waiting to be paid. A film. The word slowly seeps into my fear, threads its way into my confusion. Followed shortly by "walk-ons" . . . and the humming of Jean-Claude's camera.

Walk-ons? Were these bastards actually making a *movie?* Were they all putting me on? Just like a film, only the hero doesn't know he's being filmed? So that when I got the sensation of acting in a play, it was in fact real? Of course—Christian was reading off notes! It was a screenplay! Feeling a mix of rage and relief, I almost laugh.

"Who said anything to you about a movie?" Mercanti's saying to my uncle.

"Why, Elise," my uncle replies, sounding puzzled. "In the message that fell on the ground."

What?

I hear him fumbling through his pockets. He continues, "I admit that when I got here, I was really in despair because of Sonia, and terribly nervous. Cops everywhere, murders, bombs, wounded people, a whole production! Remarkable, really. I even wound up telling my whole life story to the guy playing sergeant!"

I'm hanging on his words, like a mountain climber to a frayed rope.

"You really had me going!" he admits, admiringly. "Even if I did find it rather cruel that I was led to believe my daughter was dead! So I was upside down, and then I found Elise's message. Wait, here it is: 'Don't worry, Uncle, it's all just a movie! In fact, everything's all right. It's all top secret, though, so please don't tell anyone, not even Justine. Pretend nothing's the matter, act as natural as possible. I'll explain to you later. I'm absolutely counting on you. Elise.'"

But I never wrote that! I scream in silence.

"I thought it was kind of twisted," he continues, "but I was so relieved! Elise always has the taste for mystery, so I told myself I could wait a few hours. You'd be through filming your little episode, and the explanation would make more sense."

Laetitia giggles. "I was sure it would work!" she calls out, startling me.

"When I found out later," he adds, "I could tell it was all a big madhouse: the sergeant who looked like a girl, all those cops scared out of their minds, the explosion scene in the snow, with Léonard, who looked like he'd been through makeup, Yvette running all over the place, the nurse with the camera on her shoulder, Mrs. Atchouel ranting, screaming, 'Let's go to the theater tonight,' or something. Anyway, I was even saying to myself that all of you were just bad actors. I felt like laughing."

"Well, Mr. Andrioli, in fact this isn't really a film . . . ," Yann starts.

Yann! *Tu quoque!*

"Rather, it's a documentary," Laetitia goes on.

"A docudrama," Francine explains, more precisely.

I'm digging my nails into the palm of my hand until they draw blood; that should do me some good.

"You see, the idea was to create a sequel to the adventures of Elise," Yann continues.

"I've well understood!" my uncle exclaims. "Really, young man, I'm not senile!"

"Yes, but a real sequel," Yann goes on, "so it would add a second volume to the adventures of your niece."

"Very nice. It's a good idea."

"We all agree," says Francine, approvingly. "Let's see, what does it talk about in volume one?" she asks, in a schoolteacher's voice.

"Uh . . . murders of children in Boissy, and how Elise led the investigation, all that," my uncle mutters.

"And didn't you get the impression that its success was due to the fact that it wasn't so much a cheesy whodunit but rather a true-crime account?"

"Uh, yes, of course."

"You'll understand, then, that we decided to follow the same modus operandi. From this we gathered that (a) if you write a best-seller from a true-life tale, then first of all, it's necessary that the hero—or heroine—has lived through it. You're still with me, Mr. Andrioli?"

"Uh . . . yes," my uncle murmurs, feebly.

"Well, then, my good man, (b) that's what we've put together!" Francine calls out, triumphantly. "In fact, all this started when B* A* sent that e-mail from her publishing house," she says, finishing her point.

Where are Justine and Yvette? Come on in and have a laugh with everyone else.

"She got the address wrong, and that's how it wound up with us, at *PsyGot'yK.*"

"At what?" my uncle asks.

"*PsyGot'yK.* The magazine of Total Art. A recognition of polyexpressional art. Psycho-art, which sweeps away old concepts and outmoded prejudices, and taps the spring of synaptic, infraconscious transmissions of us all."

I say to myself with bitterness that Justine must be the editor in chief.

Besides, I remember how Laetitia found a copy in her room. I was right to be wary of her.

"B* A* came to give a lecture during a colloquium we'd organized, we hit it off, and I gave her all my whereabouts," Francine explains. "That's where the transmission error comes from. The flitting of a butterfly's wing set off this hurricane."

"What hurricane?" Christian asks. "They didn't forecast any hurricane."

"It's a metaphor!" Yann shouts. "Don't interrupt Francine. It's complicated enough as it is!"

Christian grumbles, "'plicated, 'plicated, you prick," between his teeth.

"So here's what B* A* wrote to the editor of the series," Francine continues: "'Dear R* P*, I'm sorry to inconvenience you, I know I'm very late turning in *Elise 2, Death from the Snows,* but I've been having a ton of problems and find I need to pay off huge bills for the house I bought in Cannes. I'd be forever grateful to you if you would agree to send me a substantial advance to help me keep my head above water. In any case, be calm in the knowledge that everything is right on track. I think I'll be finished in two months. Attached, please find the outline of the new novel.'

"Clearly she was stuck," Francine sneers. "Attack of the blank page. It's normal: she took the first book from a true story. And Elise isn't just a character, she's a real person who belongs to no one, you're following me?"

"Of course," says my uncle, apparently lost. "So what's this outline?"

"A synopsis, if you'd prefer."

I don't think he'd prefer it, but he says "Mm-hm," and Francine goes on talking as if it's been eating her up for months, which may be the case. "I'll read it to you."

"What are you reading?" asks my uncle, all mixed up.

"B* A*'s text."

"But you *have* read it to me."

"No, the foundation text. The one that determined the series of events leading up to here and now."

My uncle asks no more.

"All right, I'll read it to you!" Francine repeats firmly. "'It's winter. Elise has to leave for winter sports in Alpes-Maritime, in Castaing, at her uncle's.'"

Obviously Yvette told her.

"'In Castaing, she will stay at an institute for handicapped adults.' That's because I advised her that I was director of MRCHA, and that—this is a funny detail—it was located in the native village of Elise's uncle!" she explains. "Imagine how that would ring a bell for an author. Which goes to show how people are inspired by reality," she murmurs dreamily, before continuing. "'Elise makes friends with the residents. Shortly thereafter, horrible murders occur, signed by one D. Vore.'"

"I've always thought it was kind of thin as a point of departure," Mercanti shouts scornfully.

"Maybe so, but at least it was a basis," Francine retorts. "It followed a rather muddled development, which we've decided to set to work, literally. And then to write it down and get our hands on the jackpot!" she continues.

"But we needed a solid story for that!" Yann says.

"Something that holds together!" Laetitia confirms.

"A true story that Elise will truly live—one she'll write down in her true little notes. And in order for her to truly live it, neither Elise nor B* A* may know!" Francine emphasizes, as if my uncle were either deaf or senile.

"Well, that we can agree on!" he replies.

"I don't think you've quite understood," Mercanti pipes up. "In a film, you have actors. We on the other hand have chosen to stage a novel, with nonprofessionals, to make it more authentic. Get it?"

"Nonprofessionals?" my uncle repeats.

"It's about the triumph of fiction over the inert matter of reality!" Laetitia exclaims. "We've incarnated, in the literal sense, the novel's hero. We're rewriting life, all live!"

"Whose life?" asks my uncle.

"Everyone's life! You know what a snuff movie is?" Yann says, excited. "It's a film in which people are really killed. That's worth billions. We, on the other hand, are making a snuff book."

"That's disgusting," my uncle says. "Who are you?" he adds brusquely.

"We've just told you: characters in the novel!" Martine snaps.

"I mean, are you really actors?" my uncle asks, his voice suddenly changed.

"*Si, signor!*" Francine answers. "We're the actors of the *commedia della vita*. Friends of Art, with a capital A for Action, Adventure, *Amour.*"

"Assassination," Christian says proudly.

"What I'm trying to make you understand, Mr. Andrioli," Francine continues, carefully pronouncing her words, "is that we've just put on a reality show. With Elise, yourself, Yvette, Justine, and our darling residents, all playing themselves."

"Well, that's okay. But what's this bit about . . . uh . . . "

"Snuff movies," Christian repeats. "Snuff, snuff, snuff, ah-choo!"

"As I was starting to explain," Francine goes on, sounding annoyed, "we've decided to give a little push in the right direction for an author lacking inspiration. Christian, would you keep quiet two seconds, please—"

"Plea, plea, plea, *plaisir d'amour*," Christian sings in falsetto.

"Ha, ha, ha, very funny! As I was saying, we were looking for a plotline that would throw Elise into battle against the famous D. Vore."

"But who is D. Vore?" asks my uncle.

"The killer dreamed up by B* A*. But it's not enough to have a killer. You also need a story. Shh! Don't interrupt, just listen! By some fortunate coincidence, one day when Léonard was in the hospital in Nice for his treatment, he heard a drug addict introduce herself by the name Marion Hennequin. The name is uncommon enough to make him wonder if she was related to an old friend from high school. He engaged her in conversation and, yes, she was Hennequin's widow. They hit it off, and Léonard introduced her to Yann, who's secretary of our association in the southeast of France. By another coincidence, it just so happens that at the same time she received a visit from our adorable little Sonia, who informed him that she's her sister: old Mauro coughed up that little morsel.

"In one shot, we had our plot! A bloodthirsty killer murdered Marion, then her half sister, but far from being the work of some demented character, it was committed by their half brother, who had his eye on their inheritance! A half brother living at MRCHA, killing under the identity of D. Vore! Get it, pal?" she adds, with vulgarity, for my uncle's benefit.

So I guessed the . . . script. My satisfaction is bitter.

Fernand's incredulous voice rises through the self-satisfied silence: "Still, you didn't . . . Sonia . . . Marion . . . They're . . . they're not—"

He doesn't finish his sentence, so overwhelmed is he by the conversation.

"You haven't read the papers?" Martine asks.

"I was in Poland! I went straight to Italy, and I got the messages on my cell phone."

"What about dear Justine? Didn't she tell you anything?"

"Well, yes! I was worried sick," Fernand protests vehemently, "but again, Elise's little note helped me understand that I'd arrived in the middle of filming and that Justine wasn't aware anything was going on, either!"

I'm hot and I'm cold. I feel sick. My memories are telescoping: Yes, he did arrive after Véronique Gans's cadaver was taken away. Truthfully, he never saw anything. Not even the explosion in the kitchen.

"You're not telling me that *you killed them?*" he suddenly says.

"Of course we killed them," Christian exclaims.

"And we're going to kill you, too, and sell the filmed journal of your redemption to the TV stations!" Martine interrupts. "They'll pay millions to run it on the news!"

"Because nothing's a trick. That's the beauty of it!" Laetitia says, impassioned. Now I'm really feeling ill.

"And I'm really crazy!" Christian replies.

There's laughter. Where are all the other residents? Emilie, Clara, Léonard, Jean-Claude, Bernard . . . Are they all dead? What about the lab technicians? Did they kill everyone?

"You told me Elise was going to solve a mystery live, that we were going to win lots of cash!" my uncle mutters, crestfallen.

"But we are gonna make lots of cash!" Christian shouts. "Cash, cash, cash, Johnny Cash!"

"Let's not count our chickens before they're hatched," Mercanti returns. "We still haven't come up with her downfall."

"We've spoken about it a hundred times!" Francine snaps. "Listen: Elise discovers that Léonard is Fernand's son and therefore Sonia and Marion's half brother, and that he killed them to grab hold of the Gastaldis' inheritance."

"And he shoots down Elise before fleeing," Martine explains.

"You're forgetting that that jerk Léonard doesn't want to know about it anymore," Mercanti says.

Léonard refuses to go on with this game of theirs? A glimmer of hope.

"We don't care. We can use him anyway!" Yann replies in an icy voice.

"Who are you?" my uncle repeats like a drunken parrot. "Who are you? Tell me this is a joke, will you. It's a joke, that's what it is?!"

"It's true, we haven't made our introductions!" Laetitia exclaims, clapping her hands. "Go ahead, Yann."

"Very well. Ladies and gentlemen," he begins proclaiming in a stentorian voice, "you've just come to attend a performance of *Death from the Snows,* with Elise Andrioli, the world-renowned star-on-wheels, playing herself!"

Applause.

"Playing Francine Atchouel: Thérèse, the literary director of *PsyGot'yK.* Ah! Thérèse! Our muse and inspiration. In addition, she's the director of

MRCHA, thanks to her background in special education for the severely handicapped. Thérèse leads clandestine research in sculpture from living matter—"

Sculpture from living matter . . . oh, no!

"—and in her passionate devotion to theater, she has expanded on the concept of 'little lived plays,' as she calls them, which is to say plays where everything is really happening, inspired by plays in ancient Rome in which men sentenced to death were really tortured."

It takes a few microseconds for the meaning of the sentence to take shape.

"And in the role of leading lady, Laetitia!"

Laughter.

"At the age of fifteen, Laetitia was given her first role in *Helene and the Boys,* when her unfit, alcoholic father's drunk driving forced her to give up all her dreams. Laetitia's been laboring for a just reward: She tampered with the brake wire of her ghastly father's car, which in one single stroke melted, literally, out in the boonies. She spent four years in a depersonalization cell before she could join us here once again."

A girl filled with malice who lost her future as a sitcom heroine. Four years of internment before she mastered her role as a normal young girl who had been cured. I can still hear the joy in her voice as she spoke to me about her father, just as if he were alive. The father she in fact killed.

"Playing Dupuy," Yann goes on, with a note of sadness in his voice, "was our dear Gégène, who could raise the function of a homeless person to the level of poet by writing the state of his soul on the skin of his fellows, all with the help of a broken bottle."

"May he rest in peace!" Martine whispers in her mother-superior voice.

I can see myself again, surprised at how this Gégène's language lacked the military note I would expect. And yet I was unable to draw any conclusion from it that would have saved lives. "Elise, you're just a miserable asshole!" I scream to myself from inside my temples, clenched tight from a migraine.

"Playing the crazy savant, here's Léonard!" Yann brays. "A pioneer who predicted the action of mass well before American high school students. Léonard's a specialist in converting the energy of cloth by combustion. He allowed nearly fifteen of his schoolmates to free the whole of their corporeal energy by setting fire to his high school the year he was prepping for Polytechnique. It was an act of scientific audacity that earned him ten years of the noxious influence of group therapy."

Suddenly I remember Hugo telling us how Léonard's classroom burned down. What he didn't know was that Léonard was the one who set it on fire!

"In the part of devoted nurse, we have a divine emissary," Yann continues, rattling off his sinister litany with obvious pleasure. "Martine used to wipe old people in an old folks' home when God came looking for her. Now she works directly with Him, watching over souls in danger, whom she removes from this low world, to send safely to our Father. She worked in several hospitals before meeting Francine in a center for autistic children."

A nurse who's not wrapped too tight, euthanizing her patients.

"And in the part of Christian, a victim of standardizing totalitarianism: Christian spent his whole life in institutions because his mother was a junkie whore. His sad experience inspired him to write a novel, which higher minds rejected. So Christian attacked the problem of feminine redemption with some success. And finally," he concludes, "in the part of Mercanti, a great artist, whom I've named DJ KO, our sound man. With a background in electronic and concrete music, yet too innovative, he never caught on with the imbecile public. Tirelessly continuing his research, he works on the frequencies and sounds emitted during corporal distortions, especially among children."

Corporal distortions. I feel like throwing up.

Christian imitates a drum roll, and everyone cheers.

These are dangerous psychopaths frustrated in their "artistic" ambitions. Who have come across one another through an art revue that considers itself subversive. Using its concepts to satisfy their perverted instincts.

Without realizing it, we've just attended the performance of their masterwork: *Elise and the Death from the Snows.*

A work whose ending remains to be written.

It's unlikely to be a happy ending.

What about Yann? Who is he? And how were Mercanti and Dupuy able to get onto the police force? It's funny that the pen and pad are still in my lap. My fingers are trembling, and for a moment I'm afraid I won't be able to write.

"Hey, our favorite Elise wants to intervene! Let's see—'Yann?' And then, 'How are Mercanti and Dupuy cops?'" Yann reads. "Mercanti will explain it to you while we see to some details."

They go off in a consultation. I hear objects moved around, doors shutting. Mercanti comes close, close enough for me to get a whiff of his strawberry chewing gum.

"My little darling," he whispers, without noticing my revulsion, "I'm the true Mercanti! There are plenty of priests who are pedophiles, so why not a policeman who's a murderer? The trick is to stay clean on the surface! And as for the true Officer Dupuy, he's lying at the bottom of the gorge, though his surface is in a pretty sorry state, ha, ha! Thanks to Léonard, who snuck onto the computer in the barracks, we knew that he should be rejoining his company, to which, it just so happens, I recently managed to have myself appointed by falsifying a transfer order, at darling Francine's request. Gégène pretended to be stuck at a bend in the road. His future alter ego stopped to help him out. I jumped out from behind a mass of fallen rocks, holding him by the cheek. I've fashioned a pretty smile that will never leave him."

I listen with disgust, all the while wondering who has just limped in, breathing so heavily next to me. Is it Justine? No, I'm sure it's a man.

"Francine, can you pass me the new notebook over there?" Yann asks.

Someone leaves a notebook in my lap.

"We're not going to deprive ourselves of the advice of the pro!" he jeers.

I shake my pen as an officiating priest would his bell. Again and again, to buy some time.

Vore: a disguise worn one by one by members of the group?

"No, do a little reasoning!" Francine yells.

If it were a disguise worn by everyone, then Magali would never have recognized anyone in particular. So it's a single person who held the role most of the time. And that means it can't be anyone from the center, because Magali would have said his name; it must be an outsider, thus Dupuy or Mercanti, since Magali never saw them at the center; she died before they arrived as police officers. Given Vore's voice and size, I would say Mercanti.

Mercanti.

"Bingo! It's true, you're very talented."

"Where's Justine?" my uncle suddenly asks, sounding lost.

"She's where she ought to be!" Yann replies in an unyielding tone. "Great. Now, let's get down to work: How are we going to finish up?"

"All we've got to do is hold on to what was predicted: Léonard kills everyone," Christian suggests.

"Pfff! That's pretty dull! What did B* A* already predict?"

"Well, not much. 'A resident sees the killer on TV.'"

"We really sweated over that one!" Laetitia exclaims. "We should have skipped that passage, it was pretty lame: The girl sees some guy on TV and recognizes him, but in fact she doesn't recognize him because he was wearing a ski mask! Great, a sudden new development!"

"What's more, I was dying of heat under that ski mask!" Mercanti growls.

"'Elise receives a volley of darts . . .'" Yann goes on.

"Magali didn't want to come see you pushing Elise on the terrace, so I had to drag her," Martine exclaims. "In the first episode, Elise was already getting pricked by needles," she continues. "This doesn't have much variety."

"Haven't you noticed how mystery authors are always writing the same book in various disguises?" Laetitia calls out. "It's because they're really a bunch of hacks. Obsessive neurotics."

Their conversation's giving me goose bumps. I'm their prisoner, of course, but they're also logical in their madness. These aren't just madmen, these are beings with perverted psyches. For whom we are subjects for experimentation and amusement. Perhaps even disgust?

No, they're not immoral, nor are they amoral. They're no more insane than the dignitaries of the Third Reich. They're self-styled eugenists. Who hold us in their power and rejoice over the idea of killing us as cruelly as possible. It's the absolute nightmare: being delivered, bound hand and foot, to armed sadists who double as spurned artists.

My pen again. Every passing second is one extra second of life, one second of respite before pain. What should I ask for? Oh, yes.

Elise eating human flesh?

"Oh, that, that was dear Francine's good idea!" Yann says joyously.

"It's a change from tea," Francine says, approvingly.

"There was also that passage in which Elise's wheelchair took off when someone sets off a bottle rocket!" Christian cries. "That was beautiful!"

"That was asinine!" Francine replies. "We replaced that with the explosion in the kitchen."

"Asinine!" Christian shouts back. "Ass, ass, asshole—"

"Christian!" Martine lets out mechanically.

I'm wondering if I would have preferred taking off with a bottle rocket up my ass than to be here, at the mercy of their experiments, like a lab animal. I think back to Pavlov and his work on animals and experimental neuroses. Sick. Rationalized torture. And I'm the one in the cage.

"Why didn't we make her sleep with Vore?" Christian's asking.

"I was going to do that, but Schnabel disturbed us," Mercanti explains, giving me retroactive shivers.

"The cops are going to be here in two hours. We've got no more time to pussyfoot around!" Yann calls out nervously.

"Are Elise's fingerprints on our good Dupuy's weapon?" Martine asks.

"They're erased," Laetitia answers.

"Stop this stupid game!" my uncle suddenly calls out, with the frenzied optimism of a man condemned to die persuading himself it's all a dream.

"Go and take a walk outside and see if this is a game! Mercanti, take him!"

Mercanti drags him out of the room, despite his protests. My uncle suddenly seems very old. I write, *Where is Yvette?*

"Out in the cold, in the water tank!" Yann sneers. "No, rest assured, she's with the others, no one's touched a hair on her head, *yet,*" he says.

What are you doing with us?

"We've told you, you're going to finish this up as a thing of beauty! As grandiose as Waco! Twenty-odd cadavers consumed in a fire at the center, and Léonard will personally shoot you down before the National Police make their final assault," Francine puts forward, enthusiastically. "This could be an exclusive scoop for *PsyGot'yK,* a book, a film, sales of the live recording of anything that happens. Don't you realize we're in the middle of writing a slice of history? And what's more, one hell of a slice."

Outside there are shouts and curses, and I go tense, waiting for the gunshot; the door flies open and a body falls to the floor.

"This asshole tried to get away. I must have beaten his brains out," says Mercanti, no doubt speaking about my uncle.

"You must have hit him hard. He's bleeding all over the place," Christian observes.

"Old people bleed easily," Mercanti says. "What's more, their blood stinks. Not like kids. When kids bleed, it's like angel pee."

"All that idiot Lorieux's got to do is shoot one bullet into Uncle's face," Christian continues. "Elise in tears, the whole thing . . . Damn! It would be really heavy!"

Lorieux! I completely forgot about him. Is he part of the band?

"Let's not sacrifice verisimilitude for ratings!" Laetitia's saying. "Why would Lorieux shoot Elise's uncle?"

Christian mumbles a pouty "I don't know." I let out an inaudible sigh. This is like a creative writing workshop given by psychopaths. Our lives are hanging by their plotline. I'm struck by a gust of hatred, superimposed over fear to form a sickening, bitter-tasting mixture that makes me feel I'm going to implode.

"What's wrong with what was predicted?" Christian asks.

"I think it's mushy," says Mercanti. "No surprises. And Elise has done practically nothing. Talk about a heroine!"

"All right, all we've got to do is keep the passage where she discovers the policemen's bodies. She realizes that Léonard is the guilty one," Christian proposes.

"Why?" Martine asks, cutting him off.

"How do I know? Because he's her uncle's son."

"And how does she know that?" Martine insists in her sugary voice.

"Well, shit! Because she's the heroine. Otherwise, what good is she to us, huh?!" Christian protests.

For ten seconds they all rack their brains.

On the pad I write, *I'm guessing because I've guessed. See my notes. Deductions.*

"There. She's guessed because she's guessed!" Yann says approvingly, irritated. "Shoot, had you guessed?"

"Well, what did she guess, since there was nothing to guess?" Christian gurgles.

"She guessed what we wanted her to guess," Francine explains. "Our dear Elise really is a great detective."

"Well, okay," says Christian. "She guessed, so she calls the cops and—"

"She . . . can't . . . speak!" Laetitia articulates.

"Ah, I forgot! I gotta say, she doesn't make things easy for us," he mutters. "What's more, she's not that sexy. Why didn't we get Pamela Anderson?"

"We're not going over that again!" Yann cuts in. "It just happened we knew Elise's uncle through Francine, and not Pamela's."

"Such a charming man, Mr. Andrioli," Francine simpers. "Who wants some more tea?"

"We've got no more time!" Yann snaps, a bit annoyed by the playful mood of his band of killers.

"I've got an idea," says Martine, "a trick that's truly brilliant: Why not make Elise the murderer!"

"Oh, yeah?" Christian calls out. "She kills with her wheelchair?"

"No, she financed the murders. She uses a professional killer to have new adventures and make a big pile of cash for herself."

"And who's this professional killer?" Yann asks, interested.

"Léonard! That way, we'll get back on our feet."

"No one could ever tell me how Léonard was supposed to have killed all these people!" Mercanti gripes. "What I mean is, he's not exactly mobile . . . "

"People with limited mobility are just as capable as anyone else of rubbing out someone next to them!" Laetitia retorts, furious.

"In fact, your idea's shit!" Christian's saying to Martine.

"I won't stand for that!"

"I say Lorieux's the murderer," he goes on.

"Yes. That's beautiful! It's subversive! Law against order!" Francine says, clapping her hands with approval.

"And Elise guns down Lorieux!" Yann cries enthusiastically.

"But who shoots Elise? We can't keep any witnesses!" says Francine, frustrated.

"What if the uncle were the murderer?" Mercanti suggests.

"Too old!" says Laetitia. "Lorieux's more sexy."

"We need a method!" Francine cries. "Without a method, we're not getting out of this. Speech influences form, and form reveals speech. We need an aesthetic credo!"

There's a brief silence. I can almost hear their distorted thoughts swirling through the room. They're brainstorming, in the literal sense of the word. By the way, has Francine ever been committed to a psychiatric hospital? If so, how was she able to get authorization to direct a health care facility? I scrawl, *Francine not in psychiatric hospitals?* on my pad.

"Good little Elise is inquiring after darling Francine's mental health!" Yann declares.

A hand smelling of disinfectant seizes my chin and forces it up. Lips as cold and wet as slugs brush my cheek. The chewing gum lets through a sharp, suffocating stench. My skin bristles.

"It's a long story. Francine almost experienced being locked away," he whispers, his mouth pressed to my ear, "but she was saved in time."

I try to turn aside but he tightens his grip and licks me with the tip of his tongue; it feels as if a fat worm is trying to make its way into my ear.

"It was in a center for vegetable children. The director, a real sycophant, was a bit concerned about her excesses and wanted to denounce her to the authorities. But the poor dear had an accident before there was time. An overdose. You know, most doctors take drugs, my little angel. Sensing that she'd been given a mission, Francine-Thérèse left her position and founded the journal. In a way, she's a holy mother to us all," he adds, passing his tongue over my cheek, eyes, and lips, desperately shut.

Deliberately refusing to shudder under his touch, I scribble, *My uncle?*

"Oh, you'll never guess, my little sugar doll! It was Justine who introduced him to Francine at a private art viewing. He was looking for someone to run the center. She had all the references he wanted. You see how it's a small world," he says ironically, trying to stick his serpent's tongue into my mouth.

"Until we can all agree on the final sequence, why don't we arrange all the cops in the van, in such a way that no one would notice when first approaching?" Laetitia suddenly proposes. "It would be funny: 'Nothing to report, Commander!' and then, all of a sudden, one of them opens the car door, and *pow!* Madame Tussaud's Whacked Museum! Poetic and effective!"

"Wax?" Christian asks.

Laetitia, all proud of herself, spells out her play on words.

"Yes, a bit of a stage production wouldn't hurt," Martine approves. "It'll give us some time to think."

In the commotion, amid the laughter, exclamations, and doors slamming shut, Mercanti gets up again, and his voice is like a scalpel making an incision in my flesh: "See you soon, dearie!"

My uncle, lying at my feet, is breathing with difficulty. Someone else is next to me, someone who hasn't opened his mouth until now: "I understood too late."

Lorieux.

"When I saw one of the floodlights knocked over and Martine with Jean-Claude's camera on her shoulder, I don't know, I got a bad feeling. And when Schnabel said something to me about GPOS, I was certain we'd been caught in a trap."

GPOS?

"Group portable out of service. It's a code we use to signal that our radio transmissions have been totaled. That means he couldn't contact anyone. The cavalry's not going to arrive, Elise."

I silently digest this.

"I told myself that we mustn't awaken any suspicion from the person or people working in the shadows. I tried to act normal. When I went out, I saw you covered in blood, with a weapon in your hand, my men shot down, and everything got muddled in my head; I went back inside to get help and came across Schnabel's machine gun, pointed right at my chest. 'A beautiful mechanism,' Laetitia said to me, 'and it makes some lovely holes; I've just tried it out on Hervé Payot.'

"Everything became clear. All the convergences always leading me back to MRCHA. That feeling of being manipulated, speaking to people who recite texts learned by heart, these coincidences that were a bit too obvious. Life's never written like a novel, with all the major developments programmed in, and asides from the author."

Yes, I've gotten the same sensation. Yet I didn't trust him. Now we're all going to pay. Lorieux continues speaking in a monotone: "They've locked up everyone else in the basement. They've put my own handcuffs on me, my arms behind my back."

What about Hugo?

"I think he's dead."

The tone in his voice leads me to guess he knows so, but he doesn't want to talk about it. As if I could panic even more!

"They showed me a copy of their rag, *PsyGot'yK: The Review of Total Art.* You'd think it was Justine's, but more twisted. Besides, there was a piece on one of her shows on the first page. According to Payot," he continues, jumping from one subject to another, "Véronique got someone to talk. That's why she came here this morning. This morning! My God! You'd think it was a hundred years ago! Payot thought it was tied to her stay in the psychiatric hospital, when she was held as a matter of course after an acute fit of delirium."

This must be the famous stay in the psychiatric hospital when all the main protagonists met: Marion, Sonia, Véronique, and Yann. The three girls are dead. And Yann is obviously demented. Certainly he was not there in the capacity of caregiver, but rather as a patient. Dr. Jekyll and Mr. Yann, the two-faced seducer. He's schizophrenic. No, from his overestimations of me, his authoritarianism, his feelings of persecution, and his conduct as a persecutor, I'd say instead a paranoid psychotic. Okay, Shrink, all this is gibberish, and I've got no time to lose analyzing their case!

Still, how was he able to deceive Lorieux?

Yann sick?

"I didn't know about it! He told me he was pursuing his studies to be a teacher, with frequent internships in psychiatry. What he didn't tell me was that he was the object!" he confesses bitterly.

The herd of psychopaths stampedes back in, letting in gusts of cold air, rife with commentary, trampling across the floor of this cursed center like the incarnation of all my childhood fears.

"Have courage!" Lorieux whispers.

I'm gonna need it.

"Aren't they both cute!" Laetitia calls out.

Dirty little bitch.

"Christian's proposal has been adopted unanimously," says Yann, his long hair sweeping against my face, with his deceitful smell of fresh shampoo. "Lorieux will be our murderer, and you'll shoot him down before perishing in flames."

Get them into a dialogue. Make them lose time. My notepad.

"'Flames again? That was already done in the first volume,'" Yann reads aloud.

"She's right," Martine observes, "that would be copying. What's more, there's a book by Cornwell called *Combustion.*"

"What if she committed suicide, having discovered that everyone is dead? She could be facing the camera, with a sign around her neck that reads, 'The world is just a pile of crap'?" Mercanti suggests.

"Pie-pie-pie-pi-lo-nests!" Christian calls out.

"I've got it!" cries Laetitia. "She drowns in the snow!"

"She drowns in the snow?" Francine repeats. "Yes, that's pretty romantic. With all the bodies around her, half buried, her arms lifted to call for help, a sort of *Titanic in the Alps.* Yes, I like it."

That dream in which Magali dies eating snow.

Magali?

"Oh, that was me," says Martine. "While I was supposed to be arranging the cabinet in the pharmacy, I saw Hugo going off to listen to the match. I told Magali to go up to your room, quickly, that we were going to make a surprise for you. She was so happy at the idea that she would soon see Jesus, thanks to the magic rope!"

"What about Véronique?" asks Lorieux, vibrating with hatred.

"Oh, look, our pretty little sergeant's found his tongue again!" Francine says, mockingly.

"Véronique, that was me!" says Christian. "That's why you found the bolt cutter under my bed. That was a stroke of genius, wasn't it? The murder weapon in the murderer's room. Damn, she was nice! And I swear to you, I took advantage of her long ago."

"Marion Hennequin?"

"We all got down to it," Yann says. "The bitch wasn't looking as pretentious as she did when she was in the hospital. We had a good time. But she didn't hold out that long. Not like Sonia."

"Sonia? Was that you?" asks Lorieux, trying to make his voice sound firm.

"Yeah! You were right to suspect me. The doggy in the kepi should have followed his nose!"

A conversation suddenly springs back to mind, in a sinister new light: Sonia's sad voice addressing Yann: "You know, terrible things are going to happen." "What are you talking about?" "I'm talking about madness, destruction, evil. That's what I'm talking about." "Do you know something?" And then: "You know that nothing can stop forces of evil once they've been loosed. They're on their way, Yann. They've already struck, haven't they?" "But . . . " "No, be quiet. Haven't you learned that words mean nothing?" "That's stupid. Trust me, Sonia!" "Trust is a luxury beyond my means. Let me go!"

Sonia knew! She knew he was crazy! She suspected him of killing Marion, that's what she meant, but she was too afraid!

"I spent the whole night getting drunk, until I was found nearly comatose the next morning," Yann explains for Lorieux's benefit. "But that didn't stop me from doing a lovely job. I was thinking of you, you see. It was stimulating."

I hear a suppressed sob. Lorieux, no doubt.

"Look, the little asshole's crying!" Christian says, snickering.

They're going to torture us. Torture us, kill us in a small fire, write their sick fantasies in our fragile flesh. We've got to buy some time!

Why did Sonia run away?

"She was at the end of her rope," Yann sneers. "Drugged up to the bone. I got her anything she wanted, but she had no more will, and what's more, she was sick. She knew she didn't have much time left."

"You're lying!" Lorieux cries.

"If there's really one area where I see no point in lying, it's this one. She didn't want to wind up as a bag of bones in a hospital bed. That's why she stayed in the nightclub—because she knew it was the end, and because she loved me. So why not me in the role of Merciful Death?"

"You piece of trash! You tortured her to death. Is that what merciful means to you?!"

"Do you know the tale about the scorpion and the frog?" Yann replies.

I've got a vague memory of the story of a scorpion who swears he won't sting the frog, and then kills him, and as an excuse tells himself: "It's my nature. What made you think it wouldn't prevail?"

"Well . . . ," Mercanti starts, cracking his rubbery fingers.

Quick!

What about the dog? Didn't he recognize Yann?

"Ah! Now, there's a good question from Elise!" Yann exclaims. "From this we can tell we're dealing with a pro! When I showed up at the club that night, I made a point of wearing the ski instructor suit, the ski mask, and 'Vore's' gloves. The dog didn't make out my scent. That little bitch Sonia let him out the window before I could get to him. That's why he attacked Mercanti when he was disguised as Vore on the terrace. He'd recognized 'Vore's' silhouette."

Another question.

PsyGot'yK?

"It's a contraction of 'psychotic,' that ridiculous name they attach to us, and of 'Gothic,' in the sense of eighteenth-century horror novels," Francine explains in a refined voice.

My uncle seems to be regaining consciousness; he moves, gets back to his feet, and says a few incomprehensible words.

"The farm, Grampa!" Christian shouts.

Then nothing else. He must have hit him again. Provided that his heart didn't give out.

"Okay, let's get back to what we were doing," says Mercanti.

"Baaack, baaaack, baaa, baaa . . . "

"Shut up, Christian!" Laetitia snaps.

"Shut up, yourself!"

"Time's running out!" Yann reminds them for the umpteenth time. "First question: What do we do with supporting characters?"

"We'll eliminate them little by little. Let's worry first about the main characters," Martine suggests.

"So we're going with the idea of putting in technicians, as if they were picking up clues, with their tools and all?" Laetitia asks.

"Yeah, that was nice!" Christian says with approval.

"What about the others?" says Francine.

"I like retards," says Mercanti. "They're like kids. They die with eyes filled with reproach."

How I regret that I didn't empty my weapon into *your* guts.

"Gotta kick 'em! Kick 'em good, 'cause that's the only way we can sell videotapes and make the max."

"Money is not our sole motivation!" Francine cries. "What we want is to reach a previously unknown level of expression."

"You can trust me there," Mercanti says, sniggering. "You hear me?" he goes on, suddenly.

I hear faint cries, furtive steps. I can make out Clara's sharp tone of voice.

"You'd think there were some young ladies out rambling!" Mercanti continues.

There's a click of something metallic, the sound of footsteps fading in the distance.

I start having wild visions of the two young ladies escaping, running into the woods, out of reach, toward freedom, life.

Christian hums, "Plaisir d'Amour." Mercanti returns, shouting, "Look what I found in the rec room!"

I hear Emilie, with her flutelike voice, protesting, and Clara asking where Hugo is.

"He's gone up to Heaven with Magali," Martine whispers. "Don't be upset. You'll be joining them soon, dear."

"Me too! I want to go to Heaven!" Emilie cries. "Me first!"

"If that'll make you happy, my little jewel," Mercanti shouts. "But until then, you'll have to be good, very good, my little angel," he goes on. "Okay, you'll be very good . . . "

He continues, sugary sweet, amid Emilie's protests, Clara's squeals, and the rustle of clothing as it's put on.

"You think it's normal for that little asshole Emilie to be putting on airs?" he suddenly asks. "As if clay refused to be sculpted!"

"Good God, if you must use them, then use them! But don't let it take a hundred years!" Yann growls.

"I want some too!" Christian clamors.

"Would you mind doing this in the next room?" says Francine, sounding annoyed.

"Ah, women!" Mercanti murmurs.

"Let's get going, Phil. No reason why you should get any."

He drags Lorieux off. His boots make scraping sounds as they fumble across the wooden floor.

"Okay, straight ahead!"

"I think this is childish," says Martine, "all this corporal agitation."

"You cunt!" Mercanti suddenly exclaims from the other side of the partition.

Emilie starts screaming right away. Real screams, the kind you hear in the worst nightmares. They get more and more strident. I'm trying not to hear them. I dig my fist into my mouth until I'm choking and bite down. Francine's coughing nervously. Laetitia's turning the pages of a magazine. Emilie's giving out only a long plaintive wail now, the monotone wail of a being who's reached the end of her suffering.

A detonation. Her wail is cut short.

Martine starts singing, "Closer to Thee, O God, closer to Thee . . . " I've got the urge to crush her head under my wheels.

"You don't get much with bad material," Yann asserts, coming back into the room. "Step forward, you asshole! This big asshole tried to beat up Mercanti with snowballs. This little cop of ours is a real hero!" he explains.

Lorieux's pea coat brushes against my cheek, and after a heavy impact, he stumbles and collapses, half on top of me; he smells of vomit and Yann of menthol. A deluge of blows rains down on Lorieux, who never unclenches his lips; his head bobs against the wheel of my chair, shaking it, until I hear the bones in his face crack.

"He's passed out, the jerk!" Yann finally growls, smelling sharply of sweat, as if dementia and cruelty could have an odor.

"Where's my little Clara?" Martine asks.

"She's next door, shaking her friend's hand, trying to make her get up!" Christian jeers.

"Well, when you're done playing around!" Francine spits out. "I thought we were here to make something that would count in the history of art! You think raping and killing a poor retarded girl is meaningful? That's the suburban subculture of shit. Go find the other main characters instead. Let's get moving! In groups of four," she adds.

The men leave. For the first time ever, I think I understand what subjects of experiments in the medical block of concentration camps may have experienced: absolute powerlessness and fear.

Oh, God, give me my eyes, my fingers, a gun, for just a second, just a second, and I'll never ask You for anything else, I swear to You!"

Obviously, no one answers. Has there ever been an answer to cries raised in torture chambers or before open ditches and bullet-riddled walls?

Francine's shrill voice bores into my ears: "There! I've completed the final draft of our declaration. The PsyGot'yK manifesto. Listen up, girls: 'We, PsyGot'yK, declare war on normality, rationality, and a whole society devoted to equalization through standards. We demand our difference and our right to use peoples as we intend, in the name of the superior race we represent, free from any moralizing obstacles. Long live murder! Long live crime! Long live freedom!"

"You've forgotten 'with the greatest glory to our Eternal Father, to Whom we owe it to be above the herd,'" Martine whispers.

"I thought we might read this in front of the camera, while a policeman is burned alive on a background canvas."

"The auto-da-fé of Order. Not bad," Laetitia says approvingly while chanting, "Lorieux on the stake!"

I feel myself shaken by spasms of hatred.

There's a clamor of voices in the hallway as the others return. I'm so tensed so as not to miss a thing that it feels as if the volume inside my ears has tripled. Every sound has importance. My life, our lives, may hang on a tiny detail I manage to capture. The first four "characters" enter.

"When the time hasn't come, the time hasn't come," says Bernard, "and chatterboxes love anything that shines."

"Thank God you've got nothing!" Yvette cries, and then lets out a scream as, I suppose, she recognizes Emilie's body in the adjacent room, with Clara howling by her side.

"The poor thing! The poor thing!" Mrs. Raymond says.

I hear the dull clap of two slaps: Yvette hiccups, and Mrs. Raymond chokes back a sob, stammering, "But, Madame Francine . . . "

"No more 'Madame Francine,' you fat bitch!" Christian screams. "And we're going to cook you in your shitty oven!"

"Christian! No vulgarity!" Francine admonishes. "Our little subjects are traumatized enough as it is."

Justine calls, "Fernand? Fernand?" and Mercanti imitates her, snickering. I hear Justine stumble, then cry out piercingly. "Blood! This is blood! There's a man lying on the floor, covered in blood!"

"'Fernie! Fernie!'" Mercanti says, simpering.

"Fernie! No!"

"Quit your squawking or I'll finish him off!" Mercanti snaps. "I can't stand nervous breakdowns."

Justine stays close to my uncle and speaks to him in a low voice.

"Why isn't our brother Léonard with us?" Martine suddenly asks, sounding as if her mouth were full of sacrificial wafers.

"Good question. I'll go see!" Mercanti calls out.

"They forced us down into the basement, threatening us with machine guns. They took away Jean-Claude's camera and locked the boys from the lab in empty casks," Yvette whispers. "And Hugo's dead! They hung him in the stairway!" she adds with a note of hysteria in her voice.

Breathe in. Calm down. My pen: *Tintin?*

"He's in the cellar. They beat him and his wound reopened. Why are they doing this?" she goes on, her voice ragged. "Francine, Yann, little Laetitia, they're so nice, and then all of a sudden you'd think they were monsters. Just a little while ago, your uncle was telling us some preposterous story to the effect that these are actors. But players don't kill people!"

"Unless they're 'slayers'!" Christian, who's overheard, shouts, and then laughs at the good joke he's just made. "Slayers!" he repeats. "Come here, Yvette dear, I'll explain it to you."

"He won't drop it," I hear Yvette cry each time he says it, followed by Christian's heavy laughter. Others around us are starting to bicker.

I can hear my heart beating a rapid rhythm in my throat. I feel the curious double sensation of having undergone general anesthesia and being in a heightened state of alert.

"Elise?"

It's Justine.

"What have they done to Fernand?"

What do you want me to tell you?

"Who are all these people?" she continues. "They exude evil. I recognize their voices, but not their souls. I've heard them; they're going to kill us, but why? Are these demons who have come out of hell?"

Sort of.

On my pad I write, *PsyGot'yK.*

Yvette, just returned, reads it aloud.

"PsyGot'yK!" Justine exclaims. "I've done art shows with them! They're charming people! We served cucumber with rhubarb at the opening."

She must realize that this isn't an entirely infallible criterion for judging other people; she goes silent a minute, and then, in a low voice, continues,

"Fernand admitted the truth to me a little while ago, before they took him away. It was a film, unbeknownst to us. He found out from your message. He loves playing in comedies, you know."

Yeah, except he thought he was playing in a comedy while the truth was playing a trick on him.

"But this isn't a farce, is it?" Justine goes on.

Yes, in a sense it is a cruel farce, and we're the pigeons.

Everything since our arrival in Castaing is playing itself out inside my head. I can hear every sentence again, see every act in the new light of the plot. All these inconsistencies, all these sentences uttered dispassionately, the feeling that no one really felt sad. The facts fit together like pieces in a construction game. Suddenly I stumble over one point that remains obscure.

"'Cigarette case?'" Yvette reads.

"Ah!" says Justine. "That was from Fernie. I didn't understand how it could be in the possession of that Véronique person, and I was afraid they were looking for a link between him and the victim, so I said it was stolen from me."

"How was it in her possession?" Yvette asks.

Maybe Fernand gave it to Sonia, and Sonia to Véronique? I scribble, thinking how I racked my brains over that one or, in other words, for a lot of hot air.

Yvette reads it for Justine, who approves.

"It's plausible, but at the time, I didn't understand anything."

That makes two of us.

Suddenly I hear footsteps. Two men. One who smacks his heels against the floor, the other who seems to be constantly stumbling. Léonard.

"Leeb me 'lone!"

"Where were you, Léo?" Martine asks in a honeyed voice.

"Tie-uhd . . . ," Léonard mumbles.

"Poor dear!" Christian snarls. "You think we aren't tired, with all these assholes who won't stop jabbering?"

"Who are you talking about?" Laetitia asks, icily.

"Let's not get into any arguments!" Yann cuts in. "Léonard's here, and that's what counts! And we're going to celebrate his return!" he adds, in a nasty voice.

Mercanti lets out a sinister chuckle. "Did you see Emilie, Léonard?" he asks. "There's a little of her left, if you're interested . . . "

"I wasn't thinking about Emilie. Cadavers aren't of interest to men of action!" Yann snaps. "No, I was thinking of our dear Justine."

"You're mad!" Yvette cries.

"Shut up, you old bat!" Christian shouts. "Yeah, the blind woman and the paralytic. That'll be a hoot!"

"Let go of me!" Justine suddenly cries. "You're hurting me."

I turn my head around in all directions, following the sounds—stampeding, gasps, chairs clattering, feet on the furniture.

"First one who moves, I'll blow your head off!" Christian cries.

"So you like your little slut?" Laetitia asks Léonard. "You like her naked? Does it bring back nice memories?"

"We must punish her according to her sin!" Martine decrees.

"Exactly," Yann approves. "Pass me the poker. The one that's white-hot."

"Oh! You're more than just a little crazy!" Mrs. Raymond cries.

The sound of a slap is followed by the noise of a head violently clashing against a wall.

"Go on, Léo, go on. Give her a good, hot one. Good and hard!" Christian growls.

Laetitia chuckles.

"Léonard? Léonard?" Justine stammers. "Léonard, what's going on?"

"Take the poker, damn it!" Yann thunders.

"Nooo," Léonard suddenly shouts. "Nooo!"

"What? You don't want to?" Yann asks in a threatening voice.

"Done enough bad!" Léonard manages to articulate. "Don' want no more!"

I suddenly remember his odd intonation when he told Laetitia he wasn't feeling well.

"Léonard?" Justine calls again, sounding lost.

"Take a look at that old tramp!" Laetitia spits out.

"You! Twash!" Léonard snaps.

"Miserable wretch!" Laetitia retorts. "Subhuman!"

"Do you know what fate lies in store for traitors?" Yann continues, sounding like an actor in a Z-grade film.

They're enjoying themselves! They're permanently acting out one sentiment or another, deprived of any real emotions. Or more precisely, deprived of any emotion that doesn't concern their own precious egos.

"Go hang yourself, Léonard!" whispers Martine, whom I can't picture as anything but a roach in a cassock.

"The hell with you!" Léonard articulates distinctly. "I'm a fre-e-e being!"

"Free to die like an asshole!" Yann returns, his voice climbing into the upper registers.

The superman must be having a hard time hearing his homicidal dogma put in question again.

"We're changing the script!" he adds abruptly. "Elise thinks Léonard is Vore and kills him!"

He points the barrel of his weapon against my temple while someone forces open my hand and closes my fingers around a fluted metal grip. What? What did Yann say? I can feel the blood draining from my veins. Anyway, they don't want me to . . .

"Léonard's right in front of you, my little love doll, you can't miss him!" Mercanti whispers, his pungent breath now prevailing over the smell of chewing gum. "If you could see him, you'd think he was a saint ready for martyrdom!"

"God loathes the halfhearted!" Martine calls out with conviction.

I open my fingers and the pistol falls to the floor.

Slap. Violent enough so that all I hear now is a sharp hissing. Suddenly, Yann's voice is booming like thunder: "Mercanti, if she starts up again, you'll take care of darling Yvette. You'll give her the special treatment—massage with a drill."

Someone grabs my hand again, and puts my fingers around the metal grip. My index finger is placed on the trigger. The index finger I spent hours reeducating. Not knowing that it could go from being an instrument of liberation to being an instrument of death. Had I known, would my desire to live have been the strongest?

I've got three options:

1. Fire in Yann's direction. What would it change? Whether or not I shoot him, it would be the signal for the grand massacre.

2. Turn the weapon on myself.

3. Pull the trigger. Would it save Yvette? I don't think so.

Three options, and not four. I don't think it would be useful to fire at Yann or anyone else. I haven't got the courage to kill myself. I can't accept the idea of pulling the trigger.

So I'm in disarray.

"Go ahead and fire, Elise. Léonard's getting impatient. He can't wait to join his Creator," Martine says affably.

Somebody starts to sing. The voice is contralto. Handel. *"Lascio ch'io pianga."*

"This is a miracle!" Martine cries. "God has given his voice back to him! Oh, what a beautiful angel he'll make!"

"Wait, we've got to film this!" says Laetitia.

Jean-Claude's camera starts humming.

I feel like vomiting.

"Léonard's death. This'll be the only take!" Laetitia announces.

Justine mutters something in her mysterious language. Mrs. Raymond won't stop sniffling. My hand's trembling so much, I'm having a hard time holding the weapon. And I still feel like throwing up.

"What am I doing? Am I starting with the old lady?" Mercanti asks with avid interest.

"Go ahead."

Yvette groans. A real groan of panic-stricken pain.

I don't know what that son of a bitch is doing to her, but I know it's hurting her. I don't want to hear her groaning like that. I'm getting auditory flashes of Emilie being killed. I *can't* hear that.

Handel fills the silence, which exudes blood and fear. The voice runs with ease through melodic lines, turning into pure crystal, running water, a gushing spring, an angelic breath.

My nausea's building.

The drill starts whirring.

The spasm is followed by evacuations and the spray of something hot and sticky on my chin and hands.

"Damn it, the bitch is puking!" Christian cries.

Yvette screams.

The scream is for real.

Scream, scream, scream.

My finger squeezes the trigger.

An explosion.

The voice stammers, gurgles, and goes silent.

"Bull's eye!" Yann calls out, tapping me on the shoulder.

The weapon is pulled out of my hand before I can even think about shooting again and again, all around me. Nervous twitching runs through my eyes, cheeks, and chest, I feel shock waves shaking me like a rattle; I'm suffocating, trying to breathe through the layer of phlegm; help me . . .

I've killed Léonard.

My hand wipes my mouth and nose; the sleeve against my dirty lips has a horrible taste. I feel a great coldness within. My faculty for thought returns, intact, detached, objective.

I, who feel guilty whenever I swat a fly, have just voluntarily squeezed down on the trigger of a firearm to protect Yvette, killing my second human being in two hours.

Dupuy was legitimate self-defense. This is murder.

At this moment I know I'm from the race of survivors, those ready to do anything to survive. That I, too, am a predator. Yes, my desire to live will always be strongest.

Yanking me out of my dazed confusion, Yann calls out, "Okay, let's go, everybody outside!"

15

$\mathcal{S}$OMEBODY GRIPS MY wheelchair. It's Yvette, crying, her hot tears falling on my cold hands. I'd like to cry. To empty out the glacier creeping through my veins and lungs.

"I'm sorry," she says, sniffling, "but he started cutting into my hip with a concrete tip. I'm sorry for the poor boy, I didn't want to cry out . . . But I couldn't help it . . . He was lifting the drill toward my belly and . . . "

I'm the one at fault. I'm the one who fired.

I can hear Justine's teeth chattering; she's naked.

"Take my coat," says Yvette, "you're smaller than me. This should cover you."

Bernard's beside me. He's breathing heavily, his emphysema and obesity catching up with him in all the stress. He's muttering, "One goes to sleep at night. Chocolate hurts your teeth," as if it were his mantra.

"You can be a real asshole, Bernard," Francine whispers. "I can understand why no one wants anything to do with you."

"I've got to wash my hands, and a family's forever!"

"Oh, shut your mouth, will you!" Martine shouts. "Come on, keep going! When I think how I should have taken care of this fat pig during all this time! May God gladly take him!"

"God loves those with simple spirits," Mercanti jeers.

"God loves to have them up on high, beside Him, the way a Father gathers in His turbulent children," she replies with unctuousness.

Mercanti chuckles. Martine mutters, "Ungodly!" between her teeth. If there's life after death, I hope I'll be there to see you arrive before the Holy Father, your mouth turned up, all bright and expectant. And see you cast into the abyss.

For a moment I'm tormented by the idea that cruel beings may be the ones God prefers and that I'm the one who'll be going to hell.

The proof is that I'm already there.

They're making us go out into the cold night, striking us because we're not moving fast enough. Pistol-whipping us, kicking us. We get used to their blows. Is tonight a nice night to die? The storm has calmed. Perhaps the stars are out.

The subject of their conversation moves on to how our bodies should be laid out in the snow. Should they be naked? Should we be left to die in the cold, or should they kill us, bury us under the snow, as though under the flow of an avalanche?

"The house on fire was better," Christian complains.

"We told you, it was déjà vu!" Laetitia shouts. "You're really brain-damaged!"

"Don't ever say that again! You hear?"

"Brain-damaged!"

"You cunt, I'm going to make you eat your walker!"

"Stop!" Yann screams.

No one listens.

Bernard's beside me, muttering words that make no sense. Quick, my pad.

"'Save yourself. They're going to kill us all!'" Yvette reads in a low voice. "I'm not leaving you!"

"I've got to wash my hands," says Bernard. "When the reservoir's empty, you fill it up."

"'Bernard must leave!'" she reads again, bending forward. Yes, you've got to leave. Go quickly! Quickly! Straight to the village! Run!

"I'm dirty," says Bernard, "I'm so dirty, I have to go to the bathroom. There are sixty seconds in a minute."

He's going away! He's going away! Make sure they don't see him! Someone bumps against me, a hand's feeling around on my knees.

"Ah, it's you," says Justine. "The dark legions have regrouped, they're growling like chained-up hellhounds. This whole zone's going to be submerged by Evil!"

"We should pray," says Yvette. "Our Father, who art in Heaven . . . "

Give us this day our daily horror . . .

"Hallowed by Thy name. Thy kingdom come . . . "

The kingdom of stupidity. That's what's coming to us. Justine joins her voice to Yvette's. Then there's Mrs. Raymond, whose accent I no longer find comical as she recites, "Forgive us our trespasses as we forgive those who trespass against us."

I hear Laetitia giggling.

"You'd think they really were a flock of bleating sheep!"

Martine's waxing ecstatic: "In the most difficult moments, one comes closest to God."

"Where's the fat guy?" Christian suddenly asks.

I press the button and make my wheelchair lurch forward.

"Hey, calm down!" he cries. "She almost knocked me down!" he shouts to no one in particular, before repeating, "Where's the fat guy?"

Once again I lurch forward, and receive a hard blow across my face; I feel my nose bursting from the impact, and tears are gushing from my eyes.

"I told you, go slow!" Yann shouts.

"Wait, I'll calm her down," Mercanti whispers as he picks me up.

I try to fight back, but it's no good. He throws me into the snow, lies on top of me, snickering; as long as Bernard's far away; blood's running down my nose, flooding into my mouth, I'm going to choke, I'm—I hear Justine, Yvette, and Mrs. Raymond cry out; Mercanti's grumbling on top of me; I'm not here, in my head, I'm far away; shots are ringing out; each report makes me feel like throwing up; I'm reduced to rejoicing over their cries and being able to hear them, their pitiful cries of terror that mean they're alive. "Hey, hey!" Christian cries. They must be having fun making them run through the snow; inside, there's a brief pain; I turn my head to escape his breath, which smells like a rotting corpse; Mercanti gets back up with a satisfied chuckle, picks me back up, and says, "So you're happy?" and throws me into my wheelchair. I don't give a shit!

My pad. Don't give in. Never give in.

What's the reason for all—I sniffle and wipe my nose with an angry swipe of the hand—*these murders? I thought Léonard was killing to seize an inheritance. In fact, he's a poor nut job.*

I hold out the sheet. Christian reads it aloud, in a faltering tongue.

"Hey, she's insulting us!"

"Not in the slightest. She's right!" says Martine. "What does *massacre* rhyme with?"

"Well, if someone's a murderer, it's normal for him to murder!" Christian cries.

"But not just anyone, you retard!" Laetitia shouts at him.

"Good Lord! I warned you!"

The loud *smack* sounds hard enough to knock out a bull. Laetitia lets out a sharp cry. Immediately followed by a gunshot. One single thud. Whose echo rings long and loud in the small courtyard. The smell of burned gunpowder is so familiar now. Christian's roar of pain crescendos like a siren.

"You're sick!" Yann roars. "Can't you see what you've done? Christian! Christian! She blew off his knee!"

"It hurts!" Christian yelps. "Oh, it hurts!"

"Let's calm down," says Francine, sounding appeasing, like a schoolteacher. "Let's calm down. Christian, stop crying, please! You can see for yourself that crying never changes pain."

"That should teach him to strike a lady!" Laetitia snaps.

"You cunt!" Christian brays.

"You're not going to go on!" Martine cries.

Yvette, Justine, and Mrs. Raymond, terrorized and trembling, are right beside me; I grab Justine's hand, and Yvette whispers, "I hope they'll kill each other." There may be a chance of that. But right now, we've got to take our own. I advance my wheelchair just a little. Thank God, Yvette understands my intention and points me in the right direction. We inch forward, dragging behind a sniffling Justine, who remains silent.

The PsyGot'yKs are hollering over their psychoartistic theories, while Christian moans like a wounded animal.

"The fundamental question is the motive!" Yann screams. "The fucking motive!"

"Logic is the imperialism of the norm!" Francine retorts. "Long live libertarian art! Down with the diktats of reason!"

"You're just amateurs," Mercanti says, deploring. "Fucking amateurs. You don't make art with theories, you make it with guts!"

"Our goal was a polyexpressional work!" Laetitia enunciates.

They continue that way for a moment. They suddenly remind me of a class I took in college: "Too often, perversion finds aid and emulation in its association of evildoers who extend its field of action and exalt its harmfulness." A very closed club of bloodthirsty people.

Francine starts pacing back and forth, spouting snatches of sentences: "Our darling residents . . . just a little more tea . . . It's so darling, my darling, you darling thing, may we fall to the ground . . . "

Yann asks her if she's lost her mind.

"I'm putting my text back into my mouth, for the cops," she replies.

"But we're not waiting for the cops!"

"Speak for yourself! I don't know. After all, I've never been convicted, and I don't feel like escaping with a bunch of normalists."

While they exchange their wild imaginings, we're still moving ahead. Climbing up the ramp for the handicapped, Yvette leads us into the house. No, we should have fled into the woods, in the snow, under the cover of trees and darkness. What's she doing? She's fiddling with something by the wall, and it emits a metallic grating noise—the mailbox? She takes my pen and taps it against an object. "The light's gone out again!" "We can't see a thing!" "The clouds are covering the moon, we've got to wait a minute." "Be careful. Don't just shoot anywhere!"

"Don't leave me here, you guys!"

"I've busted the circuit breaker," Yvette whispers. "Okay, listen carefully. Just over to the side, the ground slopes down toward the woods. Justine, sit in Elise's lap, and Mrs. Raymond will push you."

What about her? It's out of the question for her to sacrifice herself, I—

"I'm going to look for the sergeant or your uncle," Yvette adds. "We're not leaving them behind enemy lines."

Yvette's in a war movie! If the circumstances weren't so tragic, I'd smile.

She points the wheelchair toward the slope, and Justine, a packet of cold flesh and chattering teeth, sits in my lap. Mrs. Raymond launches into a "Hail Mary" after "Credo," obstinately droning on like a fly bumping against a window.

"Fernand; we've got to get Fernand out of here," Justine stammers.

"I'll take care of it!" Yvette says. "Come on, Mrs. Raymond, push!"

With a vigorous shake, I accelerate and immediately begin to roll downward.

"Hey! Stop! Over there! Stop!" Yann cries. "I've just seen something move in the dark," he says to his acolytes.

"Where are the hostages?" Martine asks.

"Shit! They've taken off!" Laetitia exclaims. "All because of that circus Christian put on."

"I'd like to see you in my place, half pint!" Christian says through his teeth.

"You know what? I'm going to film you as you die!" Laetitia snaps.

"Obviously, if we don't keep an eye on the characters, we risk not writing the book!" Martine remarks, sounding irritated. "What if God had done the same with Creation . . . "

Their voices grow distant.

Our flight picks up speed, and Justine hangs on to my neck, half choking me as the wheelchair skips, reminding me of other dizzying descents, other falls, other fears I hoped I wouldn't have to confront again. The wheelchair swings back and forth, almost topples over, rises again, and hits an obstacle, sending us flying head over heels into a good yard of fresh snow.

"Elise! Elise!" Justine whispers.

I wave my arm about to keep my head above the snow, with no desire to be in their *Titanic in the Alps,* and latch on to something hard and gnarled— a branch, whose evergreen needles prick my skin; Justine's beside me, gripping my shoulder; I can hear her feeling around, grabbing a branch, and we remain here, huddled and breathing heavily, half buried, our teeth chattering as we listen to the night.

The wheel of the chair is making grating sounds. Where is it? I crawl as best as I can, bumping against metal and leather, and lift my arm to stop the wheel, my fingers getting caught among the spokes. Sometimes it's good not being able to scream. I manage to pull them back, and the wheel stops creaking.

"They've cleared out, I'm telling you!" Yann's calling. "Can somebody put the lights back on?"

I'm wondering where Mrs. Raymond went.

"The circuit breaker's burned out!" Martine cries to Yann. "It's impossible to get the current back on. We've got to use the cops' flashlights."

"We'll all be caught!" Francine forecasts, grimly. "Would you like some tea, Captain?"

"Bless me, Father, for I have sinned . . . "

"Mrs. Raymond! We're over here!" Justine whispers. "Come quick!"

"I'm up to my ears in snow, poor thing, I'm going to stay by this tree."

Laetitia's clear voice carries perfectly to us: "We've got to catch up with them. It's out of the question to leave any witnesses."

"Good Lord, we were so close to succeeding!" Yann fulminates. "The first live book!"

"With nothing but photos that would have blown away the Elise fan club," Christian observes between two groans.

"We'd walk away with the Goncourt!" Francine adds.

"Amateurs!" Mercanti says through gritted teeth.

"Where's Lorieux?" Yann suddenly asks.

"Inside, with Andrioli," Martine replies.

"I'm going in. Pass me a full clip."

Justine and I are listening for the slightest sound, and all time stands still when Yann enters the house to kill Lorieux and my uncle. Has Yvette been able to help them get out? Seconds turn into eternities. I notice that I've crossed my fingers and that Justine's murmuring "please, please, please," over and over.

"They're not here anymore!" Yann screams. "Get the flashlights. We've got to find them! Shoot on sight!"

Someone's panting to the left of me. People are stepping heavily, cracking branches underfoot. Justine digs her nails into my wrist. Fear is shrinking my skin to the point where I'm choking.

"Are you there?"

Yvette! The relief makes my skin relax until it may crack.

"Fernand?" Justine murmurs.

"He hasn't regained consciousness. I had some trouble getting him onto the shoulders of our sergeant, whose hands are cuffed; I couldn't find the keys to the handcuffs," Yvette says, all in one breath.

"Fernand?" Justine repeats, feeling around.

"There . . . at the foot of the tree . . . ," Lorieux enunciates in a husky voice.

"Don't be getting tired, Sergeant!" Yvette orders, her teeth chattering.

The cold. I'd forgotten I was cold. Justine's trembling like a generator. We must present quite a funny spectacle, disheveled, hiding in the woods, next to a handcuffed man in a tattered uniform with another lying unconscious at our feet.

"Where's Mrs. Raymond?" Yvette asks.

"I'm right here! Hanging on to the branches. I'm not moving, seeing that I'm buried!"

"They've got flashlights!" Yvette exclaims. "They're going to find us. We've got to go down to the village."

"We can't leave Fernand!" Justine protests.

"Shut up!" Lorieux orders through his teeth.

How many are on our heels? Laetitia, by necessity, must remain above. Christian's out of action. That leaves Yann, Martine, Francine, and Mercanti.

"They're making circles with their flashlights," Yvette whispers in my ear. Suddenly Martine's voice rings out nearby.

"They shouldn't be too far away, especially with Elise," she says to an unknown companion.

I hold my breath. She's really quite close. Branches and twigs crack. Her boots are making *crunch, crunch* noises in the snow. My heart's beating too loudly. She's going to hear it. She's big and strong. Can Lorieux neutralize her with his hands tied?

"Yvette!" Lorieux whispers. "Throw a stone . . . to the right . . . hard!"

Yvette fumbles around, then I hear the clear impact of a stone against a tree on our right. A burst of machine-gun fire is followed by shouts of surprise and pain.

"What is it?" asks Francine, giving away her position, just above us, more to the left.

"This thingamajig almost took my hands off!" Martine shouts. "I heard some noise about ten yards to my left!" she continues.

"Damn it, would you stop yelling like that!" Mercanti orders. "They're going to spot us!"

"Like you're really so discreet!" Laetitia calls out from the esplanade. "I'm going to see if there are any flares in the van."

How could I ever have found her so nice?

We hear them trudging ahead, hunters tracking the big game, defeated.

Somebody advances toward us, rapidly, powerfully. Breathing heavily, through the crackling underbrush; the heat of his light beam passes over my skin; I try to transform myself into a root, but something next to me moves, making me feel like an insect caught in a trap; I don't know what's advancing toward me, I don't know if anyone's pointing a gun at my head, I don't know if a shot will go off, if I'm living my last second. I'm nailed in the dark with the sensation of a halo of light beaming down against my skin . . .

"Hello there, my heart!" Mercanti exclaims.

He leans toward me, his breath warm, the barrel of his gun brushing against my temple.

"Happy to see Papa Mercanti again?" he says. "You know you're going to be beaten to death?"

Whatever you want. Go ahead, just get it over with!

"Ooof!"

With the sound of a deflating balloon, something hard lands on my head —the pistol! I hear Mercanti groan, followed by dull noises, like crashes against a bag of sand, and finally after a loud crack he goes silent.

"The sergeant threw him to the ground with a kick to the chest, and knocked him out with blows to the head. Wow! You should've seen it when he hit him with the tip of his boot! You'd think he was puncturing a lung!"

"Handcuffs . . . put on . . . ," says Lorieux.

"Right away!"

Yvette uses Mercanti's handcuffs to attach him to the tree, and we start to wait again.

"I've got his weapon. If he moves, I'll smash his brains in with the grip," Yvette murmurs.

I hope he moves.

We hear Martine, thrown off by our lure, continue to flounder about on our right. These aren't exactly guerrillas. I can hardly imagine Francine trudging through the snow in her high heels. Yann's the most dangerous one. He's used to the mountains, and he's athletic.

A gunshot!

I think I felt the bullet whiz past me.

At the same time, nearby, again too close, is Martine's voice: "It's nothing! I just slipped! The shot went off by itself!" and on my left, somewhere uphill, someone has let out a long sigh.

"Mrs. Raymond?" Yvette whispers, in the direction of the sigh.

"I think I'm dead!" she answers, surprised.

Nothing else. Only the noise of crushed branches, as if someone were falling. Above, Laetitia's hollering, "I've found the flares!"

"We mustn't alert the village!" Yann cries back.

"But it would be a beautiful finale, a fusillade under a fireworks display!" Laetitia responds, her voice distorted in the wind.

"That's true," says Francine approvingly, keeping to the embankments just above us. "It would be grandiose!"

"You assholes!" Christian roars. "It'll lead the cops right to us, that's all."

"Too bad there's not enough light to do any filming," Laetitia complains again.

The rumble of thunder prevents me from hearing Yann's reply. A flash of lightning follows not too far behind. I barely have time to count to one.

"The storm's starting again!" Martine's voice leads me to believe she's afraid of them.

Thunder. A flash of lightning. These damn flashes are going to replace the flares! And the noise drowns out everything; we can't hear anything else. Snow starts falling again.

"I can't feel my limbs anymore," says Justine. "I think I'm going to sleep a bit."

"No! No! You mustn't sleep! Rub yourself! Get some friction going!" says Yvette.

I can't feel my limbs anymore, either. It's true, sleep is tempting. Like Uncle Fernand, who's resting . . .

I must have dozed off a few seconds. Everything's quiet. Have our tormentors left? Is it all over?

"Hi, gang!"

Yann! I raise my head so quickly that it bumps violently against a branch. The pain wakes me completely.

He came from behind. He must have spotted us and maneuvered to get around us. I can feel his breath on the nape of my neck, which bristles. Snow is crunching beneath his moon boots.

"Yvette, why don't you drop that weapon you're holding all wrong anyway? Otherwise I'll be forced to blow off Elise's head, which won't do much for her diction!" he says, giggling.

The object makes a dull thud landing in the snow. There goes our last chance.

"All my nice little characters are here!" he says, mockingly. "The Valiant Caretaker, Uncle Shot, Sleeping-Eyed Beauty, and last but not least, Ben Hurette, without her chariot! Ah, I forgot . . . the Gallant Knight. Now he's got a dirty little face. You really do upset me, Philippe," he goes on, delighted. "And I thought I was doing you a favor by snuffing out that bitch Sonia. She was cheating on you with everyone. You even told me one day, 'I'd like to kill her!' But like all weaklings, you're incapable of going into action. That's the difference between us. We speak with our acts. Our words are gestures. We write *with* and *in* the flesh. And it serves no point anyway, because no one will ever get it."

The hammer is pulled back.

"Which of you should I take down first?"

"You're nothing but trash!" Yvette shouts.

"Oh, but the old lady really does scare me!"

"Your soul stinks!" Justine snaps.

"And isn't the masked cucumber ferocious! But enough joking around. Oh, I forgot to tell you . . . I've found a really super ending. Elise resolves the mystery: Lorieux is in fact the mad killer, and she shoots him down! And she remains alive! Isn't that lovely? That way, she can serve us another time. I know you're going to say, 'She'll turn you in.' I say nay, my little sweets! Because before he dies, Lorieux cuts both her hands off with an ax. This guy's a real son of a bitch! And so how will our brave Elise, mute and deprived of her little hands, turn us in? Especially with Yvette dead, she'll have a new caretaker. Extremely nice and very, very chic."

"Would you like a bit of tea, Elise? Hot or iced?"

Francine.

"We'll have so much fun together!" she adds, in her affected tone. "For years and years! But, getting back to the business at hand, my dear Yann, it seems that now is the time to put an end to the tribulations of our heroes. It will be, in order, Andrioli, Justine, Yvette, and, finally, the very handsome Lorieux," she concludes, suavely.

"What about Mercanti? What'll we do with him?" Yann asks with a hint of doubt.

"He tried to rape dear Uncle, and our darling Justine blew his brains out?" Francine suggests, sarcastically.

Laetitia's voice reaches us over the rumble of thunder: "What the hell are you doing?" she cries.

"We're coming!" Yann screams back. "We've found them!"

"How will you get away?" Lorieux manages to ask, despite his broken jaw.

"Huh? Oh, no problem. Remember the snow scooters? We'll drive to Seille, and there we'll pick up an all-terrain vehicle."

Isn't it going to dawn on them that the backup will be here before too long?

"Hello, hello, this is Earth calling!" a bullhorn suddenly roars. "Tango-Charlie, please respond!" It's Laetitia, being facetious.

"The wind might carry the sound as far as the village!" Yann says in a rage. "Go tell her to cut it out!"

"Go tell her yourself. I'm pooped!" Francine protests.

From somewhere in the woods comes Martine's voice, sounding close and far away at the same time: "Yoohoo! Where are you? I can't see a thing!"

Now's the time to act, but I may as well dig a hole in my head; though my life may depend on it, no idea comes to mind. Especially none I could execute. I don't even know what sort of weapons they've got, or on whom they're trained. Yvette and Lorieux, I suppose.

Someone's approaching. Someone heavy, whose bulky gait makes snow fall from the branches. Apparently I'm the only one to hear it, because Yann and Francine continue to argue. I'm hoping for a police commando in uniform, an assault rifle clutched to his chest.

"The light was off in the bathroom. Whoever has drunk will drink."

Oh, no! Bernard!

"Naughty boy," he adds. "You'll go without dessert."

"Hey! What's that?"

It's Yann's voice, sounding tense.

"That's a machine gun, which this fat asshole's pointing at your right ear," Francine explains in a low voice.

"Yann's got blood on his hands, and he ought to wash them," says Bernard, learnedly. "On Christmas Day, we eat Yule log."

"Okay, but lower that fucking rifle. It's dangerous!" Yann calls to him.

"I want you to put the light back on!" Bernard protests. "I don't like dark! Why can't we go to the movies?"

"Anything you want, right, dear Francine?"

"Of course. Bernard, darling, why don't you give the rifle to Aunt Francine, and we'll all go to the movies?"

"'Fat asshole, fat asshole!'" Bernard screams, imitating his voice. "For the police, it's number seventeen!"

"Martine!" Francine calls out, trying to appear cool, "we've got a little problem with Bernard."

"Never any problems with Bernard!" she cries back. "Bernard's not retarded!"

"Of course not!" Francine replies.

"Bernard," Justine says suddenly, in her deep, calm voice, "you know Yann says you're fat, and that all fat people stink."

"You cunt!" Yann shouts.

"Don't move!" Bernard orders. "I'm Mommy's barley sugar! You want me to wash out your mouth, Yann?" he adds.

"She's lying!" Yann assures him. "Come on, put down the rifle."

"Bernard," Yvette says, "what if we all got undressed to wash in the snow? Tell them to put down their weapons."

"Yes!" Bernard cries enthusiastically. "Everybody, naked in the snow! Get undressed! Apple pudding's much better."

"No. Aren't you being a little silly?" Yann replies. "Can't you see it's snowing, what's gotten into that fat-lump head of yours? Come on, put down the rifle!"

Yann's spoken in his authoritarian voice, his leader-of-the-pack voice; he's risking it all.

Bernard hesitates. He's always so obedient. And yet he must be confusedly sensing that he's got power, that the others are afraid of him. Afraid of the "fat guy who stinks," whom Yann makes fun of so often, affectionately, no doubt . . .

A branch cracks. Someone approaches on the sly. A whiff of sugary-sweet perfume tells me it's Martine, Mother Superior of the Sickies. While I'm wondering how to warn Bernard, she exclaims in a piercing voice, "Ber—"

"*Yiiii!*" Bernard cries; I can literally hear him jump.

Then comes a deafening blast of gunfire.

A startled cry of pain.

Bernard's incredulous laughter.

"You saw that Yann? Pow! Pow! Films aren't like the real thing!"

"Martine?" says Francine in a hesitating voice. "Martine?"

There's no response.

"That fat asshole hit her!" Yann whines. "I can't believe this! This is turning into a nightmare!"

"In any case, I knew this would go bad," Francine retorts, sounding irritated. "No one ever wants to reflect on the deeper meaning of our artistic commitment. You're nothing but a bunch of petit bourgeois criminals."

"I think I forgot to turn off the faucet," says Bernard. "Two plus two still makes four."

"I'm coming with you," says Yvette. "That way I'll give you a hand."

"Okay, come on. Then we'll both wash."

Yvette passes before me, her frozen hand brushes over mine in a sign of encouragement. Yes, go on, get going.

"Can we come, too?" asks Yann.

"No. Whoever kills his dog accuses him of rabies, and during the summer you go to the beach."

"What about me?" asks Francine, full of hope.

"You," Bernard snaps, "are going to wash out your foul mouth in the snow. Right away!"

"It's out of the question that—"

"Right away! And I want ice cream for dessert!"

Suddenly thunder is loosed, drowning out their voices. Lightning flashes come in crescendos. Bernard cries out in joy, "Fireworks! Fireworks!" Then everything explodes. When silence returns, the smell of fire is close at hand. Lightning must have struck a tree a few yards away. My ears are buzzing, and the noise is deafening. Somewhere from the other side of the cocoon surrounding me:

"God's not happy! God's not happy with you!" Justine proffers in her medium's voice.

"God's not happy with Bernard?" an anxious little voice asks.

"God's not happy with Yann and Francine!" Justine cries. "God wants you to kill them!"

"Bitch!" Yann shouts.

A hammer strikes an empty chamber. Out of ammunition. But for whom? Justine throws herself against me, while Yann screams, no doubt to Francine, "Pass me that gun on the ground!" Mercanti's weapon.

"You see whom God has chosen!" Justine cries. "Shoot, Bernard, shoot! Pow! Pow!"

With all these gun blasts, screams, and cross-fires, you'd think we were on a battlefield; bullets are whistling in my ears, voices are screaming themselves hoarse. I'm waiting with a kind of curiosity for the moment when some projectile or other will be embedded in my flesh. It seems I've been waiting to die for so long that even my fear is blunted, my heart frozen.

Oh, damn it! Damn it! Damn it, that hurts! There, in my shoulder, I can feel a hole, I can feel it, I can pass my finger inside. Oh, this makes me feel like throwing up, I'm sure it's gone straight through my shoulder, leaving a round hole in my own flesh; I'm having a hard time believing this, except it hurts so much and—

There's no more noise. The rumbling of the storm is off in the distance now. Just a heady odor of cordite. And groans. It feels as if my ears were stuffed with cotton, and I swallow to unplug them, with no success. Someone's speaking through the cotton.

"Wheeere outsiide snooow?"

The cotton is suddenly torn away, and it becomes, "What the hell are we doing out in the snow?" It's my uncle's hesitant voice in the deafening silence. "Justine? My God, Justine! What's . . . what's happened? Lorieux! Wake up, pal! This is a real slaughter. Hey, somebody, come help!"

A faraway voice replies, "Go fuck yourself, you old asshole!"

Laetitia. She and Christian are cornered up there. Trapped, like rats. Uncle Fernand's going to shoot them down, and then . . .

I'm going delirious. We're not in a video game. The pain's returning in boiling waves, submerging me, yet at the same time sounds are becoming clearer; I can hear Uncle Fernand shaking Justine, repeating her name, then running toward Yvette.

Yvette.

"I'm all right," she stammers (and I start crying for joy), "it's okay, Mr. Fernand, take care of the others."

"But they're dead!" my uncle screams. "Mrs. Raymond is flat on her belly in the snow; Yann's got no face left; Mrs. Atchouel's guts are coming out of her belly; Lorieux's unconscious; the other cop has half his skull blown off; and that fat boy—"

"For roaches, you need insecticide . . . "

"He's alive!" my uncle exclaims with relief. "Are you hurt, son? Try moving your arms and legs."

"Can't," says Bernard. "My leg's out of whack. When you go to a burial, you dress in black."

"Let's have a look . . . Oh, shit! Don't move, okay? You especially, don't move. How can he stay so calm?" he asks us.

"He's not very sensitive to pain," Yvette explains, "we don't know why."

"Yvette," he calls, sounding distressed, "Justine's eyes are wide open, she's not blinking, and—"

"She's blind," Yvette sighs. "It's normal for her to be staring into emptiness! Take her pulse. At the carotid artery."

"I can hear it! Just barely, but I can hear it! Good God, I've got to get some help."

"There are two others up there, in front of the house. Laetitia and Christian. They're going to kill you."

"Oh, really?" says my uncle. "We'll see about that. I'm going to pick up their guns."

"I think those guns are empty. They fired until they were out of ammunition."

"The armies of evil are in retreat!" Bernard says with satisfaction. "But my leg hurts."

"We'll take care of it. You stay here with Elise."

Someone's groaning; it sounds like a woman's groan.

"I'm thirsty, I'd like a bit of tea," Francine murmurs in a single breath.

"Shit, she's alive!" my uncle stammers. "This isn't possible. Not in this state . . . "

"Put some snow in her mouth," says Yvette.

"You're being very kind with this piece of trash!"

"She's going to die, Mr. Andrioli. It'll do no good to make her suffer any more."

"I'm not going to die," says Francine. "I'm not going to die. Help me put everything back in order!"

As her voice skids to a higher pitch, I imagine her holding her intestines with both hands.

"I'm not going to die . . . "

"Yes, you're going to die!" Bernard assures her. "And you're going to hell! Ice melts in the springtime."

"Long live disalienation!" Francine screams, with surprising vigor. "Long live the Mental Release Center for Hallucinated Adults!"

MRCHA.

She chokes on her last word, then silence.

"She's gone," my uncle declares flatly. "When I think I trusted her! She doesn't need her cashmere coat anymore," he adds. "I'm going to cover Justine with it, and then I'm going."

"Going where?"

"To get help. Pass me Yann's parka. Let's put it over Elise's shoulders. You take my jacket. I've got some headache! Well, I'm putting the wheelchair back up, okay, here we go!"

He lifts me with great effort, sits me down lopsidedly, and covers me with a parka that's soaked and smells of gunpowder, burned flesh, and blood. Something wet's tickling my neck. Could it be bits of brain? I hold in the heaves.

Yvette checks to make sure Justine's breathing.

"She's got a nasty head wound," she says, "and one in her shoulder. I'm going to put on some snow to stop the bleeding. If only you'd seen it, you'd think we were in a western! Everyone was shooting at once, and the worst thing is they all seemed happy. Bernard as well as Yann and Francine. They were smiling. The bullets were going into their bodies and they were smiling. Even Mercanti, who opened his eyes when he heard all the racket, gave me a beautiful smile when the top of his skull flew off. I'll never say this to anyone, but it sent shivers down my spine, as if these weren't humans, you see . . ."

Maybe they weren't. Who'll ever know?

"The sergeant seems in a bad way," my uncle observes.

"Yann shot him—in the legs, the back . . . I think if it takes too long for help to get here, then . . . " She doesn't finish her sentence.

"What about that one over there? His leg's all mutilated . . . We've got to make a tourniquet for him," my uncle says in a low voice.

I gather he's talking about Bernard.

"I've taken first-aid courses," Yvette says. "I'll look after him."

"But you're hurt!"

"Just a couple of nicks, nothing serious. Just a broken thumb, I think, the left one," she adds. "I already broke it in '56, picking mushrooms."

"It looks like you just jumped on a mine!" my uncle retorts.

"In my family, we're solid. Don't you worry about me. I'll get over this better than the last time!"

Oh, right, the last time she had a fractured skull.

The warmth from the parka spreads through my veins, reviving the sharp, pulsing pain in my shoulder. My fingertips are throbbing as if they were on fire. But I'm trembling less. I imagine the other two up there, ready to greet us with rifle blasts. Through some miracle, my pad is still wrapped up in my blanket, and my pen is still hanging around my neck by its cord.

Watch out. They're waiting for you. Yann spoke of scooters. Find help.

I hold out the sheet, and Yvette runs over and reads it.

"Elise is right. Christian's hurt and Laetitia can't flee. It's better if you go for help."

"Where are the scooters?"

"Near the garage, about thirty yards away. You've got to go back up to the embankment and turn to the left. But you'll be passing through an open area."

"I've got no choice," my uncle says.

He leans over and kisses me on the head, leans toward Justine, and then says good-bye to Yvette.

"Courage!" he calls out, before adding, "I'm sorry, Elise."

Before I can hear the last of his sentence, he's started on his way.

Once again I'm waiting, with a knot in my stomach and my heart beating fast. Yvette's attending to Bernard, who's humming "Petit Papa Noël."

Slowly, I count to twenty.

A machine-gun blast. Then silence. Another sustained burst of machine-gun fire. Then silence.

Silence.

Laetitia cries out in joy. Triumphantly. Barbaric.

This can't be.

Can't be.

"Why did Yann put a mask over his face?" Bernard asks. "I think it should be nice tomorrow. Could I have a plastic leg? I like Mommy's legs."

No one answers. He starts to groan. I desperately listen to the silence. Yvette lays her hand on my shoulder. I can hear her ragged breath.

"I'll go have a look," she says, in a trembling voice.

No. Too dangerous.

"If he's hurt, we'll have to find someone else to go for help. Otherwise, we'll all die."

"You're not my mother!" Bernard screams. "Jesus died for our sins."

"I'm going," Yvette says again.

She's already left. In the time it takes to snap one's fingers.

I know my uncle's dead. I know as surely as if it were carved under my skin.

I'm not crying. I have no more tears. I'm empty. Totally empty.

I'm waiting for the blast that will shoot down Yvette. Yvette, with her broken thumb, zigzagging through the trees, like a commando. Ridiculous.

There's the blast. Rattling, familiar. My heart skips a beat. Another burst, even longer.

"Tomorrow it'll be nice," says Bernard. "You should take a shower at a hundred degrees."

A motor's purring.

A motor's purring!

Thank you! Thank you!

The scooter takes off. How long will it take to reach the village? A quarter of an hour? And to return with help? Half an hour?

The storm has moved on to the next valley, and I can hear its faint rumbling. I'm so tired, everything in my head's muddled. Was that a firefly? No, it's too cold here. I think I've been dozing off for a minute at a time, I really shouldn't—

Something's slid up furtively.

Did I imagine that? I'm listening so hard, my ears may break.

It's nothing. It must be a manifestation of my anguish.

"Why's she hiding behind the tree?" Bernard suddenly asks.

My heart jumps one more time.

"Yoohoo! Sickies!" Laetitia calls out.

Impossible. How was she able to get down here?

"You remember that whatsit Yann pilfered for me?" she says, as if she'd heard me. "It was sort of like a toboggan on skis, steered by hand? Well, it works pretty damn well! You can drive with one hand and hold a gun in the other. Shit!" she suddenly exclaims. "Yann! Mother Atchouel! Mercanti!

"What's happened?" she continues. "I heard a bunch of gunshots—"

I start writing, anything.

Yann killed them . . .

"That bastard!" she spits. "All that talk about team spirit, how unity means strength, all that 'each of us is a branch on the star of destiny' nonsense!"

Yvette's gone for help.

"What the hell do you want me to do about it? I didn't kill anybody. No, wait . . . a bout with delirium? Oh, right, I forgot. I spent four years in the psych ward. My file's this thick! I do tons of things, then forget all about them. It's because I'm naughty, 'cause I'm nuts. Is it forbidden to be nuts?"

Forbidden to kill poor innocent people.

"Innocence is a reactionary concept," she snaps. "A concept of weakness. I chew up innocence every day with my breakfast. Art is never innocent. Art is guilt in a pure state."

What are you guilty of?

"Of suffering," she answers in a sad voice. "If I didn't give a shit that my father doesn't love me, I wouldn't have killed him. I'm too sensitive," she concludes. "Not like you. I knew they were right to choose you as the heroine," she adds. "You're unflappable. What's your last wish?"

To survive.

Laetitia lets out a mirthless laugh.

"Go ahead. Ask me your questions, if you've got any. You know, the last conversation between the wicked and the kind, before the wicked one shoots."

She's in the mood to talk. She's frustrated that she hasn't been the star. She knows it's her moment of glory—and it won't last long. She's acting out Pasionaria at the same time as Bonnie, yet with no Clyde.

Why did Véronique come to MRCHA?

"To blackmail Yann, just as Payot had guessed. She recognized one of the patients from the psych ward, one of the better students in the psychodrama workshop. She knew he couldn't be a teacher."

How did you all meet?

"It was through the magazine. One day there was some colloquium on the theme of 'Mystery Novels, Skin, and Art.' We all wound up there. And it was really fascinating. We all became friends. We had so many interests in common. It was during the colloquium that we discovered your existence. B* A* came to moderate one of the debates. 'The Feminine Body and Consciousness of Self in Traumatic States.' Obviously we spoke about you. It was fascinating to us. In your body, you expressed the confinement that is imposed on our souls. When her text showed up in the magazine's e-mail by mistake, we saw it as more than just a coincidence! 'In *handicap,* is the *cap* of *capable,*' Yann told us. We'd form a group and we'd be able to change the course of things. You would be a symbol. A healthy soul in an unhealthy body. Exposed to the vicissitudes of existence. We would write your life, and we'd make a world star out of you. We'd all go to the Cannes Film Festival!"

Her pitiful delirium is grating on my nerves. But how can such dangerous people be so grotesque? How could this shop girl kill my uncle with no more emotion than she would crush a roach? Is futility the prelude to moral insensitivity?

"The funniest thing," she goes on, "is that during the colloquium, there was an exhibit of Justine's works—her study on 'sonorous dissonance in souls.' I was shocked, seeing her get off here! Fortunately, there was no risk of her recognizing us."

Too bad! Their diabolical stratagem would have been laid open, and so many lives would have been spared.

She coughs. Sadistic killers cough, sneeze, laugh, or cry. I find it obscene, this humanity in their bodies that makes us believe they're like us. Of course, we're all bags of skin filled with flesh and bone, provided with the same orifices and, sheltered inside the skull, the software that allows us to think. Yet theirs is infected by a virus that orders them to destroy. With no respite, repose, or remission.

When I think you were lounging on your bed, listening to techno, while Martine was hanging Magali in the room next door. Magali, who was forced to see Vore. Vore. My pen tears the soaked paper as I write anything that comes to mind.

The kitchen?

"That was one of Martine's idiotic ideas, with her taste for spiritualism . . . "

Mercanti/Vore in the chimney?

"Hmm. That imbecile nearly sent us up in flames. He added all the wrong amounts when he was mixing the explosives. I wanted to take care of it myself, but you know how it is with these old-style macho guys! Fortunately, you broke through the window. I ought to admit, about Vore," she goes on. "He doesn't exist, but—"

"Vore exists. I met him!" Bernard cuts in.

"You're mixing him up with God, my dear!" Laetitia replies, mockingly.

"God, too, I met Him!" Bernard confirms.

"Fine!" Laetitia says, bursting out in laughter. "What I meant to tell you is that if Vore doesn't exist—shut up, Bernard!—then all the same he was conceived, and not by us."

I know. B* A*'s manuscript.

"No, not only that. Your mercenary author had the same idea we did: to get you started in a new adventure. We were talking about it at dinner, after the colloquium. The influence of reality on fiction, and vice versa. We were a little tipsy, and she told us she was thinking of creating a virtual enemy, to see your reaction and what would follow."

She did! She sent me that phony fax.

"She must have been surprised, saintly hypocrite that she is, if she found out that her fictional Vore went around knocking people off!" Laetitia adds, laughing.

In his corner, Bernard mutters, "Mommy's a saint! You fit your breasts in a bra."

"Your mother's dead!" Laetitia shouts. "And she was completely nuts! For fourteen years, she never let you out of the house! You must have made quite a pair!"

"My father's an *entrepreneur!*" Bernard cries. "*Entrepreneurs* build houses for their retarded children!"

A very long silence follows, disturbed only by Bernard's ramblings.

"Exactly what do you mean, Bernard?" Laetitia asks, her voice quivering.

Someone's snickering. To my left, below, there's a painful laugh that ends in coughs.

"It was Bernard, not Léonard!" Justine finally manages to articulate. "Whoever listens will hear!"

"Oh, no, no more of that asshole's tirades! Explain yourself!" Laetitia orders.

"Bernard's the one. He's Fernie's son!" Justine whispers, her frozen hand brushing against my knee. It's just dawned on me this instant, like an illumination. He's the one who'll inherit the Gastaldi fortune!

Bernard is my uncle's son. *Bernard is my cousin.* This is an encounter with a black hole. From the other side, the earth is whirling around, like a rainbow-colored boccie ball thrown across space to the Great Jack. Elise Andrioli wishes she could ride horseback across the earth, her hair blowing in the wind, sparks lighting up her brain. Yet the black hole pushes me back, and I must return to the here and now, to this dirty mud of time, where reality is sucked in; to this nightmare erected in logic.

Get a hold of yourself, Elise. Listen to Laetitia cursing through her teeth: "But it was just a novel!"

And Justine hammering away: "Reality can't be molded so easily, my little one. You thought it would be enough to place Elise on the stage of your little theater and have her confront other characters so that the story you want could be written. That's all wrong! Stories are like music. They're written with silences . . . lies, omissions—"

"Shut up!"

"You wanted to make Elise into a real character," Justine stubbornly continues, "forgetting that a character belongs first to its author. I'm sure that you'll have a lot of pleasure reading about her new adventures down in your padded cell," she adds, wickedly.

Laetitia takes a few seconds to strike, then screams, "That's ridiculous! We're the ones who did everything!"

"Did too much!" Justine exclaims. "You went overboard."

"B* A* will go to jail as well!" Laetitia shouts, desperately.

"Why? She'll make a profit off the evil you've committed. No one ever prospers from ill-gotten gain, yet ill gained well will bring in a good deal!" Justine declares sententiously.

"I'm going to kill you right here, right now—shoot you down like two dogs, and then no one will profit from Elise's adventures!" Laetitia growls. "And I'm going to shoot that old asshole's son right in the face—"

"I'd advise you not to touch a hair on that boy's head!" shouts a woman's voice from behind the trees.

Yvette! She made it! Ta-da! Sound the bugles! Let the trumpets ring out!

"What the . . . ?" Laetitia stammers, taken aback.

"This is Captain Bertrand of the National Police!" a man's voice, sounding extremely flat, comes through a bullhorn. "You're completely surrounded. Give yourself up!"

It's the cavalry. Finally!

"I'm armed and I've got hostages!" Laetitia screams back. "I'm going to shoot them all!"

"You have three seconds to put down your weapon!" Captain Bertrand replies. "You're in the sights of four top sharpshooters. And I'm not in a good mood. One!"

This isn't how they negotiate in the movies. I hope he knows what he's doing.

"I want a helicopter, or else I'm killing them!" Laetitia cries, shaking from a combination of rage and despair.

"My name is Marc," shouts yet another voice, sounding just as icy. "I've got your right eye at the end of my barrel. We've just found the bodies of our comrades," he adds, "and we're in no mood for playing around. In fact, what we're really hoping is that you don't give yourself up, so we'll have the right to pull the trigger on you."

"Two!"

"Time is money," says Bernard.

Is she going to cooperate or will she shoot? Which one of us is she aiming for? Justine? Bernard? Me? Do I have the right to hope that she's aiming at one of the other two? Am I sick for hoping with all my strength that my head won't be the one that's blown off?

"Three—"

"Okay, I give up!" Laetitia cries, just like in a western.

I let out a hiccup of relief.

"All right. Get your arms up!" shouts Captain Bertrand. "Higher!"

"Assholes!" Laetitia mutters. "You can all go fuck yourselves!"

Then she starts wailing, "They forced me to, I didn't want to, I didn't know what I was doing—" Our clearing is suddenly invaded by dozens of men with rough-sounding voices.

The deafening sirens of the arriving ambulances blend in with all the exclamations and interjections, while up above, on the front walk, amid the clamor of men's voices, comes Christian's protest: "She shot at me!" Clara's shrill squeals cut through the frenetic barks and sputtering flashbulbs, while a helicopter approaches. Yvette throws herself around my neck, and I squeeze her gnarled old hand so hard it might break.

"Elise, are you all right?" asks a familiar voice.

The voice asks me questions, what I'm feeling, lending me sentiments, sensations; it's the voice that gives me back my own voice, the voice of my author.

"When my publisher phoned to tell me that all these murders signed Vore had taken place," she shouts over all the noise, "I came back on the first available flight."

That's normal. An author ought to save her heroine.

"Somebody was using my manuscript!" she goes on. "I got in touch with the police, and we were just arriving in the village when Yvette bolted into the station."

I feel so tired, with all these motors humming and everything around me ringing. "Woof!" A heavy, furry weight lands on my legs, and I hug it close, breathing in the good, warm smell of a living dog. "The dog's hurt," someone says. Bernard's crying. As the stretcher bearers carry off Justine, she suddenly asks, "Where's Fernand? Tell him I'm all right!"

No one answers.

"Tell him I'm all right," Justine repeats. "He must be worried to death!"

That's the sentence that opens the floodgates; the dam breaks, and tears pour down my cheeks, coming from somewhere so deep within that it feels as if someone has turned me upside down, like a glove, and I'm going to be emptied out; a policeman says something, and I hiccup; I hear them trying to determine whether or not Lorieux's dead; they put an oxygen mask on him, and they take him away, running; I'm crying, crying; it feels like swim-ming in salt water.

Yvette's trying to comfort me, patting me here and there, as I struggle by, continuing to cry; Tintin's wet nose is on my lap. The cops are manhandling Laetitia, and she squeals back, while someone lifts my wheelchair—no, they're lifting me out of my wheelchair; there's a pharmaceutical smell as gloved hands run over me, applying gauze and bandages. With a touch of the respirator, we're off; they stretch me out, say a few things, stick a needle in my arm, and I don't feel a thing.

Epilogue

SERGEANT LORIEUX was posthumously awarded the National Police Medal. He died without ever regaining consciousness, so he doesn't know how the story ended. With all my strength I wish for him to be reunited with his beloved Sonia inside some constellation, where they'll sniff stardust for all eternity.

He's being buried this morning with military honors. Yvette, Justine, and I will be attending the ceremony dressed in the same somber clothes we were wearing yesterday, at the burial for Uncle Fernand.

It was a beautiful ceremony. Snow was crunching underfoot; the sun caressed the crowd of villagers who showed up. Old Clary came with his herd, and we went all the way to the cemetery, accompanied by clanging bells, bleating lambs, and Tintin's panting.

B* A* was there, as were Bernard, Jean-Claude, Clara, and a teacher from social services.

Clara couldn't stop crying. Ever since Emilie's death, she's refused to speak and remains prostrate for hours on end. Jean-Claude's enrolled in a class in video editing, and in eight days he'll be leaving for Bordeaux.

"Bernard's in a wheelchair, too!" Bernard shouted when he saw us. "Plaster's for building houses."

My *cousin* Bernard.

DNA tests were run to confirm or deny the relation between Marion and Sonia, and my uncle and Bernard.

B* A* expressed her condolences in front of my uncle's casket.

"The people you love never die!" Justine said.

"Then love him with all your might!" my author replied. Before adding: "When you have strength, send me your notes, Elise."

"You're not going to write a novel with them, are you?" Yvette said, indignantly. "With a drama that cost twenty people their lives! That would be indecent!"

Twenty? In my head, I quickly take another count: Marion, Sonia, Magali, Véronique, Hugo, Payot, Emilie, Mrs. Raymond, Francine, Martine, Yann, Léonard, my uncle, and six police officers. It's true, twenty lives, brutally cut short.

"I'm only the scribe of human folly!" B* A* replies, with the smooth, ingratiating tone that seems to characterize authors of whodunits. "I'll come by to see you with the contract, Elise. You know, with the money we can continue your uncle's work, MRCHA, all that. I'm sure Justine would make a marvelous director."

Watch out for the burning tea in your lap!

It's horrible, but I'm always strong enough to laugh. It must be some kind of sickness that's carried through the genes. Fortunately, nobody knows this.

We all shook hands, like conspirators or shipwreck victims, then Bernard kissed me on both cheeks, saying, "I'm sorry, but I don't want to marry you. It's because you're not normal," he added, "but I do prefer ice cream to vanilla."

Everyone left, and the three of us remained planted there, like the three Graces painted by a hack, Tintin pressed against my legs.

So there, the circle is complete. I have indeed lived the adventures my author dreamed up for me. I've become a character in a novel. Perhaps that's why I feel so different. Different from real people. From you. From you, who walk, dance, sing, cry, turn out the light, and put down the book. From you, mobile players in a moving world.

Perhaps my condition, which unites the immobility of death with the speed of living thought, makes me into a passage, a message, a bridge between what's real and what's imaginary. A screen for you to project your fantasies (Elise, *Philosophic Thoughts,* vol. 28).

Perhaps we all go through life burying our dead. Tirelessly putting a coat of powder over our fears and sorrows, to hide them from our eyes.

The sound of the bugle echoes through the Alps' crystalline sky. Colors are raised, sabers rattle, and in the end, one single note, pure, detaches like a soap bubble and floats up into the infinite ether, searching for times to come.